THE CURSE TO ASHWATHAMA

Neeraj Bharti

ISBN 9781734162714

<u>**Disclaimer**</u>
This book is purely a work of fiction. The names, characters, places, and incidents mentioned in this book are fictitious and are the product of the author's imagination. Any resemblance to any actual event, place, or person, living or dead, is purely coincidental. Some sections of this book contain partial nudity **(The Heartbreak** and **The Enlightenment)**, strong language, and scenes of graphic violence that might not be suitable for children. Parental discretion is advised.
<u>**Credits and Acknowledgments**</u>
Writing a book is tougher than I imagined and more gratifying than I ever dreamed of. This sweet journey started about two years ago when I jotted down my first word in a book. The journey would not have been possible without the generosity of **©Chess.com, LLC**. ©Chess.com, LLC permitted me to capture and use the screenshots of the chessboards and pieces from chess.com. Chess.com is the registered website of ©Chess.com, LLC. I have used the screenshots of the beautiful boards and pieces in the back cover as well as in the text. Thank you so much, ©Chess.com, LLC, for your munificence. I am certainly obliged.

I would like to thank **Mr. Tripati Pada Dey (website: kalagallery.in)**, the illustrator of the book. He crafted the front cover of the book (the black and white sketch of Lord Krishna standing with Ashwathama). Sir, thank you for your intense and mindboggling imagination. I haven't seen such a fine piece of art in recent times.

I would also like to thank **Mr. Navnish Bhardwaj (email: navnishb@gmail.com)** for crafting the eye-catching logo of USHNAR publications for the book. Thank you, Navnish!

Lastly, I would like to thank my wife, Megha, for her continuous support. I would also like to thank my in-laws and my brother Rahul along with his family. On this occasion, I also remember my beautiful daughter Shreya and my lovely niece Nayra.

This piece of fiction is a loving tribute to my respected parents Mrs. Usha Bharti and Mr. Narinder Bharti (USHNAR PUBLICATIONS). You sacrificed your yesterday for a better today for me! God bless you with happiness and good health. I love you both.

First, I'd like to thank you for your interest in my maiden novel **The Curse To Ashwathama**. I have been working as a senior principal consultant at a reputed software firm for the past 14 years. Although writing always fascinated me, I never pursued it very seriously, being quite content with my daily job. But things changed about two years ago when I was diagnosed with acute insomnia. I remember the long and grueling nights when I would hear my family members snoring peacefully while I tossed and turned beside them. I recall the moments I would get up from my bed and tread to the couch in the living room. In those lonely nights, I used to sigh and sit on the couch and do nothing but peer into the darkness for hours until I watched an interview of an indie author. The moment sparked my quiescent passion, and I decided to utilize this awful waiting time. And I could not have found a better activity to engage myself in than writing. It was a hobby I had buried somewhere in the mists of time. I still remember the first night I grabbed a pen to jot down the number of vague ideas juggling in my mind.

I picked one idea that had always enthralled me—a scenario where life seemed more miserable than death, the moment when a sinner begs and prays for death but the Lord of Death denies the plea. Suddenly, my empty and uncertain nights seemed finite and too short as I began capturing my thoughts on paper. Soon, the words turned into sentences, sentences formed paragraphs, and the first draft came to life.

But being a first-time writer, I soon realized that editing a book is much harder than writing it, and it took Herculean efforts for me to refine the manuscript you hold in your hand today. After many rounds of self-revision to ensure that the storyline was consistent and meaningful, I distributed copies to my father, friends, and colleagues to get their honest feedback and reviews. After the initial rounds of self-editing, which included the use of online tools to correct grammar and punctuation, I submitted my manuscript to a professional editing and proofreading company called *PaperTrue*, and I was not disappointed. The final version was crisp, clear, and error-free.

Among all the characters in this mystery-thriller novel, Aurangzeb - the brute jailor, and Dara – the yeti, are my favorites. I thoroughly enjoyed jotting down their beastly sides. Although all the chapters are very close to my heart, #20 (The Exposé) is my all-time favorite, and I have loved it since I wrote the very first draft.

I believe my writing grew and matured by leaps and bounds by the time I finished the final draft. Not only did I improve my vocabulary but it also sharpened my imaginative skills. I dedicate this piece of writing to my parents, Mr. Narinder Kumar Bharti and Mrs. Usha Bharti. Witnessing their eyes fill with tears of joy when they read the dedication at the beginning of the book was a heart-melting moment.

I would love to hear your thoughts on suspense in the novel. I hope you enjoy it! Also, please let me know if some particular poignant moment brings tears in your eyes. You can also leave your comments/reviews with the Twitter hashtag **#TheCurseToAshwathama**. My Twitter handle is **@iAuthorNeerajB**. Please visit my website **www.ushnar.com** to go through the free sample chapters and the genuine reviews of the book. Readers can also visit my Amazon Author Central page at **amazon.com/author/neerajbharti**

Contents

01. Why Did He Smile?

The car cruised across the mountainous terrain at a slow pace. Due to the bumpy and risky drive, a nervous Rishi glanced at Anu occasionally while driving up the hill. But an annoyed Anu peeked out of the window at her side and sat in silence. No words had been exchanged between them for about forty minutes. Having run out of his patience, Rishi sighed in frustration and tried to break the ice with his livid wife.

Rishi: "Take it easy, Anu. You're overthinking. There is no reason to get upset about it."

With raised brows and a frown, she turned towards him and shouted.

Anu: "Let me tell you beforehand—I am NOT handing it over to anyone."

He sighed and rolled his eyes, frustrated.

Rishi: "Listen, we still don't know whom to meet. All we have is a vague address. Anyway, father didn't ask us to hand it over to someone. Why are you mad at me? I'm trying my best to solve the mystery he created. Don't you want me to decode it?"

Though still unsettled, Rishi's words calmed her a bit.

Anu: "How much longer is it going to take? I am exhausted already."

Rishi: "Me too. But according to the address, the place should be nearby."

Anu: "What's the name of the place again?"

Rishi: "Ratnagiri."

They passed a massive old jail building with high, crumbling walls. It stood at the side of the road and had an eerie feeling to it. As soon as they crossed the building, their car reached a shallow bridge. Anu stuck her neck outside the window to glimpse a water body under it. But to her surprise, there was no sign of water. The water had all dried up! Anu felt a touch nervous as they entered into a vast stretch of forsaken land after crossing the bridge. With no trace of any human activity, the barren place was a dust bowl. The dry and cracked piece of land had wilted plants and leafless trees grown all over the place.

Anu: "I have a bad feeling about this place."

Rishi: "Yeah, it reminds me of Death Valley in California."

But they both sighed in relief when they caught a glimpse of a herdsman passing by. With a thick stick in his hand, he tended and reared a bleating herd of sheep. Rishi honked to grab his attention and brought the car to a gradual stop near him.

Rishi: "Hi! Umm... We were heading to Ratnagiri mansion, but it seems we have lost our way somewhere in between. Can you please guide us?"

The herdsman frowned as he gaped at the couple in the bright sunlight. Then, he replied with a gentle smile.

Herdsman: "You are moving in the right direction, sir!"

Then, the herdsman looked around and pointed his finger ahead.

Herdsman: "Follow the road straight ahead for about three miles and you would see the mansion on the right."

The shepherd's words felt like music to Rishi's ears. With a beam on his face, he thanked the shepherd and sped the car in the direction he had pointed them in. And as they drove, their perception about the place changed.

In contrast to the parched land they had seen earlier, they now found themselves driving through a verdure of lush green vegetation. A few plants and crops flourished in the man-made lagoon areas present on both sides of the road. The scene was no less than a wonder as neither of them had expected to see any greenery. The farmers had installed webs of tubes and pipes in their lands for drip irrigation to reduce water usage. Anu also noticed some deep-dug borewells and excavations for groundwater extraction. As they drove ahead, they entered the famous open market of the place, where a huge crowd thronged and bustled. In the nearly deafening chaos, a herd of hawkers approached and hooted to passersby. They screamed the prices of their commodities to woo potential customers. Interested customers followed the hawkers to their stalls. But the others flinched and continued walking without a word. The town that had appeared to be in a slumber a little while back seemed to have awoken. From small eateries to high-end restaurants and stores, the market had all that a person could desire. The sight mesmerized Rishi and Anu.

Rishi: "I take back my words. This place reminds me of Dubai, a paradise in the desert."

After about five minutes, they reached a grand mansion. Rishi parked the car and the couple stepped out. The splendor of the aristocratic turret captivated them. But, the shambled walls of the mansion spoke of deep melancholy. They looked at each other

—

anxiously before walking to the high gate of the mansion. Rishi sighed and knocked on the door. His heart began to race as he heard someone unbolt the gate. They saw a man with grey hair push open the gate. He covered his mouth with his hand and coughed a couple of times before looking straight into Rishi's eyes. The aged man cleared his throat and introduced himself as Bansi.

Rishi: "Is this the Ratnagiri mansion?"

Bansi: "Yes, it is. But who are you? I have never seen you before."

Rishi: "Yeah, we've come from Mumbai. This is our first time here."

Bansi grinned.

Bansi: "That's nice to know. How can I help you? Who do you want to meet?"

Rishi and Anu fell silent and looked at each other in embarrassment. Rishi gulped.

Rishi: "A-actually…umm…we don't know. I mean there's someone at this address we need to speak to, but we don't know who the person is."

Bansi chortled at Rishi's confused state.

Bansi: "So you traveled all the way from Mumbai to meet someone you don't know?"

Discomfited at the jeer, Rishi sighed uneasily and introduced himself.

Rishi: "I…I'm the son of Dhananjay. Would someone in here recognize the name?"

Bansi looked up at the sky thoughtfully, but shook his head after a while.

Bansi: "Dhananjay? Hmmm… I haven't heard the name recently. I guess you came to the wrong address. But since you're already here, you are most welcome to have some tea and snacks before you leave. Please feel free to freshen up if you'd like."

Rishi declined the offer with a polite smile. Bansi's reply had left him dejected. All his hopes of discovering the truth had dashed after the long journey that had lasted over eight hours. He sighed and stated that they would take his leave. Bansi nodded with a grin and began pulling back the doors of the gate as soon as the couple turned around. But then a sudden thought crossed Rishi's mind. He turned around and gripped the closing doors of the gate.

Rishi: "Wait a minute, sir. Hold on, please. I…umm…have something that might help someone in this place recall what I seek."

He silently gestured to Anu, who stared at him with an anguished look. Reluctantly, she opened her purse and pulled out a shiny metallic case. She glared at Rishi and placed the case in his hand. Even though her furious stare made him hesitate, he decided to take his chances. He opened the case and pulled out a sparkling diamond ring and showed it to Bansi.

Rishi: "Can you tell me if anyone in this place would recognize this ring?"

Bansi adjusted his glasses and scrutinized the jewel. And as soon as he caught a glimpse of the glittering ring, his eyes grew wide with shock and despair. He howled, and his body quivered at the sight of the ring. He gasped and covered his mouth with his hand. His behavior baffled the couple. After a moment, he looked up at Rishi with a glum face.

Bansi: "Are you talking about Dhananjay…Dhananjay Verma?"

An ecstatic Rishi couldn't control himself. A wide smile spread across his face as soon as he heard the name.

Rishi: "Yes, you got it! I am talking about Dhananjay Verma, my father."

The very next moment, Rishi's smile waned. Bansi clenched his teeth, and tears of anger welled up in his eyes. His body began trembling with anger.

Bansi: "What made the rascal send you guys to Ratnagiri after two and a half decades? Isn't he satisfied with everything he's done to the family? Get out of here. Don't rub salt on our wounds."

With these admonishing words, he began pulling back the doors once again to shut the gate to them. But Rishi couldn't miss this opportunity. He held on to the gate and resisted.

Rishi: "Please sir, hear me out once!"

But Bansi was in no mood to listen. He tried his best to shut the gate.

Bansi: "I said get the hell out of here or I'll call the police."

But a determined Rishi wanted to solve the mystery once and for all.

Rishi: "Sir, please talk to me. Just once, please, sir!"

Bansi: "Go away before I shoot you. Go back to your moron father."

The man's stubborn and outlandish behavior was pissing Rishi off. Tears began streaking down his cheeks, and he yowled in a loud outburst.

Rishi: "HE DIED…HE'S DEAD… DO YOU UNDERSTAND? HE IS DEAD!"

Bansi fell silent when he heard Rishi's anguish. Stunned by the news, he calmed down and looked at Rishi with a straight face.

Bansi: "What…but…when?"

Rishi swallowed the lump in his throat and tried to get a grip on his emotions.

Rishi: "Last Sunday."

He recalled his old bedridden father wheezing loudly and heavily. A patient of monoplegia with a half-paralyzed face, he uttered his dying words to Rishi and in an unusual request in his final moments.

Dhananjay: *"ASK THEM, HHHH… HHHH… WHY… HHHH… WHY HE SMILED AT ME… WHY… HHH… GO TO RATNAGIRI MANSION… ASK… THEM…"*

The dying man raised his trembling hand with a diamond ring on his index finger.

Dhananjay: *"IF…HHH…THEY…DON'T REMEMBER…HHH… SHOW THEM THE RING…HHH… TAKE IT AWAY… HHH… MY SOUL WOULD BE AROUND YOU, RISHI, WHEN… HHH…SOMEBODY WOULD BE NARRATING YOU THE … HHHH… ANSWER TO MY QUESTION…HHH…"*

Rishi wiped his tears after narrating the moment to Bansi.

Rishi: "I haven't slept since the day he died. His dying words trouble me every time I shut my eyes. I finally decided to visit this place to find some peace."

Rishi paused for a moment and mulled over his father's query.

Rishi: "What was he asking exactly? What did he mean by the words 'WHY DID HE SMILE AT ME?'"

Bansi sighed.

Bansi: "I'm sorry for my insolence. Some old and bitter memories carried me away. Please come in."

Rishi gripped Anu's hand and followed Bansi into the mansion. The front lawn of the mansion was dull, and the flowerbed was dry and bushy. The parched yellowish grass had not been tended to. Some of the weeds in the lawn looked like they were about six to eight inches tall. As the couple walked in, they observed that the path to the front door of the mansion was through the lawn. They also noticed footwear scattered around the door.

But Bansi didn't take them inside the house. Instead, they continued ahead on a path that led them to the back of the mansion. The spacious backyard was a lot neater and cleaner than the front lawn. The excited kids from the neighborhood had gathered together in its vast compound. They screamed and ran around in the game of *'Seven Stones'*. But it was the huge mango tree in the middle of the backyard that caught Rishi's attention.

Underneath the shade of the tree, a nurse was spoon-feeding a liquid, perhaps some kind of soup, to a frail, aged man. Seated on a cot, the scrawny man had withered skin and ugly sores all over his bare chest and back. He seemed too feeble to help himself, as the nurse was also holding his back to give him support. The aged man was in bad shape. Due to his age, he was breathing at a slow pace. He took ample time to gulp down a single spoon of the soup. After a few more spoons, he closed his mouth and did not open it again. He was done with his food. The nurse then got up and laid him down on a nearby cot carefully. Once on the cot, he wheezed and looked up at the open skies through his fluttering eyes.

Bansi took the couple past the tree, and away from the man. He offered them two cozy chairs while he settled down on a chair opposite theirs. There was a small coffee table between the couple and Bansi. After everyone had settled down, Rishi began bombarding Bansi with questions while gazing out at the old man.

Rishi: "The man seems to be in a pitiable condition. But who is he? Moreover, have you seen the ring ever before? How do you know my father? And what about the question I asked you earlier about my father?"

Bansi: "I will tell you everything, sir. I have the answer to everything you want to know. But I have a small request. Can you lend me the ring you showed me a little while ago? Just for a couple of minutes."

His request did not amuse Anu. She remained silent but glared at Rishi. She had cribbed about the ring throughout the journey and hoped Rishi would bluntly refuse Bansi's request. Though Rishi empathized with her, he found it too embarrassing to refuse the man. Bansi sensed his dilemma.

Bansi: "Don't worry, sir. I will bring it back. It is yours!"

Rishi sighed and placed the ring in his hand. He was ready to take the risk. At that moment, his priority was to get answers to his father's question. He was desperate to quench his curiosity, even if it meant sacrificing the valuable ring. Anu was furious. She was certain that the ring would never come back.

With the ring in his hand, Bansi walked to the tree. As he approached the still man on the cot, tears dribbled down his cheeks. Trying to hide his quivering lips with a miserable smile, he displayed the ring to the bedridden man. And then, Rishi and Anu witnessed something unusual.

The sight of the ring snapped the old man out of the trance and he suddenly began to wail and wheeze. His eyes widened in despair, and his hands started to shake violently. He howled and snatched the ring from Bansi, then closed his fist around it. Bansi patted the man's shoulder and tried to extract the ring. After all, he had promised the couple that he would return it to them. But the sniveling man didn't want to part with the ring at any cost. His body began to flinch erratically. Unable to control the man, Bansi called a few of his helpers. A group of men came running towards them and braced their arms around the old man's waist. Then, they lifted him and helped him walk inside the mansion through the door in the front lawn. An embarrassed Bansi sluggishly made his way back to the couple.

Bansi: "I'm sorry. He refused to give it back to me. But don't worry. He will be on his tranquilizer soon. Once he goes to sleep, I will bring it to you. It might take a couple of hours, though. I apologize for the inconvenience."

The frail man's insane and weird behavior moments ago had left the duo baffled. His traumatized actions had cowed Anu into silence. Although still worried about the ring, the old man's reaction to it had perturbed her to the very core.

Rishi: "What…was that? "

With a miserable smile, Bansi wiped his tears before answering.

Bansi: "The man's last living memory! Before I tell you what you want to know, I have a question—would you believe whatever I am going to tell you? Nobody does, whenever I narrate the saga."

Rishi: "Why is that?"

Bansi looked up at him with a dismal look.

Bansi: "Perhaps because of the curse!"

Rishi and Anu threw a curious and perplexing glance at each other. Rishi gulped before he answered him back.

Rishi: "I…umm…don't have any reason to not believe you. Please go ahead. I want to hear it if it serves the purpose of my visit."

Bansi sighed and looked at the group of boys playing in the backyard. One of them stood at a distance from pebbles piled one over the other, and aimed a tennis ball at the stack of pebbles. Then, with a single and precise throw, the ball hit the stack, dislodging stones in all directions. The pebbles scattered, and Bansi's gaze became unfocused as he dived into a flashback that happened in the mists of time, about twenty-five years ago.

02. The Cloak-and-Dagger Mystery

The pellet hit the bullseye with precision, and the arena roared with applause. Sahil had won the annual 10-meter air rifle shooting championship. He had set a new record by retaining the title for the fifth consecutive year. Tall and dusky with black hair, Sahil was the heartthrob of the college. With a firm handshake, the dean congratulated the skilled shooter. Everybody on the podium was on their feet, hooting for the incredible achievement. Sahil waved his hand and thanked everyone in the podium. And he chuckled when he saw Boney and Mandana standing somewhere in the crowd.

A tall and fair-skinned hottie with blue eyes, the blonde Mandana was the bombshell of the college. But she was crazy for Sahil instead. A brown-skinned and short-statured man with average looks, Boney was Sahil's best college friend.

The arena buzzed and erupted in joy when the dean presented the sports trophy to Sahil for winning the championship. Boney smiled and applauded, while a thrilled Mandana jumped up and down, pumping her fists in the air. Although a year younger than him, both of them got along pretty well with Sahil.

It was the end of September, and the end of the shooting event marked the conclusion of the sports festival in the college. Since the exams were already over, the students were eager to go back home. Everyone seemed excited to begin his or her year-end vacations. But for Sahil, it was a nostalgic moment. With a hard-earned graduate degree in his hands after five long years, this was his last day in college. He met and greeted all his professors one by one. Since he was a bright student, the faculty members were pleased with him and shook hands with him. They wished him luck for his future endeavors. He roamed around the campus one last time, reminiscing about the sweet memories he had spent at the place. He wept when he embraced his college friends in turns. To ease the pain of parting, he had insisted that

Boney and Mandana spend the vacations with him at his native village, Ratnagiri. And after both agreed, all three of them planned to leave by the crack of dawn the next day.

Sharp at four in the morning, a cab arrived at the gate of the college. As decided, Mandana and Sahil made their way to the parked cab. They stuffed their luggage in the trunk and waited for Boney, who did not turn up, much to Sahil's frustration. Seated in the backseat of the taxi with Mandana, an annoyed Sahil sighed. He glanced at his wristwatch repeatedly. He was eager to see his family since he had not seen them in three months. A strange feeling of homesickness gripped him.

Sahil: "Where the hell is this guy? It's been twenty minutes."

Mandana: "Why don't you go to his room and check?"

Sahil nodded and stepped out of the car. But before he could walk to the hostel, he saw a disheveled Boney running towards the cab. To his surprise, he didn't have any luggage. Breathing heavily, he halted as he reached Sahil and tried to catch his breath.

Sahil: "Boney? Where have you been? And…where is your baggage?"

Boney paused for a moment and replied once his breathing had returned to normal.

Boney: "Sorry guys, but I can't come with you."

Mandana peeked out of the window and yelled at him.

Mandana: "But why?"

Boney: "I got a call from my city hospital about 20 minutes ago. My mother is not well and is in hospital. She has no one around her to take care of her in the hospital. I need to start moving to my place right now."

Sahil: "Oh, Kanta aunty? What happened to her?"

Boney: "She has mild jaundice. According to the doctors, she should be fine in about two to three weeks. But they want someone to be around her during that time. I will leave in an hour to my hometown. You guys carry on, I will join you in a month after my mother's condition gets stabilized."

Sahil: "Alright, Boney. We'll see you later. Call me once you reach the Ratnagiri bus station. I will come to pick you up. You have my home phone number, right?"

Boney grinned and nodded without a word. Sahil smiled and embraced him before settling into the backseat beside Mandana. Boney waved goodbye, and the taxi sped towards its destination. Mandana poured tea from the kettle she carried along into the two paper cups, and offered one to Sahil. They enjoyed every sip of it in the cold morning.

Mandana: "When will you talk to your parents?"

Sahil frowned.

Sahil: "About what?"

Mandana: "About us, you idiot! Dad called me up. He wants you to talk to your parents about our marriage."

Sahil chuckled.

Sahil: "You still have a year left in college to complete. I thought I'd speak to them after you finish your term. But if you are so eager, I don't mind asking Ma and Baba for it. Let's do it!"

Mandana blushed and rested her head on his shoulder. She was excited to meet his family for the first time.

After about five hours, the cab entered Ratnagiri. The beauty of the place in the bright hue of the morning sun mesmerized Mandana. The mist of the dawn freshened her cheeks. The view of the tall, green oak trees on both sides of the road enthralled Mandana. The lush green vegetation continued along the banks of River Palanharini. The sight of the river burbling its way to Ratnagiri amazed her. She also noticed the village jail at the edge of a bridge. She pulled out Sahil's imported camera and clicked some pictures just as the cab sped past the building. She was thrilled when the vehicle drove over the bridge right next to the jail. She bent forward and took some snaps of the river flowing underneath. The river water rippled over the firm stones in its way.

Finally, they reached their destination—the famous Ratnagiri mansion. Once a princely state, Ratnagiri had been ruled by Sahil's ancestors. The marvelous mansion served as home to the royal family, and his parents dwelled there. His father, Thakur Pratap Singh, was a well-known face in Ratnagiri. Although no longer a king, he served as the chieftain of the village. Addressed as Thakur by the people out of affection, he was a wise man and an able administrator. Ratnagiri had progressed by leaps and bounds under his leadership. Some intellectuals even believed that as a leader, the man was better than the earlier rulers.

Sahil jumped out of the cab as soon as the driver parked the cab near the gates of the mansion. Without any delay, he rushed inside with a wide smile on his face. I opened the door for him after I heard his loud knock on the door. As always, he greeted me with respect.

Sahil: "Hello, Bansi! How are you?"

I: "Welcome back, Sahil. Everyone is waiting for you at the breakfast table."

He chuckled at my words, then grabbed Mandana's hand and rushed inside while pulling her along. I laughed at his eagerness before walking to the taxi to collect their luggage. As soon as he stepped in the dining room, Thakur and Vidya, Sahil's mother, jumped up from their seats in joy. An ecstatic Sahil bent and touched his parents' feet and sought their blessings. Thakur cradled Sahil's face and planted a kiss on his forehead while Vidya embraced her son. Mandana joined her hands and expressed her gratitude to the elders with a gentle smile. The moment brought tears to Thakur's eyes.

Thakur: "I have missed you a lot, son! Time crawled in these past three months."

Vidya: "We have been waiting for you all morning. Let us have breakfast together."

Thakur: "Didn't you tell me two of your friends would be with you? Where's the other guy?"

Sahil settled at the table with Mandana and sat beside Thakur.

Sahil: "He couldn't come due to a family emergency. By the way, what's for breakfast? I'm starving."

Without wasting any time, he picked up a sandwich from a platter and began munching. It was stuffed with boiled potatoes and mango relish—absolutely delectable.

Sahil: "I love it, Ma! But you've never made this before. Did you learn the recipe recently?"

Vidya: "No, I didn't prepare it. Preeti did. You remember her? You used to play together when you were kids."

Sahil frowned and tried to jog his memory. After reminiscing about his childhood, he suddenly remembered.

Sahil: "Ahhh, Preeti! Do you mean the daughter of the schoolteacher? If I remember correctly, her father was transferred to some far-off place. Is she here?"

Vidya nodded glumly.

Vidya: "Yeah. She is in the kitchen at the moment. About a month ago, his sick father left her with us before passing away from a prolonged illness. She has been living with us since then. She teaches primary grade in your old school in the village. What a decent and dignified girl! I asked her to occupy a vacant room in the mansion, but she preferred to stay in the room in the backyard."

Sahil: "Next to Bansi's room?"

Vidya: "Yes, I didn't inform you about her because you were busy with your exams and I didn't want to distract you."

As soon as Vidya uttered these words, a brown-skinned and a pretty faced girl entered the dining hall. She held a platter in her hands with a teakettle and empty teacups. She had a lean figure, and her chubby face with luscious lips gave her an attractive look. Moreover, her big and beautiful black eyes made her an epitome of beauty. She smiled brightly as Sahil stood up and grinned at her. Although there was nothing unusual about the gesture, a sense of uneasiness erupted in Mandana's mind. She did not like the silent exchange of smiles between childhood friends. It evoked a sense of deep insecurity in her.

Vidya: "Here she comes! Preeti, do you remember Sahil?"

Preeti's silent smile widened before she nodded.

Preeti: "Yes, Ma! I do."

Sahil chuckled when Preeti came and stood near to him at the dining table.

Sahil: "H-Hi, Preeti. It's so nice to see you after years."

Preeti placed the platter on the table.

Preeti: "It's great to see you too. I don't have words to express the joy I am feeling from within. I can't believe we're meeting after all these years."

Her long, open hair gave her an elegant look. He took in her graceful guise and excellent fashion sense, dressed in white and pink attire. But his admiration didn't go unnoticed. An envious Mandana pursed her lips anxiously. She was not comfortable with Sahil's fascination with Preeti. She immediately rose from her seat and cleared her throat to grab everybody's attention.

Mandana: "Umm…. I-I am a little tired. Hope nobody minds if I rest for a while?"

Vidya: "Are you done? You ate so little! Do you want me to send something to your room? Your room is on the second floor, by the way, right next to the balcony."

Mandana: "No, aunty, I am done, thank you. I just need a little nap. Sahil, can you please help and show me my room?"

Before he could respond, Thakur had a suggestion for him.

Thakur: "You rest too, son. You must be tired after such a long journey."

Sahil smiled and agreed. He walked with Mandana to her room and then headed towards his room. He took a long shower to kill the fatigue before jumping into bed for a nap.

After about a couple of hours of sleep, he awoke to a street hawker's hoot. It was coming from somewhere outside the house. He yawned and went to the balcony of his room. It was a beautiful summer afternoon. He rubbed his eyes and grinned at the sight of Tatya in the backyard. Tatya and Thakur were sitting on opposite sides of a table under the shade of the large mango tree. An acquaintance of Thakur, Tatya managed a big team of men who helped him carry out Thakur's projects for the welfare of the people of Ratnagiri. He was arranging stylish wooden pieces on an elegant chessboard. On the other hand, his nine-year-old son Nitin was swinging from one branch of the tree to another. Sahil walked down to the backyard and addressed Tatya with respect. It felt good to see him after all these months. Tatya too greeted him with a smile. Sahil then walked to Nitin and planted a kiss on his cheek. In response, Nitin blushed and hid within the branches of the tree. The three men chuckled at the child's innocent behavior. Sahil walked back to Thakur and gaped at the sight of the board.

Sahil: "Wow! When did you guys start playing chess? I love the game!"

Thakur: "We started about a couple of months ago. But we play it a lot these days. And as always, Tatya will win. Let me tell you, Sahil, this guy is unbeatable!"

The polished board on the table and the glossy wooden pieces set on it enticed Sahil.

Sahil: "Oh really? That's nice to hear. May I have the privilege of playing against your man?"

Tatya chuckled at Sahil's request.

Tatya: "I've heard you are a skilled shooter with a lot of trophies and shields. But unfortunately, this is not that sort of sport. Not only do you need to concentrate on your moves but you must also anticipate the opponent's moves."

Sahil: "I'm not that bad at it, Tatya. I'll give you a tough fight."

Tatya chuckled and nodded.

Tatya: "All right, let me play black! This way, you can't blame me for not giving you the chance to make the first move or cite it as a reason for you losing the game."

Sahil grinned and took the seat next to Thakur. To witness the game, I walked and sat near them as well. And what a game it turned out to be! Sahil played the white pawn to d4 in his queenside opening.

In a classic queen's gambit, Tatya played the black pawn to d5.

Sahil contemplated for a while and played his kingside pawn to e4.

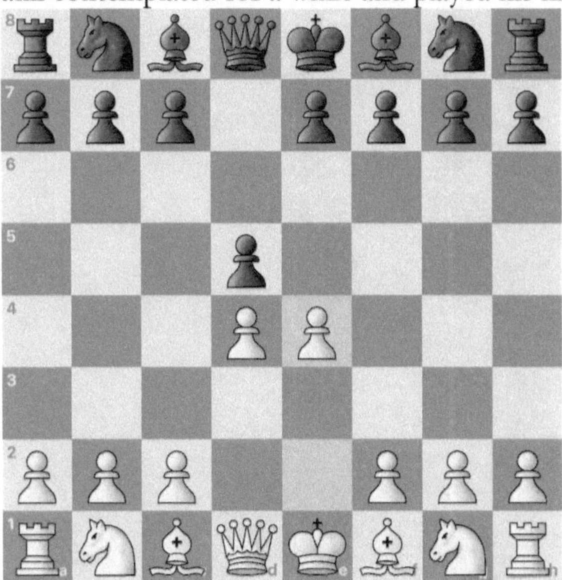

Tatya captured the white pawn at e4.

To attack the black pawn at e4, Sahil played his knight to c3. For the first time, Tatya had a genuine contender seated opposite him.

To protect his e4 pawn, Tatya played his knight from g8 to f6.

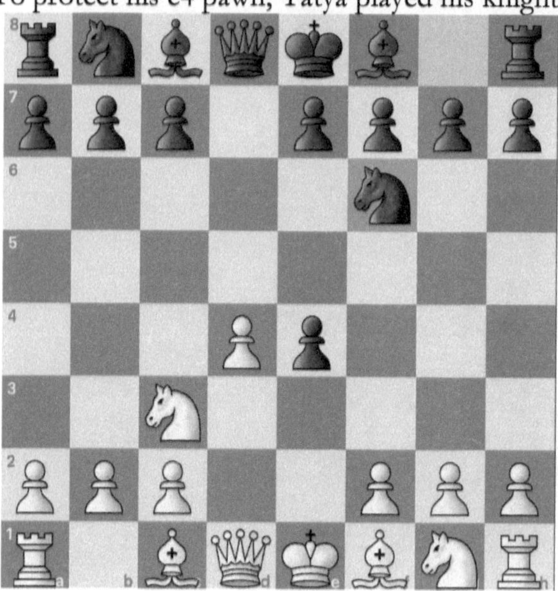

Sahil then played his pawn from f2 to f3 and attacked Tatya's pawn at e4. He was trying to gain control over the center of the board.

Tatya captured the white pawn at f3.

Sahil captured the black pawn at f3 with his queen, but frowned in disappointment as soon as he made the move. He should have captured the pawn with his g1 white knight. Now, his white pawn at d4 had a threat from Tatya's d8 black queen.

And as Sahil expected, Tatya captured the pawn at d4 gleefully.

Sahil pushed his bishop to e3 and attacked the black queen.

Tatya played his queen to b4, threatening the white pawn at b2.

But Sahil denied him the opportunity to capture his pawn and, instead, castled at the queen's side.

In his next move, Tatya played his bishop to g4.

With the f6 knight protecting it, the g4 bishop had the white queen and the white rook in its line of attack. It was a win-win situation for Tatya since the rook and the queen are always ranked higher than the bishop. Tatya was confident that Sahil would sacrifice his rook at d1 to save the queen at f3. He also knew that he would take the queen out of his line of attack.

But Sahil's next move baffled everyone. Rather than saving his queen, he played his knight, protected by his f1 bishop, to b5.

Everyone looked at him in surprise. Tatya laughed in a self-conceited manner as soon as Sahil made the move. His move left me flabbergasted too. He had been playing so well until that point. The move did not amuse Thakur either. He frowned and shook his head in dejection.

Thakur: "Why such a blunder, Sahil? You were playing brilliantly otherwise."

Tatya mocked Sahil with a jeering glee.

Tatya: "I warned you in the beginning. It is a very different sport from aiming a shot at a hard target. But I'll admit this—you played very well. Some of your moves were out of the box, especially the castling you did at your queenside. Anyway, better luck next time."

But Sahil remained silent. He held his chin and cheeks with his hand, and kept his eyes locked on the chessboard, waiting for Tatya's next move.

With a wide smile on his face, Tatya captured Sahil's white queen at f3.

As soon as Tatya made his move, Sahil smiled and sighed in relief. Then, he played his knight at b5 to c7 in a deadly move.

Then, he looked up at Tatya with a taunting smile.

Sahil: "You don't win the game by capturing the opponent's queen, Tatya. You need to checkmate the opponent's king. CHECK AND MATE!"

His confident words jolted Tatya out of his glee, and he nearly fell off his chair. He thought of moving his king to either d7 or d8, but both boxes were under attack by the white rook at d1. There was no way to save the black king, and it did not take him long to realize that Sahil had checkmated him in a brilliantly played game. An amused Thakur chuckled. I too applauded his performance. Sahil blushed as Tatya heaped praises on him for the mindboggling game.

The next few days passed in peace. Sahil often strolled to the banks of River Palanharini at dawn with Mandana. The view of the beautiful sunrise enthralled them, and the cool breeze energized their souls. With hand in hand, they chattered and sauntered along the river for hours. On their way back home, they drove through the open markets of Ratnagiri. Though not too developed at the time, it did house small eateries that offered the best food of all times. The fish-fried rice and the chicken-curry were the real specialties of the place. Crowds thronged around the famous handloom stores. The hawkers approached the passersby to woo the potential customers.

On one auspicious morning, the family paid a visit to the temple. It was Sahil's birthday. The priest tied a 108-beaded rosary around Sahil's neck to mark his blessings.

Priest: "Don't ever remove it, Sahil. It is an amulet—a symbol of power and wisdom. Things will go according to your plan as long as it stays with you. But you can gift it to your bride if you want to."

Sahil grinned and glanced at Mandana out of the corner of his eye. Though the idea seemed old-fashioned to her, she blushed at his gaze. In Mandana's company, the visit to Ratnagiri had invigorated him. He had never enjoyed his stay at the place this much ever before. But he was a naïve man. Despite spending his entire childhood here, he was unaware of a dark truth about the place. He had no idea about the hidden and dastard reality of Ratnagiri.

✳✳

It started raining cats and dogs on one cold and moonless night in Ratnagiri. Not too far from the mansion, the loud din of a thunderstorm scared the living daylights out of Mansi. Gusty winds whooshed through the window of her one-room house. Seated on the floor while cooking food on the hearth, she looked nervously through the window.

Mansi: "Looks like a heavy storm is on its way!"

But seated near the burning firewood, her husband Murari, a small-time farmer, was worried for a different reason altogether. After a brisk thought, he sighed and stood up from the cot placed in the corner of the room. Silently, he wrapped a blanket around his body and picked up a burning log from the lit firewood. Then, he put on his footwear and walked to the door.

Mansi: "Where are you going at this time?"

Murari: "I didn't put the harvest in the barn. I stuffed the burlap bags with the produce in them but the bags lay scattered in the middle of the farm. I forgot to secure them since I didn't anticipate any rain. The yield will go rancid if it rains and we'll lose everything. I need to carry the bags to the warehouse before it starts pouring."

Mansi's eyes widened with fear and she glared at her husband.

Mansi: "But it's not safe! You know I'm right! These are dangerous times. Please don't go!"

Murari smiled at her miserably before replying.

Murari: "I put my blood, sweat, and tears into the field for the past one year. Don't worry, I'll be back in a couple of hours. Lock the door from inside and don't open it for anybody until I come back."

She gulped in fear and nodded.

Mansi: "Be careful, okay?"

Murari nodded and stepped out. He fixed the burning log as a torch in the front carrier of his bicycle and left for his farm. He pedaled as hard as he could, battling the high-speed winds. The drizzle intensified once he reached the farm. Without wasting any time, he unlocked the door of the low-roofed barn and fixed the torch on its wall. Then, he sprinted to the pile of bags in the middle of the farm and counted them. He picked the first one and ran back to the storehouse. Then, he ran back to the farm to pick up the next bag after placing the first in the corner of the room. With a rumble of thunder, it started to pour heavily. With about twenty bags yet to be carried to the barn, he looked around for any possible help from anybody. But no one could be seen around! He carried the next bag and sprinted to the warehouse.

But contrary to his belief, he was not alone. Hidden somewhere, eight pairs of eyes were closely watching his every move. Eight men with balaclavas covering their faces were hiding behind the tall bushes of the farm, waiting for an opportune moment. One of the veiled men slid out a broadsword. When Murari came back to collect the third bag, the men crawled out of hiding and pounced on him viciously. Shaken by the sudden assault, he screamed for help. The hoodlums pinned him to the ground, and the attacker with the broadsword gagged him with his hand. Murari's eyes widened with fear as the man raised his broadsword. In a jiffy, the attacker stabbed him in the stomach and Murari's body flinched in pain as loud thunder crashed in the sky. Soon, Murari's body movements ceased. He died!

The men lifted his unresponsive body and placed it in the trunk of a van that they had parked next to the farm. Two of the masked men ran and settled into the front seats of the van, and the one at the wheels stomped on the accelerator. The van sped away and vanished into the darkness of the night.

03. The Harbinger

An anguished Thakur thumped the table in fury.

Thakur: "It has happened again, Inspector Sharma! One more casualty."

Mansi was wailing beside Murari's dead body in the police station. The police had recovered his mutilated body near the shore of the river two days after the goons had lynched him. After Thakur heard the tragic news, he visited the police station with Tatya and Alok, a small-time journalist and Thakur's long-time friend. In a nickel-and-dime job, Alok owned a small publishing house and published a daily newspaper. The police hired his services to take postmortem pictures of recovered bodies.

Thakur admonished Inspector Sharma.

Thakur: "How does Khatri carry out these dastardly killings with such precision? Why haven't the police managed to track him in all these years? It's been five years since anyone saw him."

Tatya patted Thakur's shoulder glumly. Sharma too tried to calm the frantic chieftain down.

Sharma: "Please don't get agitated, Thakur. I understand what you are going through, but the killings happen in the darkest hours of the night. What's more, the victims are tribal men living in the outskirts who hardly ever come forward to report their missing kin. We never get any support from their end. In any case, we don't have any evidence against Khatri, and whenever we got leads, we couldn't trace his whereabouts."

Thakur clenched his jaw.

Thakur: "That is a silly and lame excuse, Inspector Sharma. The police department should be ashamed of itself."

Alok: "He's right, Thakur. This is probably the first time that Khatri has slain a resident of Ratnagiri. Apart from his name and trade of organ smuggling, nothing much is known about him. What's worse is that there's no set pattern to his modus operandi."

Thakur: "A-and what about M-Murari?"

Alok: "L-Lungs, eyes, heart, kidneys—almost everything you can think of. The bastards ripped off everything they could get their hands on."

Thakur shook his head as he heard the grisly details. Though Sharma had assured him of stern measures being taken to nab Khatri, he was not convinced. Dejected, he walked out of the police station with Tatya and Alok. Thakur's misery was evident.

Alok: "Let's hope for the best, Thakur. I'm sure that the police will nab Khatri some day."

Thakur: "I hope whatever you said comes true, but I'm a little worried for Sahil. All these years I made sure that the news of all these killings never reached his ears. I wanted him to concentrate on his studies. I don't know how he'll react if he ever comes to know about Khatri and the murders."

Alok patted Thakur's shoulder.

Alok: "Relax, Thakur. I'm sure everything will turn out well."

Thakur: "Yes, I hope so too. Anyway, how are Dhananjay and Suhasini?"

Alok shook his head and sighed when he heard the name of his children.

Alok: "Dhananjay is still looking for a job. I wish I could have offered him some profile in my publishing house, but it isn't doing great either. I am planning to sell it off, as it has become a mere liability to me. "As for Suhasini, I'm on the lookout for a suitable groom for her."

Thakur: "That's nice to hear. I wish you get to fulfill your responsibilities well and soon."

Alok: "And I will keep a close eye on things and let you know if I find anything on Khatri."

****

Preeti drew the curtains of Sahil's room apart and entered with a smile.

Preeti: "Good morning!"

Though still in bed, Sahil was wide-awake. He yawned and grinned at the sight of her.

Sahil: "Good morning, Preeti!"

Preeti: "Here's your tea."

Sahil: "Why do you make the effort of serving me tea every morning? You know Bansi can do it."

Preeti: "I like doing it for everyone in the morning. It's become a habit now."

Sahil chuckled.

Sahil: "Alright. Let's have tea together then."

He swiftly picked up an empty cup from the tray and poured half of the tea from his cup into it. The old friends laughed and chatted after years as they enjoyed their morning tea.

Sahil: "How's the school?"

Preeti: "Going good. Why don't you pay a visit? I think you'd like it."

Sahil: "Yeah, I will. I'll come by someday."

After spending some quality time with Sahil, Preeti got up and turned around to leave. But to her surprise, Mandana was standing at the entrance to Sahil's room. With her arms crossed and back leaned against the wall, she glared at them. Sahil and Preeti's proximity irked her. She gave Preeti a tight smile as she greeted her before she headed back to the kitchen. Mandana's presence at his doorstep had surprised Sahil as well.

Sahil: "Mandy? When did you come? Come in!"

But an annoyed Mandana huffed before replying curtly.

Mandana: "I was waiting for you in my room for our routine morning walk. But I see you were in the company of the maid instead. Didn't you know I would be waiting for you?"

Sahil turned pale at Mandana's admonishment. Her vicious words offended him when she called his friend a maid.

Sahil: "Mind your language, Mandy! I spoke to her out of courtesy. Anyway, the chat didn't last more than ten minutes. Give me a few minutes, I'll get ready."

But Mandana was in no mood to listen.

Mandana: "I don't want to go anywhere. Go and be with that maid."

With these harsh words, she stomped back to her room. Sahil hadn't expected such scorn from her.

****

On the same morning, Vidya entered the study to have a word with Thakur.

Vidya: "Did you get a chance to talk to Sahil about Preeti?"

But as soon as she looked into his eyes to get an answer, she gasped as his reaction scared her to the wits. With eyes widened in fear,

Thakur was frowning. A thick drop of sweat ran from his forehead to his nose, and his lips winced in disarray. Vidya screamed at his miserable state.

Vidya: "W-what happened? Are you okay?"

Thakur: "Who…who are you? Wh-where am I?"

Vidya: "What are you saying? Have you lost your mind? I am Vidya, your wife!"

Thakur: "Vidya? Who Vidya? I don't remember any Vidya."

She held his shoulders in despair and shook him violently.

Vidya: "What has happened to you, Sahil's father? Don't you recognize me? Are you alright? Don't you remember me?"

Vidya's loud and high-pitched words snapped him out of his trance.

Thakur: "Oh, Vidya! I…I'm sorry. I don't know what happened to me. My mind went blank for a few moments. I forgot everything and everybody around me. Perhaps my age is catching up to me."

Vidya sighed in relief after she heard his sensible words. She held his hands and caressed them.

Vidya: "You scared the life out of me. I'm going to add almonds to your diet henceforth. It'll boost your memory. Why don't you take a break for a day or two? You need to take care of your health. And don't work so hard—you know I can't live without you."

Thakur smiled and cradled her hands in his as they both locked eyes.

****

Since Mandana refused to accompany Sahil on the morning walk, he decided to tread alone. Instead of his routine walk to the riverbank, he decided to walk towards the bridge. It was not a romantic venture like the riverbank, but the place had fascinated him since childhood. The gush of water underneath the bridge had always left him spellbound. It was built near the tribal area of Ratnagiri in the outskirts, right next to the jail. As soon as he started to walk on the bridge, he saw two children, a little boy, and a girl, walking towards him from the other side. They had stepped out of the police station located on their side of the bridge. He caught the shrill voice of the boy when they approached him on the bridge. From their conversation, he could gather that their names were Kaju and Muniya. It appeared that Kaju, along with his sister Muniya, sold tea for a living. And before Sahil could have passed them both, Kaju looked up at him and spoke out in a loud voice.

Kaju: "Sir, would you like to have some tea?"

The sight of the little tea sellers surprised him. The boy had worn-out shoes and baggy clothes on him. On the other hand, Muniya had rubber slippers in her feet and wore a knee-height pink-colored frock. Kaju was carrying a teakettle while Muniya held a pouch of disposable paper cups stacked one within the other.

Kaju: "Would you like to have the large cup?"

Sahil smiled in slight embarrassment. The morning tea he had shared with Preeti was still splashing in his stomach.

Sahil: "Umm…I don't need any for now. I already had some before I left home."

But the kid was not ready to give up. He proposed an alternate offer.

Kaju: "I have a small cup too. It is cheaper by a rupee."

Sahil beamed at the kid's innocent persuasion. With a smile, he took some coins out of his wallet and placed them in Kaju's hand.

Sahil: "Give me the large one, and keep the change."

With a gracious grin, the child grabbed a cup from Muniya, filled it to the brim, and handed it to Sahil, who sipped the hot aromatic cardamom tea.

Sahil: "Ahhh! The tea is fantastic. But what were you both doing in jail? I saw you both coming out of the building. It's not suitable for children."

Kaju: "We both work in *The Aroma* tea shop located across the bridge. Every morning, we deliver tea to all the guards in the jail. It helps us make some money. Everyone is nice there except for the bald jailor. Everyone pays us right away, but he delays our payment for days."

Sahil: "Aren't you guys feeling cold? It's freezing out here today."

Kaju: "If we start thinking about the cold, how will we make our living, Sir? Moreover, I need money to buy pencils and some notebooks. The school has already begun, and I am still falling short of money to buy my Science and English books."

Sahil: "Do you study in Ratnagiri School?"

Kaju: "Yes. I attend my classes after selling tea for a couple of hours in the morning."

Sahil: "What about your parents? Don't they work?"

A grim expression clouded his face when he heard the question.

Kaju: "They are no more. I live with my aunt and sister in a locality near the jail."

The locality, that Kaju referred, was located in the tribal area. Unknown to Sahil, the place had been demarcated as one of the most dangerous areas in police records. Kaju's pain wrenched Sahil's heart. He cleared his throat and assumed a neutral expression.

Sahil: "Hmm…do you know a teacher with the name Preeti?"

The boy jumped up in excitement.

Kaju: "Oh, yes! She taught me last year. She is very nice to me."

Sahil: "I can buy your books, and you can collect them from Preeti. How does that sound?"

Kaju: "Can I come to your house to pick them up? I don't want my friends to know that I got the books for free."

Sahil smiled at the boy's innocent but frank plea.

Sahil: "Yeah, sure. Let's do one thing. Next Sunday, come over to Ratnagiri mansion at around eight…emm… not eight…. around five in the evening. Eight in the evening would be too late for you! I will keep your books ready."

Kaju's face lit up when he heard Sahil. He cheerfully nodded and then continued walking ahead with Muniya. After the siblings left, Sahil began pondering. The conversation with the kids had evoked a deep sense of nostalgia in him for his school days. He remembered the sweet old memories he had made in school with his friends. Moreover, it had been a while since he had entered the school premises. With nostalgic thoughts playing in his mind, he turned around and walked towards the school.

The morning session had just begun when he entered the building of the school. He looked around the premises. Apart from the newly painted walls, everything else looked pretty much the same. In the middle of the playground, a few boys were playing football. Also, some girls had gathered near the corner of the ground and played hopscotch among each other. And then, Preeti's familiar voice snapped him out of his reverie. Startled, he turned around immediately as he hadn't expected to see her.

Preeti: "I didn't know you were desperate to have breakfast with me too after tea."

They both chuckled as they looked at each other.

Sahil: "Hey, Preeti. I took a stroll to the school for no reason. It feels so good to step into the school after so many years. I think I should visit the place more often."

Preeti nodded with a smile as she pulled out her tiffin box from her bag.

Preeti: "Would you like to join me for breakfast in the canteen? I couldn't have it at home as I was getting late for school. I have about thirty minutes before my next class. And guess what! I brought your favorite potato and mango relish stuffed sandwiches!"

Even though he was not particularly hungry, he thought it would be rude to refuse her. As they walked towards the canteen, Sahil caught a glimpse of the locked door of the school basement. The basement never had a door when Sahil studied in the school years ago. It used to be an open basement in those times, with no doors installed to it. In those days, it housed school equipment such as benches and blackboards, and everybody had access to it.

Sahil: "When was the door installed? I've never seen the basement locked before."

Preeti looked at the basement and shrugged.

Preeti: "I don't know, but I've always seen it locked."

They entered the canteen and settled down. She placed her purse on the table and opened the lid of the tiffin box. He cleared his throat as she placed a sandwich in front of him on a napkin.

Sahil: "Umm… Preeti… I am sorry to hear about Uncle. I wanted to talk to you about this before, but I didn't have the guts."

With a dejected smile, she nodded.

Preeti: "Yes, Sahil. It was a difficult time for me. But fortunately, I had everyone around me to help overcome the grief. Ma, Baba and…"

Preeti held back her words and looked up at Sahil with a mesmerized smile. A naïve Sahil frowned, as he wanted her to complete her answer.

Sahil: "And?"

Preeti: "Umm…and…Bansi…Bansi Uncle."

Sahil rolled his eyes and nodded. While he concentrated and munched on his sandwich, she secretly gazed at him with a slender smile. She had hidden the truth from him. In reality, she had managed to overcome her grief mainly because of him. And in her tough times, the sweet memories of the time spent with him in their childhood days had given her strength. Though she never told him, she had always loved him since her childhood.

Sahil: "Ma was all praise for you the other day."
Preeti: "And what about you? Do you admire me?"

Sahil blushed at her frankness, then chuckled and replied after some hesitation.

Sahil: "Umm… Y-yeah, I do. You are doing a good job."

Preeti giggled, while Sahil smiled and shook his head. It was time for Preeti's class. He thanked her with a smile and started walking back to the mansion. She too ambled her way to the class wearing a grin. Although he didn't notice, she turned around to look at him with a gaze filled with love. She wanted to profess the love she had for him since childhood. She wanted to confess to him the dreams she had woven of being in his arms one day. But she wanted him to make the first move, and she was ready to wait for it.

04. The Heartbreak

Vidya: "How much longer will it take, Harak? The guests will be here soon."
Harak: "D-d-done, a-a-almost!"

A doltish character who stuttered his words, Harak was one of the finest *Rangoli* artists in town. Like with every year before, Thakur had invited a bunch of people in the evening to the mansion to celebrate Diwali. He had organized a lavish party for the guests and hired Harak to create the *Rangoli* on the floor. Though he carried out petty, clerical jobs for Tatya most of the year, he was in high demand during festive seasons. As expected, Harak didn't disappoint Thakur. He had created a fabulous masterpiece—a beautiful peacock in green and blue, with a crooked beak, twisted tail, and opened feathers.

The distinguished attendees included Inspector Sharma and renowned advocate Tara Chand. Alok, Tatya, and his subordinates were some of the other invitees. Alok occupied the front row of seated guests with his children, Dhananjay and Suhasini.

Suhasini was a brown-skinned attractive young lady with long unbraided hair and big breasts. She dressed herself nicely in a yellow coat. But Dhananjay did not maintain himself well, and had a poor dressing sense. The obese man had rough and uncombed curly hair. Moreover, he had out fashioned plastic eyeglasses on him and wore rugged sports shoes.

People talked and laughed as they enjoyed the crispy spring rolls. I still remember the aroma of delicious fried potatoes in the air.

The sweet fragrance of espresso coffee permeated every corner of the front lawn. Thakur stood at the gate of the mansion to welcome guests, while Vidya helped the crowd settle down on the vacant seats in the lawn. Tatya and his men were busy arranging extra chairs as more and more people started pouring in.

Once the place was buzzing with guests, Sahil and Mandana walked downstairs to the lawn. Sahil looked handsome in his black formal suit and maroon spruce tie. And Mandana looked gorgeous in her short green-colored western dress with full sleeves. She looked a fashionista in her untied long hairs and high heels.

But everyone's eyes turned to Preeti when she made her way to the lawn and walked towards Sahil and Mandana. Dressed to the nine, her elegant traditional attire suited the occasion. She wore a black saree with heavy kohl eyeliner. She had a bold and bright lipstick applied to her lips. Also, she had worn two glittering bangles with one in each forearm. To counter the cold night, she wore a shimmery and stylish jacket over her outfit. With her long hair combed to one side, she had a complete makeover. Sahil smiled in her admiration when she came and stood next to him.

Sahil: "You're a real knockout today!"

While Preeti blushed at his praise, their chemistry was eating up Mandana from the inside. She gave him a veiled look as a deep sense of jealousy gripped her. Meanwhile, in one corner of the hall, Thakur was congratulating Tara Chand on a case victory.

Thakur: "It was a hands-down victory, Tara. Your arguments in defense of your client left the prosecution speechless."

Tara Chand: "It's all because of your aid, and thanks for that. The testimonies of your men and the other pieces of evidence helped me tremendously. They were great alibis. They compelled the court to drop all charges against my client."

Thakur: "You would have won it anyway!"

With those words, the two men raised a toast to each other and clinked their whiskey glasses. On the other side of the lawn, Dhananjay and Suhasini sat and enjoyed the mouth-watering snacks. Alok was keeping himself busy by clicking pictures of the event. A journalist by profession, he was also a seasoned photographer and loved to take pictures. He captured everything that fascinated him at the ceremony— the decorations, the vibrant lights, the extravagant gifts. He walked around and asked children and couples to strike various poses. He clicked their pictures, as they obliged. But as he did this, a sudden discovery shook him, and his smile vanished. Something he recalled sent shock waves through him. His eyes widened with fear, and his lips trembled. He rushed towards Dhananjay and Suhasini.

Alok: "W-w-we need to go back home. Right now!"

Their father's awkward behavior left them astounded. Although they both wanted to spend more time at the grand event, they agreed to go home halfheartedly. Along with Alok, they made their way to Thakur who stood at the gate and was busy welcoming the guests.

Alok: "I…umm…need to leave, Thakur. I have some urgent work to take care of."

His pale face perturbed Thakur.

Thakur: "All okay? You haven't eaten much. Let me get you a drink at least."

But an anxious Alok gulped and refused humbly.

Alok: "Umm…some…some other time, Thakur. I-I-I really need to leave. Please!"

Thakur stared at him with a puzzled look. He frowned, and then nodded.

Thakur: "Alright! Take care, Alok. I wish you a happy Diwali again!"

Alok greeted him and left the venue hastily.

After he left, I placed two buckets filled with water at a safe distance from the crowd. Tatya stacked low-intensity crackers near the water and asked everyone to step forward. He handed gold sparklers to everyone and cautioned the children to be careful. He requested the parents to take care of their young ones before he lit the sparklers one by one. Within no time, the area was aglow with the blaze of the sparklers. Parents and adults alike enjoyed the sparkles and the festivities.

But the heavy smoke from the crackers irritated Mandana's eyes and throat. The smog turned her eyes red, and she began to cough nonstop. Unable to endure it any more, she ran back to her room with no intention of coming down again. In any case, she had no interest in the event. She felt bored and tired all that while. Meanwhile, Sahil walked towards Preeti amid the loud cheers.

Sahil: "Won't you light any sparklers?"

Preeti: "No, I won't. I am a little scared."

Sahil: "Would you like to talk?"

Preeti agreed with a smile, and Sahil looked around with his brows raised.

Sahil: "This place is too noisy. I can barely hear you. What about the backyard near your room? Should we go there?"

Preeti smiled and nodded. Sahil carried two cups of tea and handed one to her as she settled on a bench in the backyard. He sat on the chair next to her and sipped his tea.

Sahil: "You know Preeti, I'll be honest with you. I never missed you when you left us along with your father. But there were occasions, I would recall some of the moments we spent as children together."

She looked up at him and grinned.

Preeti: "Let me be honest with you too. I always missed you."

His cheeks turned red when he heard this. She gauged his discomfort at her words and changed the course of the conversation. She pointed to the mango tree.

Preeti: "Umm…do you remember it? Do you remember when I used to make you climb it to get some mangoes?"

Sahil: "Yes, I do. And I clearly remember the day I fell off the tree during one such attempt and nearly broke my leg."

Preeti, embarrassed at this, grinned.

Preeti: "Oops! Sorry."

Sahil: "But only because of that effort of mine do you have the recipe for the best sandwiches I've ever tasted."

She covered her mouth with her hand and giggled. Sahil chuckled and finished the last sip of his tea.

Sahil: "What time do you eat lunch at school?"

Preeti: "Lunchtime starts at 12 sharp."

Sahil: "Would you mind if I come over to school around lunchtime someday?"

An ecstatic Preeti immediately agreed, trying to contain her excitement.

Preeti: "Yes, sure. My schedule right after lunch is free all five days of the week. If you come by 12, we will have a good hour to spend with each other."

Sahil: "Great! I'll walk to the campus whenever I feel like."

She took his hands in hers and looked straight into his eyes. As they both sat enjoying each other's company, Mandana glared at them from the balcony of her room. She always hated the moments they spent together. Tears of agony flowed down her cheeks. She clenched her teeth and slammed the window shut before running back to bed.

****

One afternoon, Sahil parked his bike outside the open gymnasium under the bright sun. It was one of his favorite places, and he knew the area like the back of his hand. As a child, he used to love playing cricket with his friends in the spacious field of the open gym after school. But Thakur had summoned him here for a different reason. As soon as he stepped inside, the cold breeze tickled his face and refreshed him. The sight in front of him took Sahil by surprise. Thakur was seated on a chair along with Tatya near a tree and enjoyed a friendly ongoing wrestling match.

In a routine duel, three men held Dara's arms and legs as they tried to pin him down. Dara – the yeti, was a nine-feet-tall beast with an ape-like appearance. With a broad chest and bulky shoulders, he was unbeatable in hand-to-hand combat. His tight, dark green skin set him apart from others. Thick, long hair densely covered his bare chest. A single stare from his big red eyes was enough to create havoc among his enemies.

Tatya stood up and greeted Sahil with a smile as he walked towards them. Thakur beamed when he saw Sahil and gestured to him to occupy the seat next to him. Without a word, Sahil sat down next to him, captivated by the friendly contest. As per the rules of the duel, the men had to pin down the beast by pulling him by his limbs. The pet had been tamed to endure the mischief.

But the three men wrestling him turned out to be a bunch of amateurs. They defied the rules! In their excitement, they flung a rope around his neck like a noose. This irked the creature, who felt threatened when the men began applying force and yanking him down. But with strength enough to uproot a tree, the monster was too big and too powerful for them. He gripped the rope around his neck and tugged at it. Two of the men slackened their grip on the rope and fled in fear, not wanting to come any closer to the angry monster.

But the third one wasn't as lucky. He stumbled and fell on the floor. Before he could get up and run for his life, Dara stomped forward and stood next to him. He looked down in fury and bared his fangs at the man on the floor, which scared everyone. Tatya and Thakur stood up from their chairs, and Sahil's face turned pale. The lips of the man on the floor were quivering, and he began to wail. He knew that his end was near. He folded his hands together and begged for mercy, but Dara was in no mood to spare the mischief. He groaned viciously and stared at the man in anger. Then, he lifted his giant foot in the air intending to drop it to smash the man's face. But Thakur intervened in a flash before the beast could inflict any harm on the man.

Thakur: "Dara, stop!"

He stopped in the nick of the time as he heard his master's command. Much like his ancestors to Thakur's predecessors, Dara was a slave to Thakur. The ape-man was Thakur's tamed beast, and he followed his instructions blindly. Once Thakur assigned him a task, he executed it without a second thought. After a few men tethered the beast to a nearby tree, Sahil walked to the perturbed Thakur and patted his shoulder.

Thakur: "With their walnut-sized brains, these creatures can be tough to control sometimes. They become too wild at times."

Sahil: "Oh really? I never knew that."

Thakur: "But there is a bright side to their low brain-to-body mass ratio. Their extrasensory sixth sense compensates for their small brain size. They have the terrific quality of being able to sense danger to their masters."

Sahil raised his brows, finding it hard to believe his father's words. But he was more interested in knowing the reason for which Thakur wanted to meet him.

Sahil: "So, why did you call me here?"

Thakur: "The tradition!"

With these words, Thakur handed Sahil a heavy metallic bangle. His words and actions did not make sense to Sahil until he caught sight of a baby gorilla, lying near the tethered Dara. With maroon skin, the toothless baby was squealing in fear. Dara, the baby's father, licked his face to calm him down. Named Zola, he resembled Dara a great deal, barring his maroon skin and small build. Sahil looked at the leg bangle around Dara's leg and understood the reason Thakur had summoned him. Like Thakur had put the bangle around young Dara's leg years ago, it was time for Sahil to do the same with Zola. The bangle was a symbol of loyalty. It reminded Dara, as it had his ancestors, to remain faithful to their master in the Thakur dynasty. Once a family member placed it on the ape's leg, he would protect his master from all the dangers and obey him for eternity. He would strictly and blindly follow the master's instructions. But Sahil was reluctant to follow this tradition, considering the act inhuman.

Sahil: "But Baba, he is too young and feeble. I don't want to put the heavy metal on him."

Thakur: "They grow really quick. You will see the difference within the span of a few months. Now get on with it."

Though Sahil had no wish to torture the little one, he agreed at Thakur's insistence. Upon Thakur's instruction, Dara grunted and moved away from Zola. The baby opened his toothless mouth wider and began crying in despair. Sahil smiled and bent down to look the knee-high ape in the eyes. To pacify the scared baby ape, he picked up a banana from a nearby table that had been kept to feed Dara and offered it to Zola. And the ploy worked. The baby stopped whimpering and grabbed the fruit from Sahil after a moment's thought. Next, he put his hand forward and caressed Sahil's cheek. This gesture brought a smile to Sahil's face. And then, he placed the bangle around the infant's ankle. Thakur and Tatya smiled at Sahil's actions.

Thakur had arranged for tea in the gym itself. Seated around a round table, Sahil and Thakur enjoyed some salted snacks along with tea.

Sahil: "Baba, what were the old days like when our ancestors ruled Ratnagiri as the kings?"

Thakur smiled and looked up at the sky. Though he had been suffering from dementia for quite some time, the query evoked some nostalgic memories in him.

Thakur: "I have heard a lot, but I don't remember much. With monarchy in place, those times were completely different. The people were fond of their king. People celebrated the occasion when the king tamed his beast, as you did today. The addition of the giant to his army strengthened him, making him invincible. The monster led the king's chariot whenever he marched into the battlefield. Until the king returned from the battle, his people offered prayers in the temple for his safe return. And when he returned victorious from the battlefield, his subjects danced in the streets to mark his victory. But should he return dead and mutilated, the grieving people would stand in solidarity and glorify their dead king. Masses would throng the king's cremation site and sing about his splendor."

Thakur frowned and closed his eyes, trying to recall the words the locals would sing as a tribute to their brave king.

Thakur: "What were the words? Righteous king…glory…hill…born again. Ahhh! I don't know what is happening to my memory. I feel it slipping from my grasp further and further with every passing day."

Sahil held his hand and smiled to calm him down. Thakur sighed before gulping his remaining tea in a single sip.

****

It was 9'O clock in the night when Kaju and Muniya returned home. It turned out to be one of the busiest days for both of them at the teashop. Muniya unlocked the door of their home, but Kaju turned around and started to sprint away from home. He had hardly taken a couple of steps when a surprised Muniya called out to him loudly.

Muniya: "Wh-Wh-Where are you going?"

Kaju: "I came home just to drop you. And now, I am going to the Ratnagiri mansion. Don't you remember the man we met back on the bridge? He asked me to visit him today at the mansion. He said he would keep my books with him. I am going to get them from him."

His words scared Muniya.

Muniya: "But you had to go at five! It is too late and dark now. You can pick them tomorrow."

But the boy was in no mood to listen. He was desperate to get the books that Sahil had promised him.

Kaju: "My science teacher won't spare me if I don't carry the book to school tomorrow. I'll be back soon. Bolt the door and don't step outside till I come back."

He began sprinting to the mansion. With about one mile to cover on foot, he expected to reach the mansion in half an hour. But he soon realized that leaving his house had been a mistake.

Walking through a deserted street on a moonless night, he panicked when he heard owls hooting from the trees. Their loud *hoo-hoo-hooooo* sounds scared him to the core. A dog whined in the distance, which made him tremble. Suddenly, he felt as though someone was walking behind him. Stranded in the tall bushes on the way, he heard someone stomping on the fallen dried leaves behind him. With his heart thumping loudly, he turned around amid his loud and erratic breathing but couldn't see anyone. He turned around and resumed walking towards the mansion again. And once again to his despair, he heard the sound of stomping footsteps. He turned around a second time, and this time, his eyes widened in fear.

A tall man wearing a balaclava and gloves was standing right in front of him. The masked man glared at Kaju, who gasped at the sight of the threatening figure. He opened his mouth to scream for help, but before he could get any sound out, the man gagged the kid's mouth with his hand. Kaju tried his best to free himself from the man's hold, but his efforts were in vain. The man lifted him in his arms and vanished into the bushes. Kaju never reached the mansion.

****

On the same night, Sahil entered his room and switched on the light while taking off his jacket. But much to his surprise, Mandana was sitting in his room with tears streaming down her cheeks. Her pathetic condition disturbed him.

Sahil: "Mandy? What happened? Why are you crying?"

Mandana: "Where were you the whole day?"

Sahil: "I was with Preeti in the morning. Then, Baba had some work for me in the afternoon, after which I drove to Tatya's place. The school equipment needs a few upgrades, and we spoke about it for a couple of hours. I'm just getting back from there."

But his sincere response did not calm her down.

Mandana: "I wait every day just to get one glimpse of you, but you spend the whole time of yours either with your family or with that maid. If this is what you were going to do, why did you bring me here along with you? I never expected such a cold response from you, Sahil. I will be leaving for my native town tomorrow morning. Goodnight!"

She turned around and stomped to the door, but before she could exit the room, Sahil ran to her and gripped her hand. He caressed her cheek.

Sahil: "Hey, listen! I'm sorry if I hurt you, Mandy. You are right. It is my fault. I know that I should have given you more time. But trust me, it wasn't intentional. Give me one more chance to correct my mistakes. I promise I won't disappoint you."

Though livid a while ago, his sincere apology pacified Mandana. She nodded and her smile broadened, as they both hugged each other.

Mandana: "I called up Dad. He'll be here next week."

The news startled Sahil.

Sahil: "Uncle?"

Mandana: "Yes. You don't want to talk to your parents and you won't let me initiate the talks either. So, I called the best man possible to take over the responsibility."

Sahil blushed and kissed her cheek as they tightened their embrace.

The next morning, Preeti served tea to Vidya in her room. A smile flashed on Vidya's face as she picked up the cup from the tray.

Vidya: "I heard you took the first half off from work yesterday?"

—

Preeti blushed before replying.

Preeti: "Umm…yes, I did. I roamed around with Sahil till late afternoon."

After taking a sip of her steaming tea, Vidya spoke.

Vidya: "I think he likes you. Why don't you talk to him?"

Preeti's heart skipped a beat. She blushed and tried to push her hair, which was gathered on one side, back over her shoulders. But before she could do this, Vidya stopped her.

Vidya: "Don't! Your new style mesmerized him on Diwali. Don't mess up your hair."

Despite her effort to control it, Preeti burst out laughing, and her face turned red. She picked up the serving platter and rushed out of Vidya's room. Vidya chuckled at her coyness, shaking her head and taking another sip of her tea. After serving tea to Thakur, Preeti decided to serve morning tea to Mandana and Sahil. She was in a trance-like state and had a wide smile on her face. Vidya's words kept playing in her mind.

She knocked on Mandana's door, but no one answered. And after a couple of minutes, she knocked on the door for the second time. And when Mandana didn't open the door, Preeti assumed her to be in deep sleep and decided to serve tea to Sahil first.

On Vidya's suggestion, she had decided to talk to him about their future together. Though she had always wanted Sahil to propose to her, she thought to confess her love to him. Going by her cozy chats with him recently, she had a gut feeling that Sahil won't refuse her. She recalled the warm moment on the night of Diwali when both sat together in the backyard of the mansion. That night, they held each other's hands and reminisced the nostalgic memories of their childhood. The good times that she had spent with him during school hours recently brought a wide smile on her face. With fantasies crowding her mind, she pushed open the door to his room. But when she saw the visual in front of her, she gasped and her eyes widened in despair.

With her naked breasts pressed against Sahil's bare chest, a topless Mandana was lying on top of him. Her head was nestled into his shoulder, and they both snored together in a feeling of peace. Preeti's widened eyes welled up as she saw both of them glued to each other in bed. She gasped and covered her mouth before running out of the room. She closed the door with care—she didn't want either of them to awaken. Then, she turned around and rested her back against the door. Tears streamed down her cheeks. Her dream of being with him all her life had shattered. She stood there sniffling and sobbing with a broken heart. Finally, she gulped down her sorrow and composed herself. In her miserable state, she wiped her tears. After a brief moment, she held her hair and threw it back over her shoulders, before making her way back to the kitchen with a heavy heart.

05. The Pull

With a glum face, Preeti packed lunch in her bag. The sight in the morning, when she saw Sahil and Mandana together in the bed, still played in her mind. And seated beside her on the dining table, Mandana sipped her tea and glanced at her gleefully. Once Preeti packed her stuff, she picked up her bag and looked at Mandana before walking to the door.

Preeti: "I'm leaving for school. Bye!"

But before she could leave, Mandana called out to her.

Mandana: "Preeti!"

Mandana's loud and shrilled voice startled Preeti, and she turned around in a jiffy.

Preeti: "Yes?"

Mandana got up from her chair and walked to her with a conceited smile on her face, and looked straight into her eyes.

Mandana: "I'm sorry for what you had to see today."

Preeti frowned, trying to understand what she meant.

Mandana: "I was awake when you entered Sahil's room. I know it must have broken your heart."

Preeti's gulped and her lips winced, as she stood silent and tried to conceal her melancholy. Then, without saying a word, she turned around and walked out of the kitchen to the school. Mandana stood there, and her smile widened as she watched her leave.

****

A couple of days passed by, and Sahil did not see Preeti anywhere in the mansion. On a Sunday afternoon, as everyone sat together on the dining table for lunch, Sahil looked around the hall. Preeti's absence started to bother him.

Sahil: "Ma, where's Preeti? I haven't seen her for the last couple of days. She used to meet me every day, at least to serve the morning tea. Is she okay?"

Vidya: "She has some important school assignments to take care of. And she doesn't want anyone to disturb her for a few days."

Sahil frowned in surprise as he found Vidya's words rather strange.

Sahil: "Doesn't want anyone to disturb her for a few days? Hmmm…"

Though a little hesitant, Mandana looked around the table and intervened.

Mandana: "Also, emm… it doesn't make sense for her to sit among us, the family members. I don't get good vibes when she sits next to me at the table."

Her obnoxious words did not go down well with anyone. Everybody stopped eating and glared at her. Her behavior embarrassed Sahil in particular, as the words were uncalled for. Though Vidya and Sahil remained silent, her insolence drew sharp criticism from Thakur.

Thakur: "Let me make things clear here. In this home, Preeti is just as important as the people seated in front of me at the moment."

Then, he gave her a stern gaze to Mandana before turning away his eyes to Vidya.

Thakur: "Vidya, can you please pass me the pickle?"

Feeling humiliated, Mandana swallowed her food and looked down.

****

It had been four days since Sahil had seen Preeti. Feeling concerned, he stopped by the school at recess time. He knew that she had some free time during that hour of the day. Preeti was sitting in the staffroom along with the other teachers when a peon walked in and saluted her.

Peon: "Good Afternoon, madam! Thakur's son is waiting for you in the canteen."

Seated at a table in the canteen, Sahil grinned as he went through the lunch menu. He thought of ordering fried lentils with steamed rice, a dish he knew Preeti loved. She had ordered it quite a few times whenever he came to see her at the school. But to his surprise, things did not turn out the way he had hoped. He saw the peon alone walking to his table in the canteen.

Peon: "Sir, she is busy right now and cannot come to the canteen. She has asked you to go back home."

With these words, the peon turned around and left. Sahil clenched his jaw and fixed his gaze at the menu card in his hand. He sensed that she had declined his request for some specific reason. He understood that she was trying to avoid him and something was terribly wrong.

It was nighttime, and there was a mild drizzle in the air. Preeti was preparing dinner in her room when she heard a knock on her door. She wiped her wet hands on a towel and hurried to the door. She opened it and felt a jolt of unease. Sahil stood in front of her.

He looked at her straight in the eye. She could not utter a word and took a step back to let him enter. He entered her room with a nervous smile. He then walked over to the mini-stove she had set up in her room.

Sahil: "Hmm…so you shifted the kitchen to your room, huh?"

She remained silent and continued looking at the floor. An annoyed Sahil spoke out in an irritated pitch.

Sahil: "May I know why? What happened to you in these past few days? Why are you avoiding me? Did Mandy say something to you? You have to tell me, Preeti!"

But she remained silent. Sahil heaved a deep sigh and anxiously bit his lip.

Sahil: "Your behavior is giving me the heebie-jeebies. I…umm…I'm sorry if I made any mistake, Preeti, but trust me, whatever mistake I might have done, would be completely unintentional."

His touching words made her sigh. She looked up at him glumly.

Preeti: "You haven't made any mistake, Sahil. I'm the one who made a mistake. And trust me, it was unintentional too. I never had any control over it."

Sahil: "Sorry, Preeti, but what are you trying to say here? I…I don't get you."

She digressed from the subject since she had no intention of creating a storm in his life. Even though she loved him, she decided to hide it from him.

Preeti: "Forget it, Sahil! Now, if you don't mind, I need to have my dinner and go to bed. I have a couple of meetings in the school early in the morning."

He nodded and sighed dejectedly. With a heavy heart, he started walking back to the door. As he was stepping out of her dingy room, his state melted Preeti's heart. She did not want to stress him out by keeping him in the dark. Although she had no intention of proposing to him, she decided to clear the air between them. She walked to the door and called him out in a trembling voice.

Preeti: "S-Sahil!"

Her fragile voice snapped him out of his thoughts. He turned around to face her. Without a word, he stood at the door while trying to read her face. Preeti swallowed a lump in her throat, and tears began dripping down her cheeks. Then, in a trembling voice, she opened up to him.

Preeti: "Make sure to shut the door the next time you and Mandana are in bed together!"

Her words sent shivers down his spine, and he looked at her in disbelief. He had no idea that she had come to his room while he was in bed with Mandana. Moreover, he began wondering about the reason behind her melancholy even if she had seen them together. He put two and two together, and things became crystal clear soon enough. And her behavior made so much sense when he recalled some of her banters. He remembered what she had said to him on Diwali.

Preeti: *"Let me be honest with you too. I always missed you."*

Preeti: *"I don't have words to express the joy I am feeling from within."*

Preeti: *"But fortunately, I had everyone around me to help overcome the grief. Ma, Baba and…"*

Sahil: *"And?"*

Preeti: *"Umm…and…Bansi…Bansi Uncle."*

He now understood the reason behind her abrupt pause that day. It wasn't me but him, who had given her strength in her tough times. His lower lip quivered. He continued looking straight into her eyes as she shut the door to him with a miserable smile on her face. Sahil stood outside her room for a while. Tears trickled down his cheeks. Though he had never been aware of it before, he realized now that she had strong feelings for him deep in her heart. He sighed before turning around and walking back to his room. Though he never intended it, he had somehow broken her heart.

****

As the days passed, it became clear to everyone that Sahil and Mandana were more than just friends. Even though Sahil never admitted it to anyone, Mandana was quite vocal about it. Vidya, too, held back her thoughts about Preeti and Sahil's relationship. Though she desired to see Preeti as her daughter-in-law, she did not want to push Sahil against his wishes. It was a matter of his personal preference and choice. On the other hand, a distressed Preeti stopped engaging in the activities of the family. She confined herself to her room and kept herself busy with school affairs. Perhaps it helped her to stay away from depression.

One Sunday morning, the family planned a picnic on the banks of River Palanharini. There was a gentle, cool breeze despite the bright sunny morning. Vidya helped me arrange vibrant colored mats on the banks. Once they all had settled down, I served them warm snacks along with hot tea. Mandana smiled as Thakur held the cup from my hand and passed it over to her. Despite her initial difficulties in adjusting to the place, she had developed a good rapport with Thakur and Vidya in the past few days. The elderly couple, too, seemed fond of her and had started to get along pretty well with her. The three of them appeared to be having a good time.

But seated next to Mandana, a glum Sahil seemed to be lost in deep thought. He had been silent throughout, keeping his eyes locked on the river. He missed Preeti, and as he had anticipated, she did not turn up for the picnic. He recalled the time he had met her a few days ago in the mansion. He remembered her distraught gaze at him while he stood at the doorstep of her room in the backyard.

Thakur's loud words jolted him out of his recollection.

Thakur: "Sahil? Are you alright?"

Sahil: "Y-y-yes, Baba! Umm…I'm just admiring this lovely weather."

He tried his best to hide the turmoil he was going through.

Thakur: "Yes, I am pleased with the weather as well. As a child, I used to sit here for hours in such weather. I used to close my eyes when the breeze tickled my cheeks. Then, I used to lift my face in the air, and tried to think about someone I had always wanted in my life."

Vidya: "Really? You've never told me this before! Let me try it."

She shut her eyes with a grin and lifted her face to the cool breeze. And she saw a much younger Thakur in front of her, the first time she had seen him years ago. And it happened when Thakur's parents visited her native village, and met her parents to finalize their wedding. A young and handsome Thakur had smiled and had offered her a red rose, as they stood face to face in a beautiful garden of her house. A young Vidya had blushed before taking the flower from him. The nostalgic moment brought a smile to Vidya's face as she sat by the river with her eyes closed. She grinned and opened her eyes, and looked straight into Thakur's eyes.

Vidya: "I saw you standing in front of me!"

Her statement brought a smile to everybody's face. Thakur, too, chuckled before controlling himself. Sahil couldn't hold back either, and smiled, rolling his eyes in amusement. Mandana closed her eyes next and felt the tickle of the breeze. As soon as she closed her eyes, she saw Sahil aiming at his target during the championship. She snickered, recalling their first kiss in college. She opened her eyes and laughed at her heart's content before pointing at Sahil.

Mandana: "That was you!"

He smiled and blushed at her gesture. He looked at Thakur, gesturing to him that he should go next. And Thakur did not disappoint him. As soon as he closed his eyes, a mild grin spread across his face as he saw Sahil seated on his shoulders as a kid. He savored the memory and opened his eyes.

Thakur: "Sahil!"

Mandana whistled and hooted after hearing Sahil's name yet again. We all cheered, as it was Sahil's turn next. He sighed and took a deep breath. Then, he closed his eyes and went into a meditative state. Our eyes were fixed on him, and we were eager to hear his reply. And as Mandana hoped for, he did visualize her smiling face as soon as he closed his eyes. But to his surprise, her vague image did not indicate any particular occasion. It was merely a blurry image, and he found it hard to keep his focus on her. Her image flickered, and soon, it disappeared in the darkness. He clenched his eyes and frowned as he concentrated hard to revive her image. But it did not help and darkness swamped in front of his closed eyes.

But then, something spectacular happened. The darkness faded into a dim light, and a vibrant picture of Preeti emerged. Unlike Mandana's fuzzy image, Preeti's image was crystal clear. He visualized her smiling face when she had walked to him in the dining hall the day he had returned from college. The next moment, he saw her gorgeous ensemble on Diwali eve. When he recalled her love-filled gaze at him, he gasped and opened his eyes. His lower lip trembled as he looked at Mandana, seated beside him. She giggled and had her gaze fixed at him.

Mandana: "Was that me?"

Out of sorts, he gulped at her naïve inquiry and pondered in confusion. Since he did not want to break her heart, he looked straight into her eyes and nodded with a nervous smile. She embraced him in response. Sahil's arms were around her back, but he looked around nervously. He knew that Preeti loved him. But he was surprised to realize that, in the past few days, he had developed some feelings for her as well. Though he had remained committed to Mandana all these years, he had always searched for the qualities in her, the ones that he witnessed in Preeti in the past few days. He never felt earlier, but he realized his love for Preeti once he closed his eyes and visualized her.

****

Boney jumped out of his seat when he heard Sahil.

Boney: "What are you saying, Sahil? Your words would shatter Mandy! Have you spoken to her about this?"

Sahil shook his head as he stood in the living room with the phone in his hand.

Sahil: "No, I haven't. I am not able to muster the courage to talk to her. I don't know what to do! That's why I called you up. What should I do, Boney? My brain has gone blank."

A perplexed Boney sighed deeply.

Boney: "I think you should talk to her, buddy."

Sahil: "Umm…b-but will she be able to handle it? I hope you understand what I'm talking about. You know she has some serious temper problems."

Boney: "I know she will get aggressive. She might turn violent, too, since she loves you. Regardless, you need to talk to her. There is no point in going ahead in a relationship if you don't feel the spark anymore. The earlier you guys sort it out, the better it would be."

Sahil nodded. The chat with Boney had turned out to be the perfect stressbuster for him.

Sahil: "Perhaps you're right, Boney. I should talk to her."

Boney: "Yeah, but take your time! Don't take any decision in haste. Else, it will only jeopardize the situation."

Sahil: "I won't. By the way, how's Kanta aunty?"

Boney: "She is much better now. The doctors will hopefully discharge her in a week's time."

Sahil: "That's nice to know. I hope she recuperates soon."

After a few more exchanges, the two friends hung up. The chitchat with Boney had rejuvenated Sahil. It gave him a clear direction. He decided to talk to Mandana in a day or two. But first, he decided to talk to Preeti about his intentions.

****

Preeti heard a knock on her door in the middle of the night. Settled at her study table, she was reading an article in the newspaper. She got up to open the door but was taken aback when she saw Sahil at her doorstep. Unlike his desolate look a few days ago, he seemed quite cheerful this time. His eyes were glittering, and he beamed when he saw her.

Sahil: "Can I come in?"

She gulped and nodded anxiously, allowing him to enter. He looked around with a smile, thinking of a way to break the ice.

Sahil: "Hmm…I wanted some help from you, but you don't bother to meet me these days."

Preeti: "Help? What happened?"

As soon as she said these words, he removed a unisex and a glittering diamond ring from his ring finger. Then, he gulped and looked into her eyes with a smile.

Sahil: "Baba has asked me to get married, and has bought me this ring. As per the tradition, I need to exchange this ring with my wife-to-be. I need your opinion about the ring. Do you like it, Preeti?"

He was holding the ring with his thumb and index finger. Then, he closed one eye and peeked at her through the metallic hoop of the ring. She fixed her gaze at him as well. Preeti, with her wide reading glasses, looked spectacular to him through the hoop of the ring. After a brief moment, she gulped and looked away.

Preeti: "W-w-why are you showing it to me? You should ask Mandana. She's the one who'll be wearing it."

Sahil opened his closed eye and ambled towards her after he heard her words. In an innocent gaze, they looked at each other lovingly. At that moment, because of her large emotive eyes, she looked like a paragon of beauty to him. All those days, he found her to be the epitome of feminine virtues because of her strong character. Though he never wanted to hurt Mandana, Preeti's demeanor convinced him that she was the only one for him.

Preeti's heart began to race when she felt his warm and heavy breath on her face. Lost in her eyes, he confessed his feelings to her.

Sahil: "Preeti, I am not talking about Mandy! I…I was talking about someone else."

Preeti's eyes welled up as she grasped the hidden meaning in his words. Lost in each other's eyes, they slowly moved closer to each other. They breathed heavily as their parched lips came closer and closer to each other. But before their lips could touch, I knocked on the door of her room. The sudden noise jolted them out their trance and they moved away from each other. Preeti blushed and turned around before she opened the door for me.

I: "Thakur wants to see you right now, Sahil. He is waiting for you in the living room."

Sahil smiled and looked at Preeti, who blushed and lowered her head, finding it hard to hold his gaze. In one moment, the stress the two had carried in the past few days vanished. Without saying anything further, he turned around and headed back to the mansion. He made up his mind to spill the beans to Thakur.

I made my way to the kitchen, while Sahil marched to the living room. Seated on the couch, Thakur was signing a bunch of papers. He nearly jumped up when he saw Sahil walking towards him.

Thakur: "Come here, my boy! Sit next to me. I have some news to share with you."

Sahil: "Good evening, Baba. I have some news for you too."

Thakur: "Oh, yeah? Tell me!"

But Sahil couldn't bring himself to say the words to his father.

Sahil: "Umm…first you, Baba! Tell me. What is it?"

Thakur: "Alright, but before I break the news, I need your help with something. I need to dispense some payment checks to a store in Khandala by tomorrow. It is about eight hours of drive from Ratnagiri. We recently bought some school equipment from there. The payment is still pending. Generally, Tatya takes care of it. But he isn't in Ratnagiri for a couple of days, so I need you to deliver the checks to the store manager. You need to leave for Khandala tomorrow in the morning itself. But you need to use some sort of public transport, probably a bus. Tatya took one car, and I need the other one for my work. If you want, you can book a room in some decent lodge once you reach there. You can board the train to Ratnagiri, which starts from Khandala in the evening. You would reach Ratnagiri on the morning of the day after."

Sahil: "Don't worry, Baba. I'll take the bus on the return journey, and I would be back by tomorrow evening. The Ratnagiri bus stop is close to the clock tower, hardly a mile away from home. I'll manage. Now, what is the news you wanted to share with me?"

Thakur chuckled and held Sahil's hand.

Thakur: "I spoke to Mandana's father today. He wants you two to get engaged next week, and I accepted his request. He will be here next week for the occasion."

Thakur's words sent shock waves through Sahil, who looked at his father in despair.

Thakur: "Frankly, I and Vidya weren't very fond of Mandana when we first met her. But as we spent more time with her, she mingled well with us. Don't hurt her, Sahil. Make sure you always keep her happy."

Though he had come to tell Thakur about Preeti, he remained silent. Also, whatever Thakur had said made complete sense. Mandana's father had known about their relationship for a long time. All her college friends were also aware of the intense chemistry between the both of them. He did not want to make her the laughing stock of the college. With a heavy heart, he held back his emotions and agreed to get engaged to Mandana. An ecstatic Thakur embraced him.

Thakur: "That is wonderful! By the way, you had some news too, didn't you?"

With a lump in his throat, Sahil held back his tears and replied with a miserable smile. He did not want to give any stress to Thakur.

Sahil: "N-N-Nothing, Baba. Even I came to talk to you about Mandana. I'll leave for Khandala tomorrow morning."

With those dismal words, he turned around and walked back to his room and bolted his door. He sighed deeply and sat on his bed. Miserable and confused, he cradled his head in his hands. Though he had agreed to get betrothed to Mandana, he knew that leaving Preeti would wreck him. Deep in the same thought, he was jolted when he sensed a tender touch on his neck. He looked to his side and frowned in surprise when he saw Mandana seated beside her. She threw her arms around his neck, grinned, and looked into his eyes.

The news of their upcoming engagement had reached her ears. It thrilled her to the core. Unable to control her excitement, she had come running to his room and hid in his closet to surprise him. And as soon as he entered his room, she crept out of the closet and walked towards him in silence. Astonished by the move, he looked at her with a straight face. Unaware of his misery, she leaped forward and kissed his cheek.

Mandana: "I have been waiting for this moment for a long time!"

With those words, a randy Mandana bit her lower lip and gave him an enticing gaze. She took off her robe, exposing her lingerie. She cradled his face in her hands and passionately pressed her lips against his. As she intensified her kiss, Sahil felt uneasy. The moment was making him uncomfortable, which was unusual as he craved her on earlier occasions. He grabbed her shoulders to stop her. But thinking it as his frenzy reaction to her seduction, she tightened her arms around his waist instead. He found it harder and harder to bear it further. An excited Mandana shut her eyes and swept her tongue in his mouth. But the feel of her wet tongue disgusted him. Hence, he pulled back in abhorrence and shoved her away. Fortunately, she maintained her balance and did not fall to the floor. Stunned, she looked at him with wide opened mouth. Sahil gulped and immediately rendered an apology in a quivering voice.

Sahil: "S-sorry, Mandy! I hope I didn't hurt you."

Baffled by his actions, she raised her brows and gaped at him. She frowned, unable to understand his weird behavior.

Mandana: "Are you okay? What happened?"

He stole his eyes away from her.

Sahil: "Umm…I-I'm a bit tired today. I-I-I need some sleep if you don't mind."

She felt humiliated by his words and glared at him.

Mandana: "But you loved it, right?"

Sahil: "That's right, Mandy. But as I said…I'm sapped today."

Mandana: "Alright, Sahil! Thanks for such a beautiful gesture."

With those words, she picked up her robe from the floor and put it back on. After one last glare at him, she stomped out of his room. A despondent Sahil sighed and lay down on his bed. The harder he tried to shift his focus away from Preeti, the more he thought about her. Tears trickled down his cheeks as he thought about her again and again. After regaining some composure, he wiped his tears and switched off the lights of his room. Then, he lay on the bed and slipped into a disturbed sleep.

06. The Divulge

The bus halted at Ratnagiri station, where Sahil got down. As per Thakur's request, he had gone to the store earlier in the day and handed over the checks to the owner. After completing the formalities by noon, he decided to visit some of his old school friends who lived in Khandala. By the time he met them all, it was too late in the night for him to return.

Standing alone at the empty station, he looked around for any taxi that could drop him home. He sighed, as there was no sign of any public transport around that time of the night. He noticed a public telephone booth on the other side of the road. At first, he thought of calling Thakur to pick him up, but he changed his mind. He did not want to bother his aged father that late in the night. Thus, in the moonless night, he decided to walk home instead. He took the shortcut that passed by the clock tower to save time.

It was 23 minutes past 11 when he reached the tower. Soon, he began walking through the dense bushes around the place. But before he could cross the place, a bloodstained hand clutched his foot, due to which he tripped and fell to the ground. He gasped at the sight before him. Alok, the journalist, lay in front of him. His throat had been slit, and a thick jet of blood was flowing out of it. He looked at Sahil with tears in his eyes and wheezed in agony amid wild and erratic hiccups.

Alok: "S-S-S-Sahil l-l-listen… I want I-I…"

Sahil: "Sir, what happened? Who-Who did this to you?"

Alok's terrible state horrified Sahil. Sahil gasped in panic and his lips quivered in fear. He pulled out a handkerchief from his pocket and, without wasting any time, tied it across the incision on Alok's throat. To minimize excessive blood loss, Sahil covered the wound with his hands. In the process, Alok's oozing blood stained Sahil's hands, arms, and shirt. Yet, even Sahil's best attempts to help Alok were in vain. Alok began to lose consciousness and his breathing slowed down. Sahil bawled and looked around for possible help. Though a few passersby drove their cars and went past him, none of them stopped for any aid. Perhaps, the visual in front scared the commuters where Alok lay in a pool of blood.

The situation worsened when he started vomiting blood and sniveled. Sahil screamed in agony, as the old man needed urgent medical attention.

Sahil: "IS ANYONE THERE? SOMEONE HELP ME!"

But it was too late. Alok's hiccups subsided, and his body became still. His breathing ceased, and he fell into Sahil's lap with a thud. He died! Unable to believe what he had just witnessed, Sahil's mind went blank for a moment. In his state of grief, he was unable to think of the next step he had to take.

****

Inspector Sharma opened the door of the cold storage in the morgue. Then, he slid out the locker wherein the police had placed Alok's dead body. As soon as Suhasini and Dhananjay saw his body, they clung to each other and began lamenting. Grief-stricken and in bloodstained clothes, Sahil stood near the body as well. After Alok had died in his lap the night before, he ran to an unmanned payphone at the tower and rang up the police. Once the police arrived at the location and collected the body, he had accompanied the cops to the mortuary.

In the morgue, he stood silently and watched Alok's children grieving. Dhananjay's agony and anger, directed at Inspector Sharma, disturbed him.

Dhananjay: "Will this spree of murders ever come to an end? Khatri has been abducting and killing people for years. Is the Ratnagiri police a bunch of spineless men who cannot catch one predator? When will this malevolence end?"

The statement made Sahil wince. With widened eyes, he looked at Sharma, shocked. He had spent his entire childhood here but had never heard of any such act of savagery. Even his father, the chieftain of Ratnagiri, had never mentioned anything of the sort to him. Sharma sympathized with Dhananjay and patted his shoulder to console him.

Sharma: "I understand your pain, Dhananjay, but trust me, the police have tried everything in its power to nab Khatri. He is a shrewd man. Somehow, he gets the information about the moves we plan every time. Having said that, I doubt that someone from Khatri's gang killed your father. In horrible torture, his men extract eyes, heart, and pretty much everything from the victim. Hence, I don't think that your father fell prey to the hoodlums. It looks like a case of personal animosity instead. We did find a dagger at the crime scene. Though it looks to be the murder weapon with traces of Alok's blood on it, police didn't find any fingerprints on it."

As soon as Sharma said these words, a bereaved Thakur entered the morgue. He wept when he saw his old friend lying dead in front of him. He consoled Dhananjay and Suhasini before asking them to go home, as did Inspector Sharma. He assured them he would release the body to them in a couple of hours since he had some formalities to take care of. Due to the gravity of the matter, the grief-stricken siblings agreed to abide by the advice. They gripped each other's hands and made their way out of the morgue. As soon as they walked out, a perturbed Sahil grilled Inspector Sharma and Thakur.

Sahil: "W-What is happening here, Baba? Who is this Khatri? What did Dhananjay mean by 'spree of murders'?"

Thakur exchanged a grim look with Sharma. His fears had come true. Sahil had found out the truth about the grisly murders that had plagued the village for years.

Thakur: "S-Sahil, I never wanted you to know about this. I knew that the facts would leave you devastated. About five years ago, something strange started to happen in Ratnagiri. It all started around the time you joined your college and moved to the hostel. People started to vanish from Ratnagiri. The disappearances remained unexplained for some time. But soon the police began to find the maimed bodies of the abducted people on the outskirts. Though a few are still missing, the police have recovered the corpses of many others. As per the reports, the assaulters had tortured the victims to death in a barbaric fashion. The brute killers had ripped the organs out of the victims' bodies while they were still alive. Then, they strangulated and dumped them in a gruesome manner."

The news stunned Sahil. He gasped at his father's words.

Sahil: "But…why?"

Thakur sighed before replying.

Thakur: "Organ trafficking! A man named Khatri runs the racket. The police have not traced his whereabouts in all these years. No one knows how he carries out the horrific trade from hiding."

Sharma: "Sahil, I need your statement for one such case. It's one of Khatri's victims."

Thakur: "Sahil's statement? But for whom? I don't think he knows any such man."

Sharma: "He does know, Thakur. And the victim I'm talking about is not a man but a little boy."

Saying this, he moved to the locker next to Alok's and slid it out. Sahil gasped in horror when he saw the body placed in the cabin. His eyes widened, as he could not believe what he was seeing. Lying in front of him was the corpse of Kaju, the tea seller he had met at the bridge a few days back. With nostrils stuffed with cotton swabs, the corpse was in a pathetic state. The body had cuts and bruises all over it. Sahil cried out and looked away.

Sahil: "Oh…oh…my god! K-K-Kaju? Yeah, I know him. I met him once. He wanted to collect some books from me, but he never turned up."

Sharma: "That's right. According to his sister, he had left home to collect the books from you one night, but he never returned home. We think that Khatri's men grabbed him when he was on his way to your mansion.

Sahil was speechless. Thakur walked to him and patted his shoulder to comfort him.

Thakur: "I know what you're going through, son. I never told you about all this because I knew it would make you feel wretched."

He looked up at Thakur and wiped his tears. After he regained composure, he submitted his statement to Sharma in writing. He listed every minute detail of his meeting with Kaju. After completing a few formalities, Sahil and Thakur drove back to the mansion. Thakur had arranged a funeral service for Alok that evening.

Around twilight, a big crowd thronged the crematorium. Alok was a well-known man. Thakur and Sahil were the first ones to make it to the procession, and they stood with glum faces. Before reaching the crematorium, Sahil had taken a bath to calm himself down. Then, he dressed suitably for the somber occasion and drove to the cremation site with Thakur.

A group of ladies held Suhasini by her arms as she bawled inconsolably. A high pyre of wooden logs was set up in the middle of the dusty ground. A few men carried a bier with Alok's body and placed it atop the wooden pyre. Dhananjay stood near the pyre next to the head priest. The priest issued some commands to his disciples before beginning the rituals. Once silence engulfed the ground, he began chanting the purification mantra. As per the belief, spiritual verses cleansed the departed soul of all its sins. And the dead attained salvation when priests chanted *mantras* before the body was set on fire. Sahil listened to the group of priests as they spoke the *mantra* in a chorus.

"Om-Prann-appann-vyaann-uddann-smaanaa-meee-shudyantaam-jyotiraham!
viraajaa-vipaapmaa-bhuyaa-sag-svaha!
vang-mnaahaa-shakshoo-shrotra-jigvaag-grahan-reto-budhiya-kooti-sankalapa-mey-
shudhyantaam-jyotiraham!
viraajaa-vipaapmaa-bhuyaa-sag-svaha!..."

Finally, Dhananjay set the pyre with Alok's body ablaze. Everyone wept as the dark smoke from the burning pyre rose high and engulfed the place. They then consoled Dhananjay one final time before returning to their homes.

****

After a few days, Thakur walked into his study one evening and found Dhananjay seated on a chair near the safe vault. Surprised, Thakur looked at him from head to toe, as he never usually allowed anyone to walk in without prior permission.

Thakur: "Dhananjay? What are you doing here? Is everything okay?"

With a sheet of paper in his hand, Dhananjay stood up and looked at him miserably. Then, he cleared his throat and narrated the purpose of his visit.

Dhananjay: "I am sorry to have walked in without your permission. But since I need an urgent favor from you, Bansi asked me to wait in your study."

Thakur: "That's alright! How can I help you?"

A stressed-out Dhananjay sighed and handed the piece of paper to Thakur.

Dhananjay: "After the father's demise, the publishing house isn't of any use to me. I am planning to sell it off. Since you are the chieftain, I need you to sign the NOC – No Objection Certificate to permit me to sell it off. Only then I will start the talks with some of the interested parties."

Thakur looked at him with gloomy eyes. Then, he nodded and picked up a pen from his table. Finally, without saying any word, he signed the document without going through any details listed in it. He empathized with the young man and didn't want to pester him at that desolate moment. He turned emotional as he handed the document back to Dhananjay.

Thakur: "Have you gotten any buyers yet?"

Dhananjay: "Not yet. Father was in talks with a couple of parties. I need to revisit all those deals to figure out the best bid."

Thakur: "Alok's death has left a deep void in my life, Dhananjay. There hasn't been a single day when I haven't thought about him. How is Suhasini? I know it will take some time to heal though."

Dhananjay: "Yeah, we are getting better as the days are passing. Umm…I need to ask you something. I know that father was close to you. Did he ever mention something specific he was looking for in his last days?"

Thakur tried to recall some prior interactions he had with Alok.

Thakur: "Umm…not really! Though I don't remember much these days, I doubt he ever told me anything of the sort. But…emm…I remember that his demeanor changed after Diwali eve. He went into a shell after the festival. He did not talk to me, and I never saw him thereafter. I am sure that something upset him that evening."

Dhananjay: "Yes, I remember it. He did behave weirdly that day. He became quite aloof after we returned from the mansion that evening. There were days when he left home early in the mornings and returned late at night. Whenever I asked him the reason, he would reply that he was in search of some peculiar information. But he never revealed anything more than that. I will take your leave now, Thakur. Suhasini is alone at home, and she will be waiting for me."

With these words, Dhananjay walked towards the door. But before he could exit, Thakur called out to him.
Thakur: "Dhananjay?"

Dhananjay halted and turned around to face Thakur.
Dhananjay: "Yes?"

Thakur gulped and looked at him with a straight face.
Thakur: "Are you sure you are not hiding anything from me?"

Dhananjay's eyes widened at Thakur's blunt words. He smiled nervously.
Dhananjay: "N-n-no. I…I don't have any reason to hide anything from you."
Thakur: "If you recall anything, please let me know. I would be happy to offer any help."

Dhananjay thanked Thakur and left the room with an uneasy expression.

****

Sahil parked his car outside the mansion on a late evening. He stepped out and saw a red German car in the parking lot. He had seen Mandana drive the same car around the college campus on a few occasions. He understood that her father had arrived for their upcoming engagement. He sighed and hung his head in melancholy because of his feelings for Preeti. Engrossed in his thoughts, he started walking towards the entrance. But before he could reach the door, he heard Preeti's voice. He turned around and saw her standing in front of him with her eyes locked at him. She had an innocent look and a slight smile on her face. Sahil had been in a dilemma for the last few days, as his last encounter with her had been quite romantic and loving. He had avoided her post their last conversation as his conscience asked him to marry Mandana. He knew that the news of him getting engaged to Mandana had broken her heart. He looked at her in melancholy and stammered since he had no words to say to her.
Sahil: "P…Preeti?"

She gulped and walked towards him with a miserable smile.
Preeti: "Umm…Sahil, I just came to tell you that… emm…d-don't get sad or angry with yourself. It is not your fault."

A sad Sahil heaved a deep sigh and nodded in dejection.

—

Sahil: "I know that, Preeti. The mesh of mistakes and regrets has entangled our feet."

It was an emotional moment for the two of them. Though she tried her best to control herself, her eyes welled up. She wiped her tears and replied to him with a quivering smile.

Preeti: "I know, Sahil. Moreover, certain things are not written in the stars, no matter how much we yearn for them. But I will always cherish your friendship. I am lucky to have you as a friend."

Sahil couldn't say a word. He looked at her with a glum face. It was time for them to get over each other and move on. With a rueful smile, she extended her hand to him and looked at him despondently. After a pause, he acknowledged her gesture with a gentle handshake.

Preeti: "All the best, Sahil. I wish that you both stay blessed and happy forever."

With these words, she turned around and hurried back to her room amid sobs. A perplexed Sahil stood at the door, holding back tears, and watched her leave. Then, he turned around and entered the mansion with a heavy heart.

As soon as he stepped into the living area, he saw a couple of travel bags on the floor, and beside them were two huge fruit baskets. The sweet aroma of ripe mangoes engulfed the room. Sahil looked up, and as expected, he saw Mandana's cardiologist father, Mr. Dilshad Kapoor, seated on the couch. Thakur and Mandana were sitting next to him on an adjacent couch. They were all busy chitchatting when Mandana caught sight of Sahil. She leaped out of her seat and ran up to him to embrace him. Sahil patted her shoulder with a nervous smile and walked to her father. He touched his feet and paid his respects to him. By this time, Vidya and I had walked into the hall as well. She carried a tray with tea, while I carried and served the warm snacks. And after everyone agreed, Thakur finalized Sahil and Mandana's engagement date, two days later in the mansion itself.

07. The Jeopardy

Finally, the day of the ceremony arrived. The preparations had been in full swing since early morning. Thakur had planned the ring ceremony for the evening, and he had too much work to complete before sunset. He ran around scolding the electricians, as they had not set up the string lights around the mansion. I worked with the hired cooks and Ratnagiri's most famous confectioner. Thakur had arranged for a grand feast for the elite guests in the evening. Vidya and Preeti, on the other hand, were busy decorating the place with garlands. Also, Tatya and all his men took care of the seating arrangements in the front lawn of the mansion.

Seated in the living room, Thakur and Dilshad roared with laughter. They were discussing the evening's festivities when they heard the loud ringing of the phone. Thakur picked up the phone and chuckled when he heard Inspector Sharma on the other end.

Sharma: "I called up to congratulate you, Thakur!"

Thakur: "Thanks, sir! The party will start at seven, and the exchange of the rings would happen at eight, sharp. I will be waiting for you."

Sharma: "I wish I could come, Thakur. But unfortunately, I just got my transfer orders last evening. I am leaving Ratnagiri by train in the afternoon."

This piece of news came as a rude shock to Thakur.

Thakur: "W-what? This is terrible news!"

Sharma: "Yes, it is. But let me be honest, I failed to nab Khatri all these years, so I knew I would have to bear the brunt one day."

Thakur: "And who is going to take charge as your replacement?"

Sharma: "His name is Khan. An honest and brilliant officer, I'm sure he will be able to crack the case."

Thakur: "I will miss you, Inspector Sharma. And I wish you luck in all your future endeavors."

They exchanged greetings and bid farewell before hanging up.

****

By the evening, Tatya and his men installed two tall floodlights in the spacious backyard. Moreover, they did set up a huge banquet table under the bright floodlights. On the front lawn, a raised dais had been set up near the chairs of the audience. A lavish red carpet covered the entire floor of the elevated podium. It had two stylish high chairs next to each other in the middle amid the floral décor. The background of the podium was lit up, and soft music was playing on the speakers, which added to the ambiance. As it grew darker, the crowd started to grow. Along with me, a few hired waiters served drinks and appetizers to the guests.

When it was time for the ceremony, Mandana and Sahil stepped onto the stage. Dressed to match the occasion, Mandana dazzled in an embroidered net jacket gown. Mr. Dilshad, in smiles, walked along with her from the left side of the dais to its center. Also,

Sahil looked suave in a blue open-neck suit. Vidya and Thakur escorted him to the center of the dais and walked on to the stage from the right side. Then, Mandana and Sahil came together and stood next to each other in the center of the raised podium. A professional photographer climbed onto the stage to capture a few of their poses.

Preeti walked to the couple with an ornate tray in her hand that held two glittering rings. But before she could offer the rings to the couple, she caught a glimpse of Sahil's ring on the tray. She recalled the time he had looked at her through the ring's hoop a few days ago. She swallowed the lump in her throat and looked at Sahil glumly, but she was not the only one feeling the pain. Sahil fixed his eyes on her too. But she was wise enough to turn her eyes away from him in the nick of time. Then, with a miserable smile, she offered the platter to both of them. With joy on her face, Mandana was the first one to pick up her ring. Sahil sighed and picked up the ring, trying his best to smile. Finally, amid loud applause, both of them held each other's hand and exchanged the rings. The crowd erupted with joy as Sahil and Mandana were formally engaged.

****

At the same time, a bus arrived at the Ratnagiri bus station and Boney got off. The doctors discharged his mother from the hospital that very day. But by the time he dropped her home, the first bus to Ratnagiri had departed. He managed to catch the next bus only a couple of hours later and ended up reaching Ratnagiri late in the night. After the bus drove off, he picked up his bag and walked out of the station. He looked around in the hope of finding some conveyance to the mansion. But the deserted street in front of him surprised him. Except for a whining dog under a tree, there was no sign of any life around him. He could not see any means to get to the mansion, but he noticed a payphone booth on the other side of the road. Since he had Sahil's home number noted in his diary, he thought to call him.

In the silence of the night, he made his way to the booth. But before he could enter it, someone gagged him and hauled him back. His mind went blank for a moment when he saw four men with balaclavas covering their faces in front of him—they belonged to the same posse that had mowed Murari down. He lost his grip over the flower bouquet that he had carried for Sahil and Mandana. Also, his bag slid out of his hands and fell on the dusty floor. Unable to speak, he wriggled about fearfully when he saw one of the men pull out a broadsword. With his broadsword raised high in the air, the man walked towards him swiftly. The sight of the approaching man, who looked like a Grim Reaper, petrified Boney.

In a last-ditch effort to escape, he back-kicked the man holding him. The action flustered the man, and he moved his hand away from Boney. Getting an opportunity, Boney then grabbed the man's index finger and bit it hard. And as he had hoped, the man loosened his grip, setting Boney free. Boney then ran for his life. Though unfamiliar with the geography of the place, he ran as fast as he could straight ahead, desperate to get out of their reach. The masked men were hot on Boney's trail. They seemed eager to nab him as a feed to their trade.

Running for his life, Boney gasped in despair and came to a halt. The dusty road ahead of him was split in two different directions. He gulped in confusion, and little droplets of sweat trickled down his face. But without the luxury of time, he took a gamble and sprinted towards the road on his right. He hoped to find someone who could help him out. Then, a feeling of optimism ran through him. He saw illumination a few meters ahead of him and a couple of tall streetlights. To his relief, a couple of buses were parked there as well.

As soon as he reached the lit area, he looked around in haste. His eyes desperately searched for someone to help him. Surprisingly, the place felt familiar to him. He frowned as he walked amid the parked buses. Suddenly, something on the floor caught his eye. He shuddered at the sight of his handbag and the bouquet, the same ones he had carried to Ratnagiri. The forked road had led him back to the bus station. He had landed up at the same place he had started from. The dog was still sitting under the tree and whining. His heart pounded in fear, and he looked around in terror. That's when he caught a glimpse of the payphone booth. With his life at stake, he decided to call Sahil for immediate help.

He scampered to the booth, pulled out a diary from his shirt's pocket, and turned over its pages with trembling hands. He panicked for a moment when he couldn't find Sahil's listed number. But then heaved a sigh of relief as he caught sight of it on a random page. With his heart thudding in his chest, he dialed the mansion. Once he heard the dial tone, he frisked all his pockets for some coins for the payphone. And he found a few when he slid his trembling fingers into the back pocket of his trousers.

Back in the mansion, it was the feast time! All the guests had gathered in the backyard near the dining table and were enjoying the dinner. Thakur greeted every single guest with a smile, but he was in a hurry. He had an urgent meeting in the chamber of assemblies at the same time. After interacting with all the guests, he asked me to take care of things in his absence. Then he left for the chamber with Tatya.

On the stage, Mandana was sitting with Sahil and Mr. Dilshad, chuckling as she chatted with her father. But Sahil wasn't paying heed to their banter. He sat slumped in his chair, unable to stop thinking about Preeti. He missed her and had a sudden urge to talk to her at that very moment. Mandana glanced at Sahil, gesturing for him to engage in the conversation. But her smile waned when she found him lost in some vague thoughts with a glum face. She held his hand.

Mandana: "Are you fine, Sahil? You look disturbed."

Her words snapped him out of his daze, and he looked at her, disoriented. Then, he cleared his throat and tried to excuse himself.

Sahil: "Umm…n-n-nothing. I'm a little tired though. Would you mind if I got some water from the kitchen?"

Mandana: "Do you want me to bring it for you?"

Sahil: "No, I'll go myself. I don't want to disturb you and your dad. I would be back soon."

With these words, he got up from his seat and made his way to the kitchen. As she watched him leave, Mandana sensed that something was wrong with him for sure.

Stranded in the phone booth, Boney lamented as nobody had picked up his call. He decided to try once again, praying and wishing for someone to pick up his call. This time, the Almighty accepted his prayers. As luck would have it, Sahil entered the kitchen just as the phone began to ring. He picked up the call.

Sahil: "Hello?"

Unable to control his emotions when he heard Sahil's voice, Boney stuttered in despair.

Boney: "S-Sahil…"

Sahil beamed upon hearing Boney on the other side of the call.

Sahil: "Boney? Where are you? I've been waiting for you all this time. Mandana and I just exchanged rings a few moments ago."

But his joy turned to horror as he heard Boney's story. Sahil connected this to the recent attacks on Kaju and Alok. And he understood that the same group of men had attacked Boney as well. His friend's life was in grave danger.

Sahil: "Don't you worry, Boney. I-I-I'm coming. Don't step out of the booth until I reach!"

Boney: "Come soon, Sahil. These guys will kill me otherwise."
Sahil: "I'm leaving, Boney! I'll be there in a few minutes. Don't worry."

With these reassuring words, he put down the receiver and hurried to the backyard. He looked around for Thakur or Tatya in desperation, but they had both left for the chamber already. With no other option, he ran to his car and sped towards the bus station. Mandana caught a glimpse of him as he drove out of the parking lot. Earlier, when Sahil had left the stage in a glum mood, she had thought of talking to him. And so, she had walked off the stage and walked towards the mansion as well. She wanted to know the reason behind his melancholy. But seeing him race away in his car and disappear into the darkness stunned her. Worried for him, she pondered about what to do for a moment. Then, she hurried to her father's German car and drove off behind Sahil. But she was not the only one to witness Sahil's wretched state. A baffled Preeti, who had been in the balcony at that time to fix some of the garlands that had fallen off, watched the whole episode unfold.

****

Stuck in the booth, a terrified Boney abided by Sahil's advice. He sank to the floor of the booth since the top half made of glass would have exposed him. The thick wooden walls of the lower half helped him conceal himself. He tried to control his breathing, as it was too loud and audible. He closed his eyes and leaned his back against the wooden wall.

Meanwhile, Sahil was driving as fast as he could. He crossed the clock tower and had almost reached the bus station. The car screeched and took a sudden halt outside the booth. Boney heard the sound and smiled in relief. He knew that Sahil had reached the station. But before he could stand up and leave the booth, a masked man slammed opened its door and entered. The sight of the man sent chills down Boney's spine and his feet went numb. Boney grumbled in fear as he looked up at the masked man. He joined his hands and begged for mercy.

Boney: "No, please! What have I done to you? Why are you people behind me? Leave me alone, please!"

But his pleas did not deter the masked man, who pulled him up by his collar. Then, he pulled Boney out of the booth and shoved him to the ground. Boney jolted in horror when he saw three other masked men standing near a van. Though the men covered their faces, Boney

—

66

identified the man who had held a broadsword in his hand. He was the same man who had tried to kill him earlier. He couldn't forget his angst-filled stare and red, watery eyes.

The assailant who had hauled Boney out of the booth gripped his arms and pinned him down. Then, he jerked his head towards the three waiting men. They nodded in response and walked towards the duo, and surrounded them in a circular formation. Boney howled as the man with the broadsword knelt and raised the weapon to strike him. In his last attempt to escape death, Boney grabbed the hilt of the weapon and applied all his strength to push back the hand of the man. But he started losing strength when the other hooded men bent down and held his arms. His grip on the weapon loosened, and he could no longer hold back the man with the broadsword. In one quick motion, the tyrant with the broadsword slit his throat. Boney's eyes widened in pain as a fountain of blood spurted from the incision.

Tears trickled down his face as he saw a fast-approaching Sahil at a distance. Unable to breathe, he held his lacerated throat with both his hands. He knew he was going to die. The visual sent tremors through Sahil. He saw Boney lying on the ground, surrounded by four men with covered faces. His fears had come true. Sahil's sudden arrival stunned the hoodlums as well. They had not expected any human interference at that time. They looked at each other in confusion. He brought his car to a sudden halt and jumped out of it and ran through the assassins towards Boney. Sahil held a wheezing Boney in his hands and cried out aloud.

Sahil: "Boney…no…no…no! Boney…ahhh…no…no!"

But it was too late! Boney looked up at Sahil, and tears continued to flow down his cheeks. Suddenly, his body convulsed for a brief moment, and then he went motionless. A mournful Sahil began to wail in agony. He couldn't believe what had just happened in front of him. But mourning quickly turned to rage as he looked up at the masked men. He cradled Boney's face and rested it on the ground, then pounced on the man with the broadsword.

Sahil: "YOU BLOODY SWINE! YOU KILLED MY FRIEND! I'LL KILL YOU, YOU SCOUNDREL!"

His attack took the men by surprise. They had not expected such aggression from a common man. Sahil tried to pull the balaclava off the man with his hand, and they both rolled over each other's bodies in a fierce scuffle. The other three gripped Sahil by his arms and shoulders and attempted to free their companion. But the furious Sahil did not give up. He needed to see the man behind the mask, and in one desperate attempt, he got a good grip on the balaclava and pulled it off. He flung the mask in the air and looked at the man, and the sight before him left him thunderstruck. His eyes widened in shock when he saw Harak Singh in front of him.

Sahil: "H-Harak Singh! You? You're the one behind all this?"

But Harak did not reply and merely glared at Sahil. Then, he picked up his hood from the ground and pulled it back on himself. Then, he looked at one of his acquaintances and tossed his broadsword to him.

Harak: "K-k-kill him!"

His words sent tremors through Sahil. He could not believe his ears. The words were coming from a man the world had always known as a doltish person with no brains. Sahil had no idea that his family had a hidden ill-wisher in their ranks. The man with the broadsword started walking towards Sahil. Sahil wheezed and gulped in fear. With widened eyes, he stepped back to distance himself from the approaching attacker. Walking backward, he crossed to the other side of the road. The approaching man though was yet on the opposite side of the road.

And at that very moment, Mandana arrived at the spot and hit the brakes, making a hard stop a few meters ahead of Sahil and the hoodlum. Her eyes widened in terror when she saw Boney's dead body on the ground on one side and the masked man with a deadly weapon walking towards a helpless Sahil. It did not take her long to comprehend the situation.

The sight of Mandana gave Sahil an idea for escape. All he had to do was to get into her car and flee. Without a second thought, he sprinted towards her car. His action took Harak and the other masked men by surprise. Harak yelled at the man with the broadsword in his hand.

Harak: "K-k-kill them both! K-k-kill the girl! I want b-both of them d-d-dead!"

The loud words scared Mandana out of her wits. She winced in horror when she saw the man with the weapon chasing Sahil. But at that moment, she was not scared for Sahil. Instead, she realized the threat to her own life in that instant. Sahil was a few feet away from her, but the goon was only at an arm's distance from Sahil. She knew that if she stayed there any longer, the man would get hold of her along with Sahil. Her heart pounded, and she began to tear up. As soon as

—

Sahil reached the back bumper of her car, she hit the gas and drove out of the place, unable to contain her fear. Since Sahil had put all his weight on the bumper, he lost his balance when the car sped ahead. He tripped and fell onto the ground and gasped as the car vanished in a gust of smoke and dust. He flailed his arms in the direction of the moving car.

Sahil: "MANDYYYYY….NO….!!! HELP ME MANDY! COME BACK!"

But all his cries and pleas were in vain. She had left him to die in the forsaken place. He broke down and wept at her betrayal. The man with the broadsword had almost reached him by now. He chuckled at the plight of Sahil, who lay on the floor at his mercy. The man raised the weapon high in the air and aimed for Sahil's face. Sahil closed his eyes in the anticipation of a barbaric death.

But then, he heard a vrooming sound, and a convertible car rushed towards Sahil and the assailant at a whirlwind speed. The car did not have a roof, and the strong beams of its headlights cut through the darkness of the ill-fated night. Sahil rubbed his eyes, trying to recognize the driver against the flash of the strong beam. Seated behind the wheel, with her long hair open and tousled by the wind was Preeti. She did not halt the vehicle and, instead, accelerated towards the man with the broadsword. The man panicked and sprinted to the side of the road on impulse. Preeti then halted the car beside Sahil, whose eyes were wide with wonder at her sight before him.

Earlier, when she had seen Sahil and Mandana leaving the mansion hurriedly, she ran to the backyard, looking for Thakur or Tatya. But she did not see either of them, as they had both left for the chamber by that time. Sensing something wrong, she took the key to Thakur's car from me and sped off behind Mandana.

Preeti: "Hurry up, Sahil!"

With these words, she scooted to the passenger seat in the front. Being a newbie at driving, she wanted him to drive the car thereafter. A revitalized Sahil stood up and climbed into the driver's seat. Without losing a moment, he pressed the gas pedal as hard as he could and accelerated the car. The car took off like a projectile.

This sudden and unexpected development flustered Harak. He shuddered in despair, and his heartbeat elevated. He could not let Sahil reveal his identity to the world. He snatched the broadsword from his associate in desperation and ran behind the car. He groaned in anger as he flung the broadsword at Sahil and Preeti. The car had not picked up its full speed yet, which allowed him to reach very close to them. Though he missed Sahil, his primary aim, the blade cut deep through Preeti's arm instead. She screamed in pain and gripped her wounded arm. Luckily, the car accelerated, and they soon sped out of the place, making a narrow escape. Harak tried to catch his breath. He knew he had committed a grave mistake. He now faced the risk of being exposed as the perpetrator of the village's carnage.

With his eyes locked at the road ahead, Sahil exclaimed to Preeti in panic.

Sahil: "Preeti, do you know the man behind all these massacres? It's Harak Singh, the scoundrel!"

But when he did not get any response, he turned towards her, and the sight of her horrified him. She was bleeding profusely from her arm. A deep slash ran from her upper arm to her elbow and she was losing consciousness. He put his arm around her, placed her head on his shoulder, and drove the car as fast as possible. He was desperate to break the news of Harak's involvement in the grisly murders of Ratnagiri.

Back at the mansion, Mandana parked the car in the front parking lot. She lamented as she stepped out of her car. Unaware of Preeti's heroism, she assumed the goons to have killed Sahil. But she shook in fear when she heard the squealing tires of a high-speed braking car that halted right next to her. And when she saw Sahil at its driver's seat, her eyes widened in surprise and panic gripped her. Things began to make sense to her after she saw an unconscious Preeti in his arms. She stood there, embarrassed, as Sahil glared at her viciously. She had left him all alone to die at the hands of the brute killers. Ashamed at her behavior, she hung her head down and walked to her room.

Preeti required urgent medical aid. Sahil shouted at the top of his lungs and honked the car's horn. To his relief, a group of men came running to him from the backyard. They had heard his agonized scream despite the noise of the crowd. The stunned crowd gasped and panicked when they noticed the bloody sight.

But Mr. Dilshad Kapoor, Mandana's doctor father, kept his cool and handled the situation with diligence. Without losing time, he rushed to his room and brought his emergency kit. He always carried it along with him to tackle any emergency. The doctor and the other men helped Sahil pull Preeti out of the car. With eyes half-shut, she moaned in pain. When Mr. Kapoor assured everyone that she was not in any sort of danger, Sahil and Vidya sighed in relief. He looked around for Thakur in the gathered crowd, wanting to expose Harak to him then and there. But Thakur and Tatya had not returned from the chamber of assemblies yet. At first, Sahil thought of disclosing Harak's reality to everybody at the venue, but he then held his horses. He did not want to create any sort of trepidation in the already nervous crowd. He thought of talking to Thakur first, and hence, he drove off towards the chamber. He couldn't wait to reveal what he had found to Thakur.

08. The Honcho

A heavy storm was on the way when Sahil parked his car outside the chamber. It was too dark outside, and he rushed to the door of the building. With his heart beating fast, he gently pushed open the ajar door to the dimly lit room. He could not wait any longer to reveal Harak's truth to Thakur.

But his eyes widened and mouth opened in shock, as he was not prepared for what he saw next. Boney's dead body lay on the floor of the chamber and Harak stood beside it with his head hung in shame. Tatya stood next to Harak along with all his associates. They worked for Thakur in the mansion. Finally, his gaze rested on an enraged Thakur, his father, pacing up and down.

Thakur: "How dare you attack Sahil? Don't you know he is my son?"

Thakur's reprimand irked Harak, who looked up and bared his teeth.

Harak: "A-a-and Kh-Kh-Khatri was my b-b-brother, Thakur! Didn't your men kill him when he decided to go against your wishes?"

The din of the thunder rocked the sky. The visual in front of Sahil rattled him. Dumbfounded, he gulped in despair as he stood listening to the conversation between Harak and his father. He took note of the three men standing beside Harak. They held their balaclavas in their hands and looked terrified. They were the same men who had attacked him an hour ago near the bus station. Sahil knew every one of them. He had often seen them walking into the mansion on many occasions earlier.

A volley of alarming questions filled his mind. He wondered why Harak had carried Boney's corpse to Thakur. But it was Harak's statement, referring Thakur as Khatri's killer, which baffled him the most. A few days ago, Thakur had referred Khatri as the kingpin who carried out the killings from hiding. If the man was indeed dead, Sahil wondered why Thakur had misled him.

With his heart pounding in his chest, he shifted his focus back to what was happening before him.

Thakur: "Yes, I did, but only because he proved to be a turncoat. He had planned to disclose everything to the police. I didn't have another option. Don't you remember the rule? There is no scope for any risk in our work."

So, Khatri was in no way related to the abductions and the killings. Instead, his father, Thakur Pratap Singh, was the MASTERMIND behind the grisly murders.

Harak: "Exactly! Th-Th-there is no scope for risk. A-a-and Sahil discovered my identity, Th-Th-Thakur. I d-d-didn't have any other option."

Tatya: "Now what? How do we clean up the mess? Rajvanshi will be waiting for the heart. I need some time to work on the body before I can make a move to him. Also, it is dangerous to keep the body here for too long. People might be on their way to find you, Thakur."

Thakur nodded while glaring at Harak. After a brief pause, he issued a stern warning to him.

Thakur: "You better not repeat what you did today, Harak. I will have my men cut you to pieces otherwise."

Then he looked at Tatya and heaved a deep sigh.

Thakur: "Let Harak go to Rajvanshi this time, Tatya. Arrange for his stay in Pune for a few months. I don't want to see him around in Ratnagiri for the time being."

Tatya: "Umm…do you still want to maim the body? I reckon the boy was Sahil's friend."

Thakur sighed and nodded.

Thakur: "I understand, Tatya. But I don't want to give an advantage to Sikander by missing out on the delivery. In any case, the boy is dead, and his body would be of no use to Sahil. Let's throw his body back near the bus station after your men have removed the heart."

Tatya: "B-but what about Sahil?"

Tatya's repeated inquiries irked Thakur. He scowled at him in frustration.

Thakur: "Don't worry about Sahil! I will take care of him. But I need to know how are things going on in the mansion. I hope that he hasn't leaked the information of Harak to anyone."

As soon as he said these words, loud applause resonated in the air, stunning everyone present. Thakur's eyes widened in horror and his face turned pale when he saw Sahil at the doorstep. Tears were flowing down Sahil's face as he clapped. He winced as he walked towards his father, the man he had always considered as his role model because of his dedication and honesty. All these years, he had been an epitome of hard work. Today, Sahil was standing in front of a savage and filthy beast. Thakur's true guise had turned Sahil's whole world upside down. With eyes brimming, he looked at his father. Thakur looked at Sahil in fear. His glare and demeanor suggested to him that he had heard every word that had been spoken in that room.

Sahil blinked, and tears dribbled down his cheeks.

Sahil: "Wow, Baba! Wow! What a game!"

Thakur didn't utter a word. He continued looking at Sahil with a distressed expression. Sahil shifted his gaze from Thakur to Boney's body lying in the corner of the room. He gulped and looked at Thakur again.

Sahil: "Why, Baba?"

But Thakur remained silent. He continued looking at Sahil with a sober face. When Sahil did not get a response, he grilled his father once again.

Sahil: "Tell me, Baba! Why?"

When Thakur refused to answer him a third time, Sahil yelled out.

Sahil: "TELL ME, BABA! WHY? WHY DID YOU DO THIS TO YOUR PEOPLE?"

Thunder clapped and echoed through the walls of the room. Thakur remained silent, but a mild smirk crept onto his face. Flustered by his amusement, Sahil requested him in a quivering voice.

Sahil: "L-l-let's go to the police, Baba. You need to confess your crimes and hand yourself over to the police. I promise I'll hire the best lawyer to reduce your sentence, Baba. Come, Baba! Let's go straight to the police station."

With these words, Sahil grabbed Thakur's hand. But Thakur stood his ground and did not move his step. He kept looking at Sahil with an uncanny smile on his face. And when he did not heed to his repeated request, Sahil threatened him with an austere stare.

Sahil: "Alright, Baba! I'm going to call the police. I'll tell them what your men did to Boney at your behest."

He turned around and began marching out to the door of the room. But before he could exit the room, he heard a deafening guffaw. His feet went numb when he turned around and saw Thakur indulged in a horselaugh. Thunder rumbled in the sky, and the bright glare of lightning flashed across Thakur's laughing face. Sahil shuddered when he saw the immoral beast, he called his father. While tears of misery trickled down Sahil's cheeks, Thakur wiped tears of mirth of his face. After a while, Thakur slowed down his laughter as he tried to regain his breath.

Thakur: "No matter whom you tell, no one will ever believe you, son. I have formulated an illusion to veil the truth. I have created a delusion to deceive the minds of the masses."

Sahil stammered in a nervous pitch.

Sahil: "I…I…I will go and inform the police about this."

Thakur: "Go ahead! Any of my men will take the blame on his head, and I will continue to do what I'm doing. Everyone you see in this room would happily sacrifice his life for me."

Sahil gulped as he heard his candid words. He looked around at Tatya, Harak, and all the others gathered in the small room. Thakur whispered with a conceited smile.

Thakur: "I'm a king with an invincible army."

Sahil's body trembled with anger.

Sahil: "I will tell everyone in Ratnagiri about your illegal activities."

But his anguished words did not deter Thakur, whose smile widened.

Thakur: "Go try, my boy. And let me know if anyone believes you!"

Sahil: "What if Ma comes to know about you, Baba?"

Thakur: "I don't give a damn! Either she will die in shock or she will desert me forever. Whatever happens, I won't step back. If you still have a problem with this, you are free to abandon me as well, but I am not giving up this moneymaking venture. My ambitions are too big, son. You can never defeat me. You simply can't!"

Sahil broke down after he heard his father's callous words. Thakur's brute smile waned—he knew that the truth was too hard for his child to swallow. He walked to him and held his hand to console him.

Thakur: "Trust me, Sahil! I have done a lot for the people of Ratnagiri. I'm sure you know that. And I'm still working to make their lives better. In return, I just need a couple of them a month. And I'm a generous man, Sahil. All these years, we only abducted tribal men living on the outskirts. My men have never put their hands on any women."

After hearing his insane words, Sahil locked his tearful gaze on his face. Disturbed by his vicious and hateful glare, Thakur held his hand and walked him over to a table in the room.

Thakur: "Come with me, Sahil. Let me show you something."

The table had five large suitcases that were, to Sahil's surprise, stuffed with high-denomination cash. Sahil gasped, as he had never seen such an enormous amount of money before. He touched the crisp notes to get a feel of them. He closed his eyes and inhaled the scent of brand new notes. Perhaps, the sight of the pile of cash had lured him. Though he had stared at Thakur in disgust just a little while earlier, he seemed smitten by the wealth in front of him. A smile crept onto his face.

Sahil: "This much money, Baba! Wow! Is it all yours?"

Thakur: "Yes, yes! It's all mine! And yours too, Sahil!"

Sahil's face lit up. The desire to be a wealthy and powerful man seemed to have swayed him. In a flash, all his strong principles succumbed to his temptation for the easy money, perhaps. Perhaps, the desire to lead an easy life overpowered all his morals and values that Vidya taught him. And to everybody's surprise, a wide and evil grin widened on his face as he decided to follow his father's footsteps.

Sahil: "If I join you, what would be my profile?"

Tatya chuckled at Sahil's naïve and innocent query.

Tatya: "You need to only reap the fruits, Sahil, as Thakur does. The rest you can you leave on me and my men."

A smile spread across the faces of everybody in the room. They sensed that he liked the taste of raging and unlimited power. Sometimes, the feel of power is more desirable than any treasure. But after this joyful moment, the smile on Tatya's face vanished, and he appeared a bit embarrassed.

Tatya: "Umm…Sahil, we need to start working on the body before it starts to decay. We can't wait any longer—we have already lost a lot of time."

Sahil gasped as he heard these unendurable words. Aghast by his statement, his forehead crinkled with fury, and he marched towards Tatya, fixing his glare at him.

Sahil: "No, Tatya! Not Boney! He was my friend."

Thakur: "I understand how you're feeling, Sahil. If my men had known that he was your friend, they would never have attacked him and they would have looked for a different target. But we need his heart right now, Sahil, or we will miss the deadline for the delivery."

Sahil: "No, Baba. We won't miss any deadline. We will adhere to our deadline, just not with Boney's body though."

As soon as these words left his mouth, he pulled out Tatya's gun from his unclipped holster, and in the same breath, the champion shooter shot Harak in the head. His blood splattered on Sahil's face. Thakur, Tatya, and the other men gasped in horror as they heard the loud *crack* of the gunshot. Their jaws dropped, and their eyes widened in fear. Harak fell to the floor and gasped, convulsing in pain. Soon, he exhaled a deep breath, and his movements ceased. Sahil wiped the blood off his face with a smile and looked at Harak's accomplices, the ones who had attacked him.

Sahil: "I will spare your lives this time. I know you were under the command of Harak. And I am fond of loyal dogs."

But his act did not please Thakur. He gasped and rushed towards him. He exclaimed at him in a shrill pitch.

Thakur: "What have you done, boy? You killed him! Do you know what you've done?"

Sahil turned around and looked at his father with a clenched jaw. There was a strange glee on his face.

Sahil: "He killed my friend, Baba. I couldn't bear to see him wandering alive in front of me."

His statement flustered Thakur, who was at a loss for words. Sahil looked at Tatya with a triumphant smile.

Sahil: "I've solved your problem, Tatya. Do whatever you need to do with Harak's body, but Boney will not be maimed any further. Leave his body where it was near the bus station and pass on the message to the police and his mother."

Tatya hung his head. Everybody in the room was silent, rattled by Sahil's conduct. Harak had been their companion for years. Though they didn't express their feelings, it was evident that they were mourning Harak. Sahil was wise enough to sense this. He thought to make a joke to cheer everyone up. He grinned and pointed to Tatya's unclipped leather holster.

Sahil: "Keep your holster locked, Tatya. It can be fatal."

Tatya smiled and nodded, but he had not forgiven Sahil yet for taking the life of his companion. He gave him a sarcastic reply.

Tatya: "Old habits and old friends are alike—it is hard to forget them."

A nervous Sahil gulped. He knew what Tatya wanted to convey. Harak had been one of Tatya's oldest friends. Once things simmered down, Tatya carried Harak's body to an undisclosed location to meet the delivery. And the other men moved Boney's body back to the bus station. At Sahil's suggestion, Thakur drove straight to the bus station and prepared himself to tackle a possible inquiry about Boney's death. But Sahil headed back to the mansion—he had some unfinished business to take care of.

✳✳✳

Back at the mansion, a nervous Mandana paced up and down in her room. The moment she had fled from the bus station, leaving Sahil alone, was hounding her. After she saw him safe and sound with Preeti, she knew she had made a big blunder out of sheer cowardice. She remembered his hateful glare before he left to meet Thakur in the chamber. She knew that he was livid at her. Her heart pounded in fear. She wondered - how would she muster the courage to face Sahil in the future?

Lost in her thoughts, she shuddered when she heard a sharp knock on the door. She felt a lump in her throat when Sahil opened the door and entered. He stood in front of her with an expressionless face, and with his eyes brimming with tears. After a little hesitation, she smiled nervously and looked up at him, but her gesture did not pacify him. He continued to look at her with a frown on his face.

Sahil: "I always thought you loved me, Mandy. But I was wrong. You don't care about anyone but yourself."

Mandana: "S-S-Sahil! That's not true. I l-l-love—"

But she never completed her sentence and stopped abruptly as Sahil removed the ring that she had put on his finger at the ceremony just a few hours ago. Then, he extended his palm towards her with the ring placed on it.

Sahil: "Your ring, Mandy. And I need mine back as well."

His brazen statement devastated her. Her eyes widened in despair while thunder rumbled in the background. She bit her lower lip.

Mandana: "N-n-no, Sahil! You can't do this to me."

But her agonized plea did not deter him.

Sahil: "I'm sorry, Mandy, but it's over!"

She shuddered when she heard his harsh words. Her lips quivered, and she stared at him, shell-shocked, for a moment. Then, something inexplicable happened. To Sahil's surprise, the despair waned from her face, and she clenched her teeth in fury. Tears of anger filled her eyes.

Mandana: "You used my soul and body for three long years, Sahil. You don't have any right to dump me like this."

Sahil: "I'm sorry, Mandy, but after whatever happened today, I don't think we should be together anymore. Take the ring back and give mine back to me. You need to leave the mansion right away."

Humiliation filled Mandana as she heard his coldhearted words. She scowled in fury and tears of anger ran down her cheeks. And then, she roared in a deafening pitch.

Mandana: "I will leave this place forever! But learn to fear a wounded tigress and an insulted woman, Sahil Pratap Singh. I will never forgive you for what you have done to me today. You have savaged my honor. I promise that I will come back at the most vulnerable moment of yours and destroy you. I will be the reason for your ruin one day. I swear an oath to avenge this insult."

As soon as she finished speaking, a clap of thunder boomed in the distance. She removed his ring from her finger and placed it on his palm. Then, she picked up her ring from his palm in haste and left. Soon, she was gone from the mansion along with her father. Sahil slumped back in a chair and closed his eyes in melancholy. After a few moments of silence, he walked back to his car and drove to the bus station, where he knew Thakur was waiting for him.

09. The Fathom

At the first cockcrow of the morning, policemen thronged the area where Boney's lifeless body lay on the ground. Sahil, Thakur, and his men stood beside the corpse, while Kanta howled and cradled her son's face in her lap. She had set off for Ratnagiri as soon as she heard the tragic news. Slumped on the muddy ground with her hair open and disheveled, she moaned and beat her chest with her hands in agony. Sahil held her shoulder and tried to console the grieving mother, but Kanta was inconsolable. She held Sahil's hand and bawled.

Kanta: "Ahhh…Sahil…ahhh…see what happened to him. Why…why did someone do this to him? Why…ahhh… He was so happy yesterday…he-he couldn't wait to meet you… Why…why…ahhh…"

Sahil was speechless. He glanced at Thakur, as he didn't have words to pacify the grief-stricken mother. Thakur sighed and looked at

Sahil for a brisk moment as well, but turned his eyes away from him in sheer embarrassment. Though Sahil had agreed to work with his father, his heart bled for his best friend. He had never wanted his pal to meet such a tragic end. People gathered around the corpse and stood in solidarity. As they mourned the tragedy, they saw a police car speeding towards them from a distance. Its emergency flashers were on as it skidded to a sudden halt. With his uniform cap on him, a tall and dusky cop stepped out of the vehicle and walked towards the crowd. The young cop maintained a pencil-thin black-haired mustache. He had black hair and had small black eyes. No one had ever seen him in Ratnagiri ever before. Anxiously, Thakur walked to him to take stock of the situation.

Thakur: "May I help you? I am Thakur Pratap Singh, the chieftain of the village."

The officer introduced himself as Senior Inspector Khan. A little perturbed by Khan's appearance, Thakur tried his best to conceal his anxiety.

Thakur: "Oh, Inspector Sharma mentioned that you would be his replacement. I'm afraid this is not a very good moment to exchange greetings. You have a murder victim right in front of you."

Khan's face softened in sympathy as he looked at Boney's body.

Khan: "The body will be in police custody. The family can claim it later in the evening once a detailed postmortem has been conducted on it. By the way, who is Sahil here? I heard that he was the last man to see the victim alive."

Thakur: "S-Sahil… He is my son. Sahil, come here."

Sahil stepped forward and introduced himself as well.

Sahil: "I'm Sahil, a friend of the deceased. Some hoodlums killed him right in front of my eyes."

Khan: "Hmmm… around what time did the tragedy take place?"

Sahil: "I can't recall the exact time since I was busy with a family function. I guess it must have been around 1 am when I heard him on the phone. As soon as I found out he was in trouble, I rushed to save his life."

Khan: "Any chance you recognized any of the assailants who killed your friend?"

Sahil's feet went numb after he heard Khan's query. He gulped in despair as he recalled the moment he had pulled the mask off

Harak's face in the scuffle. Then, he looked at Khan and uttered a lie—he did not want the police to suspect Thakur in any way.

Sahil: "Umm no, I didn't. Each of the goons was wearing a mask on his face. I panicked when they attacked me with their knives, and my mind went blank. I kept running ahead on the deserted street to save my life. Luckily, Preeti drove by at the same time and I made a narrow escape."

Khan: "And how many were they? Roughly?"

Sahil: "Around seven or eight men. Please catch them, Inspector. The beasts mercilessly killed my friend."

Sahil was careful with his words as he devised a deceptive story for Khan. He wanted to make sure that nobody on his side would land in any sort of trouble. Unable to see through his sham words, Khan consoled him.

Khan: "I assure you that I won't leave any stone unturned to nab the culprits."

After taking a written statement from Sahil, Khan drove back to the police station. The constables covered Boney's body with a plain sheet of cloth before placing it in the rear section of an ambulance. Kanta howled louder and tightened her grip on Boney's corpse. To pry the body from her grasp, a few men in the crowd held her shoulders and pulled her back. Sahil put his arm around the wailing Kanta as the ambulance took off.

****

The ambulance transported the body to Thakur's house in the evening. In the funeral procession, a priest chanted the purification mantra for Boney, in the way he did for Alok. After completing all the rituals, the priest asked Sahil and a few men to place the corpse on a wooden pyre. Since Boney did not have any male member left in his family, Sahil took the responsibility and lit the wooden pyre somberly. And as he did that, Kanta bawled as the fuming pyre released dark smoke into the air. She lost her balance and fell on the ground. And soon, the flames got higher and engulfed Boney's body.

After the funeral, a devastated Kanta hired a taxi and left for her village. Although Thakur had insisted that she stay in the mansion for the night, she declined his offer. She was in a terrible state of mind and wanted some time alone to grieve her son.

****

—

The rest of the day went by without any more incidents. At night, Tatya parked his bike in the parking lot of the chamber of assemblies. Sahil had wanted to meet him there, a request that had surprised him. But the sight he saw in the hall of the chamber surprised him even more. Relaxed on a chair, Sahil sat sipping a glass of whiskey. Perhaps the day's events had not bothered him much. There was a vacant chair in front of him and a small table between the two chairs. To Tatya's amusement, there was a game of chess on the table, along with arrayed wooden pieces.

Tatya: "Hi, Sahil."

Sahil: "Ah, Tatya! Come in."

Sahil placed an empty glass on the table and poured some whiskey into it. He gestured to Tatya to occupy the vacant chair and handed the drink to him.

Tatya: "All okay, Sahil?"

Sahil: "Oh, yeah! I couldn't fall asleep, so I called you here for a game of chess since I don't have any better contenders."

Tatya occupied his seat and picked up his glass.

Tatya: "When did you start drinking, Sahil? Weren't you a teetotaler?"

Sahil: "You will witness a lot of changes in me from now on, Tatya."

Tatya: "I am sorry for what happened to your friend. My men didn't know he was your friend or they wouldn't have even touched him. As for what Harak did to you…it was out of vengeance. He was trying to avenge the death of Khatri, his brother. The other men couldn't refuse him since I had instructed them to follow his commands blindly in my absence."

Sahil: "What's all this fuss about Khatri? Everyone in Ratnagiri believes he's the man behind all the killings. But I heard Baba say he died a long time ago."

Tatya: "Basically a hooch smuggler, Khatri worked for us for a long time. He was an efficient member of the group until he lost his beloved son in a tragedy. In a coincidence, his son had died after consuming the same hooch Khatri used to smuggle. The loss of his young son devastated him. And, as a result, he put an end to his illegal hooch business and changed his demeanor. Plagued by guilt and remorse, he also refused to abduct and kill anyone. He even threatened to expose us to the police if anyone from the gang ever tried to do so. Over time, his dissent grew stronger, and he started being more vocal about it.

"One night, he decided to go to the police and expose Thakur and us. But before he could step inside the police station, we captured him. On

Thakur's orders, we killed him that very night. Although Harak begged for his brother's life, Thakur stuck to the first rule in the book—no one is more important than the business, and there is no room for any risks."

Sahil: "Hmmm…so the man that the cops are frantically looking for doesn't exist anymore. No matter how much they search for him, they will never be able to trace him. And under the garb of his fake name, Baba will run the business. Easy and efficient!"

Tatya: "That's right. This is probably the reason Harak attacked you. He wanted to give Thakur a taste of his own medicine. He wanted to harm you the same way Thakur harmed his brother. As I said, there is no room for risks in our business. That said, whatever happened to your friend was unfortunate. We certainly could have avoided the mishap."

Sahil: "I agree. It shouldn't have happened, but it was a classic case of collateral damage. Anyway, no use crying over spilled milk now. This is the time to move on and make some quick bucks. Anyway, let's play! As retribution for your earlier loss, you can play white if you like."

Tatya: "No, I would still like to play black."

Sahil: "Are you sure? You played black in the last game too."

Tatya: "Every game is a new one. I will checkmate you this time around, Sahil. I learned my lesson that day."

Sahil nodded and made a king's opening. He played e2 pawn to e4.

Tatya reciprocated with a king's opening as well, playing the black pawn from e7 to e5.

In response, Sahil pushed his bishop to c4.

Sahil: "Whatever Baba said last night was too fragmented. I still have a lot of dots to connect. I want to know everything about the trade, and I need you to give me the details. Who all are in this along with us? What's our modus operandi?"

Tatya played his knight on to c6 with a sip of the whiskey and looked Sahil in the eye.

Tatya: "My men work in a group of 7 or 8 at a time to capture potential targets. They work at night. We have two agents who keep a tight vigil for any possible targets. They inform us once they set their eyes on someone. The victims are mostly poor tribal men whose cases generally go unreported. These men are of no consequence to anyone, so they serve as ideal prey."

Sahil played his queen to F3 before enquiring about me.

Sahil: "Wow…now that's interesting. And what about Bansi and Inspector Sharma? Are they a part of the posse too?"

Tatya: "Nah, not at all. Although Bansi knows everything about us, he has no role to play in it. In fact, there is no role suitable for him in the business. Thakur has kept him only for trivial household chores, to help Vidya madam. Being a puppet in Thakur's hands, he says what Thakur wants him to say, and hears only what Thakur wants him to hear. Inspector Sharma, on the other hand, is a complete dodo. He never had the brains to crack the secret or solve any of the high-profile cases."

Sahil: "Which high-profile cases are you talking about?"

Khan: "The case of Murari, a farmer, and Alok, the local reporter."

Sahil nearly fell off his seat in shock when he heard Alok's name.

Sahil: "What? You guys took down Alok too? But why? He was still alive when I saw him at the clock tower. You didn't have any intention of maiming him, did you?"

Tatya finished his remaining drink in one sip and played his knight from c6 to d4, threatening Sahil's queen.

Tatya: "He was not killed for the trade. You need to talk to Thakur for more details, as I wasn't here the night he was killed. As far as Murari is concerned, we had to mow him down when one of our informers notified us about his presence on one stormy night. That night, we couldn't get ahold of any tribal men.

"But we soon realized that we committed a blunder, as the police became extremely vigilant after this case. Fortunately for us, it turned out as one more unsolved case in the police records. The cops believed the untraceable Khatri to be the one behind this killing."

Sahil: "And who is our regular client?"

Tatya: "A fugitive named Rajvanshi. He's a big fish in the international market and makes millions out of the trade. He lives in hiding somewhere in Pune. Only a few of us know about his haunt in Pune. Though I visit him to deliver the organs, Thakur has visited him at times as well."

Sahil: "Hmm…does he have any rivals or competitors?"

Tatya: "Negative. He enjoys a monopoly in the trade. But we have one competitor for us. Named Sikander, he ships consignments to Rajvanshi too. He is a direct competitor to Thakur and is well-known to Rajvanshi. There is a perpetual tug of war between us to nab the victim first."

Sahil: "Do Sikander and his consortia know about Baba?"

Tatya: "Yes, he does, but our secrets are as important as his and Rajvanshi's. As an informal treaty, no one in the trade exposes any details to the outside world, and everyone follows this rule without any protest."

Sahil shook his head. He was beginning to comprehend the peril growing slowly and steadily around his father.

Sahil: "Do you understand the little piece of dynamite you guys are sitting on? What if someone turns out to be a squealer?"

Tatya: "I understand what you're getting at, but this is a different world altogether. Even rivals protect the identities of their enemies in the business. Anyway, the sham of Khatri as the kingpin of the business shields everyone like armor. And if they expose us, we will expose them. Those who live in glass houses don't throw stones at other's homes. By the way, your queen is in danger."

Sahil: "Hmmm…I don't agree with everything you said. An eye for an eye can't always keep growing dangers at bay. Can you please elaborate on the process once more?"

Tatya: "We work on a demand basis. Once Rajvanshi puts forth a demand, both our agents go on the lookout for a target. Once they guide us to a probable target, our men capture the victim and slay him. Then, our team operates on the body and preserves the organs, which we then ship to Rajvanshi. Finally, my men dump the maimed body in some fields nearby. Sikander does pretty much the same. The informers pass on the information to him as well. Whoever captures the target first rewards them with some share of the money. The process may seem cumbersome but it is quite simple."

Sahil: "And who carries out the surgeries on the bodies? Any doctors in our team?"

Tatya shook his head.

Tatya: "No. But Rajvanshi's medical team has rigorously trained a couple of our men to operate on the bodies. We do not need any doctor in our team."

Sahil: "Hmmm… I have a 360-degree view of the trade now. Everything is crystal clear to me. I have one last question though. Where are the dead bodies operated on? Is it somewhere inside Ratnagiri Hospital?"

Tatya shook his head.

Tatya: "The hospital is too open and risky a place to carry out such activities. The operations need a solitary location that doesn't interest anybody, especially at night."

Sahil gawked at Tatya with a mischievous smile for some time and made a wild guess.

Sahil: "Is it the school's basement?"

Tatya looked at Sahil with surprise.

Tatya: "That's right. Wonderful! We operate on the bodies in the school's basement."

Sahil: "What about Sikander? Where does he operate on the bodies? He too must need someplace to work on the corpses, right?"

Tatya: "No, unlike us, he carries out nickel-and-dime operations. With no machinery, he transports the bodies to Rajvanshi, who funds a medical team that performs the operations. He prefers our system, though, since it makes his job easy. That's why Thakur gets paid double the amount Sikander does for the same assignment."

Sahil: "Would you mind taking me to the basement right now? It should be safe to visit it at this time of night."

Tatya frowned in surprise at Sahil's strange and untimely request.

Tatya: "Now? Yeah, of course, we can. But don't you want to finish the game first?"

Sahil chuckled.

Sahil: "The game? It's already over…for you."

Before Tatya could understand what was happening, Sahil unleashed his queen from f3 to f7 in a deadly move.

Sahil: "CHECK AND MATE!"

Tatya stared at the board in disbelief. He contemplated for a while for some possible way to avoid the defeat but soon realized that he had lost to Sahil once again. His c4 bishop protected his f7 white queen. He praised his skills before they both left for the school.

****

Tatya opened the door of the basement and switched on the lights. The sight of the exorbitant surgical equipment in the room stunned Sahil. He looked around the room, mesmerized. It was a spacious and well-lit hall with a polished marble floor. Being a sealed room with no windows, the basement served as an ideal place for the operations. Under the mounted surgical lights was an operating table in the center of the hall. On one side was a bulky and state of the art machine with its rear end connected to the wall. The corner of the room had a backup system to tackle any electricity blackouts during surgery with a massive network of wires meshed around it. In the other corner of the basement, a spacious lab had been set up with restricted access. Sahil peeked at the lab through the glass wall. The lab contained numerous glass vessels filled with vibrant, colored chemicals meant to store human organs. Unknown to outsiders, this was a different world altogether.

While Sahil looked around at the spectacular hardware, Tatya ran back to his bike. He had forgotten to pull out the bike's key from the ignition switch. But as soon as he yanked out the key, he heard the rustling of leaves somewhere near him. He looked around in a panic, but it was too dark for him to see anything. Assuming it to be some sort of fox in the forest that might have stepped in the tall bushes around the school, he made his way back to Sahil.

After spending considerable time in the basement, they both stepped out of the school. Tatya dropped Sahil to the mansion and turned around to ride back to his home. But before he could leave, Sahil caught sight of Tatya's unclipped leather holster and smiled.

Sahil: "I told you last time, keep your holster locked."

Tatya looked down at his unclipped leather holster and smiled back.

Tatya: "Old habits die hard! Take care, Sahil. Thank you for the drink and the wonderful game of chess."

Tatya kick-started his bike and went on his way. Instead of heading back to his room, Sahil walked to the study. It was late in the night, and he knew it was where Thakur would be. And he was right. Seated at a table, Thakur sipped his tea and was reading a book.

Thakur: "Ahhh… Sahil! Come, sit with me."

Sahil slumped onto the chair next to Thakur and sighed. He spread his legs and shut his eyes. Thakur was anxious about starting any conversation with Sahil. He knew that Boney's untimely death had perturbed him. But to his immense relief, Sahil broke the ice.

Sahil: "What are you reading, Baba?"

Thakur: "It's Mahabharata, the epic. I love it."

Sahil nodded with a smile.

Sahil: "Me too. Who's your favorite character?"

Thakur: "There are a number of them that fascinate me, it's tough to single out anyone. Bhishma, Bheema, Arjuna, Karna, and Lord Krishna—they all had unique traits of their own. Who's yours?

Sahil: "Hmmm! I like Ashwathama. His character always fascinated me."

The answer surprised Thakur.

Thakur: "Ashwathama? The man who had a boon to live an immortal life since his birth? You like him? But why? Though his immortal life and Lord Krishna's curse on him are the prominent episodes in the Mahabharata, he is not very well known to most people.

Sahil: "Don't forget the festering and septic wound on his forehead. It got inflicted after Krishna snatched the diamond attached to his forehead after cursing him. The curse tormented him for the rest of his immortal life."

Sahil's knowledge of mythology impressed Thakur.

Thakur: "Hmmm…one second."

He got up from his chair and walked to the bookshelf. After sifting through piles of titles in the mythology section, he finally pulled out one book. He walked back to Sahil and handed the book to him.

Thakur: "Read it! You will love it."

Sahil glanced at the brightly illustrated jacket of the hardcover edition titled *'The Curse To Ashwathama.'* It had a picture of a furious Lord Krishna, dressed in his traditional yellow clothes, cursing a young prince Ashwathama in wrath. With a peacock feather in his crown, Krishna on the cover picture had pointed his index finger at the prince in an angry stance. On the other hand, Ashwathama lamented in misery and had a festered wound on his forehead. A wretched Ashwathama sniveled and looked down on the floor, while the drops of blood dripped down his septic wound.

Thakur: "The curse verbatim has an energizing start…something…umm…I don't remember it now. Umm… 'O Ashwathama…' My goodness, I don't remember it now. My memory is fading day by day. But you should read it."

Sahil nodded in silence as he went through the blurb of the book. Then, he sighed before posing a question.

Sahil: "Baba, how did Alok die?"

Thakur: "Alok? Who Alok? I've heard his name…why don't I remember anything?"

Sahil: "Alok, your friend, the journalist! Don't you remember? I found him in a pool of blood with his throat slit."

His pushing finally helped Thakur recall the man and the events leading up to his death. He sighed deeply as he replied.

Thakur: "Oh yes…I remember now. We-we met each other that night near the clock tower."

Thakur's statement was a stunning piece of news to Sahil. He exclaimed in shock.

Sahil: "What? You met him? When? The same night I found him?"

Thakur: "Yes, the same night! The bastard had plans to go to the police and hand over a piece of damning evidence against me."

Sahil: "What exactly happened that night?"

Thakur: "When you left for Khandala that morning, he called me up, asking to meet me near the clock tower. He had some secret information to share with me. As he requested, I drove to the place at night and waited for him. I looked up at the clock of the tower, and I remember it was exactly 11 in the night. I sat on the nearby bench to kill time. To be honest, I was a little scared and curious to hear what he wanted to tell me. About ten minutes later, I saw a man walking towards me in the darkness—Alok. He was holding a paper packet in his hand and walked to me with a smile on his face."

Alok: *"Hope I'm not very late, Thakur. But excuse me for that. I had to cover the distance by foot as I don't own fancy cars like you."*

Thakur: *"Come straight to the point. Why did you call me here at this time of the night?"*

Alok: *"I wanted to show you something that might be of immense interest to you."*

Thakur (narrating to Sahil): "With a mysterious smile, he opened the package and slid out a newspaper cutting. The listed article had a picture of Rajvanshi printed on it, and declared him as a known fugitive."

Alok: *"Do you recognize the man?"*

Thakur (narrating to Sahil): "I coughed anxiously when I saw Rajvanshi's picture right in front of me and denied it."

Thakur: *"Umm…n-n-no, I don't. Who is he?"*

Alok: *"Oh, don't you know him? He's Rajvanshi, the famous organ smuggler in international markets. He is a known fugitive, and the police haven't been able to catch him till date—he is too clever a man. He conducts the trade under many fake names and lives out of a lot of undiscovered haunts. Do you recognize him now?"*

Thakur: *"I-I already told you I don't. But why are asking me this?"*

Thakur (narrating to Sahil): "But he did not answer my question. Instead, he smiled at me and tore up the news article he had shown me. Then, he pulled out a picture from the same packet and showed it to me. It sent shivers down my spine. In the photo, I was standing next to Rajvanshi and we were shaking hands."

Alok*: "Now what? Would you still say you don't know the man?"*

Thakur (narrating to Sahil): "I began to panic. Before I could defend myself, he proclaimed the awful truth."

Alok: *"Khatri died a long time back, Thakur. Your men act per Rajvanshi's wishes and carry out all the killings in Ratnagiri. You are the one behind all the massacres. You are the kingpin of the racket."*

Thakur (narrating to Sahil): "I went numb and froze in horror after I heard him. I panicked, unsure of what to do next."

Alok: *"I am heading straight to the police station from here. I will make sure you pay for your sins, Thakur."*

Thakur (narrating to Sahil): "With those words, he turned around and started walking, probably to the police. His words had rattled me. The world was about to know my real identity, and I could not let that happen. In despair, I slid out the dagger hidden under my shirt and ran after him. He turned around in alarm when he heard my footsteps, and his eyes widened in terror. The poor fellow had never expected that I would attack him. I slit his throat in one quick motion. He held his slashed throat with his hands and looked at me with a shock-filled gaze. Soon, he lost his balance and fell onto the ground.

"Without losing any time, I wiped off my fingerprints on the dagger and threw it beside Alok's body. Then, I collected the envelope and the picture that had slipped out of his hands. It was the first time I had ever killed someone with my own hands. Moreover, he was my old friend, and I never wanted to kill him. I left the place with my heart pounding. You know the rest of the story. I made one small mistake, though. I had assumed him to be dead until I came to know you met him in his last few moments. I was just relieved that he died without revealing any details to anyone."

After hearing the story, Sahil went silent for a while. He shook his head, picked up a glass of water, and gulped a few sips anxiously. Then, he exhaled.

Sahil: "You did make a blunder, Baba."

Thakur wasn't pleased with his criticism.

Thakur: "The man was going to the police. I had no other option but to mow him down."

Sahil: "'I don't own fancy cars like you.' Hmmm… Baba, what was his financial condition like? He owned a publishing house, didn't he?"

Thakur: "Pretty bad! The publishing house was in shambles and generated negligible revenue. What's more, he had an unemployed son and a daughter of marriageable age. He was working on a deal to sell off the publishing house."

Sahil picked up the heavy glass paperweight from the table, lost in deep thought. He looked straight into Thakur's eyes and spoke after a brief pause.

Sahil: "If he had any intentions of going to the police, he would not have met with you in the first place. He could have simply gone to the police."

Thakur: "Umm…perhaps he wanted to confirm if I was the culprit indeed."

Sahil chuckled.

Sahil: "No, he didn't. He met you for a different reason altogether. He had come to make a deal. He wanted to make a fortune in return for the picture he showed you."

Sahil's theory took Thakur by surprise.

Thakur: "B-but he had already started walking back."

Sahil: "It was a ploy to get a higher bid. But you didn't understand the poor man's thought process. You never gave him the chance to explain what he intended to do. You should have held your horses, Baba."

Sahil's words made sense to him. Baffled, he held the plastic arm of his glasses between his lips, lost in thought. He was cursing himself for handling Alok the way he had.

Sahil: "And what did you do with the picture you took from him? I hope you destroyed it?"

Thakur tried to recall the events after he grabbed the picture from Alok but failed to recollect anything. His dementia had worsened with time. In desperation, he held his head in his hands and cried out in frustration.

Thakur: "Ahhh…what…what did I do? I don't know. I think I destroyed it…b-but I don't remember."

Thakur's answer did not amuse Sahil. He frowned at him.

Sahil: "Baba, that's a dangerous piece of evidence against you. It can land us in trouble."

But his push went in vain. Despite Thakur's best efforts, he failed to recollect the details. Sahil sighed and shook his head.

Sahil: "Alright Baba, let me know once you recall it. Meanwhile, can you arrange for a meeting with Sikander and Rajvanshi? Just a small get-together for everyone to know each other better."

His request surprised Thakur.

Thakur: "Meeting with Sikander and Rajvanshi? Is that required?"

Sahil: "Yes, it is. You are walking on thin ice, Baba. There are too many people in the world who are aware of your dark side. One mistake, and everything will go haywire. I want to socialize with everyone in the business to get a sense of their intentions."

With these words, he headed towards his room. Thakur, on the other hand, dived and lost into a thought. He wondered if the mistake he had committed by slaying Alok would haunt him forever.

****

Drained by the day's events, Sahil changed into his nightclothes and sat on his bed. It had been a traumatic day with no rest, and he had developed a mild headache. In the past 24 hours, his world had turned upside down. The sight of everyone singing and dancing around him the previous night was still fresh in his mind. His heart sank as he recalled the murkier events that followed—Boney's petrified voice on the phone begging for help, his brutal murder in front of him, Mandana's selfishness, and Preeti's bravery in saving his life. The visual of Boney's lifeless body on a pyre with his nostrils stuffed with cotton balls agonized him. He remembered the wailing Kanta beating her chest in grief when the pyre was set on fire. The bitter memories plagued him until he heard a knock on the door. He was in no mood to talk to anyone and responded in an irritated tone.

Sahil: "Yes? Who is it?"

Swathed in bandages, Preeti opened the door and entered the room. Her visit was a complete surprise to him. He immediately got up from the bed and onto his feet.

Sahil: "Hey, Preeti."

Preeti: "Hi, Sahil."

Sahil: "S-s-sorry, Preeti, I couldn't meet you at all. Today, I had a lot of things to take care of. How are you feeling now? How is your injury?"

Preeti: "I'm fine. It's just a mild gash."

After a brief pause, she looked up at him with a little hesitation.

Preeti: "Umm… I'm sorry about everything that happened last night."

He nodded at her sympathetic words but remained silent with a glum face. She knew he was upset over the series of dreadful events that had transpired in the last few hours.

Preeti: "I-I just wanted to tell you that…that…I…umm…I'm with you, always. You won't ever find yourself alone."

As she uttered these soothing words, they both looked at each other with a love-filled gaze. Then, she held his hand and squeezed it.

Preeti: "Rest, Sahil. I will catch you tomorrow. Goodnight."

With these words, she smiled and turned around to leave his room. But she halted her steps when Sahil called her out.

Sahil: "Preeti, thanks for your help last night. It is a favor that I don't know how to repay."

To cheer him up and lift his mood, Preeti smiled mischievously.

Preeti: "Don't worry, one day I will definitely ask you for something in return. But you can't refuse me at that moment."

It worked—Preeti's banter brought a small smile to his glum face.

Sahil: "I promise. Let me know when you want me to obey and surrender to you, my savior."

Preeti: "When the right time comes, I certainly will."

She smiled and left for her room. Sahil switched off his room's lights and went to bed. With the hope of encountering a better morning the next day, he closed his eyes and sank into a deep sleep.

10. The Snitch

As Sahil asked, Thakur arranged for a meeting with Rajvanshi and Sikander. Tatya reserved a party hall on the outskirts of Ratnagiri as the venue for the meeting. Everyone in the trade often met at the place for the gatherings and the parties. In the darkness of the night, the forsaken haunt was a safe place to meet, and never had any threat from the police.

Over the past few weeks, Sahil had undergone a complete transformation in terms of his gait and appearance. He had grown a bulky beard, and his overgrown mustache now merged with it. The backward-combed slick hair added to his imposing look. He was sitting on one side of a wide table, beside Thakur and Tatya. And on the other side was a clean-shaven man around fifty years old and dressed in a royal blue suit. And he was Rajvanshi, the notorious and wanted organ smuggler. With the butt of an expensive cigar pressed between his lips, he puffed smoke out from his mouth into the air. He remained mum and seemed miffed for some reason.

Thakur: "Is everything alright, sir? You look troubled."

Rajvanshi glared at Thakur and scoffed.

Rajvanshi: "I've been sitting in this dingy place for an hour. You people may not have any work but my time is very precious. Now tell me, why did you call me here?"

Tatya: "Let's discuss it once Sikander arrives. We are waiting for him to—"

But Rajvanshi stared at Tatya with widened eyes and roared in anger.

Rajvanshi: "SHUT UP, YOU BLOODY DOG! I don't talk to proletariats. Let your master answer me, or else I will leave."

Though his rebuke subdued Tatya, his attitude irked Sahil.

Sahil: "The door is open, you bighead! Get out of here if you want to, but take it from me, it will mark an end to our business deal as well."

Rajvanshi turned his attention towards Sahil and furrowed his eyebrows. He had always thought of himself as superior to others and never expected resistance from any of them. He stood up in a rage.

Rajvanshi: "What? What did you just say? Are you telling me to—"

With the things getting heated up, a nervous Thakur jumped in and admonished Sahil.

Thakur: "Are you out of your mind, Sahil? Do you know whom you are talking to? Apologize to him right now."

Thakur tried his best to calm things down, but Sahil was in no mood to call a truce.

Sahil: "He sits idle and reaps the fruits of all the hard work we do, Baba. We risk our lives and face all possible dangers while he takes the lion's share. If he thinks he is superior to all of us, then I would rather prefer to sever all business ties with him."

Sahil's bitter words infuriated Rajvanshi, but he was a shrewd businessman too. He had ruled the business like a sovereign and taken over the international market. He certainly didn't want all the years of effort going down the drain. He swallowed his anger, readjusted his suit, and sat back on his seat, not wanting to create a fuss after Sahil's reprimand.

Just then, the door burst open. About 12–14 armed men rushed in and occupied every corner of the room. Guarded by this group, a tall man with dry and permed hair entered the room and looked around. The fair-complexioned and broad-chested man looked to be in his mid-forties. He maintained a brown handlebar mustache and was chewing a piece of gum. The man was Sikander, Thakur's fierce competitor. He greeted Rajvanshi, and settled on a vacant chair next to Tatya. Sahil looked Sikander up and down. He appeared filthy to him since he had an unshaven face and plaque on his teeth. He had a crumpled shirt on him and wore old blue jeans. Moreover, he looked funny in unpolished black dress shoes. After everybody had settled down, Sahil came straight to the agenda.

Sahil: "Welcome, friends! I thank everyone for his presence at such short notice. From what I've been told, we have been together in the business for a long time. And with impotent police and inconsequential victims, it has been a real cakewalk in the past. But the scenario has changed now and things have gone for a spin. I hate to say this, but the conditions aren't as conducive as they used to be earlier. Under the leadership of Inspector Khan, the cops are on constant vigil. It will be tougher to carry out operations in the coming days under such tight scrutiny."

Sikander: "I second your opinion. The new inspector is too smart. It's getting tougher and tougher these days."

Rajvanshi: "Even I'm struggling to meet the demand in the market these days. It's getting hard for me to sustain this venture as the demand for organs is exceeding the supply."

Thakur: "Is there anything we can do to save and maintain this profitable business? Khan has asked all his constables to educate the tribal men about the potential risks posed by our men. And because of those precautionary measures, it has become tough to get our hands on them."

Sahil: "Yes, there is, and that's the sole purpose of this meeting. We need to take some severe steps and follow some basic rules. First, we all need to work together, and this is especially for you, Sikander. I know we have been competitors, but it's time to join hands. Why don't we work in collaboration?"

Sikander was silent for a moment. He had some serious doubts about Sahil's intentions. He chewed on his gum as he thought about the proposition. Then, he sighed and looked up at Sahil.

Sikander: "I don't trust you guys."

Sahil: "Consider it a compromise out of compulsion. Sometimes it's worth taking a risk. It's certainly better than sitting idle and swatting flies."

With these words, Sahil extended his hand to Sikander. Sikander looked at him with uncertainty and pondered for a bit. Then, he gripped Sahil's hand and returned a firm handshake. Two mighty forces had joined hands. Rajvanshi continued puffing on his cigar. The topic was of no interest to him. He couldn't care less about what cooked up between Sahil and Sikander. But Sahil's next recommendation irked him.

Sahil: "Until the situation eases, there won't be any further abductions. That's rule number two. Patience is key here. We need to hold our horses for the time being until police activity subdues."

Rajvanshi did not approve of this proposal.

Rajvanshi: "Nonsense! It will hit my market share. I-I'll be ruined."

Sahil: "Don't kill the goose that lays the golden eggs. Trust me, no one will be more grateful to me than you. But like I said, we need to cease all operations for some time."

But Rajvanshi was displeased. Sikander, too, wasn't convinced of Sahil's idea.

Sikander: "I don't think it's a good idea. The show must go on, Sahil."

Sahil: "It will, I promise. But before we do that, we need to understand Khan's thought process. I don't want anyone of us putting the head in lion's den. And until then, I want everyone to hold his horses. Am I clear to everyone?"

Though half-heartedly, everyone agreed to his proposition. But he was not done yet.

Sahil: "As for rule three, Rajvanshi, Sikander, and Baba will be equal partners in the business from now on. The money earned from a body will get split into three equal portions."

Rajvanshi clenched his teeth and banged on the table.

Rajvanshi: "You want my money to be divided into equal shares between us? Have you gone nuts? I object to this."

Sahil frowned and screamed at Rajvanshi.

Sahil: "Your money? What do you mean it's your money? We put our sweat and blood into hunting down someone in return for peanuts while you weigh yourself in gold. Now it's no longer about making quick money. It's a matter of survival for every one of us. Do you agree to this, or do you want to break ties?"

Rajvanshi: "B-but…this is not…"

Sahil: "Yes or no?"

A nervous Rajvanshi puffed the cigar and stared at Sahil's unflinching face. He knew he had no option but to agree to whatever Sahil dictated. He cleared the sweat off his forehead with his handkerchief and then nodded in agreement.

Sahil: "Rule four—we won't perform operations on the dead bodies in Ratnagiri anymore. Once we kill a target, we will ship the body to Pune, where Rajvanshi will take care of it. Only after Rajvanshi gets paid in the international market will we ask for our share."

Though Rajvanshi was not in agreement, he no longer had energy left to argue. He simply accepted the condition with an exhausted nod. But Sahil's next words brought some relief to him.

Sahil: "I will gift the surgical equipment installed in the school to Rajvanshi. And as a gesture of goodwill, I won't charge anything for it."

Rajvanshi rejoiced after he heard this condition, as the equipment was quite expensive. Thakur and Tatya looked at each other in surprise. They had never expected Sahil to make such an unfavorable deal. The equipment was far too costly to be gifted to someone. But Thakur remained silent, not wanting to create a scene.

Sahil: "Finally, we have rule number five. I call it the 'Three Black Box' rule. Going forward, the transactions will be done in a three-way process. First, my men will take down any possible victims and transport the body to Rajvanshi. After he removes and sells the organs, Sikander or any of his men would travel to Rajvanshi in Pune. And there, Rajvanshi would dispense him the money along with the receipt and the postmortem report of the body. Then, at an appropriate time, I will arrange for a meeting with Sikander to receive our share. The security of the cash will be the sole responsibility of Sikander going forward."

But Tatya had a concern.

Tatya: "But some of the organs have to be removed within a certain timeframe of the death of the person. Taking the bodies all the way to Pune may hamper their usefulness."

Sahil frowned and shrugged his shoulders.

Sahil: "I understand what are you saying, Tatya. But we need to live by that. We would make less money, but the process would be much safer. Moreover, to cover the losses, Rajvanshi needs to increase the prices of the organs in the market. It would also bring down the demand for the organs without compromising on our profits."

Tatya sighed and nodded. This was the only rule that everyone accepted with no objections. It seemed like a streamlined and smooth process.

Also, since it was Sahil's first meeting with everyone in the trade, Thakur decided to celebrate the moment. He ordered some wine cartons and some fried snacks from the nearby open market. The party went on till late in the night. After several rounds of snacks and drinks, Rajvanshi bid farewell to everyone and left. As the party wrapped up, two informers, Shaleen and Appu, got up and walked to Sahil. They worked in tandem with both Sikander and Thakur. They folded their hands as a mark of respect to him. In a state of complete inebriation,

Sahil stared at them in an unfocused way.

Sahil: "Yes?"

Shaleen: "Ummm…you didn't talk about our roles, sir. If we see any potential targets, whom should we report to—you or Sikander?"

Sahil: "You don't need to inform anyone. My people will take care of it. I relieve both of you of all your duties. You can go…"

Sahil's statement left them confused.

Appu: "Go? But where?"

Sahil sniggered at the innocent question, and his laughter scared them out of their wits. The very next moment, his smile vanished, and his expression grew stern.

Sahil: "To hell!"

With these words, he pulled out the gun from Tatya's unclipped holster and fired two successive shots into their heads. The informers fell to the floor, dead. The sizzling and noisy environment suddenly turned silent. Shaken, everyone in the room jumped from their seats in horror. Thakur couldn't believe his eyes and marched towards Sahil to rebuke him.

Thakur: "What have you done, boy? Have you gone insane? Why did you kill them? What wrong did they do to us?"

But Sahil remained calm.

Sahil: "Why did you need such dubious men to stalk the targets? It's a petty job that we can take care of it ourselves. With no loyal roots, these guys could have proved deadly for any of us in the future. That's why it was necessary to eliminate them."

Though not entirely convinced, Thakur didn't have any response to Sahil's explanation. He slumped back on his seat, while a distressed Tatya gestured towards the corpses.

Tatya: "What about these now?"

Sahil: "I never thought you were that dumb, Tatya. We are thirsty for deliverables while we have two right in front of us."

Sikander: "So do you want me to pass these on to Rajvanshi?"

Sahil: "No. It looks as though you've forgotten the rules, I drafted just a little while back. You will go and get the money once Rajvanshi receives it. Tatya will travel to Pune tomorrow morning to hand over the bodies to him."

Fate can be cruel at times. The two dead men had been singing and dancing just a couple of hours ago. Neither could have anticipated the ill-fated death that awaited them.

Sahil turned to his side and looked at Tatya.

Sahil: "Head for Pune at the crack of dawn. It's going to be a long trip for you tomorrow, Tatya. Why don't you rest in the guest room? And be careful with the bodies! Though this place is on the outskirts, you would still need to cross the Ratnagiri checkpoint while you drive to Pune."

Tatya nodded and left to the guest room. A few of Thakur's men dragged the dead bodies and stuffed them in the trunk of a van. When it was time to leave, Sikander greeted the father-son duo and walked with them out of the hall. But something had been nagging him from within. He halted and faced Sahil.

Sikander: "Are you sure I can trust you?"

Sahil smiled and placed his hand on Sikander's shoulder affectionately.

Sahil: "Do you think I would harm you?"

Sahil's counter-question intrigued him. He remained silent, as he did not have an immediate response. Sahil understood his dilemma and cleared the confusion lingering within Sikander.

Sahil: "I promise, I will never point my gun at you—cross my heart and hope to die."

Sahil's words brought a smile to Sikander's face. He felt a sense of sincerity in Sahil's eyes. They embraced, after which Sikander left the party hall. The father and son were the only ones in the hall after everyone else had left. Concerned by the uncertain expressions that reflected on Thakur's face, Sahil turned his attention to him.

Sahil: "Baba! Are you alright?"

A dejected Thakur sighed and shook his head.

Thakur: "You shouldn't have done what you did today. I can understand why you shot Harak, but there was no need for you to kill anyone today, at least with your own hands. You probably don't realize this, but you have plunged yourself too deep into this world. I don't see any way for you to return from here."

Sahil was silent for a moment.

Sahil: "Baba, have you by any chance felt belittled or patronized by my bold decisions? I know I didn't consult with you on them, and I am so sorry if..."

Before he could complete, Thakur placed his hand on Sahil's shoulder, and his eyes welled up. He struggled to control his emotions.

Thakur: "You have bettered me, Sahil. But I have been a little scared ever since you entered the arena. It is a lucrative but dangerous game. I wasn't afraid all these years when I was alone in it, but now I am worried about you, son. I am concerned about your safety these days, that's all."

Sahil chuckled at his father's apprehension.

Sahil: "Don't worry, Baba. I'll be all right. And I won't let anything bad happen to you either. Trust me, all will be well."

They held each other's hands affectionately. Soon, they started to drive back to Ratnagiri. While Sahil drove the car, Thakur slumped in the comfortable backseat of the car and spread his legs to relax. Sahil switched on the car's radio and began enjoying a melodious song. The female singer was crooning a famous regional folk ballad. Wary of the complete darkness due to the lack of streetlights, Sahil drove the car slowly. Since it had rained heavily in the morning, the road ahead was bumpy and craggy.

Sahil: "Ummm…Baba?"

Half asleep, Thakur responded with his eyes closed.

Thakur: "Hmm?"

Sahil: "What if…umm…the police come to know about our activities in the school?"

Thakur yawned and replied with his eyes still shut.

Thakur: "Don't worry, boy. Nothing of that sort will ever happen. In any case, we will remove the equipment and dispatch it to Rajvanshi in a few days. Though I was not in agreement with you over this during the meeting, I understand its importance now."

But Sahil remained perturbed for some reason.

Sahil: "I-I have a strange fear inside me…a weird feeling as though two hidden eyes are watching us closely. I feel as if someone is keeping an eye on us. I don't know if I'm correct in my assessment, but my sixth sense warns me that something is not right."

Thakur opened his eyes and replied with a grin.

Thakur: "As I said, nothing of that sort will ever happen. But if it does, the police would nab the custodian of the school."

Sahil was too curious to know the person.

Sahil: "And who is it? Someone in the government?"

Thakur shook his head with a relaxed smile.

Thakur: "No. My right-man!"

A rattled Sahil looked up at the rearview mirror with widened eyes.

Sahil: "Tatya?"

Thakur: "That's right! He is the custodian of the school. Being the chieftain, I signed the appointment letter myself. Except for Tatya, you and me, no one else knows that he is the custodian of the school. If such a time ever comes, it will be he who would face the music, not us. I have secured the sealed probate in the safe vault of the study and it remains there all the time. I will expose it to the world in our hour of need."

Sahil smiled and admired Thakur's shrewdness. But as soon as the car crossed the police station and reached the bridge, his smile waned. The sight of Dhananjay passing by them in the opposite direction surprised him. He looked tense as he pedaled his bicycle. Slightly suspicious, Sahil murmured to Thakur.

Sahil: "Dhananjay? What is he doing here at this hour? Do you think he is going to the police station?"

Thakur opened his eyes and glimpsed Dhananjay. Then, he leaned back and shut his eyes again. He didn't pay much attention to it and seemed relaxed.

Thakur: "He might be on his way to his publishing house, which is nearby. I heard he is in talks with some dealer to sell it off."

But the explanation did not satisfy Sahil. With a strange feeling within, he drove the car back to the mansion.

****

It had been a long and busy day for Khan at the police station. He was sipping tea and going through a file related to the spree of murders in the town. To his relief, the number of killings had gone down during his short tenure. Suddenly, his desk phone began ringing. With his eyes locked at the file in front of him, he picked up the receiver in a relaxed manner.

Khan: "Officer Khan here. How can I help you?"

But no one spoke, and there was pin-drop silence at the other end. Khan frowned.

Khan: "Hello? Is someone there?"

With no reply the second time, he almost put down the receiver when someone's heavy voice fell into his ears.

Man: "Listen carefully, Khan. Tomorrow at 6 in the morning, a van with two dead bodies will make its way to the Ratnagiri checkpoint. Nab the van, and you'll get the man you are looking for."

The news stunned Khan.

Khan: "Whom are you talking about? A-A-Are you talking about Khatri? You mean the man behind the murders in Ratnagiri?"

Man: "Yes. Remember, tomorrow at 6 am. Break a leg, Khan."

Khan: "But…but how do you know this? A-and who are you?"

But the anonymous man didn't say anything further, and hung up. Khan pursed his lips. The information baffled him, and he wondered if it was genuine.

****

After supper, Sahil lay on his bed. The day's events were replaying in his mind one after the other. A strange feeling was eating away at him. He kept thinking about Dhananjay crossing their path at night. With the same uneasy feeling, he got up from his bed and dialed Tatya's number in the guest room of the party hall. Tatya awoke at the ring and rubbed his groggy eyes. He walked to the phone on his bedside table and pressed the receiver against his ear. And when he heard Sahil on the other end, his words surprised him.

Sahil: "Tatya! I want you to leave for Rajvanshi's place right now. Start moving!"

Tatya: "Right now? But why this sudden change in plans?"

Sahil: "I have a bad feeling, Tatya. I can sense that someone has set up a trap for us, and I don't want to take any chances."

Tatya was not amused since he considered Sahil too amateur to pass him any orders.

Tatya: "But Sahil…"

Sahil: "I'm not asking you, Tatya. I'm telling you. Leave right now. Understood?"

Tatya rolled his eyes in frustration. At first, he thought to refute and tell Sahil that he would only act on Thakur's orders. But then, he realized that Sahil was trying to takeover Thakur's position. He had no other option but to agree to him since he didn't want any sort of criticism from Thakur. He heaved a sigh and agreed.

Tatya: "Hhhhhh…Alright. I'll start right now!"

Sahil: "Sounds good. Try to be back by tomorrow afternoon, and don't bring the van back. Park it somewhere in the city and hire a cab for your return."

Tatya: "Yes, I'll do that."

****

At around five in the morning, there was heavy police activity at the Ratnagiri check post. Police vans swarmed the place. About a dozen policemen were guarding the entry and exit points. In a precautionary measure, police deployed barricades and barred all the exits from Ratnagiri. Khan and his men were keeping a close eye on the passing vehicles. They frisked every vehicle that arrived at the check post. But to Khan's disappointment, they didn't find any van with corpses, as the anonymous man had conveyed to him. After an exhaustive operation that lasted for four hours, Khan called it off and returned to the police station. He ordered a cup of tea and a sandwich from a nearby eatery. As soon as he bit into the crispy toast, his desk phone rang.

Khan: "This is Inspector Khan."

He lost his temper when he heard the voice of the man on the other side. It was the same man who had given him the sham piece of information the prior night.

Khan: "You cheat! You gave me false information. Do you know that it is a crime to mislead the police?"

Man: "My apologies, Khan. Looks like there was a sudden change in plans at the last moment. But it won't happen again, I promise you. Next time, my information will be precise and accurate."

Khan: "And why should I trust you?"

Man: "I swear on the soul of my dead father, Khan. One day, I will hand over the culprits to you. Trust me, Khan."

Khan: "Hmm…but why don't you reveal their names?"

Man: "It won't be of any help even if I do. They are too powerful to be nabbed. You need strong evidence against them before you can tie a noose around their necks. Wait for my tip. Break a leg, Khan."

The man hung up. Though the call lasted about a minute, it stirred up hope in Khan. He hoped his informant to get back to him with some strong evidence against the culprits.

11. The Bung

The news of heavy police deployment in the morning reached everybody's ears. Gathered in the party hall, a contentious argument broke out between Sahil and Thakur. Tatya and Sikander stood silent though. Miffed at Sahil, the recent development had not amused Thakur.

Thakur: "How the hell did the police know about our plan, Sahil?"

Sahil replied with a straight face, embarrassed.

Sahil: "I-I don't know Baba. I'm just as clueless…"

Thakur: "What do you mean you don't know? It was your plan, boy. My men were doing their job perfectly. You're the one who changed the structure of the business. So, it was your responsibility to make sure things went as smoothly as planned."

Sahil: "I…didn't intend it, Baba. Do you really think that the changes I suggested led the police to Tatya? I don't think so. Instead, I feel like we have a spy somewhere in our ranks who passed on this information to the cops."

Tatya: "I think so too. Perhaps we had a turncoat among us at the party yesterday."

Tatya pondered over this and gave Sikander a stern gaze.

Tatya: "Looks to me like someone at the venue overheard the plans and informed the police."

Sikander was quick to sense his suspicion and dismissed it immediately.

Sikander: "You are mistaken if you think I'm the one behind this, bald man. I never turn my back once I give my word. This unknown renegade is definitely from your side."

Sahil tried to calm them both down and defuse the tension.

Sahil: "Let's call a truce. Give me some time. I'll nail the culprit soon. I assure you, Baba."

Thakur sighed and issued an advisory to Sikander.

Thakur: "Until things go back to normal, don't visit Rajvanshi to get the money. Let all the money remain with him for the moment. Let's refrain from meeting each other for the time being too. I'm a little concerned about what happened today. It is not a good sign."

Sikander nodded in agreement. Tatya turned to Sahil in admiration.

Tatya: "Although your command to leave Ratnagiri in the middle of the night annoyed me at first, I am grateful to you. You saved my ass."

Sikander: "I second Tatya's opinion. Sahil was right in changing the plan last night. I'll admit that I had doubts about his suggestions. But after I heard what happened today, it seems that he was right in his assessment of the situation."

With these words, Sikander bade farewell and drove back to his hideout. As Sahil suggested, things were at a standstill for the next few weeks. The men did not kill anyone, despite Rajvanshi's demands for delivery every other day. Sahil refused these demands, being apprehensive about the intensive police activity.

****

Sahil entered Thakur's bedroom one morning to get his signature on some documents. But he frowned when he saw Thakur seated on a chair and moaning with his head in his hands.

Sahil: "Baba? Are you okay?"

Thakur: "Yeah, I am alright, just a little headache. My glasses fell off the table last night. Probably, my hand knocked them over accidentally while I was in my deep sleep. I tend to get a migraine if I don't wear them for long. Bansi is already on his way to the optical store to collect my new glasses. By the way, what about Rajvanshi's demand? The poor guy must be in a pitiable condition. It has been about a month since we made any delivery to him. Help him out, Sahil."

Sahil: "Alright! Even though it is risky these days, I'll do it if you insist."

Thakur: "Pick some low-profile tribal man from the outskirts. Their disappearance generally doesn't get reported."

Sahil: "I'll go with Tatya in search of somebody tonight. We can't trust anyone else at the moment."

Thakur: "Okay, but let Tatya go to Pune alone. You won't go to Rajvanshi with him. Am I clear?"

Sahil smiled and nodded before explaining the purpose of his visit. He placed a bunch of papers in front of Thakur.

Thakur: "What are these now?"

Sahil: "You remember we decided to remove the equipment from the school and ship it to Rajvanshi? We need some sophisticated tools to remove the machinery. Hence, I need you to sign some payment checks that I would dispatch to the store in Khandala. Do you remember the store? We always order school equipment from there."

Thakur nodded and gazed at the checks piled in front of him. Without his reading glasses, the words were too blurry for him to read.

Thakur: "I….umm…don't have my glasses on. How will I—"

Sahil smiled.

Sahil: "It's just a matter of a couple of signatures."

Thakur: "All right. Hold my hand and place it where you need my autograph."

With a chuckle, Sahil held Thakur's hand and got the checks signed. After spending some time with his father, he left with Tatya in search of a target.

****

Back at the police station, Khan was going through some papers when a constable came running to him. He struggled to control his panting.

Constable: "Sir, do you…remember…t-the man who called the other day with a tip?"

Khan: "Yeah. What about it?"

Constable: "There's a letter from him in our mailbox."

He placed an open letter in Khan's hand. The single sheet of white paper contained a small handwritten paragraph.

"Inspector Khan,

I will soon have some evidence that will help you nab the culprits in the case you are investigating. I am sure that the documents will give a whole new direction to the case. Once I get ahold of it, I will send it to you through the mail. Please be alert and keep an eye on your mailbox henceforth.

- Your well-wisher"

Khan smiled after he went through the letter. He folded it and placed it in the drawer of his table. He was overjoyed by the new development in the case.

Khan: "Finally, I see a ray of hope. I have solved numerous cases in my career, but I have never faced such a tough case before. I hope my well-wisher helps me out."

****

Tatya parked his van near a tree and got out of the vehicle along with Sahil. They covered their faces with balaclavas and moved towards a battery farm. They hid behind a large bamboo basket, waiting for their target.

Tatya: "I don't see signs of anyone. Are you sure somebody will pass by?"

Sahil: "Hold your horses. I've observed an alcoholic man passing by this place around this time every day. According to my sources, he is a recluse and leads a solitary life. Nobody will make a fuss about him."

After about half an hour, their patience finally paid off. As Sahil speculated, they heard the sound of footsteps. Hidden behind the large basket, they peeked at the intoxicated man. Tatya went numb when he saw the drunkard haphazardly walk towards them.

Tatya: "But Sahil, he is not a tribal man. He is…"

Sahil: "Shh…quiet. To catch a tribal, we need to cross to the other side of the bridge. And that is risky because of the heavy police deployment around the area these days. He is our man for now. There is no better option at the moment."

Tatya went silent after Sahil's explanation and decided to follow his command. When the inebriated man passed them, Sahil pounced on him and gagged him with a thick towel. When the man was in his grasp, Sahil shouted.

Sahil: "Come on Tatya, take him down. Kill him!"

Tatya clutched the man's throat and throttled him. Gagged and held down by Sahil, the intoxicated man was helpless. His inebriated state made it harder for him to escape their stranglehold. He twitched and flinched erratically. But soon his strength waned. With eyes wide open, he passed out. With sweat beading their faces, Sahil and Tatya placed the body in the back of the van carefully. Tatya puffed his cheeks out and exhaled deeply. But he was taken by surprise when Sahil's next words fell in his ears.

Sahil: "Tatya, can you click my picture with the body?"

Tatya frowned and raised his brows in hesitation. The picture, if obtained by any wrong person, could bring their empire down. He protested in a loud voice.

Tatya: "A picture? That too with the body? I don't think it is a good idea. What if the picture falls into some wrong hands?"

But Sahil did not heed to his advice. Instead, he replied to him with a conceited smile.

Sahil: "Don't worry, Tatya. I would never hand over the picture to anyone, and it would always remain with me. It's my first stint on the field, and I want to capture this moment. It won't ever come back."

Tatya sighed in frustration at his strange request but somehow agreed to it. He picked up Sahil's imported camera from the backseat of the van and clicked a picture of him. First, Sahil placed one foot on the chest of the corpse. And then, he made a victory sign with his fingers with a wide smile, and Tatya captured the moment.

Sahil: "Don't tell Baba about the man. I don't want to stress him out. Am I clear?"

Tatya: "Okay, I won't. But do you really feel like we did the right thing? What if…"

Sahil: "I will deal with it. Don't worry. Now leave. Cover your license plate number, and call me once you deliver the body to Rajvanshi. Please be safe. I need you, Tatya."

Tatya sighed and nodded with a smile. Finally, he dropped Sahil at the mansion and left for Rajvanshi's place to deliver the body.

It was a busy day for Khan at the police station. He held the letter in his hand and was lost in deep thought as he went through it over and over again. The loud ring of his desk phone snapped him out of his thoughts.

Khan: "Officer Khan here."

Man: "Hope you recognize me, Khan."

Khan jumped up, eager for more information.

Khan: "Absolutely, my friend. I received your letter about the evidence to nail the killers. When can I expect it to be in my hands?"

There was a brief pause at the other end, and silence prevailed for the next few moments.

Man: "Ummm…you need to wait a little longer. For now, I have some other news for you. A blue van is heading for Pune. It should cross the checkpoint in about fifteen minutes. Get ahold of it. You will get everything you need to nail the bastards."

Khan's heartbeat increased after he heard this.

Khan: "A-are you sure? I hope this doesn't turn out to be a hoax call like it did last time."

Khan's taunt did not go down well with the anonymous man.

Man: "You are losing precious time. Remember, a blue van, fifteen minutes! Break a leg, Khan."

With these words, the unknown man disconnected the call.

Unaware of this exchange, Tatya was on his way to Pune. On his way, he saw Dhananjay stepping out of a public telephone booth on the other side of the road. He stepped out of it, climbed on his bicycle, and rode away. Dhananjay's presence at the deserted place and at that time of the night raised doubts in his mind. Sahil had mentioned his presence around the party hall the night of the meeting. And the very next morning, Khan had deployed police forces at the checkpoint.

And soon, his fears came true. He saw a massive gathering of policemen at the checkpoint. He put on a maroon balaclava and covered his face. As the van approached the checkpoint, Khan signaled him to stop the vehicle. But Tatya was in no mood to surrender. He accelerated his vehicle, and the van crossed the checkpoint. It made a roaring sound and left behind a cloud of black smoke.

The driver's actions proved to Khan that the information provided by the snitch was true. He decided to chase the van and ordered his men to block the alternate exit. His entire force made for a different route while he chased the felon at a brisk speed. Khan fired at the rear tires of the van to blow them up, but he missed his target every time he fired. It wasn't easy for him to shoot and drive at the same time. To add to his woes, he couldn't overtake the van, as the road was narrow, with thick forests on both sides of it.

Tatya was a skilled driver. He drove fast and with excellent control over his vehicle. The jet of smoke and dust from the van's rear exhaust hampered Khan's visibility. Tatya pulled out his gun from his unclipped holster and fired back at Khan. Khan ducked at appropriate times to dodge the shots. He was determined to catch the culprit and wasn't in any mood to give up the chase.

Finally, luck smiled on Khan. Due to the heavy rain the previous night, the van's rear tire got stuck in a quagmire as it drove through a damp area. A rattled Tatya stomped on the accelerator in panic but failed to get out of the quagmire. Khan smiled when he saw the vehicle struggle in the muddy marsh. He played smart and, instead of driving through the bog, decided to walk through it. He didn't want his car to get stuck in the marsh as well. With the gun in hand, he got down from the car and stepped towards the van. And as he moved closer, the sight of a masked man at the driving seat of the van shuddered him. He wheezed and pointed his gun at him before issuing a stern warning.

Khan: "Whoever you are, surrender right now! I promise I won't harm you if you surrender. But if you play dirty, I won't spare you. If you defy my order, don't blame me for what I will do to you."

But Tatya was unnerved by Khan's threat. Sweating profusely, he continued to try getting out of the quagmire. When Khan was barely at two arm lengths from him, his efforts finally paid off. Thick mud swept out from underneath the captive tire, and with immense momentum, the van sped away. Khan's chase had gone horribly wrong.

A baffled Khan ran after the vehicle and attempted to fire at it. Everything happened so quickly that he didn't get any time to recover. He ran back to his car and chased the trail of mud left behind by the van's tires. But in no time, the van had vanished into the darkness of the night. It was too late. With several detours in front of him, Khan had lost the track of the vehicle. He ceased his unsuccessful chase and looked around in disarray. Then, he sighed and shook his head in disappointment. Finally, he drove back to the station empty-handed.

Back in his office, the failed chase continued to haunt Khan. As he grappled with his thoughts, he heard his desk phone ring. With a sigh, he picked up the receiver.

Khan: "Officer Khan here."

He felt a pang of embarrassment when he heard the voice of the mysterious informer.

Khan: "Sorry, friend, but I failed to nab him. I ran out of luck at the very last moment."

———

112

Perhaps, the news did not amuse the mysterious man.

Man: "You know what, Khan, I risked my life to give you those leads. But if you keep failing, it is not worth putting my life in danger any longer."

Khan gulped with a lump in his throat.

Khan: "Listen! I tried my best, but I lost him at the very last moment. I promise I'll catch the bastards this time. Give me one more chance, just one!"

The man went silent. But after a brief moment of silence, he agreed to Khan's request.

Man: "I like your honesty, Khan. All right, I will share the details soon. As I mentioned in my previous letter, I will dispatch the evidence in a few weeks. Wait for my next clue. Break a leg, Khan."

With these words, the anonymous man hung up. Khan sat back and held his head in his hands. He was still troubled by his futile effort in apprehending the driver of the van.

****

Meanwhile, back in his bedroom, a nervous Sahil sat on a chair and waited for Tatya's call. He was jittery, as he hadn't heard from him for about 12 hours now. Ideally, it shouldn't have taken him more than 9 hours to reach Rajvanshi's place in Pune. But then, the loud landline ring jolted him out of his trance. As soon as he heard it, he rushed and picked up the receiver.

Sahil: "Hello?"

He sighed in relief and his rattled nerves calmed down when he heard Tatya's voice.

Sahil: "Where are you, Tatya? I was desperately waiting for your call. Is everything alright?"

Tatya replied amid heavy panting.

Tatya: "I delivered the body to Rajvanshi. I'm at his haunt right now. Sahil…there's definitely a whistleblower. I had a near-death encounter with Khan on my way here."

Then, in the same breath, he explained his horrific and nerve-wracking encounter with Khan. Sahil sighed and nodded in empathy.

Sahil: "Take it easy, Tatya. Relax. I knew you would make it. That's why I assigned the task to you. Let's think about who this man is once you come back."

Tatya: "I think I know who it is."

And when Tatya revealed his suspicion about Dhananjay, Sahil's eyes widened in shock.

Sahil: "I suspected him too. Let me deal with him. Meanwhile, stay in Pune for a few days, and inform Sikander to refrain from visiting Rajvanshi for a few days. Dump the van somewhere in Pune, and come back by train or bus."

Tatya nodded and disconnected the call while Sahil stroked his beard, lost in deep thought.

✳✳✳✳✳✳✳✳✳✳✳✳✳✳✳✳✳✳✳✳✳✳✳✳✳✳✳✳✳✳✳✳✳✳✳✳✳✳✳

The next evening, Dhananjay stepped out of his publishing house and walked to his bicycle leaning against the wall of the building. He looked around anxiously as he walked. With a small parcel in his hand, he seemed nervous and scared. Before he could mount his cycle, a speeding van emerged from somewhere and made a harsh stop beside him. The skidding sound of the van petrified him. Two masked men jumped from the van and grabbed Dhananjay's arms. They gagged him and dragged him into the van. Once inside, a masked man slid shut the door of the van as it accelerated towards an undisclosed location.

After a couple of hours, somebody removed the scarf tied around Dhananjay's eyes. He rubbed his eyes to counter the sudden glare of light in his eyes. Though he saw a flock of people around him in a lit room, everything looked blurry and grainy to him. But a chill ran down his spine when his vision cleared up. About a dozen masked men, armed with guns, surrounded him. Moreover, the sight of Sahil on a chair opposite him stunned him to the core. Sahil picked up the brown envelope his henchmen had collected from Dhananjay. He opened the sealed packet and went through the documents in it.

Dhananjay: "Sahil? W-what is this all about? Why have these men brought me here, and that too, in this fashion?"

Instead of replying, Sahil merely grinned viciously. His behavior frightened Dhananjay.

Dhananjay: "Why…why are you laughing?"

This time, Dhananjay's query irked Sahil. His smile vanished.

Sahil: "Are you the one trying to pass information to the police?"

Dhananjay frowned in confusion at his words.

Dhananjay: "Information? What information are you talking about?"

Sahil: "Aren't you in contact with Khan?"

Dhananjay: "Yes, I am. But how is that related to you?"

Sahil: "Just like your late father, you know a bit too much about certain things, the things you shouldn't have known about. It is time for you to meet the same fate as your father."

———

Dhananjay's eyes widened when he heard Sahil's words. He raised his brows in surprise. Things suddenly became crystal clear. Tears of anger began running down his cheeks.

Dhananjay: "What? Same fate as the father? You're the one behind it? Oh, the son of a nobleman! Are you the one who killed my father? But why?"

Though Sahil didn't say a word, his vicious smile confirmed Dhananjay's fears. To avenge his father's brutal murder, he charged at Sahil in an attempt to knock him down. But before he could touch Sahil, the henchmen in the room pinned him to the floor. After Sahil's men pummeled him down on the floor, he sat back on the floor and broke down.

Sahil: "But you won't be as lucky as your father. He was given an easy death, but you will get a brutal one, where my men will rip the organs from your body."

Dhananjay: "What did you just say? Men ripping off organs? Father was tracking the same case. Oh my God! Are you the one behind it? I can't believe it's you! And if I am not wrong, the parcel has something that can put you behind bars."

Sahil: "What do you mean, 'if I'm not wrong.' Don't you already know what's in it?"

Dhananjay shook his head as he wiped his tears.

Dhananjay: "No, I don't."

Sahil: "Are you telling me that you don't know what's in the packet you were holding? I don't like jokes, Dhananjay, especially bad ones."

Dhananjay: "I'm telling you the truth. Today was the day I found it in my father's office. In fact, I haven't entered the place since the day Father died. I did this as per his instructions."

Sahil: "What do you mean?"

Desolate, Dhananjay's lips trembled as he looked up at Sahil with tearful eyes. He recounted his conversation with Alok the night he was killed. He recalled his last moments with his father.

Alok: *"Listen carefully, boy! I need to go out for a couple of hours. But I need you to remember what I'm about to tell you."*

Dhananjay: *"What happened, father? Are you okay? You look nervous."*

Alok: *"Yes, I am, but I am excited as well. What if I tell you that we would make a fortune tonight? What if I tell you that once I'm back, we're going to be rich?"*

Dhananjay (narrating to Sahil): "My heartbeat increased when I heard him. I asked him what he meant repeatedly, but he didn't reveal anything more."

Dhananjay: *"What kind of get-rich-quick scheme are you talking about?"*

Alok: *"I'll give you the details once I come back. I promise you one thing—once I'm back, we will have enough money to leave our woes behind."*

Dhananjay (narrating to Sahil): "But suddenly, his smile waned. I could see a strange fear on his face. He choked up."

Alok: *"But...I have something more important to tell you. In case I don't come back, I want you to retrieve a sealed envelope from the cupboard in my office. But don't do it immediately after—wait for an appropriate time, when things simmer down. Don't even go to the publishing house for about a couple of months. Then, grab the sealed envelope from my office, and post it to an honest and capable cop. I have doubts about Sharma's capabilities, so wait until some efficient officer replaces him."*

Dhananjay: *"You're scaring me, father. What exactly are you trying to say?"*

Alok: *"Let me get straight to the point. Over the past few days, I have gathered substantial evidence against some very powerful people. They are the ones behind the spree of killings in Ratnagiri. The evidence is good enough to send these horrendous people to the gallows. Tonight, I'm going to cut a deal with the mastermind and trade the evidence for a lump sum of money. But in case I don't come back, I want you to carry out my instructions."*

Dhananjay (narrating to Sahil): "I freaked out when I heard him."

Dhananjay: *"No, father, I won't let you go. You don't need to risk your life."*

Alok: *"Don't worry, son. There's no chance he will reject my offer. Everything will be settled peacefully. Trust me, it will be worth the risk. These people are too smart to refrain from a settlement."*

Dhananjay: *"Who are these people you're talking about? Let me come along."*

Dhananjay (narrating to Sahil): "But he didn't reveal any name to me. He just caressed my head with a miserable smile."

Alok: *"Stay home with Suhasini. I don't want to jeopardize something that will otherwise go smoothly. I'll be back soon."*

A nostalgic Dhananjay wiped his tears as he recalled his last moments with his father.

Dhananjay: "But he never came back. I curse myself for letting him go."

After he said this, Dhananjay stared at Sahil with fluttering lips.

Dhananjay: "So you were the one who killed him after he asked you for some money in exchange for the evidence?"

Sahil didn't pay any heed to Dhananjay's question, not feeling the need to give him an explanation. Instead, he placed a loaded gun on the table, which scared Dhananjay out of his wits. He stood up in fear.

Dhananjay: "Come on, kill me. Because if you set me free, I will run to Thakur before I go to the police. He will disown you once he comes to know the kind of devil that was born to him."

Sahil got up from his seat and walked to him with a smirk on his face.

Sahil: "Don't worry, Dhananjay. I won't give you that chance. But my retribution won't end even after I bludgeon you to death. You'll be paying for this even after you are dead and gone. Don't you want to know what will happen after my men kill you?"

With eyes widened in fear, he silently tried to anticipate Sahil's threat.

Sahil: "In the darkest hour of one night, a dozen of my men will enter your home through its backdoor. All alone in her room, Suhasini would be in her disturbed sleep, after the death of her beloved brother. Stealthily, my brutish men will circle the sleeping beauty. She will snap out of her slumber when she feels two strong hands holding her upper arms. Her eyes will widen in fear, much like yours right now, at the sight of muscular men standing around her. She will scream in agony when one of them pulls out a broadsword from his scabbard. He will proceed to slit her dress from her thighs to feet. He would then hold the torn ends of the slit and rip them apart."

These words were unbearable to Dhananjay.

Dhananjay: "Shut up, you bloody…"

Sahil: "Does your sister wear any panties or a bra at night? If she does, my next man will tear off her undergarments."

Dhananjay lost his mind after he heard those vulgar words about his sister. He clenched his teeth in anger and lunged at him. He grabbed Sahil's collar and punched his face in disgust. Sahil's men rushed towards Dhananjay, but Sahil gestured them to stop. Perhaps, he did it for a purpose.

Sahil: "Imagine her fear and embarrassment in finding herself naked in front of all these men. Try to feel her melancholy when each of the men would fondle her breasts and suck her soft nipples."

His obscene words against his sister's modesty traumatized Dhananjay. In a rage, he unleashed a volley of punches at Sahil. Sahil's nose began bleeding profusely from the blows. But he was not done yet.

Sahil: "Each of them would then loosen his pants and bring down his underwear. In turns, they will place their hairy thighs on her butter-smooth thighs. And every man would take turns to be on top of her, in ultimate pleasure as he penetrates…"

But Dhananjay's scream cut him off. His obscene words about his sister had shattered him. Visualizing the assault made him go pale. He began to wail and dropped to his knees. Amid sobs, he folded his hands and pleaded for mercy.

Dhananjay: "Stop it, please! I beg of you, Sahil! Please stop it. Kill me if you want to, but don't drag my sister into all this. She is just an innocent and naïve child. Please don't do any harm to her. Think of her as your own sister. Please!"

Sahil shook his head and shrugged.

Sahil: "I can't. I don't trust you. You or your sister might turn us in any day."

Dhananjay: "I swear upon my dead father, she has no idea about my conversation with him. Please spare her life. I beg of you, Sahil."

As he watched Dhananjay's wretched expression, Sahil paused briefly to think. After a moment, he sighed and nodded.

Sahil: "Alright! Not just hers, I will spare your life as well. But I have one condition. You need to leave Ratnagiri forever along with your sister and never return."

Dhananjay looked up at Sahil in despair.

Dhananjay: "But…where should I go?"

Sahil: "Anywhere on the planet. But I don't want to see any trace of you in Ratnagiri after today."

Dhananjay: "I don't have anywhere to go. I don't have any resources. The publishing house is the only asset I have. Give me some time till I sell it off."

Sahil: "No, no, no! You need to leave Ratnagiri by today."

Dhananjay: "But how will I survive? I'm broke and…"

Sahil: "Two million."

Sahil's interjection left him astounded.

Dhananjay: "What?"

Sahil: "Take two million rupees from me and leave this place. That should be enough to cover the combined cost of your home and publishing house."

Dhananjay was baffled. He started to think about the offer, as he had doubts regarding Sahil's intentions.

Dhananjay: "I-I am not sure… "

Sahil: "Four million."

This bid flabbergasted not only Dhananjay but Sahil's men as well. They looked at each other in shock. Dhananjay's mouth fell wide open in disbelief. He wanted to accept the offer, but something was hindering him from within. Sahil picked up the gun from the table and aimed at his head.

Sahil: "Last offer—five million or a cheap bullet for your head."

Dhananjay chickened out at the sight of the gun aimed at him. The lump sum of money was the best option in these circumstances. He nodded.

Dhananjay: "Okay, okay. I agree. Please don't shoot, please."

Sahil retracted his gun. He arranged for a big suitcase and stuffed it with three million rupees. Then, he zipped it and handed it over to Dhananjay in the presence of his masked men.

Dhananjay: "B-b-but the deal was for five million, right? The bag has only three."

Sahil: "This is all I have with me in the bank. But don't worry. I will hold up my end of the deal."

With a thought to hand over his diamond ring to Dhananjay, Sahil slid it out from his finger. But before he gave the ring to him, Sahil looked at the ring and went into a trance. He recalled some of his nostalgic memories related to the diamond jewel. It was the ring that he had planned to gift it to Preeti. He gulped in melancholy and gave a miserable smile to Dhananjay. Then, he handed it over to him and choked up.

Sahil: "Take it. The value of this ornament is much more than the deficit amount."

Dhananjay couldn't believe his eyes and ears. The sparkling jewel dazzled before him. With quivering hands, he took it from Sahil and wore it on his finger. Next, he picked up the bag stuffed with money and turned around. He looked back at Sahil one last time and then left the location.

After he left, an argument broke out between Sahil and one of his men. The henchman did not agree with Sahil's decision to let Dhananjay walk out alive.

Henchman: "You have made a grave mistake. He can pose a threat to us. You loaded him with money instead of killing him? We will all be in some serious trouble if he goes to the police. I'm sorry to say this, but it was a bad decision on your part."

Sahil: "A gun is not always the best solution. His love for his sister is stronger than the vengeance he seeks for his father's death. Moreover,

I don't want to hand yet another high-profile case to Khan. I'm sure that as long as I roam free, this man will not dare go against me. Let him go."
Henchman: "What do you mean by 'as long as I roam free'?"

Sahil smiled and shook his head.
Sahil: "Nothing. Now let's pack up and leave."

12. The Celebration

In the cold night, Thakur was enjoying the warmth of the fireplace in his room. He jolted in surprise when a brown envelope landed on the coffee table in front of him. He looked up in a jiffy. A smiling Sahil stood at the doorway, and he had his left hand concealed behind his back.
Thakur: "What is this, Sahil?"
Sahil: "Our providence!"

With a frown, Thakur grabbed the envelope and opened it carefully. A chill ran down his spine when he slid out one picture from the envelope—the one where he was shaking hands with Rajvanshi.
Thakur: "This…this picture?"

Sahil sighed and replied as he walked closer to Thakur.
Sahil: "You guessed it right, Baba. It's the replica of the picture Alok showed you at the clock tower. There is a lot more evidence in the packet."

A rattled Thakur adjusted his glasses and went through the other evidence. The next two pictures he pulled out answered a question that had haunted him for a long time. He had always wondered what led Alok to suspect him in the first place.

The first picture was of a rangoli on the floor—a peacock with a twisted tail and spread-out feathers. Harak Singh had created it on Diwali eve. He remembered Alok's zeal as a photographer. Dazzled by the rangoli, he had captured it from all possible angles. The next picture was of Murari's dead body. In a close-up shot, a red marker pen demarcated a section on the picture — an inked sketch on the right shoulder of the corpse. After careful scrutiny, he made a disturbing discovery. The small doodle on Murari's shoulder was a replica of the rangoli; a peacock with a twisted tail and spread-out feathers. He remembered that the police had hired Alok to capture Murari's photos during his postmortem. He had recognized the design as soon as Harak finished the rangoli and concluded that Harak had something to do with Murari's murder. Since Harak worked for Thakur, Alok guessed that he could be a collaborator in the crime as well.

With a sigh, Thakur flipped both pictures repeatedly. And every time he looked at them, the designs looked more and more alike. He cleared his throat and looked at Sahil.

Thakur: "Harak had a habit of scribbling on the corpse when he traveled to deliver it. And probably, he did the same with Murari. Bloody goofball!"

Sahil: "After this, Alok started stalking you. In one such attempt, he followed you to Pune and captured your picture with Rajvanshi in the same frame. It was the same picture he had shown you the night you killed him. You grabbed the picture from him and destroyed it, but he had kept a replica safe. Luckily, I got ahold of Dhananjay today and snatched it from him before he could hand it over to the police."

Thakur nodded and looked at his picture with Rajvanshi.

Thakur: "You're right, Sahil. The bastard had come to make a deal that night. I miscalculated his ploy. What else is in the envelope?"

Sahil: "It has all the addresses of Rajvanshi in Pune and documents related to the school's basement. The pictures confirm that our men used the basement for illegal surgeries. There's also a list with the names of everyone involved either with us or Sikander in the trade."

A flustered Thakur issued an immediate command to him.

Thakur: "Go… go and destroy everything you have with you."

Sahil smiled and replied in mischief.

Sahil: "Okay, Baba. I'll need a good quality matchbox."

Thakur: "I heard your encounter with Dhananjay. In addition to the lump sum of money, you gifted him your ring too? Instead, why didn't you ask any one of our men to kill him? Now, he knows everything about you. We are at a high risk to get exposed."

Sahil looked at Thakur with a smirk.

Sahil: "But the good thing is that he does not suspect you to be the part of the trade. Moreover, I am not fond of unnecessary bloodshed. I know that he won't dare to go to the police after he heard my threatening words for his sister."

Thakur sighed and nodded in anxiety.

Thakur: "I am so glad you decided to remove the machinery from the basement. Good, timely decision! By the way, where were you? I haven't seen you since yesterday evening. You look worn out too."

Sahil: "I went to Khandala to finish the task you just appreciated! Do you remember the paychecks you signed for the tools to remove the machinery?"

Thakur: "Yeah, blindly!"

Sahil chuckled at his father's banter.

Sahil: "I went and delivered the checks to the store manager."

Thakur: "Hmmm…good that you got the tools. Now wrap it up!"

Sahil shook his head.

Sahil: "I wish I could, but the manager needs some notarized documents before he releases the delivery. Since you are the chieftain, he needs you to be present when he gets the documents notarized. I have made the payment and handed him the checks, but he hasn't released the tools yet."

Thakur: "I have never been asked for any such supporting documents before. Why now?"

Sahil: "Rules are always subject to change."

Thakur frowned and nodded.

Thakur: "Alright, I will go. Sometime next week."

Sahil shook his head.

Sahil: "No, Baba. You need to leave for Khandala tomorrow. I have already booked your train tickets."

Thakur: "Tomorrow?"

Sahil: "There's no time, Baba. I want to get it done as soon as possible. You'll leave tomorrow morning by train. Your return train from Khandala starts in the evening tomorrow. I have a room booked in your name in a luxury hotel for a day. Once you reach the city and get the delivery released, relax in the hotel until your train leaves for Ratnagiri. You will be back on the morning of the day after."

Thakur remained silent for a few moments.

Thakur: "You don't remember what day tomorrow is, son?"

Sahil held his father's shoulder by his right hand. He had still kept his left hand concealed behind his back.

Sahil: "Of course I know. It's your birthday. We have a big party planned for tomorrow evening in the same party hall on the outskirts. Everyone involved in our trade will be part of it. Sikander and Rajvanshi will join the party along with all their men."

Thakur: "And you're still asking me to leave?"

Sahil nodded with a miserable smile.

Sahil: "I wish you could be around, Baba, but the gravity of the matter is such that I can't help it. The earlier we clean up this mess, the better."

Thakur: "Hmmm... All right, I will leave tomorrow. But I will miss the gala time that you guys will surely enjoy. Anyway, I'll celebrate my birthday next year."

But Sahil was quick to refute Thakur's conjecture.

Sahil: "Life is short, Baba. God alone knows who will step into the next year. Besides, who told you that we wouldn't celebrate your birthday?"

Thakur: "What do you mean?"

Sahil's smile widened and he flashed his teeth. Then, he brought his concealed left hand in front of Thakur. And to Thakur's surprise, he held a wine bottle in it along with two trendy wine glasses. He handed the bottle to Thakur with delight on his face along with the glasses. At that very moment, the clock tower of Ratnagiri struck twelve and buzzed aloud. With a wide smile on his face, Sahil embraced his father and kissed his cheek. Thakur chuckled and planted a gentle kiss on Sahil's cheek as well. Thakur poured wine into both the glasses, and they raised a toast to each other. Sahil switched on the stereo and played a melodious old song. Both held each other and danced to the tune of the song. After about half an hour of merrymaking, they sat next to each other. Inebriated, Sahil raised his glass one last time.

Sahil: "To your long life. Happy Birthday! I hope God gives you a long life, similar to Ashwathama's!"

Thakur laughed out loud.

Thakur: "Ashwathama?"

Sahil: "Yes, Ashwathama, the immortal!"

Thakur: "Seems like you are reading too much about him these days, huh?"

Sahil smiled and sipped his wine.

Sahil: "Since Rajvanshi is coming to the party, Sikander doesn't need to go to him in Pune to collect the money. Instead, I have asked Rajvanshi to bring the cash to the party. We will divide and distribute the money at the party itself."

Thakur smiled in his tipsy state and pointed at Sahil.

Thakur: "I'm not very fond of nepotism, Sahil. I'll admit that when you joined me, I had doubts about your capabilities. But you have the zeal for business, my boy. I was impressed by the way you rescued Tatya. It was prudent of you to ask him to leave early when you foresaw danger. You are now ready to take over all the responsibilities I have shouldered all these years. It's time for me to take a permanent break."

Sahil burst out laughing as he picked up some roasted peanuts from a plate. He replied as he munched.
Sahil: "In that case, you're in for a disappointment. Your new assignments haven't even started yet."

Thakur smiled at his jest. But when he lifted his glass to take another sip, he suddenly recalled something important.
Thakur: "Umm… S-S-Sahil… I remember now… The picture I snatched from Alok…I kept it in…umm…in the…s-safe vault of the chamber… at the mercy of the Death Lord. After I…umm…return, l-l-let us go to the chamber…destroy it…umm…destroy everything you see that can be used against me. The picture is in the safe vault in the chamber…"

Sahil jumped up from his seat when he heard this. The information chased away the effect of the alcohol.
Sahil: "What? Instead of putting the evidence in the vault, why didn't you destroy it immediately?"

But Thakur did not reply and fell asleep instead. A frustrated Sahil sighed and shook his head. Then, he held his father by his shoulders and lay him down on the sofa bed. He removed his shoes and covered him with a warm quilt. He gazed at his father with a smile for a couple of minutes. Then, he picked up the envelope, switched off the lights of the room, and walked back to his room.

A few moments later, he stepped out of his room with a matchbox in one hand and the envelope in the other. He made his way to the corner of the backyard. There, he slid out the picture of Thakur and Rajvanshi. After staring at the picture with a stern look for a couple of minutes, he slid it back into the envelope and set it ablaze. After the papers had turned to ashes, he headed back to his room.

Though he was unaware of it, Preeti saw him burning the papers from the window of her room. She frowned out of concern for him, finding his actions strange. After he left for his room, she sighed and closed the window of her room.

Back in his room, Sahil lay on his bed and looked up at the ceiling with a smile. He thought about the private celebration moment that he shared with his father a while ago. Then, he closed his eyes and fell into a deep slumber.

✶✶

Khan held a gun in his hand and chased Thakur on a deserted street on a moonless night. Thakur, finding it hard to maintain the lead against the younger and stronger Khan, huffed and panted. As he increased his pace, Khan issued him a stern warning.

Khan: "Stop, Thakur! Stay right where you are."

Despite hearing Khan, Thakur did not stop his sprint. Khan warned him one last time.

Khan: "If you take one more step, I will shoot you."

But the warning did not deter Thakur. He continued to run as fast as he could. After Thakur had defied all his warnings, Khan took a position and loaded his gun. He aimed it at Thakur and pulled the trigger. The bullet hit Thakur in the back. He howled in pain and fell on the road. He flailed his arms and legs in agony and, soon, succumbed to the injury.

****

Sahil: "Ahhh!"

Sahil woke up in a panic and gasped when the alarm of the clock buzzed. With sweat beading his face, he panted and looked around the room. He grabbed the glass of water on his bedside table and gulped it all in one go. He sighed in relief. The visual about Thakur and Khan had merely been a nightmare. After his breathing turned normal, he puffed out his cheeks, he lay back down and went back to sleep.

That morning, Vidya awoke when she heard a feeble knock on the door of her room. She sat up in bed.

Vidya: "Yes, Bansi? Is that you?"

Since I awakened everyone in the house with the tea in the mornings, she thought me as the one standing at the door. After Preeti sustained the wound on her arm after Harak's assault, I took over the job from her. But she was a little surprised when she saw Sahil opening the door and entering inside. The sight of her beloved son early in the morning filled her with joy.

Vidya: "Sahil, what a lovely surprise! I'm seeing you after so many days even though we live under the same roof. Your Baba isn't here. He left for Khandala due to some urgent work half an hour ago."

Sahil: "I know, Ma. But today, I came to see you."

His eyes welled up as soon as he uttered these words, and he began crying like a baby. Vidya had never expected such an emotional outburst from Sahil. She stood up and cradled Sahil's face in her hands.

Vidya: "Arrey…what happened, Sahil?"

After a few moments of emotional vulnerability, he regained his composure. He wiped his tears, held her hands, and planted a kiss on them.

Sahil: "I'm sorry, Ma. It's just that we are talking to each other after such a long time."

Vidya: "I understand. I know you're working very hard, and it seems to have taken a toll on you. Why don't you take a break? Take some time off."

Sahil: "Yes, Ma. I will take a long break in the days to come. But right now, I'm here to tell you something more important."

He sat her down and looked into her eyes.

Sahil: "You are my guru, and you have been my strength all these years. I promise I won't let anything bad happen to Baba."

Though he did not reveal to her, the nightmare that he had about Thakur rattled him and scared him out of his wits. Unaware of the dreadful feelings running within him, she smiled and cradled his face in her hands.

Vidya: "Did you take the trouble to visit me early in the morning just to tell me this? I know it already. I'm a proud mother. Your Baba told me about your efforts to scale up the facilities in the school. He is confident that people would elect you as their next chieftain as you are ready to take over his role."

With these words, she kissed his forehead. By this time, Sahil was calm. With a smile on his face, he turned around and started to walk out. But his steps froze when Vidya called him out.

Vidya: "Sahil!"

Sahil: "Yes, Ma?"

Vidya cleared her throat and gave him a saddened look.

Vidya: "Mhmm…It is…emm…about Preeti. I want you to talk to her. She hasn't said anything, but I can read the prevailing gloom in her eyes for you."

He gulped and pondered for a brief moment. Then, he nodded glumly and closed the door behind him. She continued to look at the door for some time. Finally, she heaved a deep sigh and lay back on her bed.

Sahil made his way to Preeti's room in the backyard. He stood at the doorway and peered through the partially open door. She was standing near a stove in the corner, pouring tea in the kettle. Though Mandana had already left, Preeti continued to use the little stove in the makeshift kitchen of her room. Her wound had healed, but it discomfited as it pained in the cold mornings. And since she found it hard to walk to the mansion in the early mornings, she preferred to prepare her tea in her room.

He entered and called out in a mellow voice.

Sahil: "Hi, Preeti."

Preeti whirled around as soon as she heard his voice.

Preeti: "Sahil? Why are you standing there? Come, sit."

With slight hesitation, he walked slowly to a chair in the middle of her small room.

Preeti: "Would you like to have tea? I just made some."

Sahil: "Y-yeah. It's a cold morning. I'd love to have some."

After Preeti served him tea, they sat beside each other. There was a brief pause as neither spoke a word. They sat quietly, sipping their tea. It was an awkward moment. Finally, Sahil broke the ice.

Sahil: "Umm…won't you say anything?"

His words brought a sarcastic smile to her face.

Preeti: "Don't tell me that you have some spare time to talk to me today."

Her jibe made him smirk.

Sahil: "Do you have any more words to humiliate me?"

Outraged, she banged her teacup on the table.

Preeti: "You haven't spared even ten minutes for me in the past few days. How do you expect me to talk normally? Do you even care about what I've been through all these days?"

Sahil finished his tea and gently placed his cup on the table.

Sahil: "Preeti, I admit that it's my mistake. I know that it is all my fault."

Preeti: "You behave so strangely these days. And what were you doing in the backyard last night? What did you burn? I saw you burning some piece of paper."

Her words surprised him. He hadn't expected her to see him burning the envelope. He remained silent for a few moments and fixed his gaze at her. Then, he sighed after a pause.

Sahil: "Preeti…there are things I wish I could share with you…things I wish I could explain, but…"

An irked Preeti yelled out in frustration.

Preeti: "Then please explain! What's making you keep a distance from me since the day you broke off your engagement? Things should have been better between us."

Sahil: "Do you think I enjoy doing this to you?"

His strained words calmed her down a little.

Preeti: "I know you don't, but I'm sure you are hiding something from me. Ma believes that it is because of work pressure, but I don't buy it. Tell me, Sahil. What is it?"

A distraught Sahil exhaled and looked at her with a straight face. It was hard to hide things from her. But he held his tongue. He could not risk having her as a new confidante in these risky times. He got up from the chair and headed towards the door.

Sahil: "I need to go, Preeti. I have some urgent work. I am sorry if I am hurting you. I am lucky to have a friend in my life who…umm…makes the best sandwiches in the world."

The unexpected compliment brought a smile to her face. She tried her best to control her grin but failed.

Preeti: "Don't you dare to flatter me!"

Sahil: "No, I'm not. I seriously miss those delicious sandwiches."

Her smile widened.

Preeti: "Hmmm…I'll make them for you the next time we meet."

Sahil: "Next time? Are you sure?"

Preeti: "Yeah, I will."

He thanked her with a grin before leaving her room. Though she didn't get an answer to her questions, the cozy chat with Sahil relieved her a lot. The little chat acted as a stress-buster, especially after the distance between the two in the past few days. A gentle smile remained on her face as she shut the door of her room.

That morning, since I was unwell, I was resting in my room. Vidya had given me the day off. Napping on my cot, I jolted awoke when someone knocked on the door of my room. When I opened the door, the sight of Sahil surprised me.

Sahil: "How are you feeling, Bansi? I heard you were sick."

I: "I have a fever, but I should be fine by the end of the day."

Sahil: "Yeah, please rest. But I will need your services for the party in the evening. I hope you will be feeling up to it."

I looked at him in silence. Although I did not want to refuse him, I was feeling a little tired and feeble. He was wise enough to comprehend my dilemma.

Sahil: "There is a guestroom in the party hall with medicines and a comfortable bed. After you help the guests for some time, feel free to make yourself self-comfortable. I don't trust anyone more than you right now, Bansi."

I sighed and nodded.

Sahil: "Thanks! I'll pick you up in the evening. And if someone asks you about your whereabouts, don't tell him or her that you were at the party. Tell the person that you had been in your room throughout the day."

With those words to me, Sahil headed back to his car and drove towards the chamber of assemblies. After Thakur had revealed the location of the picture in the chamber, Sahil wanted to destroy it at the earliest. But an unexpected scene awaited him as he neared the gate of the chamber. Two enormous trees had fallen and blocked the road ahead. Police had teemed the area and deployed a massive crane at the place. With its headlights turned on, the crane moved backward and forward in a maneuver, lifting the broken trunks of the trees. The cops had put up barricades in the middle of the road with a signboard prohibiting commuters from using the road ahead. The sight disturbed Sahil, and he slowly drove towards a constable standing nearby.

Sahil: "When will the road be cleared?"

Constable: "Around four or five in the evening! There was a massive storm last night. We need some time to clean up the mess."

Sahil sighed and shook his head in frustration. He decided to pick up the picture in the evening after the police abandoned the area. He did not want the police to draw any attention at him by walking to the chamber alone in the early dawn. He took a U-turn and he headed back home, as he did not want the police to suspect him in any way.

****

At around noontime, Sahil heard a loud ring on the phone in the corner of his room. And as expected, Tatya was on the other side.

Tatya: "Uhh…it's done, Sahil. We just finished the work and dispatched it. It was exhausting, and it took us the entire night."

Sahil: "Great! I hope no one noticed you guys."

Tatya: "Apart from a couple of two-wheelers that were passing by, I don't recall anyone having noticed us. Moreover, our faces were covered."

Sahil: "Hmmm…Good! Today, I have received ten cartons of liquor for the party. Take them from me before you leave for the party. I'll reach a little late."

Tatya agreed and hung up the call.

****

Thakur reached Khandala and hired a cycle rickshaw to take him to the store. With the documents in his hand, he entered the spacious hallway of the store. With elegant marble flooring, the store had exhibits of the various tools for sale, with a price tag displayed in front of each. Bright ceiling lights illuminated the place. Dressed in white shirt and blue trousers, the employees of the store conversed and engaged themselves with the customers.

Thakur looked around and spotted a neatly dressed man in a stylish blazer seated in a glass cabin. The man was sitting at his desk and going through some papers. The man gestured to Thakur to step inside when he knocked on the door. Thakur introduced himself to the manager of the store.

Store Manager: "Tell me, Thakur! How can I help you?"

Thakur: "I placed an order for some tools. I'm here to pick them up."

Store Manager: "With pleasure, sir! May I know the name under which the order was placed?"

Thakur: "It should be either under my name or under the name of Tatya."

The manager nodded and went through the logbook. He scanned all the pages from top to bottom, and then glanced at Thakur.

Store Manager: "I don't see any order placed under these names."

Thakur: "Oh really? Umm… then, it might be under the name of Sahil."

The manager went through the register again and this time, he found an entry.

Store Manager: "Ah, here we go."

Thakur smiled in relief. But the manager's next words left him stunned.

Store Manager: "But as per the record, we have already released all the tools to him. My workers handed him the tools when he visited the store yesterday."

With raised eyebrows, a baffled Thakur tried to make sense of his words.

Thakur: "What? S-Sahil picked up the delivery already?"

The manager nodded.

Thakur: "B-but, didn't you want to notarize these documents before releasing the tools?"

Store Manager: "We never require notarized documents for the items we sell. Sahil already picked up everything yesterday."

Thakur: "Are you telling me that there was no need for me to come here today?"

Store Manager: "That's right. You wasted your time traveling this far."

Flabbergasted, Thakur turned silent and dived into deep thought. Then, he sighed and looked up at the Manager.

Thakur: "Umm… All right! If that's the case then thank you very much. I'll take your leave."

After shaking hands with the manager, he walked out of the store. He sat in the same rickshaw he had hired before. In a state of confusion, he asked the rickshaw driver to drop him at the hotel. He recalled the manager's words over and over. He needed to talk to Sahil to clear the confusion.

Once he checked into his room, he dialed the mansion's number. He wanted to talk to Sahil to clear all the confusion hovering around him. He shouted his words at Vidya as soon as she picked up his call in the mansion.

Thakur: "Hello, Vidya! Is Sahil around? I need to talk to him urgently."

Vidya looked around her to catch any glimpse of Sahil, but she didn't see him anywhere.

Vidya: "Emm…I don't think he is at home. He came to meet me in the morning though. Do you have any message that you want me to pass to him?"

Thakur sighed and looked at the roof of his room in frustration.

Thakur: "Th-Th-That's alright, Vidya! Probably, I will talk to him tomorrow after I return to Ratnagiri."

With those words, both greeted each other and hung up the call. Then, Thakur took a nice, long bath to freshen himself up. After he dressed up, he ordered tea and lunch to his room, which he devoured. Being dog-tired, he decided to take an afternoon nap. At around six in the evening, a loud ring on his room's phone woke him up. He sat up in bed and put on his glasses in haste. He smiled when he heard Rajvanshi at the other end.

Rajvanshi: "Many happy returns of the day, Thakur."

Thakur: "Thank you! This is a pleasant surprise. How did you get my number?"

Rajvanshi: "I got it from Tatya. He informed me that you wouldn't be able to make it to the gathering today. I'm here at the venue with my entire crew to celebrate the occasion. Sikander will be joining us shortly too. We will miss you, Thakur."

Thakur: "I wish I were there as well. Thank you for coming, though."

Rajvanshi: "It's my pleasure, Thakur. It was an honor when Sahil visited me to personally invite me to the party."

The statement came as a shock to him.

Thakur: "What? He met you in Pune? When…when did that happen?"

Rajvanshi: "Yesterday, around lunchtime. He must have kept it a secret to surprise you."

Rajvanshi chuckled, but Thakur gulped anxiously.

Thakur: "Enjoy the party. I'm sure Sahil and Tatya will take good care of you. I'll see you soon in Pune."

After conversing for a while longer, they both hung up. Sahil's peculiar behavior was disturbing him.

Thakur: "What is this boy up to? First, the confusion with the order, and now, his meeting with Rajvanshi! More importantly, why didn't he tell me about this? Why is he keeping secrets? And why doesn't he want me to attend my own party?"

He sighed and began packing for his return journey. Unanswered questions hovered around his mind, and he was desperate to seek clarification from Sahil.

13. The Catastrophe

In the darkness of the night, Sahil parked his car outside the chamber. As soon as the police opened the road up, he picked me up from my quarters and set off for the place. Since I was unwell, he suggested that I rest in the passenger seat. While I was slumped in the seat, he jumped out of the car and entered the chamber through the front door. He shut the door and entered the building. He needed to retrieve the envelope from the safety vault before he could have destroyed it.

The atmosphere inside the chamber seemed too silent. In a gust of breeze, a patch of dry leaves swept through the door's entrance. Suddenly, he heard a savage bellow from somewhere around him. Sahil gasped in fear. It wasn't the first time he had heard it. He remembered hearing it when he had invited Tatya for a game of chess in the chamber. But just like the last time, Sahil ignored it. His heart began to pound when he caught sight of the safe vault. To grab the lethal evidence against Thakur, an anxious Sahil ran towards it with a nervous smile on his lips. The numbers in the sequence of 1,7,2,4,3,6,8 had always been the combination to unlock the safe.

But to his surprise, it did not require him to enter the code in it. The vault's door was unlocked, and Sahil's gentle pull opened it up. The sight of vault's unlocked door rattled Sahil. For a moment, he thought as if someone had nicked the picture from it. But to his much-needed relief, the brown envelope lay right in the center of the vault. Apart from the envelope, the vault didn't contain anything more in it. Sahil noticed that the locking mechanism of the vault had a glitch, and did not work for some reason. Perhaps, that was the reason Thakur couldn't lock the door when he placed the envelope in the vault.

A delighted Sahil puffed his cheeks out in respite. He caught hold of the last remaining piece of evidence that could have sent Thakur to the gallows.

But unknown to him, a hidden pair of eyes were watching his every move. As soon as he reached out to pick up the envelope, he felt someone lift him in the air and throw him against a wall. The impact was so powerful that everything went dark for a few moments. He lost his grip on the envelope, which fell to the floor. When he regained his senses, his eyes widened in horror—Dara, Thakur's pet beast, was towering over him. The tall and gigantic monster roared at him in fury. Sahil gulped in fear when Dara bared his long, razor-sharp canines at him. Terror-stricken, he recalled Thakur's words.

Thakur: *"The picture I snatched from Alok…I kept it in…umm…in the…s-safe vault of the chamber… at the mercy of the Death Lord."*

And Dara's presence in the chamber made it clear to Sahil who the Death Lord was. Thakur had commanded Dara to guard the vital evidence. He must have instructed him to bludgeon anyone who sneaked into the chamber and tried to open the vault without his consent. Though Thakur had forgotten his command due to his memory loss, the slave-monster had followed it to the T.

Breathing heavily, Sahil looked the fiend in the eye. Outraged by his intrusion, Dara growled and bared his fangs at Sahil.

Sahil: "W-w-wait Dara! I am…I'm here to-to help…help y-your master…l-l-let me go…please!"

But his pleas did not deter the savage in any way. He was there to kill under the instructions of his master. Sahil knew that Dara couldn't be beaten in a physical fight. There was only one way to escape brutal death—somehow grab the envelope from the floor and flee. He lunged at the fallen envelope, and as soon as he picked it up, he turned around and raced to the exit. However, his attempt failed miserably. Dara grabbed the fleeing Sahil by his waist, lifted him high in the air, and flung him onto the floor. In the process, Sahil's grip on the envelope slackened, and it fell to the floor once again. In no time, Dara came close to Sahil and punched his face. This mighty blow nearly broke his jaw and his nose began to bleed profusely.

In a counter-attack, Sahil groaned and sprinted towards Dara, launching a flurry of punches at his broad and densely hairy chest. But his blows didn't affect Dara's rock-solid build in any way. On the contrary, Sahil's insolence annoyed the ogre further, and he whacked Sahil's face again. The impact cracked his lower lip. Dara then kicked him in the stomach. For a moment, Sahil felt as though Dara had smashed his intestines to a pulp. He howled in pain, then held his belly with both hands and fell to his knees.

Dara grabbed Sahil by his collar and yanked him close to his face. His mammoth face was a hair's breadth away from Sahil's. The length of Dara's nose was nearly the full length of Sahil's face. Sahil felt his warm and moist breath on his face as Dara grunted in fury. His demeanor suggested that he was going to finish the job assigned to him by his master. Dara released Sahil's collar and picked up a heavy hammer from a corner of the hall. The beast's sheer might became evident to Sahil after he saw the ease with which he lifted the hammer high in the air. The tool would otherwise require a great deal of effort to wield. Sahil recollected the moment when once five of his men had carried the same hammer together. They had been panting and gasping as they somehow carried the hammer to the corner of the hall.

With the hammer raised high, Dara now stood at a striking distance from Sahil. Sahil tried his best to get back on his feet, but he was unable to, as he had run out of energy. The battering had taken a heavy toll on him, and he was dead tired by the assault. He leaned his back against the wall, his face drenched in sweat and his lower lip quivering in fear. Thinking his end was near, Sahil gulped and closed his eyes when Dara brought down the hammer with a force.

But then, something miraculous happened. Though Sahil had anticipated a barbaric death, he heard an odd clank and loud groans. With a pounding heart, he slowly opened his eyes. And the visual in front stunned him. He saw Zola, Dara's son, firmly holding a thick iron rod in his hand, and blocking Dara's strike. In a combative stance, he was baring his teeth at his father. Dara went silent. He was evidently surprised to see Zola jump to Sahil's rescue. Even Sahil couldn't believe his luck until he recalled Thakur's words.

And Sahil was right. Zola had come prepared to save Sahil, his master, from the clutches of imminent death. It was his duty to act as Sahil's savior, even if it meant going against his own father. Sahil scrutinized Zola from top to bottom. He was no longer a feeble-looking creature. In a mere couple of months, he had grown as tall as Dara. With broad shoulders, he matched Dara's appearance with thick, masculine thighs. Unlike when he had heard him at the gym for the first time, Zola's timid whine had transformed into a ferocious roar. The toothless wimp had transformed into a monstrous beast with long and sharp canines. Sahil had doubts when Thakur boasted about their rapid growth rate that day. But this visible transformation in Zola had proved Thakur right.

They roared and glared furiously at each other, neither ready to back off. If Dara was resolved to eliminate Sahil, Zola was determined to save his life at any cost. The stage was set for a fierce duel between the blood-related monsters. They both were trained to fight to the death. Hence, a victory for one meant certain death for the other. With one powerful thrust, Zola pushed Dara away from Sahil. Though Dara maintained his balance, Zola's impertinence flustered him. In a fit of rage, he raised his hammer, lunged at Zola, and brought down his hammer with force. But the warrior son was wise enough to anticipate his move. Once again, he used the rod to obstruct the hammer. As both stood and locked horns with each other, a powerful head bump from Zola sent Dara crashing to the floor. The sight brought Sahil some relief—Dara seemed to be on the back foot for the first time. Sahil dragged himself to the corner of the hall, at a safe distance from the ongoing duel between the two giants.

Dara stood back and punched Zola's face, and the impact made Zola tumble to the floor. The fight was full of twists and turns with no clear winner. If there were moments when Zola overpowered Dara, in some others, Dara pinned Zola down. It was a struggle between an experienced father and a son with young blood gushing through his veins. The scuffle destroyed the age-old statues and the furniture in the hall. The vibrant lamps broke and the large canvassed wall paintings came crashing down.

After about half an hour of intense battle, luck finally smiled upon Sahil. Dara began to tire out. His movements slowed down because of fatigue. He wheezed and stopped resisting Zola's blows. Exhausted and unable to endure the assault any further, he collapsed on the floor. Finally, Zola turned out victorious among the two. To declare his victory, he stomped on the floor, thumped his chest in frenzy and roared. To finish the matter off, he picked up Dara's hammer and raised it high. With a wild roar, he ran towards Dara, who was lying on the floor and had anticipated Zola's intention. Though defeated, he was ready to embrace his death with valor.

But Zola halted his sprint before he could unleash the lethal blow. Dara's dire plight made him think twice. A sudden thought crossed his mind that he would never see his father again. This soul-stirring feeling shook him to the core. He whimpered, and his roar subdued. In the intense and poignant moment, his eyes welled up with tears. Dara saw his son's misty eyes and empathized with him. He grunted in agony, and his eyes brimmed with tears as well. The father bid a grim goodbye to Zola. The son lifted the hammer high in the air and, with tears in his eyes, brought the hammer down. But before he could smash Dara's face, Sahil screeched in a shrilled voice.

Sahil: "Zola, stop!"

Astounded by Sahil's command, Zola halted the hammer's downward push and looked at Sahil. The screech surprised Dara as well, and he gave Sahil a miserable look. Sahil gripped a chair for support. And with its help, he gasped and got back on his feet. He limped his way to the duo and glanced at the fallen Dara. Then, he looked up at Zola.

Sahil: "Remove his bangle and give it to me."

Sahil's request took Zola and Dara by surprise. Zola pondered for a moment, but soon abided by his master's words. He knelt and pulled the bangle off Dara's leg and placed it in Sahil's hand.

Sahil: "Zola, I need yours as well."

The words flabbergasted Zola. But, as was asked of him, he removed the bangle from his leg as well. Then, he roared and handed it over to him. But Sahil's next words surprised them even more.

Sahil: "I emancipate both of you from this slavery. This day marks an end to your bondage! You have lived enough for us. Now, it is time for you both to live for yourselves. Leave this place, and don't even think of returning. Go, go back to your people!"

By this time, Dara was back on his feet. He couldn't believe his ears. Even in his distant imagination, he had never thought of leading a free life. But since Sahil owned his bangle, Dara bowed and submitted to him. From now on, Sahil was his new master. Unable to come to terms with their reshaped destiny, the duo looked at each other and began to walk towards the exit. Though Dara left the chamber, Zola stopped to look back at Sahil. With tears streaming down his cheeks, he ran back to Sahil and hugged him tightly. Sahil tried his best to embrace Zola's broad waist, but the beast was simply too big for him. He rested his head on Zola's broad and hairy chest. It was a touching moment for Sahil. He couldn't control his tears and, with a runny nose and rueful smile, he patted Zola's furry chest.

Sahil: "Go, brother, go. I will certainly miss you. Take care of yourself and your father. Go, brother. Live your life!"

Zola caressed Sahil's cheek with his hand. Though Sahil was in immense pain, the act brought a weak smile to his face. He recollected the moment when Zola did the same after Sahil had offered him a banana a few weeks ago in the gymnasium. Then, Zola turned around and joined his father. Then, both exited from the backdoor of the building, and headed towards the mountain that everyone believed was the home of Dara's tribe. Sahil watched them until both vanished into the darkness of the night. Still dealing with his sore bruises, Sahil sat down on a chair for a breather. He closed his eyes and tried to relax.

Unaware of things that happened inside, I was sleeping in the car parked in the parking lot of the chamber. I awoke from my slumber after I felt a painful mosquito bite my cheek. I swatted it on my face and opened my eyes. But Sahil's absence made me nervous.

In the darkness of the night, the place was buzzing with the sounds of locusts. An uneasy calm prevailed over the chamber. I glanced at my wristwatch. It had been about an hour since Sahil had gone in. Though frightened, I switched on a torch, opened the chamber's front door, and entered it. I felt my stomach drop when I took in the chaotic sight in front of me. With wrecked furniture and paintings, the chamber looked like a ruined battlefield. I screamed in despair when I caught a glimpse of Sahil's bloody face in the flash of torchlight and ran to him.

I: "Wh-what happened, Sahil? Are you all right? How did this happen?"

He slowly opened his eyes and looked at me. Amid his panting, he recounted Dara's attack on him and how Zola saved his life.

Sahil: "Do you see that envelope on the floor? Pick it up and burn it. Then, let's go to the party. We're already too late."

I gulped nervously and looked around. I made my way to the battered packet as soon as I glimpsed it. Then, I pulled out a lighter from my shirt pocket and burnt the envelope to ashes. My act brought a smile to his face, and he sighed in relief. Finally, he had destroyed the final piece of evidence against Thakur. He washed his face and cleaned his wounds with some clean water. Then, I helped him walk to the passenger seat of the car before I drove the car to the party.

After about ten minutes, we reached the venue. Sahil was feeling much better by that time. He didn't ask me for support and hobbled into the party hall. I followed him.

The hall had a bar stationed near its entrance. After Tatya had collected the cartons from Sahil in the afternoon, he had arranged the bottles on the bar table with care. The assorted flavors of whiskey included Scotch, Irish, Rye, and other imported brands. As soon as we walked in, we noticed a group of acquaintances at the bar table. The known faces in the gathering included Sikander, Rajvanshi, and a few other colleagues. A few meters away from the hall, an enclosed ballroom was alive with loud music. An exhausted Tatya was serving drinks to the guests in all corners of the hall and ballroom. He grinned when he saw us, then came to me in haste and handed me the serving platter.

Tatya: "Where have you guys been? Everybody is looking for you, Sahil. And why are you limping?"

Sahil didn't want to recite the whole episode in front of the guests, so he smiled and shrugged it off.

Sahil: "Umm…that's nothing. It's just a mild sprain."

Without losing any time, I took over from Tatya and started serving drinks and snacks to everyone. Tatya rushed to the ballroom to unwind on the dance floor, while Sahil walked towards Rajvanshi and Sikander. After exchanging greetings, Rajvanshi expressed how much he missed Thakur at the occasion.

Rajvanshi: "I wish Thakur were here too. I spoke to him a couple of hours back but forgot to thank him for the surgical apparatus you've supplied to me. I will make up for it and call him up as soon as I return to Pune. And as you wanted, Sahil, I have brought yours and Sikander's share of money for the body that you delivered to me."

Sikander cheered and raised a toast at this. The piece of information relieved Sahil as well. After I served drinks to everyone for a couple of rounds, I started to feel dizzy, and my body heated up due to the fever. I asked Sahil's permission to rest in the guestroom, and he agreed immediately.

Sahil: "I know you don't partake in alcohol. Take some water and soda to the room. It also has a first aid kit and fever medicines. Rest, Bansi."

I abided by his instructions and stepped out of the hall and into the guestroom, located next to the ballroom. I shut the door to block out the loud music as it was ringing in my ears. I took the pill and lay down on the single mattress bed.

After the trio spent a few more friendly moments together, Sahil walked to the ballroom. He had something important to discuss with Tatya. It was a lavish room with vibrant roof lights. Sahil noticed that a huge crowd of men had thronged the dance floor. Tatya was busy grooving to the tunes of a sensual cabaret song. Barring him, everyone else was sipping their whiskey as they danced on the floor. Sahil moved to the dance floor and held him by his arm, then screamed into his ear to be heard over the loud music.

Sahil: "I need to talk to you. Let's go to the bar table."

Tatya hummed as he walked along with Sahil to the bar just outside the ballroom. Sahil requested all the other people at the bar to join those in the ballroom. And it was a request that everyone was only too happy to oblige. Sikander grabbed Rajvanshi's hand and they both danced their way to the dance floor. Everyone in the discotheque raised his whiskey-filled glasses in the air. The men danced and hopped on the floor under the flamboyant lights. Making sure there was no one around but him and Tatya, Sahil bolted the door of the ballroom from the outside. He didn't want anyone to disturb his little chat with Tatya.

At the same time, seated in his office, Khan was waiting for his team of constables to return from an operation. Barring one constable, all the cops were on duty to guard a cash van that was on its way to a bank. Suddenly, with a parcel and letter in his hand, Constable Manoj came running to him.

Manoj: "Sir, there's some news for you!"

He handed over the letter and parcel to Khan. He went through the contents of the letter with raised brows. Within no time, he recognized the man who penned the letter. The words had come from his old whistleblower friend. Perhaps, Dhananjay betrayed Sahil. Though he had promised otherwise, he probably shared information with the police. Though he had handed over the evidence to Sahil, he probably had a copy of it that he posted to Khan along with the letter.

"Hi, Khan,

I hope you get this letter by the 12th of February, a day many will remember as the day of reckoning. Go through the parcel I have sent with this letter. It contains pictures of the kingpin behind all the slaughters in Ratnagiri. The parcel also contains pictures of some of his other aides. Also, go through other documents enclosed in the envelope. In addition to the evidence, the parcel contains an address as well. At around ten in the night, arrive at the given address and bust the place. You will find the entire contingent behind the massacres. Raid and arrest the bastards. This is our last communication, Khan. I have shared with you whatever I could. I have nothing more. The ball is in your court now. Break a leg, Khan.
- A friend forever"

With his heart thudding, Khan opened the parcel and slid a bunch of papers out of it. When he went through the documents and pictures, his eyes nearly bulged out of their sockets. The pictures stunned Manoj as well.

Manoj: "Sir…He is…"

Khan: "Yes, Manoj. I can't believe it too. But the evidence says otherwise."

Khan peered at the wall clock—it was twenty past nine. He had about forty minutes to launch an attack on the mentioned venue. But he was short of manpower—his force hadn't returned yet. He couldn't take Manoj along, as somebody was needed to keep a vigil at the police station. But it was an opportunity he did not want to miss. He instructed Manoj to take care of the police station in his absence. He was aware of the dangers he would face at the unknown place. But he was ready to risk his life to nab the culprits who had been working under a garb all these years.

****

Sahil initiated a conversation with Tatya at the bar table.

Sahil: "No drinks today?"

Tatya shook his head with a smirk.

Tatya: "No alcohol on Tuesdays!"

Sahil: "Oops! Sorry."

After a pause, Sahil breached the issue he had wanted to bring up with Tatya.

Sahil: "Umm…What lures and enslaves you to this risky trade of organ trafficking? To be frank, I love it because there's a lot of money involved in it. It certainly is a moneymaking venture. And what about you? Are you glued to it because of the money involved in it?"

After Tatya heard him, he lit a cigarette and puffed up in the

———

air. Then, he looked at Sahil and smiled viciously. His response surprised Sahil.

Tatya: "Do you think I do this work because of the money involved in it?"

Sahil remained silent and continued to look at him with a small, uncertain smile on his face.

Tatya: "It's not the money, Sahil. It's the pleasure that binds me to this work. I wish I could explain the pleasure I feel when I throttle someone to death. I feel like a king when I see a feeble victim at my mercy when I squeeze his soft neck with my bare hands. I wish I could explain what I experience every time I slash someone's throat with a broadsword. Ahhh…it feels so good when the warm blood of the victim splatters on my face. I live for those moments in this profession."

Sahil nodded with a smile after hearing Tatya.

In the ballroom, Sikander and Rajvanshi sat beside each other and tried to catch their breaths. They puffed their cheeks and exhaled since the strenuous dance movements had tired them out. Rajvanshi suddenly recollected something important.

Rajvanshi: "By the way, the last delivery Tatya made was the body of an alcoholic. Excessive intake of alcohol had damaged his right kidney, so it was of no use to me. I deducted the equivalent amount from the expected revenue."

Sikander: "Really?"

Rajvanshi: "I understand that in our business, it can be hard to trust each other sometimes. As per the guidelines Sahil set in our last meeting, I have the postmortem report of the body, which supports my claim. I have the pictures of the body as well, in case you want to investigate further."

Sikander: "Please don't get me wrong. I do trust you, and I don't need any medical report. But yes, I am curious to know who the man was."

Rajvanshi pulled out a file from his bag and handed it to him. It contained a bundle of papers and full-length pictures of the man. Sikander gulped his last sip of whiskey in haste, then picked up the picture and brought it closer to his eyes. And the moment he saw the picture of the person, he squirted out all the whiskey from his mouth. The dead man in the picture was John, a key member of his team.

The night Khan chased Tatya, he had John's body contained in the rear of the van. Earlier that night, accompanied by Sahil, Tatya throttled John on his command, before delivering it to Rajvanshi.

In the party, a panting Sikander looked around with the hope of spotting John somewhere in the gathered crowd. But to his disappointment, he did not see John among all his dancing men. No one had seen John for quite a while. Since he often disappeared for days without informing anyone, Sikander did not care much about his prolonged absence.

But now, he realized that Sahil had tricked him and broken the protocol by hunting down his man for the delivery. Moreover, his lips quivered in horror as another thought crossed his mind. He recalled the day when Sahil shot dead both the informers who used to pass him the information about the possible target. Though he did not pay any heed at that time, John's assassination made things crystal clear to him. Perhaps in a coup, Sahil was slowly eating up his men and aides. He gasped in fear and roared at all his men in a panic call.

Sikander: "Hey! Let's get out of here now! The bastard Sahil has plans to zap all of us!"

This triggered panic among the men inside the ballroom. Sikander picked up the money-stuffed briefcase in haste and ran to the door of the room along with the others. Rajvanshi smelled a rat as well and commanded his men to vacate the place immediately. But everyone's feet went numb when they realized that Sahil had bolted the door from the outside. They banged on the door in a panic. When no one opening the door to them, they screamed in dread. The sounds coming from the ballroom confused Tatya.

Tatya: "Did you lock the door of the ballroom? It seems like they want to come out."

Sahil: "They have gone wild. They've been drinking for too long."

Panting heavily, Sikander clenched his teeth in anger and bellowed

Sikander: "Sahil, you traitor! I won't spare you. I trusted you, but you killed my man! Now I will slit your throat. Open the door before I break it down!"

The crescendo of the screaming men locked inside the ballroom scared Tatya out of his wits! His eyes widened in fear when he heard Sikander's furious words.

Tatya: "Did you hear that? It looks to me that he has found out about John."

Sahil: "Yes, I think so too."

Tatya rolled his eyes in frustration and grumbled.

Tatya: "I told you that night itself, targeting John was a bad idea. I don't know why you did it. We…we need to abandon this place before they break free and create havoc. But how do we rescue our own men? They are trapped inside with the other two parties and stand outnumbered."

But Sahil did not utter a word. Instead, he kept staring at the bar table in front of him. Disturbed by Sahil's lack of response, Tatya repeated himself.

Tatya: "Sahil, our lives are in danger. Let's get out of here before Sikander harms us in any way."

But Sahil looked up at Tatya with a tranquil smile. And his response surprised Tatya.

Sahil: "Don't worry, Tatya. Sikander won't harm you."

Tatya: "What makes you think he would spare me?"

Sahil began to laugh. The laughter was so intense that tears began dripping down his cheeks. Tatya turned pale when he witnessed his unexpected behavior.

Tatya: "Wh….why are you laughing? This isn't a joke."

But Sahil's laughter grew louder and louder. He wiped his tears and looked at Tatya. Finally, with an uncanny smile, he looked Tatya in the eye.

Sahil: "To harm you in some way, they need to catch you alive first."

Before Tatya could react to those words, Sahil pulled out the gun from Tatya's unclipped holster and shot him straight in the head. With blood trickling down his forehead, he stared at Sahil in a state of shock. His dry lips trembled and beads of sweat covered his nose, cheeks, and neck. Tears brimmed in his eyes. Finally, he convulsed and collapsed on the floor. As he lay on the floor and writhed in pain, Sahil knelt beside him and brought his face closer to his.

Sahil: "I told you so many times, Tatya. Keep your holster locked. Didn't I? For one last time, Tatya, CHECK AND MATE!"

Tears flowed down Tatya's cheeks when he heard Sahil's words. Tatya, Thakur's right-hand man, breathed his last.

Everyone in the ballroom heard the gunshot. Though Sikander had been yelling abuses at Sahil just moments ago, he fell silent now. Pin-drop silence engulfed the dance floor. Scared and distressed, the men looked at each other nervously. I, too, came running from the guestroom. The loud sound of the gunfire had woken me up. I felt squeamish at the sight of Tatya's dead body lying in a pool of his blood. Though I never approved of his actions, he was an old friend of mine. I clutched a nearby chair and wailed at the irreparable loss. Suddenly, anxiety gripped me when Sahil pointed the gun at me.

I: "No, please! S-S-Sahil, w-w-why?"

But my pleas didn't melt his heart. He loaded his gun and aimed at my head. For a moment, I thought my end was near. But to my relief, he relaxed his arms and put the gun away. He changed his mind at the very last moment.

Sahil: "Tatya once told me that you're a puppet. You speak only the words that Baba wants you to speak and you hear only the words he wants you to hear. I don't kill ingenuous loyal dogs. Go back to the mansion, Bansi. As I said earlier, if someone enquires, tell him or her that you were in your room all day. Make sure you parrot the same words no matter whoever asks you."

I had a strong urge to ask for the reason behind his behavior but I held my tongue in fear.

Bansi: "W-won't you come along?"

His smile widened. I remember his gaze on me before he replied with an unhinged look.

Sahil: "I still have some loose ends to tie up. Now, get out of here before I change my mind and add you to my hit list."

With heavy emotions and a torrent of unanswered questions, I followed his orders. I drove the car back to the mansion.

Meanwhile, everybody was getting restless in the ballroom, desperate to get out of the locked room. They knew something terrible was in store. Then, they jolted in panic when the lights of the room turned off and the music system went down. With uncertainty looming, a frantic Rajvanshi yelled.

Rajvanshi: "It's too dark! W-what are you guys waiting for? Light up a candle, lighter, or any damn matchstick! I shouldn't have come here to visit the bastards like you. I made a grave mistake."

Sikander pulled out his lighter and lit it up in a single click. He brought it near Rajvanshi and waved the flame at his face. He did a double-take when he saw Rajvanshi's face in the dim yellow light. And the visual in front horrified him. A thin stream of blood was trickling out of Rajvanshi's nose, and his face appeared bluish. Sikander mumbled in despair.

Sikander: "A-a-are you alright? Your face looks like blue meat, and there's blood dripping down your nose."

A stunned Rajvanshi stared at Sikander's face, which matched this very description. Rajvanshi felt a sense of dizziness. Perplexed, he feebly asked Sikander a counter-question.

Rajvanshi: "Are you t-talking about me… or… y-y-yourself?"

With his finger pointed at Sikander, Rajvanshi collapsed to the floor with a *thud*. Sikander felt his heartbeat speed up. He realized that Rajvanshi's last words were true as he touched his nose and felt the warmth of his blood. And when he brought his hand in front of his eyes, he gasped in panic and drew away his fingers stained with warm, sticky blood. Soon, he began to feel giddy, and his knees gave way. With twitching eyes, he shook Rajvanshi's shoulder but did not get any response. Rajvanshi was dead.

A scared Sikander howled when he realized this. He still held the lighter in his quivering hands. Suddenly, all his acquaintances in the ballroom started to meet the same fate one by one. The sight horrified him. Their bodies began to pile up, as they lay dead on each other on the floor. Soon, Sikander lost his senses too and fell to the floor with a *thud*.

In the hall, Sahil picked up Tatya's half-burnt cigarette. To kill time, he inhaled the smoke and puffed it out, waiting for the roomful of people to die. After about ten minutes, he crushed the burning cigarette under the heel of his shoe. Then, he puffed out the smoke up in the air and walked to the door of the ballroom. The door creaked as Sahil unbolted it and pushed it open. He looked around and found himself standing in a sea of dead bodies. Rajvanshi's was one of the few faces he recognized at first glance. His corpse lay on the floor with eyes and mouth wide open. With a mild grin on his face, Sahil strolled amid the pile of motionless bodies around him. And as he walked, he recalled the moment when he had added poison to the liquor bottles before he handed the cartons to Tatya.

But he halted his steps when he caught the sight of Sikander's body on the floor. With his eyes shut, he seemed to be dead as well. But as soon as Sahil walked past him, he staggered up, grabbed Sahil's feet, and looked up at him in fury. His dried lips quivered in pain. Amid wild hiccups, he clenched his teeth in agony.

Sikander: "S-Sahil…you-you…l-l-lied to me!"

But Sahil looked down straight into his eyes. He whispered while flaunting a stonehearted smile to the dying man.

Sahil: "No, I didn't. I never pointed my gun at you."

Sikander recollected the exchange between them.

Sahil: *"I promise, I will never point my gun at you—cross my heart and hope to*

Sikander gulped and tears flowed down his cheeks after he heard Sahil's callous words. His gasping intensified, and his grip on Sahil's feet slackened. Then, he fell back on the floor and closed his eyes forever.

Sahil stood and looked around with a smile on his face. Once he had made sure that no one was alive, he made his way to the main entrance of the party hall to abandon the premises. But before he could flee, the sound of footsteps alerted him. In a panic, he sprinted back to the hall. He pulled out Tatya's balaclava from the pocket of the dead man and covered his own face with it. For self-defense, he picked up Tatya's gun and hid behind the bar table. He guessed that some intruder had encroached upon the venue. And he was right.

With a protective helmet and a bulletproof jacket on him, Khan entered the building, which was at the address he had received in the tipoff. Khan didn't notice Sahil as he hid behind the bar table. But Tatya's body in the pool of blood sent shockwaves through him. Sensing danger around, he pulled out his gun and looked around.

And as soon as he walked in the ballroom, he gasped in shock and went numb when he noticed numerous dead bodies stacked one atop the other in the darkroom. Panting heavily, he looked around with widened eyes and shivering lips. The visual left him stunned. He had no clue about the motive behind the genocide.

He gulped and frisked the bodies, hoping to find someone alive. But to his disappointment, none of the men were alive. Amid the scattered corpses, he immediately recognized the bodies of Sikander and Rajvanshi. Khan had seen Rajvanshi's picture in the newspapers a lot of times, as he was a known absconder and a wanted felon. The packet he received a little while ago had pictures of Rajvanshi and Sikander as well. The documents in the packet mentioned them as the ones involved in the business along with the kingpin.

But he was on the lookout for somebody more prominent — the man whom the letter had mentioned as the kingpin of the illicit trade. And to his surprise, he did not find the body of the man among the bodies scattered on the floor. Taking a cue, Khan deduced that the lynchpin killed all the men, and would be present somewhere around the place. But when he did not see him anywhere, he glanced at the building's open main door. He assumed the alleged killer to have left through the main entrance. With his gun in his hand, he sprinted to the

---

main door.

Meanwhile, hidden behind the bar table, Sahil furtively peeped at Khan and aimed his gun at Khan's occiput. Unaware of the danger to his life, Khan reached the door to take the exit, but as soon as he took his first step, Sahil pulled the trigger and fired. The loud sound of the gunshot resonated across the place. But the bullet narrowly missed its target and hit an empty glass bottle placed on a table an arm's distance from Khan. The bottle blew to pieces, and shards of glass flew everywhere. Sahil clenched his teeth in desperation after his attack failed. He cringed and hid back behind the bar table. Khan took cover behind a table and fired multiple shots at Sahil, who retaliated. Soon, Sahil ran out of ammunition and, to escape the flurry of shots from Khan, he crouched down on his knees. After about five minutes of non-stop firing, the hall was filled with smoke. The strong smell of gunpowder permeated every corner of the room. With sweat on his face, Khan panted heavily. He knew that he had got his man.

Khan: "Drop your gun and walk towards me with your hands raised. I promise I won't harm you in any way."

But before Sahil could respond, loud police sirens were heard all over. Manoj had led the entire force to the hall once it returned from the assigned task. Armed with weapons, around thirty constables stomped into the hall. Once they secured the place, Khan reiterated his warning.

Khan: "Don't compel my men to take any hostile steps that might harm you. I ask you one last time. Drop your gun and walk to me with your hands raised!"

It was now evident to Sahil that there was no escape for him. He took a deep breath and abided by Khan's orders. With the balaclava still on him, he stood up and dropped his gun. Then, he raised his hands to indicate his surrender. And as Khan had asked him to do, he started to walk towards him. As soon as Sahil reached him, Khan pounced on him and pinned him down on the floor. Then, he gripped his hands and handcuffed him.

Khan: "Sahil Pratap Singh, you are under arrest for running the racket responsible for human organ trafficking in the village."

Khan's words surprised Sahil, as he still had the balaclava on. Khan then pulled and removed his balaclava in a flash. The policemen went numb when they saw Sahil standing before them. The documents received by Khan did not have any mention of Thakur. Instead, they listed Sahil as the mastermind behind the organ trade. A group of constables held him by the collar and dragged him outside the hall, and he didn't offer any resistance. They threw him in the rear of the police van before heading to the Ratnagiri police station. Once back in the station, Khan pushed Sahil into a lockup and bolted its door. Sahil stumbled and fell to the floor. Khan turned around and sighed in relief. Then, he looked around and addressed all the gathered policemen with a victorious smile.

Khan: "Congratulations, gentlemen. The case is solved!"

14. The Trepidation

After his futile journey, Thakur stepped off the train at Ratnagiri station. Unaware of the catastrophic events of the previous night, he stood on the platform with his luggage in his hands. He looked around with a smile on his face, anticipating Sahil to be standing nearby to pick him up. But his absence surprised him.

Thakur: "No one? Strange!"

When no one turned up for some time, he picked up his suitcase and walked to a nearby taxi stand to hire a cab. But as soon as he stepped out towards the stand, the inexplicable behavior of everyone around him left him baffled and confused. Everyone on the road was gawking at him. A Perplexed Thakur looked around anxiously. He had never encountered such bizarre behavior before. Even the driver of the cab he hired didn't utter a word and merely nodded in silence when Thakur asked him for a ride. And as the cab raced to the mansion, the driver kept stealing glances at him every time he glimpsed the driver in the rearview mirror. Thakur felt knots in the pit of his stomach. He got goosebumps when he noticed the intense hostile stares from everyone passing by him. Most of the commuters turned around to look at him over and over. And when the cab halted near the gate of the mansion, the driver didn't ask Thakur for the fare. Instead, he sped away as soon as Thakur stepped out of the cab. He was certain that something abysmal had occurred in his absence.

Thakur: "What's happening?"

Then, his face turned pale when he noticed about a dozen police vehicles swarming the mansion. With the emergency flashers on, a full unit of the police force had besieged the place. A big crowd of locals had thronged the place. They all watched the proceedings from a distance in disbelief. Thakur frowned and scratched his cheek anxiously. He rushed to Vidya and Preeti as soon as he spotted them in the gathered crowd. Both were sobbing and looked out of sorts. Preeti held Vidya by her shoulders to support her. Thakur gripped Vidya's hands in despair.

Thakur: "V-V-Vidya, what happened? W-what is the police doing here? Why are you crying?"

Vidya howled as soon as she saw Thakur. She fell into his arms and continued to cry inconsolably. Thakur posed the same question to Preeti, who replied amid sobs.

Preeti: "Baba, the police arrested Sahil."

Preeti's reply sent shockwaves through him. He gasped in despair.

Thakur: "What? What are you saying?"

Preeti lowered her head, unable to muster any more courage to reply to him. Thakur's lower lip quivered, and he looked around in disarray. He tried to locate Tatya but couldn't see him anywhere.

Thakur: "Where's Tatya? I need to talk to him."

By this time, Vidya regained her composure.

Vidya: "He is dead. The police recovered about 25 dead bodies, including T-Tatya's. The police say Sahil…Sahil killed them all."

Unable to believe his ears, he went numb and took a step back.

Thakur: "Are you in your senses, woman? It's not possible. Sahil can't kill Tatya…or anyone. W-when did this happen?"

Vidya: "I don't know much. The cops entered the mansion early in the morning and launched a search operation. They've sealed Sahil's room. A constable told us that Sahil carried out a mass massacre."

Thakur stood speechless with his mouth wide open. He snapped out of his trance when a sudden thought crossed his mind—he realized that I would have been at the party as well.

Thakur: "Where…where's Bansi? Is he all right?"

Preeti: "He is inside the mansion. Khan is questioning him. He has asked us to wait outside."

Vidya grabbed Thakur's collar and looked at him with pleading eyes.

Vidya: "Please bring him back. Do something! The police are wrong! My son is not a murderer. They have wrongly arrested him."

Thakur: "Get a grip on yourself! You're not doing any good behaving this way. I need you to stay calm. Let…let me do something. Nothing will happen to our boy. I…I promise."

He looked around at the police personnel gathered outside his home. He caught a glimpse of an old man in uniform with a baton in his hand. He was guarding the mansion and restraining the public from trespassing on the sealed area. Thakur gulped and walked to him.

Thakur: "Excuse me, brother? Where is Sahil?"

The constable glared at Thakur, then opened a metallic case and picked up a betel leaf from it. He started munching and chomping on it, making a loud and uncomfortable sound.

Constable: "Where have you been all this while, huh? Khan has been looking for you all morning, Thakur."

Inside the mansion, Khan was busy interrogating me. I still remember the scene. Khan sat on a chair opposite to mine and quizzed me in all possible ways. A bunch of his subordinates surrounded us and were recording my statement.

Khan: "Where were you yesterday? And I expect only the truth."

Sahil's instructions were still fresh in my mind. I cleared my throat and parroted the same to Khan.

I: "I was in my room the whole day since I was not well."

Khan: "What about the other house members? Was Thakur around?"

I: "Thakur was out of the station, and Preeti and Vidya Madam were at home."

After he asked me a few more questions about Sahil, the constable came running in and informed him about Thakur's arrival. Khan asked me to leave and told the constable to summon Thakur. As I walked out, I crossed paths with Thakur. Though he gave me an incredulous look, I averted my eyes and walked past him. He was confident that I knew a lot more than met the eye and frowned.

Thakur: "May I know what's going on, Inspector? You arrested my son without giving us any details. Can you please explain? What's the matter? Why is he being detained?"

Khan sighed and went into deep thought. He felt it was only fair to inform him about his son's crimes. Moreover, he was the chieftain of Ratnagiri. It was well within his rights to know about the crime.

Khan: "Alright! Please have a seat, Thakur."

An anguished Thakur sighed and sat on the vacant chair to hear Khan's explanation.

Khan: "All these years, the police thought Khatri was the man behind the Ratnagiri killings. But in the last twelve hours, our opinion has changed. After a whistleblower passed me an anonymous tip-off, I busted a party on the outskirts of the village yesterday night. There, we found the dead body of Rajvanshi, a wanted criminal involved in organ smuggling. We also got our hands on the corpse of Sikander, Rajvanshi's partner in the crime. Moreover, the dead bodies of Tatya and several other men sent shock waves through us.

"Sahil was the only man I caught alive at the venue, and that too with a gun in his hand. Moreover, he fired at me when I entered the building. It looks as if Sahil killed everyone at the party in the night."

Thakur's eyes widened with shock and he was speechless.

Thakur: "No…no that's not possible. Inspector…there's been some grave misunderstanding. Sahil couldn't have killed Tatya…he simply couldn't have. They were friends."

Khan: "That's something Sahil needs to explain. He hasn't said a word since we arrested him."

Thakur's eyes were brimming with tears.

Thakur: "He might be scared. Can…can I talk to him just once?"

Khan: "I'm sorry but I can't allow that, at least for a few days. Moreover, I need you to cooperate with the police. I don't want you or any of your family members to leave Ratnagiri without prior permission. By the way, I heard you were not in Ratnagiri yesterday. Where were you yesterday, all the time?"

Thakur gulped and stammered after a brief pause.

Thakur: "I-I had some household work in Kh-Khandala. I stayed in the hotel *'Royal Exotica'* at night."

A constable nodded and listed the address of the hotel in a notebook. Though Thakur visited the store to get the delivery of the tools, he did not furnish any of its details to Khan. The specially designed tools aided in the removal of sophisticated medical equipment. And Thakur did not want Khan to suspect him in any way.

After he gave the hotel's address to a constable, he gulped and walked near to Khan. He could no longer contain himself. Tears of agony streamed down his cheeks and lips. He sobbed and choked up.

Thakur: "W-w-where is Sahil? Where's my s-s-son? What have you done to him?"

Khan: "He is in our custody. That's all I can tell you for now."

Khan's statement shattered Thakur, who began to wail. He covered his face with his hands. Unable to endure Thakur's plight, Khan found it hard to interrogate the traumatized father. He sympathized with the old man and whispered to the constable in a concerned voice.

Khan: "Don't pester him much, and let him go back to his family. But do inquire about his stay at the hotel last night."

The constable did as Khan directed. He politely asked Thakur to sign his statement. And after Thakur did that, he turned around and walked back slowly to Vidya and Preeti.

I stood with them as well. I had a lot to reveal to him, but it wasn't the right time. After about ten minutes, the police cleared out of the mansion and allowed the family to enter the mansion. In haste, we all entered the mansion and I shut the main gate on the angry crowd. As soon as we stepped inside the hall, Vidya started to howl. She gripped Thakur's hand in agony.

Vidya: "What did the police tell you? How is Sahil? Where is he?"

But lost in deep thought, the last thing Thakur wanted to do was answer Vidya. Instead, he had some far more pertinent questions in store for me.

Thakur: "P-Preeti, take her to the bedroom. I need to discuss something important with Bansi."

Despite Vidya's resistance, Preeti repeatedly requested her to come with her. Finally, Vidya relented, and Preeti held her shoulders and took her upstairs. As soon as the ladies left us alone in the room, Thakur ran towards me and gripped me by my arms. Amid heavy breathing, he pulled me near him. As he panted and whispered, I felt his warm and moist breath on my face. I can still recall his distressed voice.

Thakur: "Bansi…what…happened?"

I lowered my head, as I didn't have the guts to answer his question. But my silence only frustrated him.

Thakur: "Why don't you answer me? Tell me exactly what transpired at the party!"

I lifted my face and looked into his eyes with a glum face.

I: "You may not be able to endure it."

My concern did not go down well with him. He clenched his teeth and yelled at me.

Thakur: "This is not the time to throw puzzles at me. Just answer my question. What happened last night?"

I sighed deeply before narrating the events in the order of occurrence to the best of my knowledge. My words devastated him. He was rendered speechless.

Thakur: "Why did he do this? And Tatya? He was Sahil's most trusted man!"

I: "Perhaps he sensed some danger from them? The police nabbed him before he could flee."

He looked at me in despair.

Thakur: "Bansi, I'm scared for him. I don't know how the police will treat him in lockup. I need to get him out of this mess as soon as possible. I'll call up Khan and admit that I was the one running the illicit business. Yes, I'll just tell him the truth. My son is innocent. Yes! Let me call him."

He rushed towards the telephone in the corner of the hall. But I ran to him and disconnected the call as soon as he dialed the police helpline.

I: "Calm down, Thakur. You need to be sensible here. He isn't innocent anymore. He gunned down Tatya and murdered two dozen people in cold blood. By admitting your guilt, you will further jeopardize his case. You need to think of a legal way to handle this mess."

My rational advice pacified him a little. After a brief pause, he nodded and put down the receiver.

✳✳✳

In the police station, a constable handed a file to Khan.

Constable: "Sir, the statements of the people in the house check out. I don't see any irregularities. Being unwell, the servant was in his quarters, and the ladies were at home as well. Thakur was in Khandala and stayed in a hotel *'Royal Exotica'* that night. The hotel staff has confirmed his presence."

Khan: "Hmmm… And what about Sahil? Has he spilled any beans?"

Constable: "No, sir. He hasn't spoken yet. Why don't you talk to him? He might spit out some details to you."

Khan: "I am waiting for some forensic lab reports. Then, I'll meet the man with some substantial evidence."

As he uttered these words, luck smiled upon him. Another constable walked to him and handed him the forensic and ballistics reports. A slight smile appeared on his face as he went through the reports. The reports confirmed his claim, identifying Sahil as the perpetrator of the ghastly massacre. After going through the file, he handed it back to the constable.

Khan: "Submit these documents to the court as evidence and take care of the items we recovered from the mansion. Now, it's time for me to settle an old score with Sahil."

The smile on his face vanished. With an austere expression, he rose from his seat and walked into the lockup where Sahil was detained. Under the dim light of a small bulb, soaked in sweat and slumped on the floor, Sahil looked exhausted with disheveled hair. Three policemen were interrogating him, repeating their questions while he remained mum. With a baton in his hand, Khan entered the cell and stood next to him. He gestured to the constables to vacate the cell. As they left, Sahil looked up at him with terror in his eyes. Khan slowly removed his wristwatch.

Khan: "Were you the one I chased that night when your van got stuck in the marsh?"

Sahil remained tight-lipped. He understood that Khan was mistaking him for Tatya. Khan displayed the balaclava Sahil had worn in the party hall when he was caught. It was the same mask Tatya had worn on his way to deliver John's corpse to Rajvanshi. Though Khan had failed to nab Tatya that night, he had not forgotten the mask. The memory was still fresh in his mind.

Khan then removed his ring and folded up his sleeves.

Khan: "You have troubled me a lot, Sahil. But now it's my turn."

With these words, he raised the baton high in the air and brought it down on Sahil. Sahil moaned and gasped in pain, but this didn't deter Khan. He thrashed Sahil mercilessly without pause. His excruciating screams echoed throughout the station for the next couple of hours.

****

In the evening, Thakur visited the police station with Vidya and Preeti. Khan was at his desk scribbling some data in a register. Thakur gulped and walked to Khan's desk and cleared his throat before he spoke.

Thakur: "Hello, Inspector. Can we see Sahil?"

Khan: "Didn't I tell you in the morning? His case is still under scrutiny. I can't let him meet anyone until the investigation is over."

Khan's stubbornness frustrated Thakur. Unable to control his emotions, he slammed his hand on the table.

Thakur: "Do you know who you're talking to? Instead of going after the real culprit, you have made my son your scapegoat."

Khan: "I understand what you all must be going through, but I'm sorry. I can't let anyone besides his lawyer meet him."

Vidya broke down when she heard these words. She folded her hands.

Vidya: "You are like my son too. I am begging you. Please, let us see him once. Otherwise, I will kill myself right here in front of you. I beg you to accept a mother's request at least."

The agonized and distressed plea of a mother melted his heart. After a brief pause, he sighed and nodded.

Khan: "Alright! I can give you only fifteen minutes. Moreover, my two constables will be there with you the whole time."

After Khan's permission, the three of them rushed to Sahil's lockup alongside two constables. He was lying on the floor with a bruised face, inflamed eyes, and swollen lips, moaning in pain. Vidya, Preeti, and Thakur gasped in horror when they saw his plight. He was almost unrecognizable. Vidya wailed and sobbed in despair. A semi-conscious Sahil opened his eyes when he heard her sobbing. He looked up at them through blurry eyes. Unable to stand or walk because of the bruises, he crawled close to them using his elbows and knees. A sobbing Vidya dropped to her knees and cradled his cheeks through the bars. Preeti and Thakur held the bars and knelt as well. Sahil broke down after he felt the warmth of his mother's touch. He kissed her hands and looked up at her through his swollen and blackened eye.

Vidya: "Sahil…who…who did this to you? This is inhuman!"

Tears flowed down his cheeks, and his agonized words lisped due to his sore lips.

Sahil: "Ma, theeshh (these) guys beat veee (me) sho (so) bad! It ishh (is) sho (so) fainful (painful)."

Vidya: "Why don't you do something, Thakur? Why are you just sitting idly?"

But Thakur remained silent. Sahil's plight had left him in shock. Though he wanted to talk to him about the ill-fated night, he stopped himself, being aware of the constables standing beside him.

After fifteen minutes, the constables asked the family to leave. Thakur held Vidya's shoulders as she bawled and helped her stand up. Devastated, the elderly parents turned around and walked back to Khan. Preeti was the last one to leave. Before she walked out, she turned around and exchanged a grief-stricken look with him. Though she remained quiet, tears dripped down her cheeks. Sahil's eyes were brimming as well. She touched his hand before sobbing and running out.

It was nighttime, and Thakur was sitting on his chair in his study. I offered Thakur his medicine and a glass of water, but he didn't pay me any heed. Instead, he picked up the phone and dialed Sharma's home number. He sighed in relief when he heard his voice at the other end.

Thakur: "Do…do you have ten minutes to talk?"

Sharma: "It is my bedtime. But yes, I can talk for some time."

Thakur: "I won't take up much time. D-d-did you hear about Sahil?"

Sharma sighed as he sympathized with the respectable man.

Sharma: "Hmmm…it's the front-page news these days. The whole world knows about it."

Thakur: "I need your help. I know you have connections with higher authorities in the judiciary. Going by the cordial relations we shared in the past, I request you to bail out Sahil."

Sharma: "What can I do here? The police caught him red-handed at the crime scene. He even fired at Inspector Khan. He is the perpetrator behind all the murders in Ratnagiri all these years."

Thakur clenched his teeth after he heard Sharma's insensitive words and freaked out in anger.

Thakur: "That is rubbish! He doesn't have any role in it."

Sharma: "Yes, he does. He camouflaged himself under Khatri's name and carried out all these gruesome murders. Since he was working under a garb, I was unable to identify him as the real mastermind. I am sorry but I cannot help you here. It's a high-profile case. I advise you to consult a good lawyer."

With these curt words, he hung up. His unexpected and rude behavior left Thakur shaken. He couldn't bring himself to put down the receiver. He dialed Tara Chand, the well-known criminal defense lawyer. Tara was his friend, and Thakur was sure he would help him out in those dire times. As expected, Tara Chand picked up his call and greeted him with respect. Moreover, he empathized with him and consoled him. Thakur nodded and sighed before he got to the point.

Thakur: "Tara! I want you to take up Sahil's case. I know you will win it."

Thakur expected his agreement, but the silence on the other side flustered him. Tara Chand's words rattled Thakur.

Tara Chand: "I wish I could say yes to your request, but…umm…this is an open and shut case, Thakur. I doubt any lawyer will take up such a hopeless case to end up on the losing side. I don't want to risk the credibility I have built over the years."

A distraught Thakur made a last-minute plea to him in a trembling and choking voice.

Thakur: "Help me, Tara. I'm sure the court will acquit Sahil if you fight his case. I need your help today."

Tara Chand: "I understand your situation, Thakur, but it is impossible to win this case. I would advise Sahil to admit his guilt in court. The court may be lenient when deciding his sentence."

Tara's words irked Thakur. He yelled at him.

Thakur: "I don't need your frivolous sermons! How much money do you want? Tell me. I-I-I will pay you whatever you want. But please don't refuse…"

But his efforts were in vain. Tara disconnected the call before he could complete his sentence. This came as a bitter jolt to him after his cold conversation with Inspector Sharma. A disheartened Thakur looked at me with terror on his face.

Thakur: "Bansi, Tara is refusing to take up Sahil's case. I want you to arrange a meeting with Mr. Gokhale. He is also a prominent lawyer. Tell him I want to talk to him about Sahil's case."

I stood silently with shoulders drooping. I had bad news in store. I looked at him glumly and gulped.

I: "I already spoke to him today when you went to meet Sahil at the police station. He…he also refused to take it up."

I could see that my words broke his heart. He slumped back in his chair in disappointment. He cleared his throat and pursed his dry lips. I patted his shoulders and tried to console him. A distressed Thakur gulped in misery.

Thakur: "All these guys, bloody Inspector Sharma and that coward Tara Chand, were once my petty pawns. They wagged their tails before me like dogs. I've done so much for them all these years. But today, when I need them, they have all turned their backs on me. Bloody bastards!"

15. The Trial – The Beginning

Days passed by. The cops beat Sahil day and night, but he didn't confess any wrongdoing. Khan did not allow any of the family members to meet him.

Thakur wandered from pillar to post to save Sahil. He contacted the best lawyers around the place. But to add to his woes, no private lawyer agreed to defend Sahil in court, and all his efforts went in vain. None of them wanted to jeopardize their careers by taking up a hopeless case. Hence, the court assigned a public defense lawyer, Batuk

Lal, to take up Sahil's case. Moreover, the court decided to fast-track the case due to the raging public anger. Upon Thakur's request, Batuk visited the mansion.

Seated in the living room in front of Thakur, Vidya, and Preeti, he cracked some silly jokes and laughed out loud. He picked up some salted cookies from the platter placed in front of him and munched on them before slurping tea in haste. Preeti was keenly observing his imprudent behavior. The short man was stout and had a bald crown. He maintained a bushy chevron mustache that had a mix of black and grey hair. He chomped on his tea-dipped cookie.

Batuk: "Don't worry, Thakur. We'll get Sahil acquitted in the first hearing itself."

Thakur: "Thank you. I am counting on you. None of the other lawyers even dared to touch the case."

Batuk: "If private attorneys take everything, the public defenders will starve to death. HAHAHA!"

His foolishness did not go down well with Thakur. He looked at Vidya and Preeti in apprehension. The man wasn't giving the ladies much reassurance either. But he was their best bet at the moment.

Batuk: "Khan has levied heavy and grave charges against Sahil. But the accusations are based on one single observation—that he was present at the party. We need to convince the court that he was merely a guest at the party and that someone invited him there. If we can somehow prove this assertion, I am sure the court will acquit him."

Thakur: "But is that possible? The police nabbed him from the venue with Tatya's gun. He even fired at Khan."

Batuk: "It is not a crime for a person to fire at someone in self-defense."

Thakur: "Umm…everyone believes that a man called Khatri carried out all the massacres till date. Can we prove this in the court, which would prove Sahil's innocence?"

Batuk slurped his tea and shook his head.

Batuk: "It would be suicidal. No one has seen him in years. The police have never found any trace of him. As I said, our best bet is to prove that someone close to Sahil invited him to the event. I propose naming Tatya as the host. It would make things easy since the party hall was booked under his name."

Vidya: "What? Tatya? But he was a good man! Why do you want to blame him? Instead, you need to uncover the truth."

Batuk rolled his eyes.

Batuk: "It does not matter whether I blame him or not! The man is dead, and it will not affect him in any way. But I know it would save your child's life for sure."

With these words, he smiled at her and dusted the salt off his fingers. A reluctant Vidya agreed after Thakur persuaded her.

Batuk: "I hope you will take good care of me, Thakur. The government pays public attorneys peanuts."

Thakur sighed and nodded.

Thakur: "I understand. Before you reach home, a bundle of 10,000 rupees will be waiting for you."

With a beam on his face, he paid his regards to Thakur and left. The man's behavior discomfited Preeti, and she had some serious concerns about Batuk's capabilities.

Preeti: "Baba, do you think he will win the case?"

Thakur pondered for a moment and shook his head. He doubted the man's caliber. Perplexed and distraught, he left for his room.

The night before the first court hearing, Thakur stood in his study's balcony under the open sky. The rattled father sipped whiskey under the glimmer of the moonlight. I wheeled the dinner cart to him.

I: "You haven't eaten anything since the morning. Have a little at least!"

But he paid no heed to my words. He continued to gaze at the moon in a trance, and a small smile appeared on his face. His smile baffled me because of the dire situation we were in.

I: "Are you alright?"

Still smiling, he turned his attention towards me as he snapped out of his trance.

Thakur: "Huh? Oh yeah, I'm fine. Don't think I've gone insane. I was just thinking of something."

His bizarre words baffled me. I wondered what could amuse him, especially when his son's life was at stake. Thakur pointed to the entrance of the mansion.

Thakur: "Not very long ago, Tatya and the others would stand in a herd, cramming the place. I remember some standing and cleaning the cars while the others watered the plants and carried out their routine chores. When there was nothing more important to do, they would bicker with each other and dispute on silly matters. I remember Tatya intervening and helping them settle an argument. And this would happen right there, near the gate. But today…the place is deserted and desolate. None of them are around. They're all dead."

He laughed miserably when he uttered these words.

Thakur: "A few days ago, I was like the invincible Emperor of Ratnagiri. People bowed before me and danced to my tune. But today, this emperor has turned into a vagrant. I am knocking on all doors begging for my son's life. What a turn in fortune!"

The smile on his face waned when he said these despondent words out loud. Then, he looked at me with tears in his eyes.

Thakur: "Listen, Bansi! Can you sense the eerie and uneasy calm of this silent night? Can you hear what the night is saying about the dawn that is to follow?"

He paused briefly before breaking down in agony.

Thakur: "I don't want this night to ever end, Bansi. I just don't want it to get over!"

I: "Don't lose hope, Thakur. Let us hope that he survives this mayhem safe and sound."

Thakur sniffled before wiping his tears. Unable to withstand his condition, I made my way out of the room without saying another word. He ignored his dinner and walked to the sofa bed after he regained some composure. Then, he draped a quilt over himself, turned off the lights, and prayed silently.

Finally, the dreaded day arrived. Amid heavy security around the premises, crowds thronged the courtroom. The kin of all the murder victims had collaborated and hired Talwar, one of the top-rated criminal lawyers in Ratnagiri, as the prosecutor.

The courtroom had a spacious layout with three partitions. The front precinct had a raised dais with a mounted seat for the judge. To witness the high-profile case, people crammed the gallery at the rear of the hall. Thakur occupied a seat in the front row of the audience along with Preeti and Vidya. And I sat in the row that was right behind Thakur. A wide aisle in the middle of the hall separated the judge's dais and the gathered public. Moreover, the aisle did have a long, wide table in it. The aisle hosted both the lawyers at the table, who sat referring to their notes as they waited for the judge. Two witness boxes stood high near the judge's chair, with each located on either side of the raised dais. The court was buzzing with the loud and audible chatter of the crowd. But they all fell silent and stood up in respect when the judge entered the hall and took his place on the dais. Once he settled down, he asked the police to present Sahil in the witness box to his right. Policemen dragged Sahil out of a police van and pushed him towards the court premises.

But before he could enter the courtroom, he caught sight of Kanta, his friend Boney's mother. She was standing at the entrance, blocking his way. Though he looked at her with tears in his eyes, she glared back with nothing but fury. Her expression grew sterner, and suddenly, she smacked his cheek. The slap was so tight that he almost fell to the ground. With his hand pressed to his cheek, he looked at her in despair. Her vehement action had left him aghast and shattered. Then, he got a shock when he noticed the group of people standing beside her. He recognized Mansi – the deceased Murari's wife, and Nitin – Tatya's son. While Mansi looked at Sahil with a glum face, Nitin gave him an outrageous stare. An old lady in the crowd gripped Nitin's hand, as he looked all set to lunge at Sahil. He recognized this old lady as well—she was Nitin's grandmother. He had been living with her since the night he had killed Tatya. To them, including Kanta, he was a brutal killer who had kidnapped and massacred their loved ones without any mercy. The policemen pulled Sahil away from Kanta.

As soon as they brought him inside the packed courtroom, pin-drop silence engulfed the gallery. Every single eye was focused on him. Barring his family, everyone was looking at him with utter hatred. Distressed by everyone's deep disgust towards him, he stole a glance at everybody. Then, he gulped and walked to the witness box. Thakur, Vidya, and Preeti looked at him with a pang.

Judge: "The court asks the prosecution to put forward their opening remarks."

Talwar stood up with a smile and walked towards the judge. He bowed to the judge and marked his respect. Then, he sighed and made his opening remarks.

Talwar: "Your honor, this is an open and shut case. To provide a background, let me remind everyone here that a spree of gruesome murders rocked Ratnagiri for the last five years. The cruel kidnappings and killings of innocents plagued the village. As per the official record, some unidentified men killed about 106 people in these five years. The actual count though could be much higher since many cases go unreported. Families grieved and mourned over the mutilated corpses of their loved ones. Many a time, the police recovered the battered or maimed bodies in landfills and sewage. Often, the faces of the battered bodies had ordure smeared over them with the flies buzzing around their faces. As per the postmortem reports, the victims were tortured in the most barbaric manner. And the worst, in a few cases, to keep the harvested organs fresh and usable, they inflicted most of these injuries antemortem. In these cases, the assailants removed the body's vital organs and even hollowed out the victim's eyes before throttling them to death. So far, the police had believed a man named Khatri to be behind the killings, but they failed to trace him every time a murder was committed."

Talwar sighed and took a deep breath.

Talwar: "Your honor, the prosecution believes that Khatri never had any role in it. But, it was the accused, Sahil Pratap Singh, who masterminded the trade. He was the kingpin of the minions who carried out all the kidnappings and killings."

The stunned crowd began muttering when they heard this shocking piece of information. Preeti and Vidya looked at each other in shock. Though Thakur threw a frantic glance at Batuk, the lawyer only smiled and gestured to him to relax. Talwar continued making his statement after the noise in the courtroom subsided.

Talwar: "The accused was not alone in the crime. The game involved some other criminals as well, but his colleagues soon became a liability to him. Hence, on the night of the 12th of February, he assassinated all his collaborators in one single shot. In a barbaric and thick-skinned manner, he tricked and killed about two dozen men in a drunken orgy. He even attacked the police and fired at inspector Khan when he busted the party to catch the culprits. Your honor, the crimes leveled against the accused fall under the rarest-of-rare categories. Once the prosecution proves him guilty, I would demand capital punishment for him. That's all for now."

After he listened to Talwar's introduction, the judge scribbled some notes in his logbook. Then, he turned his attention to Batuk and asked him for his opening remarks. With an impish smile, Batuk stood up and bowed to the judge.

Batuk: "The defense does not deny the grisly murders that have plagued the village all these years. Not only the kin of the victims but also all the citizens of Ratnagiri were pained by these horrific killings. However, it is absurd to assume that my client masterminded the dastardly slayings. He was away at college for most of the duration of the killings. The prosecution is barking up the wrong tree. As the case progresses, the defense will prove that all the charges leveled against

Sahil Pratap Singh are baseless. The prosecution is right when it says that someone massacred two dozen men at the party. It is right in stating that the police nabbed Sahil at the party on the night of the 12th of February. But Sahil was a naive invitee to the party, and his presence at the party was a mere coincidence. The fact that he was the only one alive at the party does not make him a culprit by any standards. In a travesty of justice, the police made an error in charging my client. It was a sheer attempt to smear the reputation of Sahil and his family. I am confident that after the proceedings get over, the honorable court will acquit my client and that he will walk free with dignity. That is all for now, your honor."

The judge nodded and scribbled some notes in his logbook once again. With a sigh, he turned his attention to Sahil, who was standing mum in the witness box.

Judge: "Mr. Sahil, the court is aware that you have not admitted to any wrongdoing in your statement. The court would now like to offer you one last chance. If you have any involvement in the crimes leveled against your name, this is the time to admit to them. The court would consider the admission as remorseful sentiment on your part. And in that case, the court would be lenient while deciding your sentence. However, if you decide otherwise and are found to be guilty, the court will impose the harshest penalty. So, would you like to plead guilty?"

Sahil looked up at the judge with eyes filled with terror. His loud panting was audible throughout the hall. Thakur gulped and put his hands together in apprehension. Although Preeti and Vidya never believed him to be part of the grisly crime, they were gripped by fear. When there was no answer from him, the judge repeated his question in a soft voice.

The Judge: "Please, answer. Would you like to plead guilty?"

But Sahil did not answer. He licked his dry lips with his tongue and looked around at the tense faces of his family members. His continued silence made the judge impatient.

The Judge: "Answer me, boy. You are taking up too much of the court's valuable time. Would you like to plead guilty?"

Sahil gulped and his lips flinched as he looked up at the judge. Then, he yelled in panic and stammered to him.

Sahil: "N-n-not guilty! I-I-I am not guilty."

Whispers broke out across the courtroom as soon as he pleaded 'not guilty.' Vidya and Preeti sighed, and Thakur exhaled in relief. The judge then asked Talwar to proceed with his presentation.

Talwar nodded and walked near the judge.

Talwar: "The history would never forget the horrific events that befell on the night of the 12th of February. On that catastrophic night, the accused singlehandedly massacred more than twenty people. But before I speak about the ill-fated night, I would like to bring forward another incident. A few months ago, the cops recovered the mutilated body of a little boy named Kaju near the bank of the river. I would like to call Kaju's sister Muniya, into the witness box as my first witness."

An elderly lady held the hand of a scared Muniya and helped her walk to the witness box. Sahil scratched his head, unsure what the girl would say against him. Talwar approached the scared girl and tried to calm her down.

Talwar: "Don't be scared, sweetheart! Do you see that man there? Have you seen this man before?"

He pointed to Sahil. The girl hesitated to answer Talwar's question, shivering in fear at the sight of Sahil. But after a little more persuasion from Talwar, she nodded. With a shrewd smile, he posed his next question.

Talwar: "Did this man invite Kaju to his home late at night to pick up some books?"

Without saying a word, the girl nodded again.

Talwar: "Did you see your brother ever again after he left to meet this man?"

Muniya: "No, I never did!"

Talwar looked up at the judge with a conceited smile after Muniya uttered those words.

Talwar: "Your honor, as Muniya testified, Sahil lured Kaju to the mansion. Grabbing the opportunity, Sahil got the boy abducted and killed when he was on his way to the mansion. Then, his men dumped the boy's mutilated body near the riverbank. Sahil knew that Kaju was on his way to the mansion, and one of his men abducted the kid on his orders. The incident suggests that Sahil did have some connection with the trade."

Talwar looked at Batuk with an austere stare.

Talwar: "Your witness, please!"

Batuk smiled and walked near to the little and scared girl.

Batuk: "I have just a few more questions, sweetie. When exactly had this man invited Kaju to his home? Was that on the same day when he disappeared?"

The nervous girl looked up at Batuk in fear. And after a pause, the girl shook her head.

Muniya: "No, he invited Kaju about a week before he went missing."

Her statement shocked Talwar. Perhaps, Batuk was not as idiot as he thought him to be. The murmurs within the crowd turned louder. Thakur, Vidya, and Preeti sighed in relief. They had mild smiles on their faces. The day began on a promising note for them. Batuk gestured the lady to take the child back to her seat. Then, he looked at the judge with a glee.

Batuk: "Your honor, as the girl testified, Sahil invited Kaju about a week back before the boy got abducted. While the boy was on his way to meet Sahil in the mansion, someone kidnapped and killed him in a mishap. But it is foolish to believe that Sahil abducted the kid since he invited him a week back. That is all for now, your honor."

The judge nodded and noted his observations in his logbook. Batuk's defense left Talwar flustered. He gulped and summoned Khan as his witness. Khan got up from the audience and walked to the witness box to the left of the judge. Sahil and Khan stood face-to-face across the court and locked eyes. They broke their gaze when Talwar began questioning Khan.

Talwar: "Inspector Khan, you claimed that you caught Sahil at the party on the night of the 12th of February. But before we talk about that ill-fated night, I have a more pertinent question. Apart from that night, was there any other instance where you had an encounter with the accused?"

Khan: "Yes, I did. One night, after I received the news of a body being smuggled in a van, I chased the vehicle being driven by the accused. I almost caught the driver but he slipped out of my hands in the end. I am certain that the man behind the wheel was Sahil."

Sahil and Thakur exchanged looks. They knew that Khan was mistaking Sahil for Tatya. After quick eye contact with him, Sahil turned his eyes away. Thakur wanted to rebut Talwar's claim, but he remained silent.

Talwar: "And what makes you believe that the van carried a dead body?"

Khan: "I received the information in the tip-off. Moreover, the mannerisms of the notorious driver said it all. He broke the barricades and fired back at me when I was chasing him. His felonies confirm the piece of information."

After Khan's testimony, Talwar walked to the table in the aisle and picked up a bunch of papers. Then, he walked back to the judge and handed it to him.

Talwar: "I would like to submit the signed statements of a few residents who witnessed the chase."

Then he turned towards Batuk and smirked.

Talwar: "Your witness, please!"

Batuk smiled back and made his way to the witness box to cross-examine Khan.

Batuk: "You are a brave man, Khan. You freed the village from the clutches of a racket that had been in operation for a long time. But I have one question to ask—did you see the face of the man behind the wheel the night of the chase?"

Khan: "No, sir. I did not see his face. He was wearing a mask."

An astonished crowd began babbling when they heard Khan's complete version. The judge, too, frowned in surprise. Preeti and Vidya looked at each other, feeling hopeful again.

Batuk: "If the felon behind the wheel had covered his face, what makes you so sure it was Sahil?"

Khan: "He was wearing the same mask the night I captured him at the party, so I correlated the two encounters."

Batuk guffawed when he heard Khan's statement.

Batuk: "Khan, I expected much more from an intelligent man like you."

With these mocking words, Batuk walked to the table and picked up the maroon balaclava from the pile of exhibits. It was the same mask Sahil had worn the night of the party. Batuk handed it over to the judge.

Batuk: "Your honor, once a person wears it, no part of the face other than the eyes is visible."

The judge studied the woolen cap for a moment and nodded. Batuk walked to Khan and mocked him yet again.

Batuk: "Aren't you going too far with your imagination, Khan? Your accusation of Sahil being the felon you chased is hilarious. Was it based on the fact that he wore a similar balaclava when you caught him at the party? Tell me this—can't two people wear a similar balaclava at two different times?"

Khan clenched his fist. He did not want Sahil to walk free after he had poured his blood, sweat, and tears into nabbing him.

Khan: "But I'm sure he was the only one who—"

Batuk: "Yes or no?"

Khan gulped and sighed deeply before replying.

Khan: "Yes."

As soon as he uttered the word, there was unrest in the crowd. Though Khan glared at Sahil in fury, Sahil maintained a straight face. There was some relief on the faces of Preeti and Vidya. Though Thakur was smiling, his heart was still thudding in his chest. All his doubts about Batuk's caliber were cleared, and a sense of optimism surged in him. He was confident that the court would acquit Sahil in the days to come.

Judge: "The court asks the prosecution to come up with better substantiation. The evidence presented is too meager to be used against a murder suspect."

Talwar: "I agree, your honor. I am sure that the next piece of evidence will clear up all lingering doubts. Here are some pictures of the party hall after the catastrophic event. The police clicked these after Khan caught Sahil and arrested him. These pictures show some of the dead bodies recovered from the hall. I would like to point out two prominent faces among the dead—Sikander and Rajvanshi. The world knows the both of them as notorious organ smugglers. Their names top the lists of most-wanted criminals. Sahil's presence at the venue points to the fact that he knew the gangsters beforehand. Moreover, it also suggests that he also collaborated with them in the crime. The prosecution is certain that Sahil was involved in organ smuggling. The pile of the money recovered from the site further supports the claim."

Talwar handed over the documents to the judge. Thakur wondered if the truth was about to come out. He was afraid that the world would soon find out the identity he had concealed for years. But he underestimated the shrewdness of the defense lawyer.

Batuk: "Maybe the prosecution did not hear my opening remarks properly, your honor. I stated in clear words that Sahil was a mere guest at the place. Tatya was the one who hosted the party and invited Sahil. The hall is also booked in Tatya's name. Moreover, his death should not be a pretext to make Sahil the scapegoat."

Talwar: "Does the defense have any evidence to prove that Sahil was a guest?"

But before Batuk could reply, the judge intervened and issued an advisory to Talwar.

Judge: "Mr. Talwar, let me make one thing very clear. Being the prosecution, the onus lies on you to prove that the accused was not a guest but the host. The court agrees that he was at the party with some high-profile criminals. As you said, there is a possibility that someone hatched a conspiracy to kill everyone at the venue that night. Just because the police caught him alive at the venue does not mean the man is guilty. If you can't prove his guilt, the court will give the benefit of the doubt to the defense."

Talwar fell silent and sighed. After a pause, he gulped and nodded.

Talwar: "The prosecution will try its best to bring the truth to light, your honor. But before I do that, I have a small question for Sahil."

Batuk: "I object, your honor. All the questions to my client need to go through me."

Talwar: "It's a simple and direct question, my lord. I assure that I won't complicate it."

Judge: "Overruled! Please go ahead, Mr. Talwar."

Talwar stood so close to Sahil he could hear his heavy breathing. He knew that Sahil was scared. After a brief pause, he posed his question.

Talwar: "Do you consume liquor, Sahil?"

Sahil looked at him with a straight face and, after a deep breath, he nodded.

Sahil: "Yes, I do."

Talwar: "And do you consume alcohol in parties and gatherings?"

Sahil: "Yes, sir. I do."

Talwar: "Then, why didn't you consume any alcohol that night at the party?"

Batuk: "I object, my lord. The prosecution is trying to intimidate my client."

Judge: "Objection sustained! The court advises the prosecution to remain in its limits."

Talwar sighed and apologized to the court. He then walked to the table in the aisle and picked up a thick file of papers and handed it to the judge.

Talwar: "I would like to submit the postmortem reports of all the bodies recovered from the party hall. The reports state one common reason for everybody's death—cyanide poisoning."

The crowd was aghast, and Thakur pursed his lips in fear. To counter the loud noise from the audience, Talwar raised his voice.

Talwar: "I am not done yet, your honor. The night the police arrested

Sahil, they launched a search operation at his home. And from his room, they found a zipped sachet containing a white powder. I would like to submit the chemical report of the powder to the court. It identifies the encased powder to be lethal cyanide primed by scorpion venom. Your honor, postmortem reports of all victims confirm the same cyanide as their cause of death. The postmortem reports of the recovered bodies corroborate the chemical report. Hence, it proves that Sahil poisoned the men by spiking their drinks."

He brandished the sachet in the air and displayed it to the packed courthouse. Then he walked and placed it on the judge's table. Along with the sachet, he also placed an envelope with enclosed chemical and postmortem reports. The judge struck his table with a gavel many times, ordering the noisy crowd to calm down. Once silence prevailed, the judge turned to Batuk.

Judge: "How would you refute the claims of the authenticated reports? The postmortem report of the dead and the chemical report of the seized substance match."

Batuk: "The defense respects the validity of the reports, my lord. But in the sheer excitement, the prosecution failed to notice that the powder is a lethal rat poison as well. This is stated in the chemical report too. It is legal to use the chemical as a rodenticide. As everybody knows, the mansion's doors are open for everyone. Since Thakur is the chieftain, many people visit him daily. The gates of the mansion are never locked for anyone. Hence, it is possible that some wily brigand crept into the mansion and stole the poison from Sahil's room. And at an appropriate time, he later poisoned the drinks served at the party. That night, Sahil survived merely because he didn't consume any alcohol."

Talwar: "So I ask you again! What made Sahil refrain from drinking that night? He isn't a teetotaler!"

Batuk: "Because it was Tuesday, your honor. Sahil doesn't consume alcohol on Tuesdays, and the 12th of February fell on a Tuesday."

Talwar: "This is absurd, Mr. Batuk. Are you saying that some known friend of Thakur entered his home and stole the poison from Sahil's room? Why would a friend of Thakur's try to kill his son and the others at the party?"

Batuk: "I never said 'a friend of Thakur,' did I? I merely said 'wily brigand,' if you heard me right."

Talwar seemed to be out of ideas and arguments. Batuk's rebuttals in the court rattled him. He sighed and looked at the smiling

Batuk in disarray.

Judge: "Mr. Batuk, let us assume for a moment that Sahil was not connected to the horrific trade of organ trade. But he was the only one to survive the massacre. Except for him, the police didn't find anyone else alive. Someone definitely killed everyone at the party under his nose. And whosoever the person was, either he fled after killing all, or he was killed with others as well. And the court believes that Sahil should know who the man was. Moreover, if the killer was killed, who killed the killer?"

Batuk walked near to the judge with a silent and conceited smile.

Batuk: "Yes, your honor. There was definitely a killer at the venue. That night, apart from Sahil, there was one more man who didn't consume any liquor. The same man laced the drinks with poison and served them at the party. But the man faltered terribly. Unlike all the other men at the party, Sahil refrained from liquor and survived the deadly plot. And the man who hatched this plot was none other than Tatya, my lord! Tatya was the one who massacred all the guests at the party and masterminded the killings in Ratnagiri."

But as soon as these words left his mouth, a shriek resonated across the courtroom. The crowd went silent. Nitin stood up from his seat when he heard Batuk's argument, unable to control his emotions.

Nitin: "NOOO! My father was a good man. My ahhh-ahhh-father was n-not a killer."

Sahil looked at Thakur and smiled. He understood that Batuk was trying to place the entire blame on Tatya's shoulders. But Batuk did not want the judge to have any sympathy for the orphaned child. Upon his request, the judge asked Nitin's grandmother to take him out of the courtroom. The old lady held the sobbing child's hand and exited the room desolately. Once the silence prevailed in the court, the judge posted one more question to Batuk that bothered him.

Judge: "Then, who killed Tatya that night?"

Batuk: "Thakur suffers from dementia, your honor. These days, he is not as involved in work as he used to be. And Tatya took advantage of the great man's sickness. While pretending to work with Thakur, Tatya smuggled the organs and did not let him know about it. In the process, he allied with Sikander and Rajvanshi and soon, lured all of Thakur's men into the murky business. The night when Khan chased the vehicle with the supposed body, the veiled man at the wheel was not Sahil, your honor. In fact, wearing a balaclava, the man at the wheel was Tatya instead."

The crowd was atwitter again when they heard Batuk's statement. A stunned Khan looked around in despair, wondering if Tatya was indeed the man driving the van that night.

Batuk: "All was going smoothly for him until Sahil entered the arena. Things changed for Tatya once Sahil took control of his sick father's duties. The monitoring of his men by Sahil resulted in a steep slump in Tatya's trade. And as time passed by, Sahil turned suspicious for Tatya. As a result, Tatya was unable to use manpower as freely as he did when he worked under the diseased Thakur.

"Things worsened for him after Khan took charge of Ratnagiri. Also, Tatya began facing continuous and tremendous pressure from Rajvanshi as his supply to him had dried up. To add to his woes, the police trained the tribal men with some safety measures. As a result, they were no longer easy prey for Tatya and his men. Unable to pay his men anymore, he faced a rebellion from them. Thus, to get rid of all his problems, he hatched a deadly conspiracy. He decided to kill everyone including Sahil in one shot. He wanted to start the trade from scratch.

"Your honor, it was Tatya who sneaked into Sahil's room and stole the rodenticide. On the 12th of February, he invited Sahil and others to the party with the malicious intention of assassinating them all.

"He poisoned Sikander, Rajvanshi, and all the others using adulterated alcohol. But as luck would have it, Sahil survived the massacre. Tatya panicked when he saw Sahil alive. He pulled out his gun in a jiffy and aimed it at Sahil. But before he could fire, Sahil caught hold of him and they both engaged in a scuffle. In this brawl, Sahil snatched Tatya's gun and shot him to save himself. Sahil did fire and kill Tatya, but he did this in self-defense."

A rattled Talwar stood up from his seat and interjected.

Talwar: "That is ridiculous! Sahil tried to kill Khan at the party hall too. The police have already submitted the ballistics report of the gun and Tatya's postmortem report to the court. As per the reports, Sahil used the same gun to fire shots at both Khan and Tatya."

Batuk smiled at Talwar's statement and requested the judge.

Batuk: "I would like to question Inspector Khan again, your honor."

Upon hearing his name, Khan made his way to the witness box for the second time.

Batuk: "When you raided the party, did you announce your arrival to alert everyone inside the hall? Did you issue a warning through a microphone?"

Khan: "No, sir. I did not."

Batuk: "Were your emergency flashers and loud sirens on when you parked your car?"

Khan: "No, sir, they were not. I was carrying out the raid at the party alone that night. It was a covert operation, and I entered the hall stealthily."

Batuk: "Hmmm…so is it safe to assume that Sahil was not aware of your identity when you entered the hall?"

Khan sighed and nodded.

Khan: "Yes, sir. That is possible."

Batuk: "Point to be noted, my lord! Sahil might not have known the identity of Khan at the time of his arrival. After shooting Tatya in self-defense, Sahil decided to flee the building. But when he reached the door, he heard some footsteps. Being in a state of shock, he suspected some assailant coming towards him. As a precaution, he hid behind the bar table with the gun in his hand. He fired at Khan, mistaking him for an attacker. It was a classic case of mistaken identity. And everyone knows the events of the rest of the night. That ill-fated night, my client was merely at the wrong place at the wrong time and is innocent. No further questions, my lord!"

Embarrassed and annoyed, Khan stepped out of the witness box and returned to his seat. The judge glanced at the wall clock. It was time to call it a day. He scribbled some notes in his logbook.

Judge: "Alright! There is still a lot more to be discussed in the case. The court will resume on Friday, after three days, for the next hearing. The court is adjourned for the day!"

With these words, the judge struck his table with the gavel and moved out of the courtroom. The audience began to disperse. The constables held the handcuffed Sahil by his upper arms and dragged him out of the court. In despair, Thakur rushed towards him before Batuk obstructed him.

Batuk: "Relax, Thakur. It's a matter of three more days. Hold your horses till then. I won't let Talwar prove the charges against him. The prosecution doesn't seem to have any more evidence to show to the court. The judge will exonerate him for sure."

Thakur looked up at him and nodded with a sigh. After they shook hands, I drove the family back to the mansion. Though frazzled, they seemed content, as the day had turned out to be in Sahil's favor by and large.

Later that night, a desolate Khan sat at his desk at the police station. In deep thought, he recalled the moment when the masked driver's van got stuck in the marsh. The driver had pressed the gas frantically to get the vehicle out of the swamp. Khan was tossing a light paperweight up and down as he pondered. He wondered if he had erred in his judgment about the driver's identity. Then, a man's voice interrupted his thought process. It did not take him much time to recognize the man standing in front of him. He was Dhananjay, son of the deceased journalist Alok.

Khan: "Yes, Dhananjay. How can I help you?"

Dhananjay gulped and sat down opposite Khan nervously.

Dhananjay: "Sir, I-I want to help the police in the ongoing case against Sahil. I'm sorry I could not make it to the first hearing since I was too scared to reveal my identity to you guys. But since the case seems to be heading in Sahil's favor after the first hearing, I couldn't control myself. I don't want the court to acquit him. Rather, he should be hanged."

Khan frowned.

Khan: "What do you mean?"

Dhananjay: "Did…umm…did you get the letter mentioning the evidence against Sahil and his men?"

Khan: "Yes I did. But how do you know about it?"

Dhananjay: "Perhaps, you did not recognize me. I was the one who wrote it to you!"

A dumbfounded Khan jumped up from his seat.

Khan: "What? A-are you, my secret friend?"

Dhananjay: "Yes, sir."

An elated Khan stood up from his seat and walked to him to embrace him tightly.

Khan: "Thank you for all your help, my friend. I don't have words to express my gratitude for what you've done for the entire police department."

Dhananjay: "Thank you, but did you get the evidence that—"

Khan: "Yes, yes. We got it, and thank you for a zillion times for that. You are entitled to a cash reward of one million rupees. The posse carried a bounty on their head. And since you sent us the package with all the evidence, you deserve the reward. I'll ask Talwar to make a formal request to the court to declare you as the sole beneficiary of the prize money."

Dhananjay gulped with a straight face and went silent for a brief moment. But soon, his eyes glittered in delight. He accepted the offer with gratitude and made a humble request.

Dhananjay: "If you and Talwar permit me, I would like to be a witness in the case. I want to reveal my story to the world."

Khan: "That would be great! It will make our case stronger."

Dhananjay submitted his statement to Khan before heading home. Khan slumped back into his chair. He smiled and sighed in relief. He recalled the words of his anonymous friend, now known to him as Dhananjay, over the phone.

Khan: *"You cheat! You gave me false information. Do you know that it is a crime to mislead the police?"*

Man: *"I swear on the soul of my dead father, Khan. One day, I will hand over the culprits to you. Trust me, Khan."*

His palm met his forehead as he realized with an embarrassed smile. How could he have missed that? Dhananjay had used the term *'dead father'*. He should have taken a cue from that. He shook his head with a smile and dialed Talwar's home number. Although Talwar's sloppiness in court hadn't amused him, meeting Dhananjay had rejuvenated him.

Khan: "The public defender outplayed you today, didn't he? Why didn't you present the other vital pictures and documents to the judge?"

Talwar: "Do you know what Chanakya once said? Let the enemy believe he is victorious until you identify his weakness. I wanted to know what his strategy was, Khan. And I know it now. Don't worry, I'll put him in his place at the next hearing."

Khan: "Didn't you feel that the judge was biased towards the defense?"

Talwar: "Certainly not! He is one of the most brilliant and honest men in the system. Nobody dares question his integrity. The error was at our end, but as I said, I will take care of it next time."

Khan: "I have some news to share. We have a witness who can give a new spin to the case and turn the tide in our favor."

Talwar listened carefully as Khan spoke about Dhananjay. This piece of information put a wide smile on his face.

Talwar: "That's terrific! I'll ask the court to issue him a subpoena."

The two men greeted each other and hung up. After the

conversation, Khan slumped back in his chair in relief. Although he had a tough day in court, a sense of hope was creeping in again.

****

The night before the verdict, a disturbed Thakur rang Batuk's home number. His heart began beating frantically when no one picked up his call in the first few rings. But his heartbeat raced, even more, when someone finally picked up his call.

Dressed in a long nightgown with a broad bindi on her forehead, Batuk's wife picked up Thakur's call.

Batuk's wife: "Yes! Who is calling at this time of the night?"

A nervous Thakur cleared his throat.

Thakur: "H-h-hello! May I speak to Batuk? I am Thakur Pratap—"

Batuk's wife: "Your call!"

She didn't even care enough to hear him out. She thumped the receiver on the table and called for Batuk.

Batuk, laid on his bed in his loose nightdress, was watching a live cricket match between India and Pakistan. He frowned while chewing a betel leaf as his wife's interruption annoyed him. He was in no mood to talk to anyone at that time. Half-heartedly, he walked to the phone and grabbed the receiver.

Batuk: "Yes, who is it?"

He faked a chuckle when he heard Thakur at the other end.

Batuk: "Ahhh…Thakur. Tell me, how can I help you at this hour?"

Thakur: "You have become something of a celebrity these days. The newspapers are all praises for you. Umm…what do you think about the prospects for tomorrow?"

Batuk: "Don't worry, Thakur. We will get Sahil acquitted tomorrow. Didn't you see how I beat Talwar two days ago?"

Thakur: "Yes, I know. You were brilliant that day. I am pinning all my hopes on you, Batuk."

Batuk: "Take it easy, he will be a free man tomorrow. By the way, are you watching the India-Pakistan match? It is heading towards a nail-biting finish. Can I get back to my TV if you don't mind? And thank you for the wine. It's the best wine I have ever tasted in my life. Don't forget to gift me another bottle after Sahil's acquittal tomorrow. HAHAHA…goodnight, Thakur."

Thakur: "Goodnight."

Thakur hung up and sat on a chair in the study. He was beset by an unknown fear. He leaned against the backrest of the chair and closed his eyes. But his heart was beating fast and he was too restless to get any sleep that night. For a moment, he felt as though his heart would jump out of his chest. Unable to fall asleep, he gulped down a glass of water and slumped back into his chair after a while.

16. The Trial – The Verdict

Finally, the Day of Judgment had arrived. Glued to their seats, the crowd in the packed courtroom waited for the proceedings to begin. In a pensive mood, Thakur sat in the front row with Preeti and Vidya. And as I did during the first hearing, I had crossed my arms in anxiety and sat in the row behind Thakur again. The judge wrote down some preliminary notes in his official register. The attorneys settled down on their seats and waited for the proceedings to begin. After a brief and tense pause, the judge asked the cops to present Sahil in the courtroom. Just as the cops were hauling Sahil inside, Dhananjay entered the room as well. They crossed each other's paths and froze in their steps. And as they stopped, they gave a fierce glare to each other.

After a brief pause, Sahil smirked. He studied Dhananjay from top to bottom. As opposed to his earlier rough and greying curly hair, his now dyed and slicked back hair gave him a sophisticated look. He had swapped his cheap plastic glasses for stylish and expensive golden-framed ones. Instead of the worn-out sports shoes that he used to wear earlier, he had sparkling polished shoes on him that day. A black coat gave him a regal look. Dhananjay glared at his alleged father's killer, while Sahil looked back at him with a glee on his face.

Sahil: "Squandering my money, huh? By the way, how is your sexy sister?"

Dhananjay clenched his teeth in fury when he heard these words. He recalled Sahil's derogatory words against Suhasini when Sahil had abducted him. In a fit of rage, he pounced on Sahil. Gasps could be heard across the courtroom. Everyone in the hall got up from their seats and screamed. The constables guarding Sahil struggled to control the fierce scuffle. As the situation neared a stampede, the judge repeatedly struck his table with the gavel to bring order back into the court.

After some effort, the police caught hold of Sahil and separated him from Dhananjay. They hit him with their batons and dragged him to the witness box. Thakur yelled at the constables in agony when he saw them beating Sahil. Dhananjay walked to a vacant seat next to me. Finally, the crowd went quiet and things returned to normal. But the nuisance had displeased the judge. He looked at the audience with a frown and yelled a stern warning.

Judge: "Let me warn everyone! The court will not tolerate this sort of behavior again. Anyone who does it next time would be held in the contempt of court."

Though Dhananjay remained silent, Sahil looked at the judge nervously. He apologized for his behavior immediately. But the apology did not calm the judge down. He asked Talwar to begin in a vexed and frustrated tone.

Judge: "Mr. Talwar, please begin!"

Talwar bowed to the judge with a beam. Batuk had a conceited smile on his face as well. He intended to throttle every statement of Talwar's just as he had on the first day of the hearing. But this time, Talwar was better prepared and he intended to live up to his reputation. He marched to Sahil and began questioning him.

Talwar: "The defense stated the other day that Tatya possibly nicked the poison from your room. But what about the drinks served at the party? Did you order them?"

Sahil: "No, sir. I never did. As Mr. Batuk narrated, I was just a guest that night. Tatya organized and took care of all the preparations that day."

Talwar: "Hmmm… Did he mention any details about the dealer who supplied him the alcohol for the party?"

Sahil: "No, sir. He didn't."

Talwar: "Are you sure, Sahil?"

Sahil: "Yes, sir."

After he heard Sahil's reply, he turned around to face the judge.

Talwar: "Your honor, I would like to call my first witness for the day, Mr. Jitsu, into the witness box."

A lean and short man in untidy clothes made his way to the witness box. He folded his hands and greeted the judge before looking at Talwar.

Talwar: "Please introduce yourself, Mr. Jitsu."

Jitsu: "I am Jitsu, and I work as a delivery man for the local liquor shop."

Talwar: "What's the name of your shop?"

Jitsu: "*Moonlight Liquors*"

Talwar pointed to Sahil and posed his next question.

Talwar: "Do you know this man?"

The man frowned in disgust at the sight of Sahil and nodded.

Jitsu: "Yes, sir. I know this crazy man. I delivered a parcel of ten liquor cartons to him on the morning of the 12th of February."

The crowd erupted in chatter, while Thakur covered his face with his trembling hands. Unable to believe their ears, Vidya and Preeti looked at each other fearfully.

Talwar: "Date to be noted, your honor! Jitsu delivered the alcohol to Sahil on the day of the party."

Jitsu's statement was a major setback for Batuk. It overrode everything he had proved in the prior hearing. In a desperate attempt to regain his hold over the case, he stood and cross-examined Jitsu.

Batuk: "How do you remember the precise date of the delivery? What makes the date so special?"

Jitsu: "My daughter's birthday falls on the 12th of February. I can never forget the confrontation I had with such a vicious man on the day of my daughter's birthday."

Batuk: "What do you mean?"

Jitsu: "I remember the morning when I delivered the liquor to him at his home. Since it was my daughter's birthday, I was in a hurry to finish all the deliveries that morning. My boss gave me a half day's leave too. This man took the cartons from me and started to inspect it. And when I asked for money, he began a verbal confrontation with me instead."

Sahil: *"I placed an order for fifteen cartons. There are only ten here. Where are the rest?"*

Jitsu (in court): "His assertion surprised me because I knew that he had only ordered ten cartons. I was the one who took his order when he had dialed the store. I had even confirmed his order before disconnecting the call. I tried to correct him in a humble tone."

Jitsu: *"No, sir. You ordered ten cartons. I even confirmed the order with you on the phone."*

Jitsu (in court): "But I'm not sure what irked him. He snapped at me arrogantly and rudely."

Sahil: *"Don't you dare speak to me like that. Do you think I would lie to a petty blue-collared worker like you?"*

Jitsu (in court): "But he was not done. He grabbed my collar and pulled me towards himself in a fit of rage."

Jitsu: *"S-sir, what are you doing? I can get you five extra cartons by the evening if you want."*

Jitsu (in court): "But the angry man didn't pay heed to my requests and rebuked me loudly."

Sahil: *"I don't want to do any more business with rascals like you. Just take the money and get the hell out of here."*

Jitsu (in court): "He hurled vulgar and indecent abuses at me before he let my collar go. Then he pulled out a bundle of money from his pocket and flung it at me. Finally, he turned around and walked away angrily. I counted the money and it was the exact amount for ten cartons. There wasn't a single rupee extra for a tip after all the bickering. Before meeting this bighead, I had planned to buy a good gift for my daughter with the tip. But it was a disappointing moment for me. I cursed myself to encounter such an obnoxious customer first thing in the morning of an otherwise lovely day. I returned to the shop with a grim face."

With no more queries for Jitsu, a distressed Batuk returned to his seat.

Talwar: "Your honor, the shop owner has identified the labels marked on the bottles recovered in the hall. He has confirmed that the cartons were ordered from his shop. Jitsu's testimony proves that it was Sahil who ordered the alcohol and laced it with the deadly poison. He never intended to use the cyanide as a rodenticide. In a pre-planned strategy, he carried the toxic alcohol with him to the party. Once he reached the party hall, he served this to all the men present, killing them all. But, unfortunately for him, Tatya didn't consume alcohol that night. And since he survived the conspiracy, Sahil shot him dead. But whatever happened at the party was the last leg in the filthy malpractice that had been going on for five long years. In those five years, Sahil abducted and massacred over a hundred people with the aid of his allies."

Everyone in the courtroom seemed shocked, finding it hard to believe Talwar's words. The judge made some notes while Talwar sipped on some water to quench his thirst. Then, he walked to the table and diligently opened a paper packet. He carefully slid out two pictures and walked back to the judge.

Talwar: "Your honor, a few months ago, the police recovered the dead body of Alok, a local journalist. His murder had remained a mystery to the police, but his son, Dhananjay, handed us a set of documents recently. The recovered documents contain two pictures that I would like to submit to the court. Alok had captured both the pictures on two different occasions, your honor."

A nervous Thakur bit his nails as he tried to guess which pictures Talwar was presenting. As per his information, Sahil had already burnt all the evidence he had snatched from Dhananjay. And to his horror, the first picture displayed Murari's corpse with the sketch of the peacock. And the second portrayed the rangoli design that Harak had created in the mansion on Diwali eve. Talwar explained the pictures to the judge the same way Sahil had explained them to Thakur.

Talwar: "Alok used to help the police with the postmortems of bodies. He clicked the pictures of the corpses. In one such instance, he clicked the first of the two photos in your hand. Named Murari, the man in the picture was kidnapped from his farm. His maimed body was later recovered in the outskirts of Ratnagiri. During the body's postmortem, Alok noticed a sketch of a peacock on the body and took its picture. The second picture portrays the same peacock in a rangoli. A man named Harak Singh created the rangoli at the Ratnagiri mansion on the day of the Diwali function. Since Alok captured the pictures of the event, he identified the image in the rangoli as the one he found on the corpse. Hence, he deduced that Harak Singh was involved in the murder of Murari, the man in the first picture."

As soon as Talwar made the statement, Batuk jumped from his chair and yelled in Sahil's defense.

Batuk: "That is bizarre. Even if the sketches look similar, it doesn't mean that the same man drew them, just like two people can wear the same kind of balaclava at two different times."

Talwar: "I knew that the defense would repeat this point. Along with the pictures, I have tabled a report from experts that confirm that the same person created the sketches."

Batuk sighed in frustration. Dejected, and with his heart pounding, he slumped back in his chair.

Talwar: "Thakur isn't keeping well these days and Alok did not want to distress him. He called up Sahil and expressed his desire to meet him near the clock tower. Sahil smelled a rat after the telephonic conversation but agreed to meet him near the clock tower at one night. When Alok spoke to him about Harak and the sketches, Sahil knew he had to stop Alok from spreading the news to Thakur. As Harak was merely a pawn, Sahil was afraid that he would be exposed.

"In a flash, he pulled out a dagger from his scabbard and slit his throat. Then, he wiped his fingerprints off the dagger, which is why when the police recovered the dagger from the site, they did not find any fingerprints on it."

Batuk: "This is absurd! The prosecution is trying to frame my client using a false charge, your honor. Sahil visited a store in Khandala to make a pending payment. He saw Alok bleeding to death on his way back home."

Talwar: "According to the store manager, Sahil was free of all his formalities by the afternoon. But in a deliberate ploy, instead of returning early, he visited a few of his friends in Khandala to kill time. He did that to make sure that his time of return to Ratnagiri matched with the time of his scheduled meeting with Alok. He perfected his timing before he slashed Alok's throat, your honor. He tried his best to portray his meeting with Alok as a chance encounter. Otherwise, there is no reason he did not call anyone in the mansion upon his return from Khandala late in the night. To let everyone know, the bus station does have the facility of a public telephone."

Batuk: "He was the one who informed the police, my lord. Why would he commit the murder and call the cops himself? In that case, he could have simply fled from the venue after committing the crime."

Talwar: "Because he did not have any other option, your honor. A few passersby had spotted him while he faked his whimper after he slashed Alok's throat. With his hands and clothes stained in blood, he did not have any place to hide. He feared that someone from them might turn up to the police, and reveal his details if he runs out of the place. So, in a smart act, he behaved as if he was an ignorant and naïve man. After killing Alok, he rushed to a nearby telephone booth and dialed the police. He made this complicated crime look simple in everyone's eyes."

The judge turned his attention to Batuk.

Judge: "Any comments?"

A flustered Batuk fumbled as he ran out of arguments.

Batuk: "N-n-none, your honor."

Batuk's meek submission sank Thakur's heart. He gasped in frustration at Talwar's false statement. Though Sahil had seen a fatally wounded Alok near the clock tower, it was Thakur who had killed him in reality.

Then, Talwar called Dhananjay to the witness box. He got up from his seat and adjusted his coat before walking forward. Once in the witness box, he glared at Sahil, who responded with a smirk.

Talwar: "The prosecution would like to thank you for the evidence you shared with the police. Thank you for your courageous efforts."

Dhananjay: "The credit goes to my late father. Though I arranged the bits and pieces together, he found most of it."

Talwar: "What makes you believe that the defendant killed your father?"

Dhananjay: "Sahil confessed this to me the night his men abducted me. I was on my way to the police station to hand over all the evidence to Inspector Khan. And as I sat in front of him, gagged by his men, he also admitted that he was the kingpin of the organ trafficking trade in Ratnagiri."

As soon as the crowd heard this startling piece of news, it erupted into roars and hurled abuses at Sahil. Dhananjay narrated his horrific experience that night. He recounted how the men had gagged and roughed him up before throwing him at Sahil's feet. He revealed that Sahil had seized all the evidence he had with him and had asked him to abandon Ratnagiri with his family. He narrated his conversation with Sahil that night.

Sahil: *"But you won't be as lucky as your father. He was given an easy death, but you will get a brutal one, where my men will rip the organs from your body."*

As soon as Dhananjay recited those words, a curious judge intervened in a jiffy.

Judge: "If Sahil snatched the evidence from you, how did you post it to the police?"

The question was of keen interest to Thakur as well. He was eager to know how Dhananjay had managed it after Sahil had burned whatever he had confiscated from Dhananjay.

Dhananjay: "My father had maintained another copy of it. I didn't reveal this to Sahil when his men abducted me. After Sahil let me off on the condition that I abandon Ratnagiri, I mailed everything to Khan."

As Dhananjay spoke, Sahil snickered at his half-truth. Besides, he had also stuffed his pockets with a lump sum of money in return and gifted him with his costly diamond ring. The ring shone on Dhananjay's finger as he stood and spoke in the witness box. Sahil also recalled his conversation with one of his men after he had let him go that night.

Sahil: *"I'm sure that as long as I roam free, this man will not dare go against me. Let him go."*

Henchman: *"What do you mean by 'as long as I roam free'?"*

Sahil: *"Nothing. Now let's pack up and leave."*

Dhananjay's conduct had confirmed Sahil's prophecy. The coward had remained in hiding all these days. But as soon as the cops nabbed Sahil, Dhananjay sauntered to Khan and agreed to testify against him. Burning up in the vengeance to punish Sahil, whom he had thought as his father's killer, he betrayed Sahil's trust.

Sahil recalled Dhananjay's wimpy face the night he had let him off the hook. When he remembered his pale and scared face, he lost his self-control and began laughing loudly. His erratic and ear-deafening cackle stunned everybody in the court. Thakur, Vidya, Preeti, Dhananjay, and the entire crowd looked at him in confusion. His obnoxious behavior particularly irked the judge.

Judge: "What's so funny, Mr. Sahil?"

Sahil wiped away his tears of laughter and fell silent. Exasperated by Sahil's conduct, the judge reprimanded Sahil a second time.

Judge: "Make sure you don't disrupt the court any further, boy. I have already tolerated enough of your nonsense."

A nervous expression reflected on Sahil's face. Since Talwar and Batuk had no further questions for Dhananjay, he took his seat in the audience. Batuk's dismal defense distressed Thakur. He sighed deeply and scratched his cheek restlessly. That day, an aggressive Talwar was in full form and on fire.

Talwar: "Recently, a few villagers came forward to the police. They reported some suspicious activity near the school gate on the morning of the party. As per them, a few masked men lifted out some uncovered machinery from the basement and loaded it onto a truck. Finally, they drove the truck away to some unknown place before the sunrise. In their statements, the villagers have described the machinery. And when the cops busted the school, they found a network of dismantled wiring in the school basement.

"Your honor, the evidence shared by Dhananjay includes all the haunts of Rajvanshi in Pune. When the cops raided these addresses, they confiscated some disassembled surgical equipment. The description of the machinery matched with the details of the equipment as given by residents of Ratnagiri. The masked men had nicked the machines from the basement and had shifted them to Rajvanshi in Pune."

Judge: "And what are these machines precisely for?"

Talwar: "They are state-of-the-art machines for human organ extraction. Also, a few of them help in the preservation of the organs after the extraction. As Khan increased the vigil, it became tougher to carry out abductions in the village. Hence, Sahil asked his men to move the machinery from school to Rajvanshi in a planned strategy. Apprehensive of carrying out the surgeries in Ratnagiri, he wanted

Rajvanshi's men to operate on the bodies once he delivered them to him."

With these words, Talwar made his way to the aisle and picked up a few pictures, which he submitted to the judge.

Talwar: "Your honor, I would like to submit three sets of pictures to the court. The first set contains recent pictures of the basement displaying the dismantled wiring in the basement. The second set of pictures shows the machinery recovered from Pune. Finally, the third set of pictures shows the basement with the machinery installed."

The information stunned everybody in the courtroom. The shocked crowd looked at each other in disbelief. They found it hard to believe that any such surgeries were being carried out in the school where they had their children studying in.

Talwar looked at Dhananjay in the audience.

Talwar: "Mr. Dhananjay risked his life and sneaked into the basement one night. Then, he captured the images and mailed them to the police along with all other evidence. Though he could have mailed the pictures a lot earlier to the police, he held his horses. He posted them once he got his hands on all other pieces of evidence to nab the culprits. Luckily, all the shreds of evidence reached Khan on the evening of the 12th of February, the day Sahil massacred everyone at the party."

The statement flustered me. I could see that even Thakur was unsure about how Dhananjay had managed to enter the basement since Tatya kept the door locked at all times. Dhananjay could have snooped when Tatya took Sahil there for the first time. Thakur remembered Tatya telling him about the sound of leaves rustling that night. He had heard the sound when he walked back to his bike to grab his keys. Back then, Thakur had shrugged off Tatya's fears, but now he thought otherwise. He was certain that Dhananjay hid behind the bushes and clicked the pictures. Probably, he ran away when he saw Tatya heading for the bike.

Talwar: "The machinery seen in the basement is the same as that seized from Pune."

Sahil stood mum and listened to Talwar. He recalled the conversation he had with Tatya the morning of the party. With the help of his men, Tatya had removed the equipment from the school and transported it to Pune.

Tatya: *"It's done, Sahil. We just finished the work and dispatched it. It was* *exhausting, and it took us the entire night.”*

Sahil: *“Great! I hope no one noticed you guys.”*

Tatya: *“Apart from a couple of two-wheelers that were passing by, I don’t recall anyone having noticed us. Moreover, our faces were covered.”*

Sahil: *“Hmmm…Good! Today, I have received ten cartons of liquor for the party. Take them from me before you leave for the party. I’ll reach a little late.”*

Talwar: “Your honor, the door of the basement always remained locked during school hours. Only the custodian of the school had a key to the basement.”

He took a brief pause, and his expression turned dour.

Talwar: “I would like to call Thakur Pratap Singh to the witness box, your honor.”

Thakur’s feet went numb when Talwar called out his name. Silence engulfed the courtroom as Thakur stood up and walked to the witness box. Emotions ran high when he gazed at Sahil standing in front of him. Tears flowed down their cheeks as they exchanged a nostalgic look. Thakur’s lips quivered as he wiped his tears.

Talwar: “I can understand your situation, Thakur. I can imagine what you must be going through. I won’t take up much of your time. I have only three questions for you, and you can answer them with a simple ‘yes’ or ‘no.’ You are the epitome of truth and justice, and people swear by your name. Justice seeks your help today. Is it true that being the chieftain of the town, you appointed the custodian of the school five years ago? Did you sign the probate?”

Thakur merely nodded, unable to speak a word due to the emotions overwhelming him.

Talwar: “Am I correct in saying that the custodian must have known about the equipment in the basement? Nobody can install or remove such huge machinery without the custodian’s approval. Am I correct in my assessment?”

Thakur nodded again.

Talwar: “One last question. If someone used the school for some malpractice, do you think the custodian would be involved in it as well?”

Thakur nodded for the third time.

As promised, Talwar didn’t ask any further questions. He thanked him and asked him to return to his seat. Thakur looked into Sahil’s eyes one last time before walking back to his seat in the audience. There was a ray of hope now. Tatya was the custodian of the school, and Thakur was confident that the entire blame would fall on the dead man's shoulders. It was time for his move of appointing Tatya as the custodian of the school to finally come to fruition. It was the last weapon in his armory to bail out Sahil of this mess. As he walked back to his seat with renewed hope, he recalled the conversation he had with Sahil once.

Sahil: *"What if…umm…the police come to know about our activities in the school?"*

Thakur: *"…if it does, the police would nab the custodian of the school."*

Sahil: *"And who is it? Someone in the government?"*

Thakur: *"No. My right-man!"*

Sahil: *"Tatya?"*

Thakur: *"That's right! He is the custodian of the school. If such a time ever comes, it will be he who would face the music, not us. I have secured the sealed probate in the safe vault of the study and it remains there all the time. I will expose it to the world in our hour of need"*

He returned to his seat and sat back with a relaxed smile. But his face turned pale when he heard Talwar's next proclamation.

Talwar: "As per the probate recovered from the mansion, the custodian of the school is Sahil Pratap Singh! Your honor, the registered paper has Thakur's signatures on it. Sahil has been the custodian of the school during the entire period of the spree of murders in Ratnagiri."

With these words, Talwar submitted the documents to the judge. This turn of events thwarted Thakur's long-planned, devious scheme. He frowned and looked at Sahil with a shocked expression, and his son seemed equally baffled.

Thakur recalled the day Dhananjay had been waiting for him in the study. He needed Thakur's signatures on the NOC to get clearance to sell off the press. Thakur had always hung the key to the safe in the room itself. Dhananjay probably nicked the probate from the vault and tampered with it. Perhaps he replaced Tatya's name with Sahil's. Entangled in the emotional conversation, Thakur sympathized with him. And hence, he did not read and verify the document before signing it. Dhananjay seemed to have made Thakur sign the tampered probate instead of the NOC.

Thakur clenched his jaw in anger and turned around to look at Dhananjay. Dhananjay simply smirked at him. As soon as a helpless Thakur witnessed his brazen smile, his anger turned into misery. He turned around glumly to witness the ongoing proceedings. With every moment, he was losing the battle.

Seated next to him, Vidya looked at Preeti in a state of shock. She was losing faith as time went by, though she still hoped the trial's verdict to go in Sahil's favor. She never believed that her son could be guilty of any of the charges leveled against him. But Talwar's next evidence, a photograph, rocked her faith.

Talwar: "A few days ago, a family filed a missing report of one of its family members named John. An alcoholic, he usually strolled by the riverbank in an inebriated state. One such night, he strolled towards the river and never returned. There was no clue about his whereabouts until the cops recovered a camera from Sahil's room."

With these words, he waved the picture in the air for everyone to see.

Talwar: "The picture shows this ruthless man smiling with his foot placed on the chest of a dead man—the man who went missing—John. Sahil killed John and then brazenly took a picture of himself with the corpse."

The crowd jumped out of their seats to take a look at the picture, unable to believe their eyes and ears. The picture created much uproar amid the crowd. The picture stunned Thakur in particular. He had been unaware of this incident since Sahil and Tatya never revealed the details of their prey to him.

Talwar: "The night the police caught Sahil at the party hall, they got their hands on a postmortem report with the picture of John stapled to it. The report lay near a bag stuffed with cash. This proves that Sahil killed John and transported his corpse to Rajvanshi in exchange for money. It is safe to conclude that this was the money Rajvanshi owed to Sahil for John's body. But before Sahil could abscond from the venue with the money, Khan caught him red-handed."

A nervous Batuk jumped up from his seat and stammered in a counter.

Batuk: "A-an autopsy report with a loose picture stapled on it doesn't guarantee its legitimacy. The defense smells a deep-rooted conspiracy here to indict my client."

Talwar: "Your honor, according to the family, John had a bad liver due to excessive intake of liquor. The recovered autopsy report confirms this. Moreover, the blood group of the specimen in the report matched that of John."

The judge went through the report recovered from the crime scene. He also evaluated the receipt of the money recovered from the site. But what turned his stomach was the snap of John's dead body. The lifeless eyes were wide open, and the tongue was protruding from his mouth. His arms lay splayed in different directions, and his legs were parallel to each other. But it was Sahil's pose in the picture that made the judge's blood boil. With an unabashed smile on his face, Sahil was standing with his foot on the deceased's chest. An outraged judge stared at Sahil, who looked back at the judge with a grin. And this conduct annoyed the judge further. He didn't see any remorse in Sahil's demeanor.

In a last-ditch effort to regain some lost ground, Batuk stood up and screamed in a jittery voice.

Batuk: "Y-your honor! I would like to invite Miss Preeti to the witness box."

The judge tried to concentrate on Batuk's plea but he could not forget Sahil's barbaric stance with the dead body. Upon hearing her name, Preeti looked at Vidya in despair and walked to the witness box. Tears flowed down her eyes when she looked at Sahil, who stood straight in front of her. Sahil looked back at her with a miserable smile.

Batuk: "Miss Preeti, on the night of Sahil's engagement, did you chase Sahil in your car once he left the mansion?"

Preeti replied in a frail voice.

Preeti: "Yes, I did."

Batuk: "Where did you find Sahil?"

Preeti: "Near the Ratnagiri bus station. He was sitting on the ground, unarmed. A masked man stood near him with a dagger in his hand. But before he could attack him, Sahil jumped in my car and we tried to flee from the place. Though we escaped successfully, one of the brute men attacked me with a knife at the same time, and I lost consciousness."

Batuk: "Hmmm...Did you by any chance see Sahil killing someone?"

Preeti gasped.

Preeti: "No-no-no! He was nowhere near the dead body. A man with a veiled mask stood near Sahil, looking all set to kill him. Sahil is innocent, sir. He can't kill anyone."

With those words, Preeti broke down in front of everyone. Batuk looked at the judge with a nervous smile.

Batuk: "Your honor, as Preeti testified, she never saw Sahil killing Boney. She followed Sahil till the bus stop, where someone had already murdered Boney. I insist that this is a fabricated case against my client, Sahil. Hence, I request the honorable court to dismiss the case."

Talwar jumped in to refute Batuk's claim.

Talwar: "Your honor, I would like to point out a factual error in Mr. Batuk's statement. Preeti did go behind Sahil that night, but she was not the first one to do so. There was another person who followed Sahil that night before Miss Preeti. The person was none other than Sahil's ex-fiancée, Mandana. I would like to call her to the witness box next."

Preeti's eyes widened in despair as soon as Mandana's name fell in her ears. She looked at Sahil with a shocked expression before she started to walk back to her seat. After hearing her name, Mandana stood up from somewhere in the audience, and walked to the witness box. Preeti and Mandana froze as they crossed paths. They both looked at each other and locked eyes. Preeti gulped as Mandana smirked and threw a conceited grin at her. Preeti sighed and steered her eyes away from her as she walked back to her seat.

The sight of Mandana stupefied Sahil more than anyone else in the audience. His lips quivered when he looked into her eyes. She looked at Sahil with an evil grin that sent chills down his spine. She was dressed in a red saree and wore a *mangalsutra* around her neck—she was a married woman now.

Talwar: "Thank you for turning up as a witness at the last moment, Ms. Mandana. The prosecution is grateful to you. Did you get engaged to Sahil the night your friend Boney was murdered?"

Her grin vanished, and her face turned red in rage. She answered him with tears of anger in her eyes.

Mandana: "Yes, we did get engaged that unfortunate night."

Talwar: "And what made Sahil to break off the engagement?"

Insane and sadistic glee reflected on her face for a split second. Tears flowed down her cheeks and her lower lip fluttered as she replied.

Mandana: "He didn't…it was me. I was the one who broke it off!"

Her statement stunned Preeti and Vidya, who held each other's hands in disbelief. Even Thakur looked at her with a perplexed expression.

Talwar: "And what made you do so?"

Mandana: "I…I saw him killing m-my friend Boney. He slashed his throat right in front of me."

Murmurs erupted all over the hall yet again. Preeti and Vidya looked at her in disbelief. Kanta covered her mouth with her handkerchief and sobbed in agony. But her testimony shocked Sahil more than anyone. He hadn't been part of the racket until that night. Though he had been involved in the murders in the later stages, he had nothing to do with Boney's murder. The judge knocked on the table with the gavel to control the crowd. He appealed to everyone to maintain decorum in the court. Once the crowd fell silent, the judge asked Mandana to furnish the details of the incident.

Mandana: "I had been waiting for Boney since the morning that day. I was desperate to meet him, having lived among strangers all those days in Ratnagiri. I asked Sahil to take me along to pick up Boney. Toward the end of the celebrations, I saw him talking to someone on the phone. Immediately, he ran out of the mansion and drove away in haste. I thought he was leaving to pick up Boney and had forgotten to take me along. In sheer excitement, I drove my father's car and followed Sahil.

"After about ten minutes, I saw three or four men holding Boney by his arms and legs. But what shocked me most was seeing Sahil slash Boney's throat under a tree near the bus station. I panicked when Sahil turned around and saw me. Without wasting any time, I fled from the scene, fearing for my life.

"Once I reached the mansion safe and sound, I remained mum. Although people were dancing and enjoying the festivities, I ran back to my room. Soon, I heard people screaming near the front gate of the mansion. From the window, I saw Sahil helping a wounded Preeti out of the car. Then, he drove out of the mansion. My father, a doctor, treated an unconscious Preeti and tried to revive her.

"I was in a dilemma all that while. Although Boney's murder traumatized me, I never wanted the police to arrest Sahil. Once he returned, he cooked up a false story. Even though his men had attacked Preeti on his command, Sahil portrayed himself as a naive victim. He lied to everyone that he saw a few people killing Boney, the same people who injured Preeti. It was a calculated move on his part to hide his real identity. After about an hour, he entered my room and threatened me of dire consequences if I ever revealed the truth to anyone. He frightened me, so I agreed to stay silent. But I also decided to break off the engagement. With fear in my heart, I removed his ring from my finger and gave it back to him and left the mansion with my father."

Judge: "If you thought to spare Sahil then, why this sudden change of heart?"

Mandana: "I am a married woman now, and I don't have any feelings left for Sahil. Boney was my friend, your honor. My conscience haunted me day and night because I was keeping this a secret. Hence, when I heard about the ongoing trial, I decided to testify against him."

The judge pondered and nodded in empathy, before he listed her statement in his logbook. Since Batuk didn't have anything to ask her, Talwar requested her to take her seat in the audience. But before she left, her grin widened, and she looked at Sahil arrogantly. Her actions reminded him of the vow she had taken after he had broken off his engagement with her. He still remembered the tears of agony flowing down her cheeks as she swore to destroy him.

Mandana: *"Learn to fear a wounded tigress and an insulted woman, Sahil Pratap Singh. I will never forgive you for what you have done to me today. You have savaged my honor. I promise that I will come back at the most vulnerable moment of yours and destroy you. I will be the reason for your ruin one day. I swear an oath to avenge this insult."*

As soon as he recalled her words, a miserable smile spread across his face and tears flowed down his cheeks. She turned around and walked out of the court premises with a victorious smile. She had achieved her long-sought vengeance. Her testimony shattered Thakur, Vidya, and Preeti. All their hopes of seeing Sahil come out of the mess were dashed. But it was Talwar's next and last piece of evidence that proved to be the final nail in Sahil's coffin.

Talwar: "Your honor, it is now time to checkmate the master. Among the evidence Dhananjay submitted, the last piece remains to be shown to the world."

With a triumphant smile, he walked to the dais and handed a picture to the judge.

Talwar: "In the last hearing, the defense portrayed Sahil as an innocent man. The defense misled the court by stating that he had no connection with the murders. But the picture in your hand nullifies Batuk Lal's claim. Look at the man sharing the frame with Rajvanshi in the picture. Just to remind everyone, Rajvanshi was an international organ smuggler. This picture proves that Sahil was his partner in crime indeed."

The judge studied the picture silently. He frowned and stared at Thakur with an intense look on his face, which rattled Thakur. Thakur knew that along with other evidence, Sahil had burnt the picture after he recovered it from Dhananjay. I had also told him that I had burnt its copy in the chamber—the one he snatched from Alok. He wondered if

Alok maintained another copy of it, which Dhananjay had found. In one impulsive moment, he made up his mind to admit all his wrongdoings to the court. He knew that the act would besmirch his image and send him to the gallows. But he didn't want Sahil to endure the punishment alone—he was guiltier than Sahil. His lips fluttered as he looked at Sahil with a miserable smile. Sahil, on the other hand, wiped his tears and looked at Thakur glumly. But the judge's next words shook Thakur to the core.

Judge: "The picture displays Sahil standing shoulder to shoulder with Rajvanshi. It establishes camaraderie between the two."

Shock waves passed through Thakur when he saw the picture. In the picture, Sahil was standing beside Rajvanshi shaking hands with the wanted felon. Astonishingly, Sahil's pose was a replica of his own in the photo that Sahil had destroyed. Perhaps Dhananjay had secretly followed Sahil when he visited Rajvanshi in Pune. He must have been the one to click that picture of them. Thakur recalled his telephonic conversation with Rajvanshi that tragic day.

Rajvanshi: *"It was an honor when Sahil visited me to personally invite me to the party."*

Thakur: *"What? He met you in Pune? When…when did that happen?"*

Rajvanshi: *"Yesterday, around lunchtime. He must have kept it a secret to surprise you."*

A baffled Thakur looked at Sahil standing in the witness box. Sahil seemed stunned too. Perhaps the picture baffled him as well. He met Rajvanshi only after Dhananjay had abandoned Ratnagiri on his orders. Talwar smiled as he made his final comments on the case.

Talwar: "Your honor, this proves that Sahil was involved in all the murders. All these years, Sahil maneuvered the illicit trade under the name of Khatri and minted money out of it. My version of the story is almost identical to Batuk's but with some minor corrections. Sahil made a fool out of Thakur and allied with Sikander and Rajvanshi. Sahil was the one who killed locals and smuggled their organs with the help of Tatya and a few others. Sahil was the one behind the wheel when Khan chased the van that night.

"As the defense indicated, the trade went into a slump after Khan came into the picture. Moreover, Rajvanshi and Sikander admonished him repeatedly for missing delivery deadlines. Due to unpaid wages, his men revolted against him as well. Hence, to get rid of all his problems, he organized an extravagant party. Then, he served poisoned drinks to all his men and killed them all. In a single Judas kiss, he annihilated them all. He shot Tatya dead, as he did not consume the spiked liquor. He, too, was a victim of Sahil's malevolence. I believe that Sahil was aware of who Khan was when he fired at him. The shot missed Khan by a whisker, or else Sahil would have fled from the scene and succeeded in his plan."

Talwar took a deep breath and continued morosely.

Talwar: "In about five years, he has committed more than a hundred crimes in the village. In his greed for money, he didn't spare anyone— be it a good friend or a mere child. He killed and traded anyone who yielded him a good profit. Not only did he kill Kaju but he also slaughtered his friend, Boney, as Mandana testified. The man has no remorse for what he has done. His shameless picture with John's corpse proves my assertion. Alok and Murari are some more names in the endless list of his victims.

Talwar heaved a deep sigh and continued.

Talwar: "He had a team that operated on the bodies in the school basement at night. The school was an ideal place to carry out illegal surgeries, as the premises were deserted during the night. Once extracted and preserved, Sahil's men delivered the organs to Rajvanshi in Pune. The bodies of Rajvanshi and Sikander at the party establish a clear link between all three of them. Sahil sharing space with Rajvanshi in one of the pictures only proves this further."

Talwar paused after he uttered these words. Then, he gulped morosely and continued with a bitter expression.

Talwar: "The kin of all those killed and maimed by Sahil await justice, your honor. They have pinned all their hopes on you. The prosecution demands capital punishment for Sahil. He is a mass murderer and doesn't deserve a lesser sentence. With that said, the prosecution rests its case."

Talwar bowed to the judge and started walking back to the aisle. But as soon as he turned around, thunderous applause resonated in the courtroom. Astounded, Talwar looked in the direction of the sound. The sight before him stunned not only him but everyone else present in court. Standing in the witness box, Sahil was clapping with a smile on his face. He then finally broke the silence he had maintained for the most part of the trial.

Sahil: "Very good! Very good, Talwar! I am impressed. Bravo! I had heard a lot about your brilliance, but today I got the chance to witness it too. Great job!"

Talwar hadn't expected such appreciation from Sahil. His words perplexed everyone in the packed courthouse. Thakur frowned, while Preeti and Vidya looked at each other in despair. The judge adjusted his glasses and turned his attention to Sahil.

Judge: "What do you mean?"

Sahil looked up at the judge with a broad smile on his face.

Sahil: "Talwar is right, sir. I am the one who orchestrated all the killings in Ratnagiri with my allies. I alone am responsible for every single killing in the village all these years. I killed Harak, Khatri, Alok, Murari, John, Boney, Kaju, Tatya, and all others on the list. Talwar is also correct in his narration of the sequence of events on the night of the party. I am the one who masterminded the organ trafficking trade with Rajvanshi and Sikander for the last five years."

As Sahil was making his confession, the kin of all the victims who had been butchered started to wail. Many of their family members sat down on the floor, thumping their chests in agony. Kanta whimpered and broke down when she heard Sahil's confession. Preeti too broke into a fit of sobs. Unable to believe her ears, she covered her face with both her hands in misery.

But Sahil's brazen words shattered Vidya the most. She fell silent. He had broken all her trust and faith. She stared at Sahil austerely while tears of anger dripped down her face. The crowd rose from their seats and hurled frantic abuses at Sahil. A shocked Thakur merely fixed his gaze at him with his mouth wide open. Thunderstruck by his false confession, he began yelling at the judge to negate Sahil's claim. But his voice went unheard amid the cries of the crowd. He alone knew that what Sahil had said was not the truth. He hadn't started the business five years ago. He hadn't been involved when Tatya and his men had killed Khatri, Kaju, Boney, and the hundred other victims. But the lamentation around him did not stop Sahil.

Sahil: "It all started five years ago. During my college vacations, I came in contact with Khatri, a hooch smuggler. I had just finished my first year of college when I got lured into his get-rich-quick plan. At first, we preyed on the tribal men in the outskirts of the village, as they were the easiest targets. We both worked in tandem. He administered the trade while I was away at college. Being the custodian of the school, I invested money and got the equipment installed in the school's basement to extract and preserve the organs.

"Everything was going great until Khatri lost his son in a tragedy. After this, he refused to continue this work and pushed me to shut down the business. His guilt was eating him up from within. One night, marred with remorse, he even set off for the police station to expose all of us. My men gagged him and abducted him while he was on his way to the police. I tried to persuade him one last time, but he did not agree. With no other option, I strangulated him.

"Luckily, his brother Harak still wanted to work with me. I befriended Sikander, as I needed manpower to expand the business. Things were steady once again, and we minted money off the trade. Once my men abducted and killed a target, they operated on the bodies in the basement. On a few occasions, we shipped the body to Rajvanshi in Pune. He had his own medical team to operate on the bodies. But despite the risk, operating on the bodies in Ratnagiri yielded a lot of profit and was worth the risk."

With those words, Sahil sighed and shook his head in dejection.

Sahil: "Everything was going well until Alok became suspicious of me. He realized that Harak had killed Murari, a local farmer. As Talwar said, Alok met me near the clock tower one night to blackmail me. In exchange for his silence, he demanded a big chunk of money from me. Though he rebuked me for my so-called evil actions, he was in dire need of money. He needed the money to take care of his jobless son and his young daughter of marriageable age. First, I thought of agreeing to his demand, but then I realized that he was Baba's friend. I did not want him to reveal my truth to Baba. With a heavy heart, I slashed his throat with my dagger. I wiped my fingerprints off the knife and informed the police, as Talwar narrated."

Sahil paused for a while and gave an austere stare to Khan in the seated audience in the courtroom.

Sahil: "But things got out of hand when Inspector Khan took charge. He made it a hell lot more difficult for my team to hunt down victims. Khan almost caught me one night when my vehicle's tire got stuck in the mud. But luck came to my rescue at the very last moment, and I managed to escape. Business slumped and hit rock bottom because of Khan's increased vigil around the clock. We were desperate for any potential targets.

"On the evening of my engagement, I received a phone call from Rajvanshi. He was angry, very angry in fact! He was in dire need of a body by the next day and wanted me to make a delivery. He threatened me that if I failed, he would sever all business ties with me. Half-heartedly, I decided to take Boney down."

He wiped the sweat from his forehead before he continued with his statement.

Sahil: "With the help of Sikander and three of his men, we pinned Boney down. I still remember his shocked expression when I slit his throat. But the decision backfired on me and turned out to be my first blunder. Before we could ship his body to Rajvanshi, Mandana, and later Preeti, arrived at the place. Mandana had seen me killing Boney, and fled from the place. Due to the mess, I called off the delivery of Boney's body that night. To escape everyone's suspicion, I asked one of my men to injure Preeti, as I wanted to brand myself as her savior. Then, I drove an unconscious Preeti home and left to Sikander's place, where a heated argument broke out between Harak and me. He mocked me as I had failed to make the necessary delivery to Rajvanshi. In one impulsive moment, I shot him dead and asked Sikander to ship his body to Rajvanshi instead. Then, I drove back to the mansion. Luckily, a scared Mandy hadn't revealed my truth to anyone. She broke off the engagement and left Ratnagiri forever.

"Your honor, after things simmered down a little, I decided to gift the surgical apparatus to Rajvanshi as a step to cut the risks around me. I wanted his medical team to carry out all the surgeries in Pune thereafter. However, I needed more manpower to revive my dying business. I took a gamble by involving Baba's men in the business to increase the labor force. I knew Baba would have never approved of it. Hence, I deliberately sent him to Khandala under the pretext of some work. In his absence, I organized a party on the outskirts of Ratnagiri and invited Tatya and everyone who worked for Baba. I extended the invitation to the whole crew of Sikander and Rajvanshi as well. But it turned out to be my second blunder.

"As soon as I introduced Sikander and Rajvanshi to Tatya, Tatya yelled at me in disgust. Everyone from Baba's side refused to work with me. And things heated up at the party. On one hand, Tatya and his men threatened to expose me to the police. And on the other hand, Sikander and Rajvanshi wanted to kill Tatya and his team, as he knew too much by that time. Both parties were on the brink of a gang war in the party hall.

"And when I saw things getting out of my hands, I decided to put my plan B into action - to kill and get rid of them all. I couldn't afford to let Tatya and his men walk away after everything they had come to know. I was certain that Tatya would reveal my identity to Baba.

Moreover, the partnership with Rajvanshi and Sikander had begun to exhaust me. The constant bickering from both parties had been frustrating me for quite a while. Above all, I had amassed too much debt in terms of what I owed to everyone in wages. Unable to endure the stress anymore, I decided to kill everyone present at the party that night. I had my ducks in a row that evening to achieve my objective. In a stealth act, I added lethal cyanide into the opened liquor bottles.

"I calmed both the livid parties down and offered them the drinks laced with cyanide. Though Tatya's men cursed me for my involvement in this trade, they accepted the drinks. Within the next few minutes, their bodies started to drop on the floor one by one."

Sahil paused after his long speech as his eyes began to well up.

Sahil: "Batuk was right when he said I bought the rodenticide to kill rats. I killed all the bloody rats around me that night in one go."

Seated in the audience, I found it hard to stomach his blatant lies. I had been there until the end, and nothing of that sort had ever happened. He never adulterated the liquor in the party hall as he said. Moreover, his desperate attempt to paint Tatya and Thakur's men as mere innocents baffled me. I frowned and looked at him in despair. Sahil's words left Thakur stumped as well. We couldn't understand why he was trying to portray Tatya and all his men as innocent.

Sahil: "As both attorneys stated, Tatya didn't consume any of the spiked liquor and survived the plot. But it didn't take him long to guess the game once he saw the people around him falling to the ground. He panicked when he saw all his men perish one by one. He pointed his gun at me, but before he could fire, I pounced on him and pinned him down. By chance, I got my hands on his gun and I shot him in the head. After I had killed Tatya, everything looked settled to me. But I ran out of luck at the very last moment. Before I could abandon the venue, Khan reached the spot. I aimed and fired at him, but missed my target by a whisker. And everybody knows the rest of the story."

Sahil's confession brought down the curtains on the ongoing case. Everyone in the court was silent the entire time he was speaking. But a ruckus erupted as soon as he was finished. Many in the crowd hurled vicious abuses at him. To control the crowd, the judge knocked on the table with the gavel. He appealed to everyone and asked all to maintain decorum in the court. Though Batuk didn't have much to offer in Sahil's defense, the judge turned towards him.

Judge: "Any comments?"

A dismayed Batuk shook his head.

Batuk: "N-n-none, your honor."

Thakur slumped back into his seat. He knew that it was all over. The judge scribbled down some final notes in his logbook. After a break of ten minutes, he delivered the verdict.

Judge: "The court has heard all the witnesses with the utmost diligence and examined every piece of the presented evidence in detail. The evidence and Sahil's confession present a clear and complete picture to the court. Sahil masterminded the abductions and murders in Ratnagiri to feed his trade. Sahil's confession also proves that he carried out a brutal carnage on the night of 12th February, killing 25 men. He tricked and poisoned all his confidantes, and shot Tatya dead after he survived Sahil's ploy. **The court declares Sahil guilty of the grave and heinous charges leveled against him.** The court charges Sahil under IPC section 363 for kidnapping and section 302 for murder. Moreover, the court charges him under IPC section 370 for the forced removal of organs. The court also charges him under section 370A for the exploitation of human beings. The court indicts Sahil under IPC section 120-B for criminal conspiracy. The court also charges him under IPC section 419 for cheating by impersonation. Finally, the court indicts him under section 201 for tampering with evidence. For his unpardonable crimes, the court sentences him to capital punishment. **Thirty days from now, at the crack of the dawn of the 9th of April, Sahil Pratap Singh will be hanged by the neck until death.**"

After the judge signed the death sentence, he pressed his pen against the table and smashed its nib, as it was the custom. As soon as Sahil heard the verdict, he shut his eyes and smiled miserably. The courtroom erupted with hooting and applause, hailing the verdict. Tears of joy flowed down the cheeks of the victims' kin.

But the verdict devastated Sahil's family. Thakur went to pieces, stumbling out of his seat. Had I not held him by the shoulders in the nick of time, he would have fallen face-first onto the floor. Preeti whimpered in pain. But Vidya did something unexpected. With one last fierce glare at Sahil, she got up from her seat and walked out of the courtroom. Disgusted and ashamed at Sahil, she wept and walked back to the mansion. She couldn't forget his glee when he confessed his crimes to the judge in a loud and brazen voice. His obnoxious and despicable demeanor had destroyed her from within. In a silent vow, she decided to sever all her ties with him and resolved to never see his face ever again. Preeti followed Vidya after a glum look at Sahil.

———

Though she wanted to stay until the end of the proceedings, she knew that Vidya wasn't in the best state of mind. She didn't want her to be alone. The judge took off his glasses and sighed before making his closing statements.

Judge: "The court would like to thank the prosecution, the defense, the police, and all the witnesses. The court would also like to convey special thanks to Mr. Dhananjay Verma. His testimony and evidence submitted by him greatly helped the court in arriving at its decision. As a memento of his courage and valor, the court declares him the sole beneficiary of the bounty declared on Sahil's head. He made it possible for the police to crack the case and nail down Sahil, the mastermind behind the heinous crime. People like Sahil are gangrene to society and must be removed as soon as possible. Finally, the court expresses its condolences to the kin of the victims killed by Sahil and his men. Though their losses are irreparable, their future generations are safe. After this decision, they can sleep peacefully at night. The monster will be dead soon. Today is a historic day! It marks the cessation of the brutalities inflicted on the innocents in Ratnagiri. On that note, the court is adjourned. Justice has been delivered."

With these words, the judge struck the gavel on his table for one last time before he stood up and walked out of the courtroom. The gathered audience dispersed to the exit amid loud chatter. After suffering a crushing defeat, a disgruntled Batuk shook hands with Talwar. Then, he packed his things in haste and rushed out of the courtroom, embarrassed.

Satisfied with the verdict, Dhananjay rose from his seat and looked at Sahil with a victorious grin. He had accomplished his mission to avenge his father's death. Moreover, as a cherry on the cake, the court had made him the sole beneficiary of the bounty money. Dhananjay's glee conveyed a message to Sahil—he had avenged his father's murder and obtained his much-awaited retribution. In return, he expected Sahil to glare at him, furious at losing the case.

But Sahil's reaction baffled him. Sahil merely looked at him innocently with a miserable smile. Tears flowed down his cheeks, and his lips quivered as he looked into Dhananjay's eyes. The moment had tremendous sway over Dhananjay. His smirk waned into an embarrassed expression. In his desperation to send Sahil to the gallows, he had concealed some facts from the court. He had not mentioned the cash he had received from Sahil the night his men had abducted him. Out of greed, he didn't even speak about the ring that Sahil had given him. Moreover, Thakur's predated signatures on the probate were a mystery, as was the picture of Sahil with Rajvanshi. But he did not want these doubts to help Sahil in any way. Now he couldn't help but feel guilty as he saw his traumatized smile. Dhananjay adjusted his coat and turned his eyes away from Sahil in embarrassment. Then, he cleared his throat and walked out of the hall. Neither of them noticed that I had witnessed the silent communication between them. But I never thought that Sahil's cryptic smile would trouble Dhananjay for decades to come.

The cops held Sahil by his arms and dragged him out to the police van parked outside the courtroom. Thakur bawled and ran behind the cops as they hauled Sahil away. But before he could reach them, the vehicle sped away and left for the Ratnagiri police station. A broken Thakur howled and slumped onto a nearby chair in despair.

Meanwhile, Khan walked to Talwar and congratulated him for the emphatic and hands-down victory.

Khan: "You were terrific!"

Talwar: "It wouldn't have been possible without you. Thank you for all your aid."

Khan nodded, but he was engrossed in some thought, and his demeanor bewildered Talwar.

Talwar: "What's wrong?"

Khan: "Umm… I was just thinking about Sahil. I have a weird feeling. A veiled man in a crowd, who presided over a dreaded posse for years surrenders so meekly. A sly man of his stature admits to his crimes in the court with a smile and no trouble whatsoever. Don't you find it a little strange?"

Talwar: "He sensed his defeat and saw it coming. He had no other choice. But our job is not done yet. He is a crook, and I am sure he will try his best to escape his sentence. We need to be vigilant until he is hanged and dead."

Khan sighed and nodded. After shaking hands, both left for their respective homes. It had been a long and exhausting day for both of them.

A devastated Thakur wiped his tears. Then, he held his head in his hands and stayed glued to his seat long after everyone had vacated the courtroom. He was in deep shock after all he had heard and seen in the court that day. I went to him with tears in my eyes and patted his shoulder to console him.

I: "Thakur, let us go home. Everyone has left."

But he was too upset to leave. He looked up at me with gloomy eyes, and his lips were trembling.

Thakur: "I will come back by myself once I digest whatever I saw and heard today. I need some time alone, Bansi. Go to your quarters and rest. I know you are tired as well."

I empathized with the old man and understood that he wanted to live that moment all by himself. After a deep sigh, I nodded and drove back to my one-room quarters in the mansion. Thakur remained seated all alone in the deafening silence of the hall. He was a broken man. Lost in his thoughts, he snapped out of his trance when the peon of the court called out to him.

Peon: "Sir, it is time to lock the gates."

A depressed and dejected Thakur looked up at the peon. He stood up from his seat and made his way out of the hall slowly. Shaken after the court's verdict, he hired a cab to the mansion.

17. The Curse

The sun had gone down by the time the cab reached the mansion. As soon as Thakur stepped out of it, the cab sped away. The darkness of the night engulfed the mansion. Thakur sighed and looked up at his mansion with a pang. Just a few weeks ago, his friends and aides had thronged the mansion. But that day, immersed in darkness, the mansion now stood deserted. He heard a dog whining at a distance—a bad omen. He gulped, and his heart began to beat rapidly. He shook his head in dejection and walked into the mansion. Exhausted by the day's events, he craved some rest. He knew he had a Herculean task ahead of him to pull Sahil out of the mess.

But he halted when he caught a glimpse of Vidya in the dining area. With a grin on her face, she was humming a song as she arranged the dinner plates on the table. Rattled by her eerie behavior, Thakur called out to her in a quivering voice.

Thakur: "V-V-Vidya?"

She turned around, and her smile broadened when she saw him.

Vidya: "Ahh, you are here! Dinner is ready. Take a seat, I'll serve you."

Thakur: "Are you alright?"

Vidya: "Yes, I'm fine. Would you like to have your dinner at the table or do you want me to serve it in your room?"

For a moment, he thought to reprimand Vidya for her insensitivity. But he was a broken man that night. Being tired and dejected, he had no strength left in him to start an argument with her. Instead, he replied to her glumly.

Thakur: "If you can get hungry tonight, go ahead and have your dinner. I am tired, and I am going to bed."

With these words, he made his way to his room. He gulped down a glass of water, removed his shoes, lay down on the bed, and closed his eyes. Though he tried to sleep, terrible and pessimistic thoughts plagued him. The tormenting events of the day played in his mind one by one. But he jolted out of his thoughts when Vidya opened the door and entered the room in a black negligée. With a bright smile, she looked at herself in the mirror. Then, she sat at the dressing table and began to brush her hair while crooning an old classic song. To Thakur's dismay, she had a gentle smile on her face throughout. Finally, she made her way to bed and snuggled under the blanket. Thakur remained silent and kept looking at her with a pale face.

Vidya: "Ah! I forgot to tell you. I won't be home tomorrow. I would be at Mrs. Malti's house for the whole day, to attend her baby shower function. Though she hasn't invited me yet, I was thinking of going over owing to the cordial relations we share."

An edgy Thakur found her words too insensitive for the occasion. Unable to control his emotions, he admonished her for her queer behavior.

Thakur: "Have you lost your mind? How can you act so normal? It seems like whatever happened in the court didn't bother you at all."

His harsh rebuke brought a sudden change in her expression. Her face contorted with rage, and the grin she had on her face just a while ago vanished.

Vidya: "What else do you expect from me? You want me to wail and beat my chest? But for whom, the devil? The monster got what he deserved. May God forgive the sins committed by our family!"

Thakur: "F-for heaven's sake, Vidya, he's our s-son!"

But Thakur's tormented plea did not melt her heart. Tears of anger dripped down her cheeks.

Vidya: "I wish I had never given birth to him. If I had known I was going to give birth to a monster, I would have crushed my womb with my own bare hands. He is dead to me."

She fell silent after her emotional outburst.

Vidya: "Henceforth, I disown him."

She gulped and held back her tears when she thought about Preeti's feelings for Sahil.

Vidya: "Preeti! The poor girl fell in love with the devil. She waited for a crook all her life. But now I am glad that she dodged a bullet."

With these brazen words, she yanked the blanket over her face and drifted into a disturbed sleep. For a moment, Thakur thought of revealing the truth to her. He wanted to tell her that Sahil was not the only one and that his hands were bloody as well. But some force prevented him from doing so. Perhaps he was still clinging to the hope that things would turn out smooth again, as they were earlier. He sighed and closed his eyes. He knew that he had a steep road ahead in the coming days. But he was determined to save Sahil from this mess.

****

The next morning, police shifted Sahil to the jail located near the bridge on the outskirts. He had stayed in the police station the previous night as Khan had a few legal formalities to complete. Once he reached the jail, he shaved off his overgrown beard and took a bath. He submitted his wallet and other valuables to the authorities as per the rules. But the authorities did not ask him to remove the rosary around his neck. They permitted him to wear the amulet on the premises. He underwent routine medical checkups and physical examinations. He then put on the mandatory uniform for prisoners—a plain full-sleeved white shirt and loose white pajamas. The number 786 was stitched on his shirt's pocket in blue. Sahil Pratap Singh was, from that point onward, inmate number 786.

Two constables held him by his arms and made him walk to his assigned barrack. Sahil looked around to understand his surroundings as he walked. After walking through the corridor of the front office, they reached the veranda at the rear of the jail. The quadrilateral strips of the roofed and floored veranda outlined all four sides of a vast compound. Each of the four sides of the veranda hosted six barred barracks in a sequence. And every barrack was further divided into two cells. A barbed-wire, from top to bottom and left to right, separated the boundaries of the two cells in each barrack. And each cell housed two prisoners. Each barrack had a single entry and exit gate meant for all four prisoners residing in it.

Enclosed within the boundaries of the veranda, the compound was poorly maintained. It had patches of dried yellow grass scattered across, and in the middle were two small buildings. One of the buildings had a placard indicating that it was the restroom for the prisoners. There was no signboard for the other one, but the giant ladles and wide gas stoves indicated that it was the kitchen for the inmates.

As he walked to his barrack, a brief sight disturbed him. Standing in the middle of the compound, a bald policeman was ruthlessly beating a prisoner with a baton. The prisoner wailed with folded hands and begged for mercy. But his pleas didn't deter the brute, and he was in no mood to spare him. He thrashed the prisoner without a pause, landing some mighty blows on his legs and shoulders.

The constables halted when they reached the gate of barrack #3. One of the constables removed Sahil's handcuffs and unlocked the barrack's gate. They pushed Sahil into the cell on the left side of the barrack, then locked the gate and marched back. He frowned and looked around his cell. An old man sat on the floor of his cell with his legs crossed, worshipping a stone idol of Lord Krishna. Sahil did not want to disturb the elderly man, who looked like he was in his mid-seventies. Devoid of furniture and the beds, a sense of deep desolation prevailed in the cell. With no chair around him, Sahil sat down on the floor and waited for the man to complete his veneration. He sighed and looked around and saw another man in the adjacent cell covered with a blanket. With his forearm placed over his forehead, the fatso lay snoring on the floor.

A couple of minutes later, the man in his cell finished his prayers and turned around. As soon as he caught sight of Sahil, he locked his gaze on him. The stunned man looked at him with a straight face, and after a brief moment of silence, he smiled. Discomfited by the man's odd fascination, Sahil broke the ice.
Sahil: "H-hi."

The man came out of his trance when he heard Sahil's voice. He introduced himself as Chaudhary, mentioning that everyone in jail addressed him as Chachoo. Term 'Chachoo' meant 'uncle' in their language. Chachoo held Sahil's hand in affection and offered him his glass of tea.
Chachoo: "You look tired. Have some tea. They serve us tea once a day during lunch. You're a little late."

Though Sahil hesitated at first, he held the glass. Besides being exhausted, he had a mild headache due to inadequate sleep.
Sahil: "You might want to take your tea back after you hear of the

crimes I'm charged with."

Chachoo merely chuckled when he heard Sahil's honest words.

Chachoo: "There is hardly anyone here who doesn't know about you by now, Sahil Pratap Singh. The news of a hardcore criminal to be my cellmate has been doing the rounds since last night. Everyone here is eager to get a glimpse of you, Sahil."

Sahil smiled when he heard his name.

Sahil: "Yet you offered your tea to a man who has a plethora of murders listed under his name?"

Chachoo: "To be honest, until I saw you, I was wondering how a man could be so evil as to commit such dastardly acts. But after I saw you, I immediately understood…"

But he didn't complete his sentence. Once again, he gazed into Sahil's eyes. Sahil frowned in confusion.

Sahil: "You understood what?"

Chachoo shrugged and evaded the question.

Chachoo: "Umm…n-nothing. Let it be. But remember that you are in a place where everyone around you is a captive for some reason—no one is a saint here."

Sahil nodded with a faint grin and sipped his tea. He felt quite comfortable in Chachoo's company.

Sahil: "And what brings you here? You seem to be a decent and humble man to me."

Chachoo sighed and replied with a miserable smile.

Chachoo: "Perhaps I wasn't one twelve years ago. I was working as a daily laborer in a soap factory. One day, I got the news that my younger sister's drunken husband had mercilessly beaten her to death. I lost control over my emotions when I saw her lifeless body on the floor in front of me. In a rage, I stabbed the man sixteen times in his stomach. By the time I regained my senses, the court had awarded me imprisonment for fourteen years."

Sahil: "I…umm… I'm sorry to hear that!"

Chachoo: "That is all right. It was a long time ago. And I'm going to be a free man in two years."

Sahil nodded and remained silent for a few moments. After a brief pause, he looked to his side and inquired about the bulky figure asleep in the adjacent cell.

Sahil: "What's his story?"

Chachoo: "Ah! That's Bheema. He has been here for two months. The poor fellow is serving a seven-year sentence after a case of road rage. A couple of months ago, he lost his wife and son in an unfortunate car accident. They both died on the spot. And while his daughter survived the crash but developed some medical complications. When he saw the bloodstained bodies of his son and wife, he quivered in fury. In a fit of rage, he marched to the other driver involved in the crash and strangled him to death. His daughter is currently undergoing treatment at Ratnagiri Hospital. The trauma has shaken him to the core, because of which he has alienated himself from everyone. He barely speaks to anyone and keeps to himself all the time."

Sahil: "That is tragic. Is he alone in that cell? I mean, no cellmate?"

Chachoo replied with a chuckle.

Chachoo: "He has one! The guy is serving one year of jail time for an alleged bank robbery. But in only six months of his stay, he has already tried to flee about a dozen times."

Sahil smiled and looked around his cell. His gaze rested on the beautiful stone idol of Lord Krishna engraved in black marble.

Sahil: "It gives one immense peace of mind, doesn't it?"

Chachoo nodded, and the smile on his face waned as he looked into Sahil's eyes.

Chachoo: "One time or the other, he will come down from his abode in some incarnation. I always wondered if I would ever recognize him if h—"

He paused suddenly when a bald and bearded policeman unlocked the barrack's gate and pushed a young prisoner into the adjacent cell. He kicked the bruised man one last time before locking the gate and stomping away.

Sahil recognized both the men. He had seen them in the enclosed compound just a while back. He recollected the bald cop thrashing the man ruthlessly despite his agonizing screams.

The prisoner held his bruised arm and groaned in pain. The noise in the barrack awakened Bheema. In his state of half-sleep, he blinked at everyone in frustration. Then, without saying a word, he covered his face and fell into slumber again. Named Ranga, the young man was Bheema's cellmate and their fourth companion in the barrack. And as Chachoo talked about a little while ago, cops caught him as he tried to climb up the wall of the jail in a bid to escape from the place. Chachoo walked to the barbed wire boundary of the cell and looked at Ranga from his side of the fence.

Chachoo: "Aurangzeb beats you to a pulp every time he catches you red-handed. Why do you keep doing this? It's a matter of only six more months for you. Can't you hold your horses?"

With an up-to-no-good smile, Ranga crinkled his nose in pain and sat back on the floor.

Ranga: "Forget about six months! I can't stay in this cruddy place for one more moment of my life. Just wait and watch! One day, I will flee from this scum."

The name of the bald cop amused Sahil.

Sahil: "Aurangzeb?"

Chachoo: "Yeah, the cop who pushed him in. An Afghani immigrant, he is the jailor and supervises the prisoners. He's a bloody maniac and an ogre! Keep a safe distance from the ruthless man, Sahil."

Sahil looked up at the ceiling and recalled Kaju's words when they had met on the bridge.

Kaju: *"Every morning, we deliver tea to all the guards in the jail. Everyone is nice there except for the bald jailor. Everyone pays us right away, but he delays our payment for days."*

Perhaps the boy had been referring to Aurangzeb. While Sahil was lost in his thoughts, Ranga stared at him with a disgusted look. The smile on his face vanished when he heard Sahil's name.

Ranga: "Oh, is he the one?"

Chachoo nodded in response.

Ranga: "Be careful, Chachoo! You know his history."

His words annoyed Chachoo, and he rebuked Ranga for his insolence.

Chachoo: "You better worry about yourself, kid. The next time Aurangzeb catches you, he will break your bones."

Ranga sneered and lay down beside Bheema, needing some rest after the beating. He soon drifted into a deep sleep. But his scornful words had turned off Sahil a bit. A concerned Chachoo looked up at him in empathy and patted his shoulder.

Chachoo: "Don't mind his words. He is a gem at heart. I'm sure you both will be good friends soon."

Chachoo's reassuring words brought a miserable smile to his face. Moreover, he knew that he did not have enough life left to live, and he would be hung in a month. Hence, in a psychological impact, he prepared himself mentally to endure the sardonic comments from his inmates. He looked into Chachoo's kind eyes and nodded with a sigh.

****

The very next morning, Sahil understood why Ranga had termed the place as 'cruddy'. The arduous day began sharp at five in the morning for prisoners. The officers used blaring sirens as alarms to wake up the inmates. As soon as they woke up, they had to mandatorily line up outside the sole bathroom in the compound. It was, without a doubt, the worst time of the day for them all. The inmates were not permitted to use the bathroom at any other time of the day. As soon as the clock struck six in the morning, the officials locked the bathroom and blocked its access. In jail with around a hundred captives, the bathroom could accommodate a maximum of ten people at a time. Verbal confrontations between the mates were the norm at that hour.

Moreover, the toilets were poorly maintained and low on hygiene. The sanitation facilities were in a despicable state too. The strong stench of urine was unbearable. To add to their woes, most of the flushes either did not work or had a glitch of some kind. As a result, it led to the unpleasant sight of undisposed human ordure scattered all over the place.

The condition of the single-roomed hospital, located near the front office, was worse. With no electric fans or coolers, it was a living hell for ailing prisoners, especially in the summers. Moreover, it did not have a full-time doctor. The physician, Mr. Sen, visited only two days a week. Moreover, the stock of medicines was scarce, and the medical staff was inadequate and inefficient.

Every detainee had an assigned work profile tagged to his name. Due to his physical strength, Bheema worked at the construction site. Aurangzeb had deployed him along with a few others to lift heavy stones. Chachoo had been part of the cooking team for years while Ranga worked both as a locksmith and carpenter. His task was the hardest since his cabinetwork often lasted till late in the night. But irked by his attempts to flee, the officials paid him the least. The authorities had assigned the role of a gardener to Sahil on a fixed salary of forty rupees per day. But since the court awarded him with the death sentence, the jail had a different clause for him. Once executed, the officials were required to handover all his earned money to his family.

Every prisoner got back to his assigned tasks when the guards blared out the siren at sunrise. They worked through the morning till the lunch break, which was scheduled from twelve to one. Everyone craved that one-hour of a break in the afternoon. After the vigorous labor, the dog-tired inmates would gather in the compound. Thirsty and hungry, they would line up along a wide dining table near the kitchen. Standing on the other side of the table, the cooking team served food in platters to the men. As the detainees moved ahead in the queue, the cooking team poured tea into their metal cups.

The constables unlocked the gates of all the barracks at the start of the lunch break. And the gates remained unlocked during that one-hour window. With no restrictions, they were free to roam around and visit their mates in the other barracks. They had to return to their respective cells once lunchtime was over. The constables locked the gates again once the inmates made it to their assigned cells. And from there on, they remained confined until dinnertime. At nine in the night, the officials unlocked the gates again, and the prisoners marched to the kitchen. Though the cooking team did not serve tea in the supper as they did during the lunch, the pattern remained the same as at lunch. This supper lasted for an hour as well, during which the prisoners were free to roam around. Post dinner, the inmates had to return to the respective cells.

****

It was Sahil's second night in jail. He was on his way back to his barrack after finishing his dinner when a constable shouted out his name. Sahil turned around and saw the cop walking towards him. He had a visitor during the last visiting hour of the night. Every prisoner had a window of fifteen minutes to meet any of his visitors once in a day. The last slot of the day fell at ten in the night. Sahil knew who the visitor was.

A constable opened the door of the dingy visitor's room and helped Thakur to walk inside. He shut the door and left once the old man entered the room. The room was unique in that it had double-layered prison bars dividing it into two halves. The bars ran from top to bottom and left to right, and the prisoner and the visitor stood on either side of the bars. A despairing Thakur looked around for Sahil in the darkness of the silent room. Baffled by Sahil's confession in court, Thakur had a lot of questions for him. He was furious at him for misleading everyone by telling self-destructive lies to the court.

Suddenly, amid the vicious thunder, he jumped in fear when he looked at the other side of the bars. His blood ran cold when he saw his son standing with his back turned to him. Sahil's awkward stance rattled him. An apprehensive Thakur whispered his name feebly.
Thakur: "S-S-Sahil! It's me, son. Look at me."

But to his despair, Sahil refused to respond to him. He did not say a word and continued to stand in the same posture. It was a nerve-racking sight for Thakur. He tried to make out the reason for Sahil's peculiar behavior.

Thakur: "Ah! You are angry because I didn't visit yesterday. I tried my best, but these obtuse policemen did not permit me. They wanted me to take care of some legal formalities. But look, I'm here today in front of you. Look at me, son!"

But Sahil did not look back at his father. At last, Thakur lost his patience and screamed in frustration.

Thakur: "WHY AREN'T YOU TALKING TO ME? DON'T YOU UNDERSTAND HOW MUCH TROUBLE YOU'RE IN?"

But his agonized words didn't affect Sahil in any way. He maintained the same stance, with his face turned to the other side. Thakur wheezed and his lower lip quivered in anxiety. He was panicking now.

Thakur: "W-w-why aren't you talking to me? Who…who do you want to talk to? Preeti? Oh yes! You'll talk to her, right? I-I will bring her with me. I-I-I will be back soon."

Thakur sprinted to the exit. But before he could leave, a loud cackle resonated in the room from somewhere behind him. He frowned in confusion and halted in his steps. He turned around slowly, and to his horror, Sahil had turned around and begun to laugh. Tears of joy streamed down his face. The booming sound of laughter felt like déjà vu to Thakur. Sahil wiped his eyes and looked up at Thakur. And the words he spoke next intensified Thakur's eerie feeling. He had indeed heard that spooky laughter before.

Sahil: "Do you recognize this laughter?"

Thakur had been finding it hard to recollect even simple facts lately. But after the little push from Sahil, he recalled the ill-fated night when Harak had killed Boney. It was the night Sahil had discovered his father's real identity. He remembered his own laughter when Sahil insisted that he surrender himself to the police. This is what Sahil's laughter a few moments back reminded him of. But the tables had turned, as he was standing on the receiving end this time. Sahil's laughter shook him to the core. As his laughter waned, Sahil clenched his teeth in anger.

Sahil: "Do you remember the night your men killed my friend Boney? Do you remember it, Thakur Pratap Singh?"

Thakur went pale when he heard Sahil address him by his name instead of 'Baba.' Baffled by Sahil's hostility, a confused Thakur managed to utter a few words.

Thakur: "Son, why are you angry—"

Sahil: "Don't call me your son, you bloody murderer! It hurts to be reminded that I was born to an evil man like you. Your hands are stained with the blood of innocents. I get the urge to claw at my own face whenever you touch me with your bloodstained hands. I severed all ties with you the night I got to know the veiled fiend residing within you."

As soon as Sahil proclaimed his vow, a rumble of thunder rolled in the sky. The lightning flashed across Thakur's shocked face. Stunned by Sahil's uncouth behavior, his eyes widened in fear.

Thakur: "W-what are you saying Sahil? W-w-we both worked together all this while!"

Sahil burst into laughter once again.

Sahil: "HAHAHA…working together? With you? HAHAHA…you murderer! Do you think I would ever be the kind of man who has the will to kill? After you and your dogs refused to surrender to the police that night, I exterminated them all in one shot. For a while, I was concerned about them anticipating my real intentions, but I was wrong. Your brainless and dimwit dogs were nothing but a few clowns short of a circus."

Thakur: "W-what? Y-y-you mean you were an impostor?"

Sahil: "I simply followed your footsteps. Oh, don't you remember your words, Thakur? Sometimes, you need to formulate an illusion to veil the truth. And at other times, you need to create a delusion to deceive the minds of the masses."

Thakur recollected saying the same words to Sahil that night in the chamber.

Thakur: *"No matter whom you tell, no one will ever believe you, son. I have formulated an illusion to veil the truth. I have created a delusion to deceive the minds of the masses."*

But Sahil was not done yet. He admonished Thakur with a deep fury in his gaze.

Sahil: "I remember your eyes filled with greed that night. I can still recall the shameless smile on your face while you were bragging about your sins. What did you say about yourself that night? *'I'm a king with an invincible army.'* Isn't that what you said to me about your men that night? Huh?"

With extreme disgust and hate, he spat on the floor near

Thakur's feet while Thakur gazed at him with a straight face.

Sahil: "AAAK...THOOO...Today, you are all alone, Thakur. I have wiped out all your men, and your empire has crumbled to ruins."

Thakur gulped in shock and gasped in fear. Then, he tried to mollify his incensed son in a shivering voice.

Thakur: "Why this sudden change of heart, Sahil? Didn't we kill men to help our trade prosper when you were working with me?"

A glint of humor flashed in Sahil's eyes at Thakur's naive question. He approached Thakur and clasped the prison bars between them. His lips twisted into a vicious smirk.

Sahil: "Yes, we did. But did you ever stop to think who all lost their lives since the day I joined the ranks? Did you?"

Thakur frowned as he tried to recollect and remained silent at Sahil's words.

Sahil: "To revive your dying memory, I killed Harak first, the night he killed Boney. Then, I shot the informers the day you introduced me to Sikander and Rajvanshi. John, the inebriated man in Sikander's gang, was my next target. And I am sure Bansi would have narrated all that happened in the party hall. Did anyone else die, Thakur? Except for your allies, I don't recall anyone else on the list. Did I miss anyone, Thakur?"

Stunned at Sahil's mocking words, Thakur looked at him with his mouth wide open. Sahil was right! Since the time Sahil had started working with him, the only men to lose their lives had been the ones who belonged to his and Sikander's gangs. No innocent had ever lost his life after. Thakur stood speechless as things became crystal clear to him.

Gusts of strong winds continued to whoosh through the small window near the roof. A heavy storm was on its way to Ratnagiri.

Sahil: "Watching your villainous men die in front of my eyes was almost satisfying, Thakur. But in a stroke of bad luck, Khan busted the venue and caught me before I could abscond. Dhananjay turned out to be a lucky charm for him. He passed on my location to him at a wrong time for me."

Thakur's eyes welled up with tears, which then flowed down his cheeks.

Thakur: "Clean up the mess that surrounds you, Sahil. You have cornered yourself into definite death. Why did you take the entire blame on yourself in court? Tell me, son!"

But Thakur's heart-rending plea did not melt Sahil's heart. He smiled scornfully at Thakur.

Sahil: "Because I will make your life a living hell, more miserable than death. I will inflict horrendous suffering upon you, Thakur Pratap Singh! For all your crimes, it will be your son instead who goes to the gallows and not you. An aged father's pain in witnessing his young son's corpse is more than flesh and blood can endure. The day I die, I hope that someone places my lifeless body on a pyre in front of you. Just like aunty Kanta did for Boney, you will wail like a banshee when the priest asks you to set the pyre on fire. The rising cloud of thick, dark smoke will give you immense and unbearable pain. The flames of my burning pyre will eat at you from within. As you grieve for your innocent son, you will lose a part of yourself with every passing day. Being the reason behind your own child's death, you will crave for death every single moment of your life. You will spit at yourself in disgust every time you look into the mirror. I, A DYING MAN, CURSE YOU FOR YOUR VILE ACTIONS, THAKUR PRATAP SINGH."

Thakur's eyes widened in fear after Sahil's excruciating words fell in his ears. A loud din of a thunderstorm rocked in the sky and scared Thakur to his wits. He fell to his knees, wailing, and folded his hands to beg for mercy.

Thakur: "No-no-no Sahil. Kill me or skin me alive if you want to. Punish me in any way you like. B-B-But don't do this to me!"

But Thakur's pleas fell on deaf ears, as they did not affect Sahil in any way. A disenchanted Sahil fell silent. His hair blew in the strong breeze, and he looked at Thakur with a destructive rage in his eyes. The fierce storm weakened, and the thunder subsided. Finally, in a loud voice, Sahil broke the uneasy calm in the room.

Sahil: "O ASHWATHAMA!"

His loud ethereal voice echoed off the prison's walls, and his words horrified Thakur. Thakur recalled his birthday when Sahil had addressed him by the same name.

Sahil: *"I hope God gives you a long life, similar to Ashwathama's!"*

Thakur: *"Ashwathama?"*

Sahil: *"Yes, Ashwathama, the immortal!"*

At the time, Thakur believed that Sahil had addressed him as Ashwathama in a wish to him for a long life. But in reality, Sahil had never meant to wish him a long life. In the Mahabharata, in an act of cowardice, Ashwathama had slain a few men in the enemy army while they slept in their camps. And his unforgivable action had drawn Lord Krishna's wrath. Disgusted by his unpardonable crime, Krishna placed a savage curse on him. Much like Ashwathama, Thakur had never given his innocuous victims a chance when his goons strangulated or stabbed them to death.

Thakur began to tremble as he remembered the curse. He was going to share the curse that the immortal man had lived with for ages. Sahil scowled and his face contorted in an extreme rage before he roared at him in a divine voice.

Sahil: "*Filled with guilt and contrition, your boon of long life will turn into an abhorrent curse!*

Weighed down by the burden of your grisly sins, devoid of any love and peace, you will wander like a nihilist!

The ghosts of the dead standing beside you will haunt you forever!

You will outlive your kin and languish a hellish state, as all your loved ones will die one by one in front of your eyes!

Marred with rotted wounds that will never heal, an endless pain will be your destiny!

The death lord will betray you, no matter how much you yearn for it!

With no salvation, you will lead a wretched life with no reprieve!"

Thakur shivered in fear when he heard Sahil's harsh curse. He grimaced in pain.

Thakur: "No, Sahil, no! Please take the despicable curse back. I beg of you. Free me from your curse!"

But Thakur's agonized words did not garner any sympathy from Sahil. Instead, he glowered at him and reprimanded him in an austere tone.

Sahil: "Who am I to free you from it? You are indebted to mankind, and an evil man like you must pay back in the language you understand best."

With his emotions running high, Thakur looked up at Sahil and sniveled.

Thakur: "I-I-I cannot live without you, son!"

Tears of agony flowed down Sahil's face when he heard Thakur's tormented plea. With angst-filled eyes, he freaked out and shrieked in a shrilled voice.

Sahil: "You should be delighted—you will get a new body to rip out organs from, Thakur. Once you get ahold of my dead body, make sure you slit it wide open and rip it apart before gutting it. Pull out my heart, lungs, intestines, and whatever else that can reap you some money to squander around. To charm others, display my hollow body in a menagerie as a symbol of your bravery."

Down on his knees, Thakur began to wail as he heard Sahil's tormenting words. Sahil clenched his teeth in fury before he rebuked him one last time.

Sahil: "Get out of here! And if you have some shame, don't show me your hideous face ever again."

With those punishing words, he turned his back to Thakur once again and left the room. Shattered and flustered, the sobbing Thakur stood up and made his way to the exit. He knew that he might never see Sahil in his life ever again.

18. The Virtuous

Days passed by, and as Chachoo had predicted, Ranga and Sahil started getting along quite well. Both were energetic and young lads, and both had a good sense of humor too. Soon, they started to enjoy each other's company. Within just a few days, Chachoo, Ranga, and Sahil had turned into a trio of close friends. But an aloof Bheema never engaged with any of them. He remained silent, absorbed in his private affairs. One day, Sahil and Chachoo sat in their cell during lunchtime. They giggled as they exchanged a funny banter over their meal. But then, Sahil jolted in panic when he caught a sudden glimpse of Ranga. He was limping back to the cell with his arms around the shoulders of a barely conscious Bheema. Chachoo and Sahil rushed to the two and, along with Ranga, helped Bheema walk into the cell. They yanked a blanket over his body and massaged his feet once he lay on the floor.

Sahil: "What happened to him?"

Ranga: "Same old problem—anxiety and high blood pressure. It soared to 170/98 today. Luckily, Mr. Sen was in the hospital today. He has been given an injection, so he should be stable pretty soon."

Chachoo: "I don't think the guy will survive for long this way. His depression and awful thoughts about his daughter disturb him throughout the day. Anyway, we shouldn't disturb him. He needs some rest. Let's pray he gets better soon."

Ranga nodded, and the two of them walked out of the barrack. Sahil, however, continued to stand in his place. He sighed and looked at Bheema's face for a few moments before marching out.

Bheema's condition had stabilized by dinnertime. Seated at the corner of his cell, he was eating his food. Sahil, Chachoo, and Ranga held their plates and sat together in Ranga's cell as well. Seated diagonally opposite to Bheema, Chachoo and Ranga gossiped while munching on their dinner. But Sahil remained silent and he had his gaze locked on Bheema. With his stare locked at Bheema, he roared at Ranga with a slender smile on his face.

Sahil: "Ranga, have you ever killed someone in your life?"

His interruption stumped Ranga and Chachoo. They were speechless. Moreover, they had never heard such uncouth words from him before, as he had remained pretty decent in his stay in jail so far. He had steered clear of any conversations about the nature of the crimes listed under his name. But those sudden words left them perplexed. Ranga stammered in a nervous reply.

Ranga: "W-w-what? N-n-no way."

But Ranga's naive protest did not deter him. He continued with an uncanny smile.

Sahil: "Ahhh! You missed the fun, Ranga. It's a splendid moment. You get a feel of a great power residing within you. You begin to admire your strength when you see a person down, as dead as a dodo, before your eyes."

Though his statement baffled Ranga and Chachoo, the words did not seem to irk Bheema. The apathetic man continued to chomp on his food, refusing to even look up at Sahil. But Sahil's next set of loud and loathsome words evoked some erraticism in his behavior for the first time.

Sahil: "Of all the murders I've committed, do you know which one I enjoyed the most? It was when I bumped off a twelve-year-old girl."

Though Bheema didn't say anything in response, he stopped gnawing on his food. A stupefied Ranga gulped and tried to interject. But before he could speak a word, Chachoo held up his hand and shook his head in silence. He gestured to Ranga to not barge in. Perhaps he understood the reason behind Sahil's brazen words. And he was right. Sahil wanted Bheema to unleash his unspoken emotions. He wanted him to react to his words. In a ploy, he wanted to bring out a side of Bheema's personality that no one had ever seen before.

Sahil: "Poor girl! I slashed her throat in one flick. She writhed in pain for a few minutes before she finally succumbed. And I stood next to her in a triumphant smile until she breathed her last."

A smile crept onto his face. But before he could utter another word, his mind blanked out. With reddened eyes, Bheema pounced on him and gripped his neck with his strong, thick hands. Clenching his teeth in a fit of rage, he groaned as he tried to throttle Sahil. His voice shivered in anger.

Bheema: "You scoundrel! Didn't your inner conscience hound you? Didn't you feel the pain a father suffers when a fiend like you takes the life of his child? Monsters like you annihilate all the love a father invests in his child for years. You turn a man like me into the living dead."

It was the first time anyone had heard Bheema's voice. Ranga stood up and sprinted towards the duo, not wanting Bheema to harm Sahil in any way. But before he could stop Bheema, Sahil gave him an austere stare to discourage him from intervening. Though surprised, Ranga abided and halted. Meanwhile, a grief-stricken Bheema continued to yell at Sahil.

Bheema: "I will kill you as a tribute to all the grieving parents in the world. I will… I will…"

As he uttered these words, his lips fluttered before he fell unconscious. Sahil grabbed the stocky man, and with a grin, helped him lie down on the floor. Chachoo covered him with a warm blanket, and Ranga massaged his cold feet to give him some warmth. To everyone's relief, Mr. Sen was available to take care of things. He declared Bheema to be out of danger after an hour of medical supervision as his blood pressure had reduced to 123/84, which was considered normal.

****

The next morning marked the beginning of a new chapter in Bheema's life. He was a different man entirely when he woke up. Around lunchtime, he strode to the kitchen table in the compound. As opposed to his earlier dead-as-a-doornail expression, he walked around with a beam. When he caught a glimpse of Sahil in the kitchen area, he walked over to him and held his hands, marveling at his efforts in granting him a new lease of life. Sahil smiled in acknowledgment.

Bheema: "Forgive me for my conduct yesterday, Sahil. I did not know the noble intentions behind your loutish words. I am so sorry."

Sahil: "You don't need to apologize! That was the sole purpose behind my theatrics. You needed to speak your mind. And I am glad that you did. You had too many emotions pent up inside you, but yesterday, you finally let them out through your outburst. You have awakened from a long and deep slumber, Bheema. We need to fight the turbulences in life instead of submitting to them. I will pray for your daughter. I hope she recuperates soon."

By this time, almost every prisoner stood up and walked near to the duo in solidarity. An emotional Bheema wiped his eyes and smiled.
Bheema: "It is a lucky day for me for more than one reason. I have good news to share. One of my relatives visited me today, and it looks like my daughter will get well soon."

Everyone gathered around them jumped in joy after hearing Bheema. An ecstatic Sahil embraced Bheema.
Sahil: "Wow! That is wonderful!"
Bheema: "A team of specialized surgeons will operate on her next month. It will take a couple of weeks more for the doctors to discharge her though. Once discharged, she will stay with my sister."
Sahil: "Congratulations Bheema! I will apply for a day's parole and pay her a visit when she gets discharged—"

But Sahil stopped abruptly and did not complete his sentence. Instead, he gulped and looked at Bheema in despair. Even the other prisoners looked at him with morose faces. They knew that Sahil wouldn't be alive to witness the fortunate day. His execution was scheduled for the 9th of next month. After a brief pause, Sahil patted Bheema's shoulder with a miserable smile and walked back to his cell. Everyone stood silent and watched his back in melancholy as he walked away.

****

Standing in the kitchen of the mansion and engrossed in deep thought, Preeti stood over the milk simmering on the stove. She snapped out of her trance when she heard Vidya's loud voice and wiped her tears in haste.
Vidya: "Where have you been, Preeti? I have been looking for you since the morning."

Preeti did not reply and remained silent. She looked at Vidya with a gloomy face as tears flowed down her cheeks. She gulped and turned away from Vidya. Though she did not say a word, her silence said it all. Vidya frowned at Preeti.
Vidya: "D-did you go to jail? To meet Sahil?"

She looked at her nervously and nodded in silence. Vidya gulped and tried her best to hold back her tears. After a pause, she asked her the next question in a choked voice.

Vidya: "Did he meet?"

Preeti shook her head and broke down into sobs.

Preeti: "I don't know why he is doing this to me. I visit the jail every day with the hope of seeing him, but he has refused to meet me every single time. He doesn't care to meet me even once."

Preeti's words filled Vidya with rage.

Vidya: "The coward doesn't have enough courage to face you. Forget about him, Preeti. The sooner you do, the better it will be for you."

Vidya paused for a moment and uttered her next words with a little hesitation.

Vidya: "Preeti, I know this may be hard for you to endure, but I need to tell you something. Umm, we have a marriage proposal for you. I haven't said yes yet, but I haven't refused it either. I want you to think about it.

"The boy's name is Amit, and he works as a manager in a bank. I would like you to make a decision soon. You need to move on, Preeti."

With these words, Vidya turned around and walked back to her room with a lump in her throat. An astounded Preeti gave her a horrified look. Vidya was the last person whom she ever imagined to pass on such a shattering recommendation. Just a few months ago, she had teased Preeti for liking Sahil. Her witty one-liners had encouraged her to nurture feelings for him. But today, her harsh words crumbled her fantasies. A dejected Preeti continued to stand in the kitchen all by herself. She had never imagined a life without Sahil. But she knew she had to take a call. Thakur and Vidya were getting older, and with Sahil's future dangling in uncertainty, she didn't have too many options.

✳✳

It was late in the evening. I returned to my room after finishing my household duties in the mansion. I was about to go to bed when I heard a knock on the door, and I was surprised to see Thakur standing at my doorstep. He gave me a desolate look and walked inside without a word. He had already shared with me all that had transpired between him and Sahil in jail.

Frazzled and tired, Thakur sighed deeply and settled down on a chair near my bed. His demeanor rattled me.

I: "Are you alright, Thakur?"

Thakur: "Huh? Yeah, I-I was not getting any sleep, so I thought I would come here for some chitchat. I have a question in my mind that has been hounding me for days, Bansi. I was unable to find an answer, so I thought I would ask you. Perhaps you can help me out."

He gave me a perturbed look. Then, he explained the purpose of his visit.

Thakur: "You have been my greatest confidante all these years, Bansi. Be it my past or my present, you know in and out of it. I don't have any secrets from you. Sahil spat venom on me for the killings I orchestrated over the years. I see the sympathy in the eyes of Vidya and Preeti for the victims of my crimes. B-b-but I don't feel any guilt or remorse for whatever I've done all these years. Why is that, Bansi? Tell me, why? Am I a stone-hearted man?"

Sahil was right in the evening he called me Thakur's puppet when he killed all those men in the party hall. Though I never approved of Thakur's actions, I had remained a mute spectator all these years. I never had the guts to voice my resentment. As my ancestors had to the earlier generations of Thakur's family, I served him blindly. I never opened my mouth and spoke against him. However, this query from the pathetic man irked me that day. It ignited a wave of terrible anger inside my heart. For the first time in my life, I taunted him. I crossed the line and went against the protocol.

I: "It is hard to believe that a man so deeply involved in homicides is standing before me and asking me if he is cruel."

He did not take my insolence well. He got up from the chair and lunged towards me in fury. Disgruntled at my unexpected defiance, he scowled at me.

Thakur: "How dare you say that to me? Instead of offering me advice, you are making sardonic comments?"

Though he tried to disparage me, I was no mood to pamper him that night. It was a rare occasion when I was in a dark mood. I jeered back at him.

I: "Yes, I am! Don't forget, you brought death to Sahil, and if you still don't feel any guilt, then may God help you. Let me be honest, Thakur. The law should have deemed you guilty for the murders and not him. If anyone needs to be punished, it is you! If anyone needs to be hanged, it is you and only you, Thakur."

Unable to control my emotions, I broke down.

I: "That boy used to play in my lap. I don't know how I will endure the sight of his lifeless body…"

I couldn't complete my sentence as my throat choked up and I burst into tears. My rebuke had left Thakur flustered. I could tell that my words had a profound effect on his psyche. He started to wheeze and his eyes widened in despair. Then, he stood up and left my room without a word.

****

Back on his bed, Thakur looked at Vidya disconsolately. She was sitting on the bed with her legs crossed, chanting verses from the Gita, the holy Hindu scripture. After Sahil's conviction, she had made it a habit to recite the verses every night before going to sleep. It kept her calm and peaceful in turbulent times. Shaken after Sahil had rebuked him in jail, he thought to reveal the truth to Vidya. He felt an immense pain whenever he heard someone, especially Vidya, calling Sahil an evil. Ominous thoughts played in his mind. He knew that the shattering piece of news would devastate her to the core since he was no less than God to her. He knew the truth would destroy her from within. It was a bitter pill for him to swallow.

He gasped and with trembling lips, he began once she finished her prayers.

Thakur: "V-Vidya, I-I-I n-need to tell you something."

Vidya turned to him and looked into his eyes.

Vidya: "Hmmm?"

Sweat dripped down his forehead as he tried to tell her the truth. He was unable to gauge the extent to which his words would devastate her.

Thakur: "I-I-I w-want to… I mean… I w-was the… I…"

His mumbling confused her. Unable to understand what he wanted to convey, she asked in an irritated tone.

Vidya: "What's the matter? Are you alright?"

He lost all the courage he had mustered the minute she locked her gaze on him. His words got caught in his throat at the very last moment. He wiped the sweat off his forehead.

Thakur: "Umm…n-n-nothing. I won't be home tomorrow. I have some work to take care of. Don't get worried if I come home late."

She nodded in silence without any sign of interest and lay on the bed. Thakur lay down as well, exhaling anxiously. He felt his heart thudding in his chest. He puffed out his cheeks and closed his eyes amid heavy panting.

****

A couple of days later, Preeti came running to me as soon as I parked the car at the front entrance. She panted to catch her breath. She had been sitting at the doorstep the entire day waiting for my return. She knew I had gone to jail in a last-ditch effort to meet Sahil.

Short of breath, she wheezed and held my hand anxiously.

Preeti: "Uncle, d-did he meet you today? I…I…am sure he did! Did you pass on my message to him? I need to see him as soon as possible."

With tears in my eyes, I rubbed her shoulder and shook my head. As had happened in all my previous efforts, Sahil had refused to meet me yet again. My response crushed her from within. Dejected, she stared at me in despair. Tears sprung up in her eyes, and her lower lip trembled. Unable to endure her plight, I looked away and made my way to the mansion. She stood alone at the same place for a while. After gaining a little composure, she wiped her tears and walked back to her room in the backyard. Lost in deep pessimistic thoughts, she switched off the lights in her room and shut the door.

19. The Rebellion

At the dinnertime, Ranga walked to Chachoo in the kitchen. He was busy gathering the dirty utensils after all the inmates had finished their supper. Ranga looked about nervously and called out his name in an urgent whisper.

Ranga: "Chachoo!"

Chachoo turned around and wiped the sweat off his forehead. He didn't like Ranga barging in at that hectic hour.

Chachoo: "Ahhh, I don't have time, son. I need to clean up all this mess. I'll see you back in the barrack in about an hour."

But Ranga gulped anxiously and licked his lips. With his eyes locked on Chachoo, he pulled out a long metallic key from his pocket. Then, he inched closer to Chachoo and placed the key in his hand. The move took Chachoo by surprise.

Chachoo: "What is this?"

Ranga: "Umm…the-the duplicate key of the b-b-barrack."

His reply sent shivers through Chachoo.

Chachoo: "What?"

Ranga: "I crafted it for what will be remembered as the great escape from jail."

Upon hearing his words, Chachoo looked around cautiously. Then, he clenched his teeth and rebuked him in a raspy voice.

Chachoo: "Have you gone nuts? Aurangzeb will smash your skull if he comes to know about this. And anyway…why are you handing this to me?"

Ranga looked up at him with trembling lips. Then, after a pause, he made a sincere confession.

Ranga: "Because…now, I don't want to leave you guys. Since the day Sahil came here and Bheema came back to his senses, you all have been a family to me. I can't live without you guys, Chachoo. I can't."

His tender words touched a chord in Chachoo's heart. With tears in his eyes, he embraced Ranga.

Chachoo: "Good boy! Don't worry about the key. I will take care of it."

Smiles crept onto their faces as they both stood together hand in hand. But the poignant moment turned miserable when they heard an agonizing scream. They both rushed in the direction of the shriek they had heard moments ago. They landed up near a grieving prisoner.

Sahdev, as everyone called him, knelt and clung to the lifeless body of his cellmate, Namdev. The gathered prisoners tried to console the lamenting man. Soon, a policeman drove an ambulance into the compound. Then he lifted the body and placed it at the rear of it with the help of a few inmates. Sahil came running out when he heard the buzz of the crowd. Carrying the body, the ambulance sped away from the ground, possibly to a crematorium. A sense of gloom engulfed the detainees. As the ambulance disappeared into the darkness, the place began buzzing.

Gora (A Prisoner): "One more casualty! And the cause is the same again—food poisoning!"

Kuldeep (A prisoner): "He was so cheerful in the morning. But as soon as he had his lunch, that was it. He complained about mild stomach pain and slight discomfort in the beginning. But by the evening, his condition worsened. And within the next few hours, he was gone."

Chachoo: "I have complained to Aurangzeb so many times, but he pays no heed to it. The food supply is often contaminated with frogs and dead rats. I bet the supplies are not meant for humans by any standards."

Ranga: "The whole system is bloody corrupt. Just look at the despicable state of the restrooms. After using them, even a healthy man will fall sick within a few days. I have heard that Aurangzeb misuses the funds that are supposed to be spent on us. No wonder we dwell in such a deplorable place."

After Sahil heard everyone, he put forward a naïve suggestion.

Sahil: "I think it's time to speak to Aurangzeb in one united voice. He needs to take measures against these inhumane living conditions."

Bheema: "You want us to talk to the tyrant? Even if someone manages to do so, do you expect him to agree to the favors we would ask him for?"

Sahil: "We are not asking for a favor. We are entitled to these basic rights as per the law."

But his recommendation irked the lamenting Sahdev, who scoffed at him.

Sahdev: "Then why don't you initiate things? It is easier said than done. Do you have the guts to do it? Tell me!"

With a hint of anxiety on his face, Sahil fell silent for a moment and looked around at everyone. The sight of Aurangzeb had always terrified him as well. To talk to him, he knew that he would have to put his hand in the lion's mouth. But he sighed and accepted the challenge.

Sahil: "Alright, I'm in. But I need a promise from you all—until I win this for you, I need blind support from you guys. Are you all up for it?"

His proposal did not go unheard. The enthused inmates did not disappoint him. With a cheerful smile, everybody spoke in solidarity.

Everyone (in a chorus): "YES, WE ARE!"

A sense of confidence surged in Sahil. A thin grin replaced the nervousness that he had on his face a few moments back.

A guard scurried to Aurangzeb's top-floor room and knocked on the door. The loud knock jolted Aurangzeb out of his sleep. He sat up in bed and yelled.

Aurangzeb: "What is it? Don't you know that I don't like to be disturbed at this time?"

Guard: "Sorry, sir, but the prisoners want to meet you. They have gathered near the office and want to talk to you. They are adamant."

The guard's explanation irritated him further.

Aurangzeb: "At this time? What do they want to talk about?"

Guard: "I asked them but they refused to tell me the reason. They want to have a word with no one but you."

At first, he thought to refuse the prisoners' request. But considering one of them had died about an hour ago, he thought it wise to meet them. Dressed in a plaid robe, he went down the stairs and stood in front of the gathered prisoners. Being furious at them for awakening him in the middle of his otherwise sound sleep, he shrieked in anger.

Aurangzeb: "What is so urgent that you could not wait till morning?"

While everybody stood hushed in fear, Sahil walked and stood between Aurangzeb and the inmates. Standing face to face with Aurangzeb, he looked straight into his eyes. Aurangzeb's eyes widened in surprise. He stared at Sahil from top to bottom in anger.

Aurangzeb: "What do you want?"

Though Sahil felt a touch nervous while talking to him, he knew that he had to put forth the request. With his heart beating rapidly, he maintained a humble smile.

Sahil: "Sir, there have been many deaths in the jail owing to poor hygiene. On behalf of everyone, I request you to meet some of our demands. They might seem trivial at first, but we need them. Please hear us out, sir."

Aurangzeb frowned in surprise.

Aurangzeb: "Demands? Like what?"

Sahil: "Nothing much, sir. We have only six demands.

01. Provision of drinking water along with a fan, chair, and a table in each cell of every barrack.

02. Clean toilets with scheduled repairs and the freedom to use them any time of the day.

03. Access to study materials that include the morning newspaper and library books.

04. Refrigeration and better storage of vegetables and other edibles in the kitchen.

05. Use of electric bulbs and tubes in the veranda.

06. Round-the-clock availability of a doctor in the prison hospital.

After Aurangzeb heard Sahil, he paused and pondered for a few moments with his gaze fixed on Sahil. He did not say a word. All of a sudden, he unleashed thundering laughter. His ridiculous action surprised everybody gathered around him. He wagged his finger at his security guard while laughing, and issued a command.

Aurangzeb: "HAHAHA… Take them away and throw the scoundrels in their respective cells. Dinnertime is over. HAHAHA…"

His audacity perturbed Sahil. He tried to persuade him one last time.

Sahil: "B-b-but sir…"

But Sahil's intervention outraged him. He frowned his brows and roared in anger.

Aurangzeb: "Shut up before I pull out your tongue!"

Before Sahil could speak any further, the guards began pushing the inmates back to their cells. Though there was a bit of scuffle between both the parties, things did not get out of control. The prisoners returned to their barracks, and the rest of the night passed in peace for everyone.

But it was far from over. The ripple effects of the incidents of the night were visible in the next morning. Like every day, the peon pressed the buzzer and the loud siren resonated across the jail. It notified the inmates to jump onto their assigned tasks. But to his surprise, nobody turned up. Instead, they all sat idly in their respective cells, giving him dead-eyed looks. It seemed as though nobody was willing to do any work. Sensing something fishy, the peon informed Aurangzeb about it.

As soon as he heard about the disobedience, he issued an order that asked all the inmates to gather in the compound. Once they had all gathered in the ground, Aurangzeb marched to them with a thick-girded baton in his hand. He looked at everyone angrily and clenched his teeth.

Aurangzeb: "Why hasn't anyone started the work yet? Don't you remember the policy? No work, no food!"

Standing somewhere in the middle of the crowd, Chachoo spoke out with a smirk.

Chachoo: "Don't worry about the food, sir. The cooking team won't enter the kitchen today onward as well."

Many of the gathered inmates cracked up when they heard his words. The chuckles infuriated the brutish man further. Stumped by Chachoo's cheekiness, he walked to him and stood face to face with him and gave him an austere look. His stern glare scared Chachoo a little, and his face began to turn pale. But before he could inflict any harm on him, Sahil moved and stood between them. He looked straight into Aurangzeb's eyes, and the act baffled him. After a little pause, Sahil broke the silence.

Sahil: "Until you accept the demands we made last night, nobody here is going to work. Moreover, none of us will consume any water or food either. We are on an indefinite hunger strike henceforth!"

The statement came as a shock to Aurangzeb. With his vicious glare fixed at Sahil, he fell silent for a few moments. Then, a gradual haughty smile crept onto his face. He turned around and began to laugh. He paid no heed to Sahil's proclamation. Thinking it to be a joke of some kind, he started walking back to his office. But before he walked out of the compound, he offered a piece of advice to the kitchen team.

Aurangzeb: "When the hunger of these rascals crosses all limits, give them something to eat. I don't want them to disturb my sleep with their cries of agony."

But what Aurangzeb missed to gauge was the willpower that reflected on every inmate's face. As Sahil had asked them to, they skipped lunch and the tea. They refused to eat dinner as well. They knew that their defiance would put them at loggerheads with Aurangzeb. But even then, they were ready to embrace the outcome. They knew that every great victory needed a great endeavor. They boycotted work and remained confined to their cells as a mark of their protest. Though direct conflict with the brute was like skating on thin ice, none of them backed out. Twelve hours passed by, and as decided, no one consumed a single drop of water. The arrogant Aurangzeb didn't even care to inspect their health.

But things began to change when the strike entered the 24th hour. With butterflies in his stomach, Aurangzeb made his way to the compound. He was a bit worried after the inmates skipped their lunch on the second consecutive day. Gathered near the kitchen in the afternoon, and seated on the dusty floor, the inmates looked as cheerful as ever. With smiles on their faces, they crooned a folk song and clank their utensils to produce beats. The synchronized clinking of the empty plates with the empty steel mugs produced music that amused them all. The moment gave Aurangzeb the heebie-jeebies. He had not expected such jubilance from the starved and thirsty men. Flustered at their enthusiasm, he clenched his teeth in fury and stomped back to the office.

Days passed by, and with their faith still intact, the hunger strike entered its fifth day. None of them nibbled on even a single grain of rice in all those days. Soon, the news started to make the rounds. Under fire for his callous conduct, Aurangzeb drew heavy flak from his superiors. His boss called him one evening and reprimanded him for his poor handling of the situation.

Aurangzeb: "N-n-no, sir! D-don't worry, sir-yes-yes, sir! I-I ASSURE y…"

But his irked superior disconnected the call before he could complete his sentence. A distressed Aurangzeb put the phone down and held his bald head in his hands. He did not want the authorities to set up an inquiry against him, having misused the funds for years. Due to his pilferage, there wasn't any money left in the kitty to take care of the demands of the prisoners. He had no option but to persuade the protesting prisoners to call off their strike by hook or by crook.

****

At their usual dinnertime, the inmates gathered near the locked kitchen of the compound. Dehydrated and famished, they all looked feeble and frail. Though they all remained steady, Chachoo's health deteriorated. He lay on the floor while Ranga massaged his feet. Bheema and Sahil sat close to him with a concerned look on his face. Chachoo stirred and opened his eyes, flashing a tired grin when he saw Sahil. A worried Sahil caressed his hair.

Sahil: "Are you alright, Chachoo?"

Breathing slowly, he replied with parched lips.

Chachoo: "Ahhh…I-I am alright, son. D-don't worry."

Sahil: "Have some water, Chachoo! I don't think you are well."

Chachoo gave him a miserable smile.

Chachoo: "I am a tough nut to crack, son. My Krishna is with me. Nothing is…nothing will happen to me."

Sahil: "But Chachoo…"

Chachoo: "Don't insult me, son. I am all right. I won't lose the battle so soon."

Sahil sighed, and they both exchanged rueful smiles. But soon, the marching footsteps in the compound distracted the duo. A group of policemen came into view, followed by Aurangzeb. The policemen were carrying a huge wooden barrel on their shoulders. On Aurangzeb's command, they placed the barrel near Chachoo. The scene perplexed the hushed inmates, as ominous thoughts began to play in everyone's minds. Aurangzeb broke the ice with a disdainful smile by murmuring to Chachoo.

Aurangzeb: "What a pity! Why are you troubling your old and fragile body this way?"

Unable to stomach his sugarcoated words, Ranga and Bheema looked at each other in surprise. They had never heard any kind words from the rascal's mouth ever before. Then Aurangzeb looked around at the gathered prisoners and roared.

Aurangzeb: "Fellas, let's all call a truce! As a token, I will serve a delicious dessert to you all once a week. The entire expense will be on my shoulders. It's a promise. Is everyone alright with this?"

The gathered prisoners looked at him in surprise. But before anybody could respond, Sahil questioned him.

228

Sahil: "And what about the demands we asked you to consider the other day?"

The fake smile on Aurangzeb's face waned. His eyes widened in anger as he glared at Sahil. But keeping in mind the gravity of the matter, he feigned a smile again.

Aurangzeb: "Uhmmm…we are looking into them. We will take care of them as soon as we devise a plan. But until then, I want you guys to be patient and cooperate."

Sahil: "I am sorry, sir! But until you take care of our requests, the strike will not be over. We will neither work nor eat!"

Sahil's defiance irked him. Though he had been trying to veil his anger all this while, he blew his fuse at Sahil's words.

Aurangzeb: "Don't be so selfish, Sahil. Look around! Do you even care about the plight of these men?"

With these words, he walked to Chachoo, who was licking his dry lips with his dehydrated tongue. It was time to toy with the weak and hungry old man. Aurangzeb knew that Chachoo was the weakest link among all the adamant detainees. He looked at his men and gestured to them silently. One of the constables nodded in acknowledgment and took the lid off the wooden barrel.

As soon as the cop removed the lid, the aroma of boiled rice immersed in sweetened and steamy hot milk reached their nostrils. Though hunger and thirst dehydrated them, the aroma of hot milk made everyone's mouth water. All the prisoners stood up and looked at the barrel with immense yearning. The temptation was so intense that the empty stomachs of inmates began to growl audibly. Aurangzeb could see his plan working.

Aurangzeb: "Jump in, everybody! I have ordered *kheer* for you guys from the best sweet shop in Ratnagiri. Ah! It pains me every time I see you in this appalling state."

Since Aurangzeb did not take care of their demands, the prisoners thought to refuse the offer. But deep in their hearts, the starving inmates wanted to lunge on the hot milky dessert. They found it tough to endure hunger any longer. Everyone stood and looked at each other in anticipation. They waited for someone to make the first move. Sahil sensed and apprehended the feelings that played in their minds. Though he thought to ask them to hold their horses, he remained mum. He did not garner the courage after he looked at their hungry and low-spirited faces. He knew that Aurangzeb shed crocodile tears. But he left the final decision to the discretion of the inmates.

Standing at a corner, he crossed his arms and hurled a sigh in disenchantment.

Aurangzeb sensed that he was only one strike away from breaking the inmates' spirits. In the last leg of his ploy, he scooped the delicious dessert into a small bowl with a spoon. Then, with a shrewd smile on his lips, he brought the bowl close to Chachoo's lips. In a pretentious behavior, he asked the frail man to devour the sweet dish.

Aurangzeb: "Chachoo, come on, have some. Puchhh, have some!"

A flabbergasted Chachoo gazed at the milky dessert in the bowl. He held the bowl in his frail hands and looked up at Aurangzeb with quivering lips. He looked all set to consume the pudding. But then, he surprised everyone by refusing the enticing offer.

Chachoo: "I don't want it. Take it back!"

With these determined words, he handed the bowl back to Aurangzeb. Chachoo's defiance irked the tyrant. The phony smile vanished from his face and his eyes widened in fury. With a stern expression, he scoffed and tried to force the pudding into his mouth.

Aurangzeb: "Take it, I say! Don't you dare to refuse me, you understand? Take it!"

But Chachoo did not give up. Though hunger and thirst had tired him out, he resisted the man with his full might. In one defiant moment, Chachoo clenched his teeth and pushed the bowl away from him. Aurangzeb lost his grip over the utensil and it fell on the floor. The creamy pudding spilled over Aurangzeb and stained his black beard. As the milk splattered over his beard and lips, he became the butt of everyone's jokes. Not only the prisoners but a few policemen too began laughing at him.

Outraged, Aurangzeb pounced on Chachoo and held him by his collar. But his hideous action revitalized the tired prisoners. A scuffle broke out between the prisoners and the policemen. Sahil pushed Aurangzeb away from Chachoo. Soon, a few constables intervened and scooted the prisoners back to their barracks. Aurangzeb glared at Chachoo obnoxiously, but he did not say another word to him. With a fuming expression on his face, he turned around and stomped back to his office.

****

The night intensified, but there was no sleep in Aurangzeb's eyes. Dressed in his nightgown and seated in his room, he snuffed in anger. The insulting moment when Chachoo had stained his face with

230

the sweet kept playing in his mind. His body shivered in a fit of rage when he recalled everyone mocking him and laughing at him. He snapped out of his thoughts when he heard a knock on his door. He had summoned three constables. As soon as they took a position in front of him, he stared at them and issued a command.

Aurangzeb: "Pick him up!"

The guards nodded in silence. They marched to barrack#3 and unlocked its gates. The loud squeaking of the gate startled Chachoo out of his sleep. With an abrupt jolt, Sahil, Ranga, and Bheema awakened as well. The sight of the three guards frightened them all. Chachoo's behavior with Aurangzeb was still fresh in everyone's minds. With ominous thoughts in his mind, Chachoo stammered his query to the policemen in a frail voice.

Chachoo: "W-what is the matter, sir?"

But the stomping cops did not say a word and inched closer to him. They looked like they had every intention to inflict harm on him. Sahil stood up and ran to him, then braced his arms around Chachoo to shield him. But contrary to everyone's anticipation, the guards did not even touch Chachoo. Instead, they grabbed Sahil by his shoulders and dragged him out of the cell.

Stunned by their actions, Sahil trembled and looked around frantically. Chachoo, Ranga, and Bheema ran towards the guards in an attempt to free Sahil from their grasp. But they failed as the guards locked the gate in the nick of time. They clasped the prison bars and screamed at the top of their lungs. Their ear-deafening screams woke up the detainees in the other barracks too. They clung to their prison bars in horror when they saw the cops hauling Sahil to the front office. They knew something terrible was on the cards.

The guards pushed Sahil onto a single mattress bed in the dormitory of the office. Once he lay on the bed, the cops gripped his hands and legs by force. A tormented Sahil screamed in panic.

Sahil: "Why have you brought me here at this time of the night?"

But before anyone could reply, Aurangzeb slammed the door open and walked into the dorm. He stood beside Sahil with a wicked smile. Sahil looked up at the baldhead and clenched his teeth in anger. The demeanor of the cruel man baffled him.

Sahil: "What are you up to?"

Aurangzeb knelt and moved close to Sahil's terrified face.

Aurangzeb: "I know it! Everything is happening on your instructions. You have to call off the ongoing strike immediately. Tomorrow morning, I shouldn't see any prisoner sitting in agitation. Am I clear, Sahil?"

Though scared, Sahil clenched his teeth in agony and obstinately refused his command.

Sahil: "Never! Until you implement all our demands, none of us will back down."

Aurangzeb: "I say, stop them! I am asking you for the last time, Sahil. Will you call off the strike or not?"

Sahil: "No, I won't!"

Aurangzeb's anger hit the roof. His lower lip quivered with rage. He turned around and walked to a cabinet in the other corner of the room. From its topmost drawer, he pulled out a plier. He walked back to Sahil and stood next to his feet. Sahil's heart began thudding when Aurangzeb clipped the plier to one of the toenails on his right foot. The act sent chills down Sahil's spine. Tiny droplets of sweat broke out on his forehead as he foresaw the brute's next move.

Sahil: "N-n-n-no… Au-Au-Aurangzeb! This is not the way. L-l-listen you can't d-do this."

But his pleas did not melt the swine's heart, and Aurangzeb burst into loud laughter. Then, with an arrogant smile, he proclaimed loudly.

Aurangzeb: "YES, I CERTAINLY CANNNNNNNN!"

With these words, he pulled the plier with demonic force, wrenching Sahil's toenail from his flesh. A deafening and heart-rending scream of agony left Sahil's mouth. Sickened by the brutish act, even the three constables frowned and looked away in disgust. The scene was downright unbearable and barbaric.

After a while, the guards pushed an unconscious Sahil into his barrack. Though weak at the knees, Chachoo ran to him in panic. Bheema and Ranga had not slept all this while either. They came running to the fence that separated them from Sahil's cell. Perplexed, they looked at a semiconscious Sahil's face. He frowned and moaned in pain with partially closed eyes. With no provision of light in the dark cell, Chachoo touched Sahil's bloodstained foot with his finger, and felt the warmth of his blood. Bheema frowned and cried out.

Bheema: "What happened to him?"

Chachoo examined the wound on his foot and gulped in terror.

Chachoo: "The weasel pulled out his toenail, same way he had done it to many other prisoners earlier!"

Chachoo's words sent shock waves through the two men.

Ranga: "What?"

Without losing any time, Chachoo ripped off a part of his sleeve and wrapped it over the wound. He removed his own fabric cap and cradled Sahil's head in his lap. Then, he fanned Sahil's sweaty face with his cap to offer him some relief from the humidity of the night. Though weak with dehydration himself, he caressed Sahil's hair affectionately until the crack of dawn.

****

At lunchtime the next day, Aurangzeb stepped into the compound and took stock of the situation. Though uncertain at first, the sight of the fatigued men squatted on the floor of the kitchen amused him. The absence of Sahil in the crowd of prisoners pleased him even more. Thinking he would be resting in his cell after last night's torture, he laughed out loudly. With no Sahil around, he knew it would be easier for him to break and tame the protesting prisoners. With a conceited smile on his face, he roared in a rejoiced voice.

Aurangzeb: "Enough of this nonsense now! Cooking team, make your way to the kitchen. It's been a while since you guys stepped in it. Hurry!"

After issuing the diktat in a conceited smile, he turned around and started to walk back to his office. It appeared to him that he had won the battle. But he halted in his steps when he heard the shrill clang of metals. He turned around, and his feet went numb when he saw the sight in front of him. He stood shell-shocked as Sahil appeared in the crowd with a metal plate in one hand and an empty metal mug in the other. With his teeth clenched, he limped forward with a bandaged foot. His cracked and blackened lips trembled. With tears of agony dripping down his face, he beat the empty utensils together once again. The loud *clang* of the utensils reenergized the dog-tired prisoners. Every inmate picked up a plate and cup from a stack of utensils arranged on a shelf in the kitchen. As Sahil did, they struck their plates and mugs against each other aggressively, over and over. The loud clanks echoed in all directions of the compound under the open sky. The revolt was still alive, and the agitation was not going to die anytime soon.

Stunned, Aurangzeb stared at Sahil with a shocked expression, knowing he had lost to Sahil. Sahil fixed his gaze at Aurangzeb, and a victorious smile crept onto his face. An embarrassed Aurangzeb looked down and walked back to his office. The re-vitalized prisoners smiled and hugged each other in joy. Their ongoing rebellion was not over yet!

On the next day, a daily newspaper leaked and exposed Aurangzeb's barbaric reign on the first page. And soon, the appalling piece of news spread like a wildfire. And after the information went viral, the higher authorities suspended Aurangzeb immediately. Also, the officials decided to set up a probe against him for misappropriating the funds. But for the prisoners, the moment of glory arrived two days later when their strike entered its ninth day. In a remedy, the pressurized officials accepted all the demands made by the inmates. A celebration broke out when a constable walked to the inmates gathered in the compound at the night and broke the news. It was the moment every prisoner had been waiting for over a week. Their courageous uprising had finally paid off. The gathered prisoners hooted in joy and danced in the compound. An exuberant Sahil hugged Ranga and Bheema. Then, he sprinted to his cell to inform Chachoo about the same. Chachoo had been resting in the cell all day due to his poor health.

Eager to share the good news with his cellmate, Sahil ran into the cell. He placed his hands on his waist and paused to catch his breath. Then, he puffed out his cheeks and smiled when he saw Chachoo lay on the floor with a blanket yanked over his face. He pulled the blanket off Chachoo with a grin, as he couldn't wait to share the news with him.

But he gasped as soon as he saw Chachoo's face. His dried lips had turned bluish. With fluttering eyes, Chachoo was breathing erratically. Also, his body felt too cold to touch. The visual frightened the wits out of Sahil. Immediately, he began rubbing and massaging Chachoo's cold hands. He rubbed his cheeks frantically in an attempt to revive him. But it was too late, perhaps. Hit by terminal dehydration, Chachoo was breathing his last. Sahil broke down and shook Chachoo by the shoulder. He cradled his face in his hands.

Sahil: "Chachoo? Wake up, Chachoo!"

When the inmates heard his scream, they came running to his cell. Ranga and Bheema gasped at the sight of Chachoo. They sat on the floor along with Sahil, while the others surrounded Chachoo with glum faces. It was a somber moment for everyone, as all loved him. He was one of the oldest companions they had, and everybody shared a deep attachment with him. Sahil continued to shake Chachoo's shoulders and yelled at him. And as he did so, his tears dripped onto Chachoo's forehead.

Sahil: "Chachoo, ahhh…ahhh…wake up! Chachoo! Please…"

But in a miraculous moment, the sensation of Sahil's tears on his skin prompted some movement in Chachoo. His lashes fluttered and he slowly opened his eyes amid groans. He fixed his gaze on Sahil, and a shivering smile spread across his face. His lower lip quivered, and tears welled up in his eyes. Finally, amid hiccups, he stammered a few words to Sahil in a frail voice.

Chachoo: "Hic…my Krishna…hic… I have waited for you all my life…hic…for my salvation…hic… I am…hic…honored…hic…and blessed…hic… My Krishna…hic… You finally visited me…hic…"

His strange words baffled everybody around him. Sahil caressed his face and tried to bring him back to his senses.

Sahil: "Come back to your senses, Chachoo! I am Sahil. Don't you recognize me?"

But Sahil was mistaken. Chachoo wasn't hallucinating. He understood every word that he was speaking at that moment.

Chachoo: "I…hic…recognized you…hic…when I …hic…saw you for…hic…the first time in jail…hic… I knew that…hic…Krishna has visited me…"

Though no one else understood his words, Sahil recalled his first day in jail. He recollected Chachoo enchanted gaze at him when they had met for the first time. He remembered his unfinished words to him during his first day in jail.

Chachoo: *"One time or the other, he will come down from his abode in some incarnation. I always wondered if I would ever recognize him if h—"*

Sahil came out of his brief trance and looked at Chachoo. His next words confirmed his guess.

Chachoo: "You have come down to bail everyone out of their woes…hic…to annihilate the demons…hic…the preserver…hic…the protector…hic…whenever the evil threatens mankind…hic—"

But he never completed his words. With his gaze fixed on Sahil, he passed away with a smile on his face. Unable to control his emotions, Sahil buried his face in Chachoo's chest and wept. Shattered by the loss, everyone standing around began to weep. There was no dry eye at that moment. In a matter of minutes, their exhilaration had turned into grief. Though the inmates had called off the strike, none of them ate any food in the moment of mourning. The kitchen remained closed that night as well, though for a different reason.

20. The Exposé

6 days to the gallows

After Chachoo's demise, the officials implemented the inmates' demands in no time. Two deaths in a week had raised a big question mark regarding their credibility. The authorities tried their best to bring an end to the woes faced by the prisoners. The instrumental changes were visible to the public eye in a remarkable way. The prisoners were allowed to use the toilet at any time of the day, not simply for one hour in the morning. The officials restricted the inmates' movements only at nighttime. The authorities ordered the guards to keep the barrack gates unlocked from 5 in the morning to 10 in the night. It meant that during the day, the prisoners were free to roam around and visit their fellow mates in other cells.

Moreover, the officials released funds and took care of the mandatory amenities as the top priority. A few of the inmates volunteered and installed the broad tube lights in the veranda. The authorities equipped every cell of the barrack with a pot containing clean drinking water as well as a table and chair. Moreover, a pedestal fan was set up in every single cell of the barrack. They also gave all the detainees restricted access to the jail library, where they had access to newspapers and other reading materials. Moreover, a prisoner could issue any book in their name for a maximum of three days.

The officials took special care of every detainee's health and hygiene as well. A team of volunteer inmates was set up to sanitize the toilet. The authorities even hired labor to fix the glitches in the toilet equipment.

Moreover, they took adequate steps to store and preserve leftover food in a better way. The cleaning staff sanitized the entire kitchen, and a counter-depth refrigerator was installed too. The officials set up a nutritious menu for the prisoners, including a special meal for the Sunday lunch. Authorities also made it mandatory for jail officials to inspect the food before serving it to the inmates.

Going a step ahead, the authorities hired Mr. Sen as the permanent doctor for the jail hospital. They also appointed a full-time medical staff to work throughout the week.

But it was Aurangzeb's suspension that pleased the prisoners the most. Charged for misappropriating funds, the authorities set up an inquiry on him. The piece of news felt like music to the ears of the inmates. Though the officials had immediately relieved him of his duties, the substitute officer did not arrive for a few days. A sense of anxiety prevailed in the jail the day the new officer was scheduled to arrive. Nobody knew any details about the identity of the man, but a cleanliness drive was in full swing since the early morning.

Being the gardener of the jail, Sahil was hoeing the flowerbed in the lawn of the front office. Though Sahil didn't notice, the new supervisor walked and stood behind him. Then, in a heavy voice, he passed an instruction to Sahil.

Jail Supervisor: "Can you put in some white flowers too? These are too bright to look at."

Sahil frowned and turned around as the voice sounded familiar. And he was startled to see the man who had uttered these words. Holding the hand of his three-year-old son, Khan was standing before him. However, a glimpse of Sahil baffled Khan even more, and he looked Sahil up and down. Sahil now had shorter hair and a clean-shaven face. He seemed to have lost a few kilos in the past month. Moreover, he noticed that a solemn demeanor had replaced his earlier egoistic semblance. Sahil greeted Khan with a gentle smile.

Sahil: "Hello, Khan. Good morning!"

Khan: "Good morning, Sahil."

Sahil: "Are you taking over from Aurangzeb?"

Khan: "Umm…yeah, but only for a week. There will be a new custodian after that. I am here on a specific assignment."

With his gaze fixed at Khan and a wistful smile on his face, Sahil tried to guess Khan's so-called assignment.

Sahil: "To take care of my execution? That's it, isn't it?"

Sahil's words stumped Khan. He was right in his assessment. With no other officer in the reckoning, the officials had been unable to find a replacement for Aurangzeb. So, they had asked Khan to supervise the jail for a week. His job was to make sure that Sahil's hanging goes smoothly and without a hitch. Although Sahil had sniffed out his intentions, Khan found it embarrassing to confirm the fact.

Khan: "Ummm…I hope you hoe in some light-colored flowers, as I asked."

Sahil was wise enough to understand Khan's apprehension. He decided not to pester Khan much about it.

Sahil: "I need some more time, sir. I'll be able to finish it in about half an hour."

Thanking Sahil with a silent nod, Khan made his way back to

the front office with his son. Sahil turned his attention back to his unfinished work on the flowerbed. Suddenly, Khan received a phone call from his superior. Being engrossed in the call, he did not realize that his son had walked back to Sahil in the lawn. And then, an unknown fear pierced Khan when he heard his son's scream. He looked around and panicked when he didn't see his child in the office. A chill ran down his spine when he realized that his son must have made his way back to the lawn, where Sahil was. He recalled the gruesome murders that Sahil had committed. He shuddered when the appalling thought of Sahil strangling his child flashed across his mind.

Khan's eyes widened in despair, and he dropped the phone in horror. He had played a major role in Sahil's arrest and conviction and Sahil could be desperate for revenge. Khan sprinted to the lawn, convinced that Sahil would try to inflict some harm on his kid for vengeance. But as soon as he reached the lawn, the sight in front of him made his blood run cold. Sahil was standing with one arm around the little kid's belly and another over the kid's mouth to gag him.

Khan clenched his teeth in anger and unclipped his holster as he inched closer to Sahil and his gagged son. He prepared himself for a possible scuffle with Sahil. But what he saw next made him stop himself from pulling out his gun. Though Sahil was holding and gagging the kid, he didn't seem to be inflicting any harm. Instead, they both seemed terrified of something in the middle of the lawn. Much to Khan's surprise, his son did not pay any heed to him even when he stood next to him. Khan frowned and followed their gaze to comprehend the duo's strange behavior. And the sight of a big black cobra with a raised hood stunned him. The hissing snake was at a striking distance of about five feet from the trio of Sahil, the kid, and Khan. They stood at risk of getting bitten by the deadly serpent.

Khan was quick to understand the situation. Sahil had gagged his son because he didn't want him to make a sound and provoke the deadly reptile in any way. Khan thought to take action, but he halted when he noticed Sahil staring at him and shaking his head. Sahil didn't want him to act in haste. The serpent felt threatened, and Sahil knew that any wrong move could lead them to a painful death. The three of them stood still, breathing slowly. Sahil was waiting for an appropriate moment to make his next move, and he found one after standing still for a couple of minutes.

With its hood spread out, the cobra turned to its side, looking for an escape route. In a flash, Sahil pulled out the gun from Khan's unclipped holster and fired at the snake. The shot was as precise as it could be, and it blew the snake's hood to pieces. The deadly reptile lay dead in its blood on the lawn.

Once the disaster was averted, Sahil sighed in relief and loosened his grip on the kid. Being in shock, the toddler ran to Khan and embraced his legs before bursting into tears. There was a small cluster of smoke around the gun's nozzle. Sahil placed the gun on his palm and offered it back to Khan with a smile on his face. Khan gulped and looked at Sahil before grabbing the gun. Armed constables came running to the lawn upon hearing the loud gunshot. They aimed their guns at Sahil but held their horses when Khan intervened.

Khan: "Relax. Umm…this c-cobra made its way to the lawn before…umm…I shot it. Take it away and burn it."

On his command, the guards picked up the dead snake and left. Khan had lied to them since it was illegal for any civilian to use a service pistol. Sahil was already in dire straits, and Khan did not want to complicate matters any further for him.

Khan: "Thank you, Sahil! No words are enough to thank you for what you have done."

Sahil: "I am glad he is fine. My heart was in my mouth all that while."

Khan reciprocated with a smile. But then, his smile vanished, and a disturbed expression reflected on his face. He gulped and walked closer to Sahil.

Khan: "You killed Tatya in the same way, didn't you?"

Khan's query about Tatya rattled Sahil, re-opening Sahil's old wounds. He recalled shooting Tatya dead from a point-blank range, just like he had shot the cobra moments ago. The sound of the gunshot he had fired at Tatya was still fresh in his mind. That particular incident was one of the tensest moments of his life. He sighed and licked his lips with his tongue.

Sahil: "I already confessed that in court, didn't I?"

But with his gaze fixed at Sahil, Khan rebutted him.

Khan: "Yes you did, but not in the way you narrated it in court. You zapped him in a flash without even letting him know what was coming. You never wrestled with him, as you stated in your confession."

Afraid that Khan was close to the truth, Sahil avoided the question. He changed the conversation nervously.

Sahil: "Umm…I have put in some white lily and pink rose saplings. You will have a dazzling view of blooming flowers in a few days. Now, it is lunchtime. I hope you don't mind if I go and grab some food. I…umm…am starving. All the best to you for your assignment. Break a leg, Khan."

With these words, Sahil turned around and began to walk back to the compound. Khan sighed and looked down at the ground in confusion, aware that Sahil hadn't directly answered him. But as he looked down, he had an epiphany. He looked up at Sahil with a shocked expression on his face. His eyes widened in surprise. He sprinted behind Sahil and held him by his collar. His move startled Sahil, who turned around in shock. Baffled by Khan's actions, Sahil questioned his conduct.

Sahil: "W-what happened, Khan? All okay?"

But Khan remained silent. He felt choked up as emotions were running high in him. He panted audibly as his lower lip trembled in trepidation. Khan cleared his throat.

Khan: "Mhmm…Mhmm…w-what did you say?"

Khan's abnormal behavior flummoxed Sahil, especially after he had saved his son's life just a little while ago. Sahil tried to be as honest as possible in his reply.

Sahil: "I-I asked if I can have my foo—"

Khan: "No, Sahil, what did you say in the end? Your last few words!"

Sahil's face turned pale when he recalled his last words to Khan. Khan failed to control his emotions, and tears welled up in his eyes. His voice quivered as he made an assertion.

Khan: "Break a leg…isn't that what you uttered? I had never heard these words until one man started addressing them to me every time he spoke or communicated with me. The evidence supplied by that man played a pivotal role in your arrest and conviction. I recently started to believe that my faceless friend was Dhananjay. I thought it was him who helped me crack this case and guided me whenever I felt directionless."

Sahil went numb when he heard Khan's heartfelt words. Khan's lips fluttered before he broke down despite trying to hold back his tears.

Khan: "W-Was I wrong to think him as my helper, Sahil? Instead, are you…are you the whistleblower friend of mine?"

Sahil held back his tears as he felt an immense pang. He gulped and shook his head nervously.

Sahil: "I-I-I-don't know what you're talking about, Khan. You are clutching at straws."

Annoyed by Sahil's denial, Khan clenched his teeth and tightened his grip on his collar. His body was visibly trembling.

Khan: "No, no, no! It's the same tone and the same pitch. I recognize the voice that uttered these words during every call. Oh my God! H-h-h-how did I miss this? You sent the evidence my way despite knowing they would indict you as the culprit. B-but…why?"

Sahil had regained control over his nerves by this time. He loosened Khan's grip on his collar and pushed him back gently. Then, he replied with a miserable smile.

Sahil: "I don't know what evidence you are talking about. I never called you. You are mistaken. Now, enjoy the rest of the day with your son. I need to go and have my lunch, Khan. I don't want to starve to death."

With these words, Sahil turned around and walked to the kitchen. But a distressed Khan stood back and gazed at Sahil in despair.

Khan: "I'm going to dive deep into it, Sahil. It's not over yet."

With a slice of bread and curry on his plate, Sahil was lost in deep thought. He had slipped into some of the darker memories of his past. He thought about the awful night when Harak Singh had murdered Boney in front of his eyes. He recollected the moment he had seen and heard Thakur boasting about his evil deeds in the chamber. He remembered Thakur rejecting his plea and refusing to surrender to the cops. He could not forget his deception when he agreed to work with Thakur only to destroy his empire.

Then, he shifted his focus to some of the surreptitious events that he had hidden from the world. Khan had guessed right. It was not Dhananjay, but Sahil instead, who had mailed all the evidence to Khan. Sahil recalled the night he had dialed Khan to give him details of Tatya's movement with the bodies of the informers the next morning.

Sahil: *"Listen carefully, Khan. Tomorrow at 6 in the morning, a van with two dead bodies will make its way to the Ratnagiri checkpoint. Nab the van, and you'll get the man you are looking for. Tomorrow, at 6 am. Break a leg, Khan"*

Then, he had warned Tatya and asked him to deliver the bodies during the night itself, even though he had informed Khan about Tatya's travel in the morning. He had not wanted Tatya to fall into the trap.

Sahil: *"Tatya! I want you to leave for Rajvanshi's place right now. Start moving!"*

He also remembered the music he faced when Khan did not catch Tatya the next morning.

Khan: *"You cheat! You gave me false information. Do you know that it is a crime to mislead the police?"*

Sahil: *"I swear on the soul of my dead father, Khan. One day, I will hand over the culprits to you. Trust me, Khan. Wait for my tip. Break a leg, Khan"*

Then, with a grin on his face, he recalled his chat with Khan on one occasion. In an over-excitement, Khan spilled the beans about some letter that he had received. As per the letter, the man who penned it would be soon posting some evidence to Khan. In an error, Khan thought his caller friend as the one who posted it, though Sahil had never mailed it to him.

Khan: *"I received your letter about the evidence to nail the killers. When can I expect it to be in my hands?"*

Sahil always believed that Alok had amassed some damning evidence against Thakur. He had a weird feeling that Dhananjay, being Alok's son, had plans to turn to the cops with the evidence gathered by his father. And Khan's casual words vindicated his guess. After Alok's murder, there was nobody else, but Dhananjay, who could dare to share any of Thakur's information with the cops. Though Khan's words had shocked him, he handled the conversation with serenity.

Sahil: *"Ummm…you need to wait a little longer. For now, I have some other news for you."*

In the same conversation with Khan, Sahil tipped him off about Tatya's plan to deliver John's body to Rajvanshi.

Sahil: *"A blue van is heading for Pune. It should cross the checkpoint in about fifteen minutes. Get ahold of it."*

Khan: *"I hope this doesn't turn out to be a hoax call like it did last time."*

Sahil: *"You are losing precious time. Remember, a blue van, fifteen minutes! Break a leg, Khan."*

He still remembered Khan's remorseful words after he failed to nab Tatya.

Khan: *"Sorry, friend, but I failed to nab him. I ran out of luck at the very last moment."*

Sahil: *"I risked my life to give you those leads. But if you keep failing, it is not worth putting my life in danger any longer."*

Khan: *"I promise I'll catch the bastards this time. Give me one more chance, just one!"*

Sahil: *"Wait for my next clue. Break a leg, Khan."*

As he walked to his cell, he recalled the night he had abducted Dhananjay and seized all the evidence from him. Sahil was the one who had mailed that evidence to Khan. Dhananjay had neither called Khan nor posted any evidence to him. He recalled how he had shuddered while penning a note to Khan along with the evidence. He recalled a couple of lines that he had jotted in that note, *"Raid and arrest the bastards"* and *"The ball is in your court now. Break a leg, Khan."*

Since Sahil sent that letter to Khan, he had been aware that Khan had been on his way to raid the party. But he did not flee from the party, as he wanted Khan to arrest him red-handed. He had deliberately killed all the others at the party before Khan arrived at the venue. As proven in court, he did poison Sikander and Rajvanshi along with their men. The deafening sound of the gunshot that killed Tatya was still fresh in his mind.

Sahil: *"For one last time, Tatya, CHECK AND MATE!"*

He paced in his cell as he reminisced these bitter memories. Shaken by the horrific memories of his dark past, he poured some water from the pot into an empty glass and gulped it all down in one go. He wiped his mouth with his palm.

****

The same day, in the evening, Dhananjay opened the entrance door to his new home when he heard a knock. And the sight of a visibly furious Khan standing in front of him surprised him. Before Dhananjay could speak a word, Khan grabbed his neck and shoved him back with force.

Dhananjay: "Kh-Kh-Khan. What are you doing?"

Khan: "Did you post me the letters and pictures or even a shred of evidence against Sahil? Hmm? Was it you who called me to give me breakthroughs? Was it you? Tell me, Dhananjay."

Dhananjay: "Y-yes. Of course, it-it was m-m-me."

Khan: "Not a lie anymore, you scoundrel! If you speak one more lie, I will break your neck. Tell me the truth!"

Struggling to breathe, he nodded and tapped the back of Khan's hand. As soon as Khan loosened his grip, Dhananjay panted to regain his breath.

Dhananjay: "Hffff…Hffff…okay. I…I confess that I never did. I never mailed any copy of the evidence to you because I never had any. I had collected all that evidence from the publishing house with the intent of passing them to you. But before I could reach the police station, Sahil's men picked me up and snatched everything I had. In return, he offered me a sum of money."

The piece of information shocked Khan. He frowned in

despair.

Khan: "What? Sahil offered you money in exchange for the evidence?"

Dhananjay nodded in embarrassment without saying a word.

Khan: "Then why did you lie in your testimony?"

Dhananjay sighed guiltily when he heard Khan's query.

Dhananjay: "That day, when I had come to meet you in the police station, I wanted to ask if you got your hands on the evidence that Sahil snatched from me. But you mistook me for the one who helped you. Then, you notified me about the bounty declared on Sahil's head. Hence, I went along with it for the prize money, and I lied to you. Moreover, I sought revenge from Sahil for killing my father."

Khan recalled his small tête-à-tête with Dhananjay after the first hearing in court. He had proclaimed Dhananjay as the recipient of the bounty declared on Sahil's head.

Dhananjay: *"…did you get the evidence that —"*

Khan: *"Yes, yes. We got it, and thank you for a zillion times for that. You are entitled to a cash reward of one million rupees. The posse carried a bounty on their head. And since you sent us the package with all the evidence, you deserve the reward. I'll ask Talwar to make a formal request to the court to declare you as the sole beneficiary of the prize money."*

Khan cleared his throat and put forth his next question.

Khan: "Mhmm…but even before I told you about the prize money, why did you lie about the letters you wrote to me? You said you wrote both the letters that—"

But Dhananjay intervened and refuted Khan's claim before he could finish his words. He frowned at him in surprise.

Dhananjay: "Both the letters? I never said that! I wrote only one, wherein I mentioned my intent to hand over the evidence to you. But before I could do that, Sahil and his men snatched everything from me, as I have told you already."

Dhananjay's statement stumped Khan. He recalled receiving the two letters on two different days. The man who had penned the first letter had desired to meet him and did not reveal any significant details. That letter hadn't been of any use to him. But the second letter was substantial and matched the style of the man who had called him at his desk, whom he now knew was Sahil. Dhananjay was right indeed. Although Khan had assumed Dhananjay to pen the second letter, he had never made any such claim. Instead, Sahil wrote and posted the second letter to him. Khan recognized his blunder at the time. While

Dhananjay had been talking about the first letter, Khan mistook him as to have written both the letters.

Dhananjay: *"Did…umm…did you get the letter mentioning the evidence against Sahil and his men?"*

Khan: *"Yes I did. But how do you know about it?"*

Dhananjay: *"Perhaps you did not recognize me. I was the one who wrote it to you!"*

Khan: *"What? A-are you, my secret friend?"*

Dhananjay: *"Yes, sir."*

Khan let out a deep sigh. He lowered his head in shame. He gulped and cleared his throat in dejection.

Khan: "Mhmm…Did you look into the evidence contained in the parcel before Sahil snatched it from you? At that time, did it contain pictures and documents that indicated Sahil to be the kingpin?"

Dhananjay shook his head in shame.

Dhananjay: "No, I never did. I picked up the sealed parcel as it is from the publishing house. I never got a chance to open and inspect it."

Khan sighed in distress. He had a strong feeling that Sahil tampered with it before he posted the fudged documents to him. An embarrassed Dhananjay looked at Khan and spoke in nervous pitch.

Dhananjay: "Umm…if you feel that he did not kill my father, can…can I do anything to save him?"

Khan glared at him and replied in a shattered voice.

Khan: "You pushed a man into the jaws of death for a few bucks. Why do you want to save him now?"

Dhananjay couldn't explain the guilt he felt within. He gulped in shame before replying.

Dhananjay: "Because of…that smile!"

Khan: "What?"

Dhananjay: "I had been burning in the fire of vengeance since the day he admitted to have killed my father. My rage and desire for revenge amplified with each passing day. All that while in the trial, I wished he would be hung to death. I was ecstatic when the court delivered the verdict I had sought. He stood in front of me in the witness box as a few cops tried to handcuff him. Our gazes were fixed at each other. I smiled at him arrogantly and triumphantly, and I expected vicious or obnoxious behavior from him in return. But instead, he gave me a brief, miserable smile. It was an egoless and kind smile that seemed to be saying, 'Thank you'! I didn't get any sleep that night, Khan. That smile pierces my heart whenever I recall it. Perhaps I will remember that smile on his lips forever. Tell me, Khan. Can I do something to save him?"

Khan: "I wish I could answer that question, but I am not sure if we can help him hereon. Be ready to answer your conscience if something unjust or wrong happens to the boy. It will haunt you every moment for the rest of your life. If he gets what he doesn't deserve, you will not attain any peace till eternity, Dhananjay. Mark my words."

With these words, Khan exited the bungalow, while Dhananjay, continued looking at Khan dolefully.

****

It turned out to be a busy day for Khan. Later that night, he sat in the cabin of Ms. Usha, his superior. Widely respected across the department, she was a role model for many because of her trademark brutal honesty. They both sipped on tea before Ms. Usha started the conversation.

Usha: "Tell me, Khan. What brings you here? And that too at this time of the night!"

He gulped the last sip of his tea hastily and placed the cup back on the table with care.

Khan: "Uhmmm, Uhmmm. I don't know how to say it, madam. It's complicated."

Usha: "Is everything okay, Khan? You look disturbed."

Khan: "About a month ago, the court convicted a man on the charges of mass murders in an organ trafficking case. Did you follow the case? It was one of the most talked-about cases on the news."

She pondered and fell silent for a moment, trying to recall the case Khan was talking about.

Usha: "Oh, yes, I remember. It was an incredible achievement, Khan. The culprit had been eluding us for a long time, and you cracked the case within a couple of months. The department is indeed proud of you. I hope you are talking about the same case?"

Khan: "Yes, madam, I am talking about the same case. The culprit's name is Sahil, and he is currently in jail under my supervision. I…umm…I need your help in getting his hanging deferred."

His words baffled Ms. Usha.

Usha: "What? You want his execution deferred? But why? The police demanded a death sentence for him in the charge sheet submitted to the court. Why this sudden change of heart?"

Khan: "I have a feeling that there is a lot more to this case than meets the eye."

He narrated to her the incident in the morning when Sahil saved his son's life. He also described his encounter with Dhananjay earlier that day and his false testimony in court. Then, he placed the two letters side by side on the table before her. Dhananjay had already confirmed that he wrote the letter on the left. Though Sahil did not agree, Khan strongly believed it was Sahil indeed who had penned the letter on right. He had mailed it along with other evidence. Ms. Usha wore her glasses and looked at both the letters. She carefully read every single word written in both letters.

Letter#1 (Penned by Dhananjay)	Letter#2 (Penned by Sahil)
Inspector Khan, *I will soon have some evidence that will help you nab the culprits in the case you are investigating. I am sure that the documents will give a whole new direction to the case. Once I get ahold of it, I will send it to you through the mail. Please be alert and keep an eye on your mailbox henceforth.* *- Your well-wisher*	*Hi, Khan,* *I hope you get this letter by the 12th of February, a day many will remember as the day of reckoning. Go through the parcel I have sent with this letter. It contains pictures of the kingpin behind all the slaughters in Ratnagiri. The parcel also contains pictures of some of his other aides. Also, go through other documents enclosed in the envelope. In addition to the evidence, the parcel contains an address as well. At around ten in the night, arrive at the given address and bust the place. You will find the entire contingent behind the massacres. Raid and arrest the bastards. This is our last communication, Khan. I have shared with you whatever I could. I have nothing more. The ball is in your court now. Break a leg, Khan.* *- A friend forever*

After she went through both the letters, she took off her glasses and placed them on the table near the letters. She sighed, not entirely convinced yet.

Usha: "I am glad that Sahil saved your son's life, but it doesn't serve as evidence to your hypothesis. Coming to Dhananjay's statement, let us assume that whatever he confessed to you is the truth and that he lied in his testimony to the court. His false testimony still doesn't prove that Sahil mailed you the other note and the vital evidence. Why would Sahil send you the evidence when it is good enough to send him to the gallows? I doubt any sane man would do that to himself."

Khan: "I already told you, it is complicated."

Ms. Usha slumped back in her chair. She had great regard for Khan and knew that he was not one to fire shots in the dark. After a brief pause, she asked him an intriguing question.

Usha: "Are you telling me that he is innocent and had no role in the Ratnagiri killings? In that case, how do you explain the picture with his foot on a corpse? And what about his picture with the most-wanted organ trade kingpin, Rajvanshi?"

Khan: "I don't have answers to your questions as of now. But in prejudice towards Sahil, everyone overlooked some other small but crucial aspects."

With those words, he unzipped a folder and pulled out Sahil's case file. Then he handed the file in her hands. Ms. Usha was already working overtime. After a hectic week at the office, she yearned to go home early that day to spend some quality time with her family. But the closed case file was too tempting to pass up. After about an hour of going through the file, she addressed Khan.

Usha: "I have never read such an interesting case before. But which vital aspects are you talking about? The case seems crystal clear to me. Sahil admitted to his crimes in his confession at the end of the second hearing."

Khan: "I…umm…want you to go through Jitsu's testimony once again. Everyone in the court, including myself, heard and paid attention only to the first half of his testimony. His testimony was the turning point in deciding Sahil's fate. His words led the court to believe that Sahil bought the liquor from him and poisoned it. But I want you to go through Jitsu's reply to Batuk's query when he narrated his confrontation with Sahil."

Khan highlighted a few sections of the testimony with a yellow marker pen and asked her to go through it once again. She pursed her lips and looked at the marked portions again.

Sahil: *"I placed an order for fifteen cartons. There are only ten here. Where are the rest?"*

Jitsu: *"No, sir. You ordered ten cartons. I even confirmed the order with you on the phone."*

Sahil: *"I don't want to do any more business with rascals like you. Just take the money and get the hell out of here."*

Jitsu: *"Then he pulled out a bundle of money from his pocket and flung it at me. Finally, he turned around and walked away angrily. I counted the money and it was the exact amount for ten cartons. There wasn't a single rupee extra for a tip after all the bickering."*

Ms. Usha frowned at Khan after she went through the marked portions of the testimony.

Usha: "What is obscure in it?"

Khan: "I called up Jitsu today in the afternoon. He confirmed that Sahil had not counted the money before handing it to him."

Usha: "So?"

Khan: "If Sahil expected fifteen cartons, why did he have money only for ten cartons in his pocket? Jitsu mentioned in court that he did not receive any tip for the delivery. This means that Sahil knew that Jitsu would deliver ten cartons and not fifteen. The order Sahil placed was for ten cartons indeed, and not for fifteen."

Usha: "But then why did Sahil pick a fight with Jitsu?"

Khan: "Because he wanted the deliveryman to remember him. He knew that one day the police would present him in court. He wanted Jitsu to identify him in front of the judge based on his verbal confrontation. In a small goof-up, though, he paid Jitsu the money for ten cartons instead of fifteen.

"Moreover, the balaclava he wore when I caught him at the party hall was a ploy too. He knew I would recognize it at first glance, as one of his men had worn it the night I chased the van. Everything happened exactly the way he had planned it to be."

Usha: "I'm listening, Khan. Please continue."

Khan: "I spoke to Mr. Dilshad Kapoor, Mandana's father. Mandana is Sahil's ex-fiancée. As per him, she had never narrated to him any of the events that she testified in the court. Moreover, he had doubts regarding her mental state after their engagement was called off. She confined herself to a solitary room, and he often heard her lamenting in anger. As per her father, she has some serious temper issues as well. Back in her childhood, she spent fifteen days in a rehabilitation center for anger management. After her dog chewed her favorite doll, she fractured the dog's hind leg in rage. Based on her mental state, I reckon that she lied to the court. As per my guess, it would be Sahil who perhaps broke off the engagement, and not her. Humiliated and furious after he broke off their engagement, this was an ideal opportunity for her to get her revenge. On technical terms, the court should not have accepted her testimony. Though Sahil knew of her mental state, he did not contest her in court. He did this because he wanted the court to pronounce him guilty."

Usha: "Hmm…interesting! But I read here that Sahil attacked you the night you arrested him. If he wanted the police to nab him, why did he try to kill you in the first place?"

Khan fell silent when he heard her words. He recalled the night he had entered the hall and landed up amid the sea of dead bodies. Then, he recollected the instant when he ran to exit after failing to figure out where the killer hid in the hall. Khan gulped as he recalled the moment when a masked Sahil fired a shot at him that missed the target. The bullet hit an empty glass bottle instead of him, and shards of glass flew everywhere. Khan looked up at Ms. Usha with moist eyes.

Khan: "The shot he fired in the party hall that night was not to kill or harm me, m-madam. He fired it with the suicidal intention to alert me of his presence so that I could pin him down. He did not fire at me all the time I was standing in the hall in front of him. But he did only when I turned around and stepped out of the door. He did not want me to leave the premises without him. The man who precisely hit a target as small as a snake's hood missed a target as large as me, that too when I was standing at a shorter distance and in his line of fire."

Khan fiddled with the zipped folder again and pulled out a bunch of documents, which he placed in front of Ms. Usha.

Khan: "These are Sahil's records from college. He excelled in shooting and was the champion at all the shooting events with distinction."

Usha: "Well, your statements have certainly influenced me, but you cannot prove this in court, especially when the verdict has already been delivered and the case has been officially closed. Even if you prove that Sahil was the one who sent you the evidence, his fate will remain the same. He is still a murderer, no matter who posted the evidence to you."

Khan: "I understand your point, madam. But I have a strange feeling that he fiddled with the evidence before sending it to me. I just need your help to buy me some time. I need to find out what made him implicate himself. Please, help me. His hanging is in five days."

Ms. Usha remained silent for a few moments. After a brief pause, she agreed to help him.

Usha: "Alright, Khan. Let me see what I can do. This is a judicial matter and I can't assure if I can get his execution deferred. But I promise I will try my best."

Her words brought much-needed cheer to Khan's face.

Usha: "Make sure you talk to Talwar, the prosecutor in Sahil's case. He enjoys better judicial influence than me. I will try my best from my end though."

Her assurance was a ray of hope for an otherwise dejected Khan. He knew that she was a woman of her word. He thanked her, collected all the documents, and headed back to the jail. He had a small smile on his face as he drove back. He wanted to gift Sahil a new life in return for saving his son's life.

21. The Decipher

5 days to the gallows

Mr. Sen yanked the stethoscope from his ears after Bheema's routine checkup. With a smile on his face, he eased the rubber cuff used to measure the blood pressure around his arm.

Sen: "Hmm…132/91. Not bad, but still, it is a little on the higher side. Make sure you don't skip the dose."

Bheema covered his exposed arm with his shirt's sleeve and smiled.

Bheema: "Don't worry, doctor. Once my daughter recovers, I will recover completely."

Mr. Sen smiled and nodded.

Sen: "Yes, just a few more days until her operation. By the way, I saw her at the hospital. She is responding quite well to the preliminary medicines. I'm sure she will be fine."

An ecstatic Bheema stammered as his eyes brimmed with joy.

Bheema: "Oh really? D-d-did you meet her?"

Sen: "Yes, I did. Though she is still on dialysis, I spoke to her and she replied to me with a slender smile on her face. It's only a matter of days before she gets new kidneys and starts a new life."

Bheema: "I wish I could know the identity of the holy man who agreed to donate his kidneys to my daughter. I would touch his feet. I hope he gets the remaining years of my life."

Sen: "What? You don't know the man? Didn't Sahil tell you anything?"

His reply perplexed Bheema. He frowned.

Bheema: "Sahil? No, he did not. What does this have to do with him?"

Sen: "Come on, man. He is the one. He volunteered to donate both his kidneys to your daughter about three weeks ago. His blood group matches your daughter's, and all the other tests were positive too. As per the consent form he signed, the cops will hand over his body to the hospital after his execution. After the doctors transplant his kidneys, police will hand over the body to his family."

This was a shocking piece of news for Bheema. He gazed at him with his mouth wide open. Mr. Sen sighed in melancholy.

Sen: "To be honest, my conscience cannot accept the fact that he committed such horrible crimes. The boy is a gem."

Bheema had no words. Stunned to the core, he stood up and walked out of the clinic with a straight face.

With a group of about ten inmates, he made his way to Sahil in the barrack, where he was resting on the floor of his cell. Once they entered his cell, Bheema knelt beside his feet. He touched Sahil's feet gently, and his tears dripped onto Sahil's ankle. Sahil jolted out of his sleep when he felt the sensation of Bheema's warm tears on his feet. The sight of the sobbing man seated near his feet surprised him. He looked around at the grim faces of the men gathered around him.

Sahil: "Bheema? All okay?"

But an emotional Bheema could not speak. After weeping silently for a while, he broke down in front of everyone, wailing in a loud, trembling voice.

Bheema: "Chachoo was right. You are God, indeed. Even in the last days of your life, you thought about my daughter and pledged to donate your kidneys to her? Oh Sahil, how will I ever repay this favor? I don't know what to do. Should I celebrate for my daughter or weep for your sacrifice?"

Sahil's eyes welled up when he heard Bheema's touching words. He looked at him with a wide smile.

Sahil: "Obviously, you need to revel at the moment! Your daughter is getting a new life. You must celebrate it, Bheema!"

Bheema: "And what about you, boy?"

Sahil replied with a miserable smile.

Sahil: "My fate is sealed already, but I am glad that my death will pave the way for someone's life. Perhaps God will forgive some, if not all, of my sins this way."

Unable to control his tears, Bheema embraced Sahil. He continued to wail inconsolably and refuted Sahil's words in a quivering voice.

Bheema: "How can you call yourself a sinner? A pious man like you is born once in generations, Sahil. Once…in generations!"

Sahil too lost control over his emotions and broke down in Bheema's arms.

****

As Ms. Usha had suggested, Khan rang Talwar at his home with some optimism. Talwar's voice on the other side delighted him.

Talwar: "Hello?"

Khan: "H-h-hello, Mr. Talwar. This is Khan. I hope you remember me?"

Dressed in his loose nightdress and seated on the couch of his living room, he replied eagerly.

Talwar: "Indeed I do, Khan. I would never have won such a tough case without you. Tell me, what can I do for you?"

Khan: "Sir, I wanted to talk to you about the same case."

Khan began to narrate every detail the way he had explained to Ms. Usha. Talwar picked up his glass of brandy and sipped it slowly as he heard Khan's every word with keen interest.

But as he listened to him, he glanced at the bundle of newspapers strewn all over his coffee table. Though it had been a month since the court delivered its verdict, Talwar continued to earn fame for his role in it. Every newspaper heaped praises on him for putting Sahil behind the bars. Some of the headlines included *Talwar: The Crusader of Justice," "The Majestic Talwar,"* and *"Talwar, The Best."* For his brilliance, an editorial section of a paper declared him as the recipient of the award of merit. The ambitious man gazed at a printed photo where a man was garlanding him for his role in the verdict. Talwar sipped his brandy and smiled quietly. He didn't want to go out of the limelight just yet. And that too after contradicting the case he himself had built against Sahil in court. He intervened in an attempt to pacify an agitated Khan.

Talwar: "But the judgment has already been delivered, Khan. What do you want me to do?"

Khan: "I know, sir, but I am sure that if you try, Sahil's hanging will get postponed. Moreover—"

But Talwar didn't let Khan make his statement and interjected him again.

Talwar: "I wish I could have helped you, Khan. But I am sorry. There isn't much I can do now. If you don't mind, I need to speak to a client seated in front of me. I will call you later. Take care, Khan."

After he uttered these words, he disconnected the call. There was no visitor before him—he had lied to Khan. He lifted and placed his feet on the table. He then picked up some salted peanuts and munched on them, taking yet another sip of his brandy. Talwar's rude and selfish behavior had annoyed Khan. Disgruntled and disappointed, he put down the receiver and yelled in frustration.

Khan: "BLOODY BASTARD!"

****

4 days to the gallows

At lunchtime, Sahil carried his food and walked to Ranga in the adjacent cell. Seated on the floor glumly, Ranga had covered his face with both his hands.

Sahil: "Ranga? Are you okay? Why are you sitting all alone? And where is your food?"

Ranga brought his hands down and looked at Sahil with a wretched expression. He looked shattered.

Ranga: "I am not hungry."

Sahil: "Is everything okay?"

Ranga tried to choke back tears.

Ranga: "Sahil, there are only four days to go…for…"

But before he could complete his words, he broke down. Sahil gulped and patted his shoulder with a miserable smile as he tried to console the wailing man.

Sahil: "Come on! Don't act like a crybaby."

Ranga wrapped his arms around Sahil and wailed even louder. He appeared to be in a terrible state. Sahil put his arms around Ranga's shoulders and tried to console him.

Sahil: "Hey, hey, hey! Calm down, buddy. I had a good life. I have no grudges or complaints."

Ranga wiped his tears and tried to gain some control over his emotions.

Ranga: "You can say whatever you want, but I know one regret of yours."

Sahil: "And what is that?"

Ranga replied with an impish smile while wiping his tears.

Ranga: "Your love story! You will never complete it."

Sahil blushed and chuckled at Ranga's words.

Sahil: "My love story? You are mistaken, dude. I never had one."

Ranga: "I don't buy it. What about the girl who visits you every day? What's her name? Umm…yeah, Preeti! I know you love her. I can feel the pain in your eyes every time you refuse to meet her. Tell me, don't you love her?"

Unable to control himself, Sahil smiled and winked at him before nodding. The acknowledgment brought some cheer to Ranga's face as well.

Ranga: "Have you confessed to her?"

Sahil smiled and shook his head.

Sahil: "No. I once came very close though. But I missed the chance, like every other opportunity."

Ranga: "Then why haven't you met her even once all these days? You refused to meet her every single time she visited the jail."

Sahil: "I don't want her to remain absorbed in thoughts about me. I don't want to add to her suffering."

Ranga: "Do you think she isn't suffering at the moment? Meet her once at least. One last time! Give her some peace, Sahil."

Engrossed in his thoughts, Sahil sighed and fell silent after he heard Ranga. The little chat with Ranga sparked a deep urge in him to talk to Preeti. It had been more than a month since he saw and spoke to her. Moreover, he knew that he didn't have many days left to live. Though he remained silent, he missed her terribly at that particular moment.

Meanwhile, Ranga did not think it suitable to push Sahil any further on the matter. He stood up and walked to the kitchen to get his lunch. As soon as he stepped out, a constable entered the cell. He informed Sahil of a visitor, and the visitor was none other than Preeti. Though a disconsolate Sahil had a strong desire to see her, he refused to meet her once again. He wanted her to move on in her life. Also, any meeting with her at that moment wouldn't have served any purpose for either of them.

But when the constable informed her about Sahil's refusal, she became frustrated. This was her 45th visit to him in the past 25 days, but with no gain. But this time, she was determined to meet him at any cost. She requested the constable humbly.

Preeti: "Can you do me a favor? Can you pass him a message, please?"

The constable sympathized with the lady and walked back to Sahil with the message. But his presence in the cell irritated Sahil.

Sahil: "I already told you I don't want to meet anyone, didn't I?"

Constable: "The lady has a message for you."

Sahil: "A message? What is it?"

Constable: "According to her, it is time for you to obey and surrender to your savior."

The words made Sahil go silent. He gulped as he remembered the promise that he had made to Preeti after she saved his life.

Sahil: *"Preeti, thanks for your help last night. It is a favor that I don't know how to repay."*

Preeti: *"Don't worry, one day I will definitely ask you for something in return. But you can't refuse me at that moment."*

Sahil: *"I promise. Let me know when you want me to obey and surrender to you, my savior."*

Preeti: *"When the right time comes, I certainly will."*

Sahil sighed. He knew it was time for him to keep his word and repay what he owed her.

****

Seated in the visitor room, Preeti jolted out of her thoughts when someone opened the door on the other side of the prison bars. And when she saw Sahil entering through the door, her lips quivered. She gasped in anxiety and clasped the bars separating them. Her face reddened, and tears dripped down her cheeks. Sahil, on the other hand, seemed calm as he walked and stood near her on the other side of the bars. He gulped and looked at her with a straight face. With their eyes locked, she spoke her first words to him after about a month.

Preeti: "H-how are you, Sahil?"

Sahil went blank as he searched for words to say to her. He cleared his throat nervously.

Sahil: "Mhmm…I am good. You could have used my promise in so many better ways. Anyway, how are you?"

Unable to answer him, she simply wiped her tears and questioned him instead.

Preeti: "Did the constable give you the plastic bag I gave him? I brought some mango relish stuffed sandwiches for you."

Sahil nodded with a slender smile and lifted the bag in the air.

Sahil: "Here it is! Would you mind if I have one right here in front of you?"

Preeti: "Go ahead!"

With a miserable smile, he pulled out a sandwich from the plastic bag and crammed it all in his mouth. He closed his eyes, feeling immense pleasure in every bite. And Preeti witnessed the visual with a charm. As he did on several occasions before, he praised Preeti's secret recipe.

Sahil: "You've made my day, Preeti. Thank you!"

But unlike the times when his praise had flattered her, she was in no mood to accept his accolades that day. She yelled at him in a loud and shrill voice.

Preeti: "What's going on, Sahil? How did all this happen?"

But he had no intention of answering her. He tried to evade her question.

Sahil: "Umm… how-how is Ma?"

But that day, Preeti wasn't going to spare him. She had caught him in his attempt to change the topic. She frowned angrily and shrieked at him.

Preeti: "Don't play games with me! Tell me the truth."

But Sahil remained silent. He swallowed the sandwich and licked the breadcrumbs on his fingers.

Sahil: "Why are you asking me? You were in court the whole time."

Irked by his impudence, she lost her temper.

Preeti: "I don't want you to tell me the same cooked-up story you narrated in court! Tell me the truth!"

Sahil had never witnessed such an outburst from her before. Her words struck a raw nerve. Unable to bear her glare, he turned around, struggling to conceal the truth from her. With his back turned to her, he replied frantically.

Sahil: "W-what-whatever I said in the court was the truth."

But his quivering voice did not convince Preeti. She smelled a rat.

Preeti: "If that is so, swear on my name that whatever you narrated in court was true. Swear upon my life that everything happened as you confessed in court. Come on, Sahil, do it!"

Sahil: "Go back home, Preeti. At times, it is better to be ignorant of certain things that will otherwise pain you immensely. Go home!"

But she was not ready to give up so soon. She had resolved to know the truth behind these happenings.

Preeti: "Alright! I will leave if you say so. But before that, take back the promise you made to me when I saved your life. If you are true to your word, tell me everything."

His lip quivered as he turned around and looked into her eyes with a wretched expression. He tried to pacify an infuriated Preeti.

Sahil: "You won't be able to bear it, Preeti. You will never live in peace after you come to know the truth.”

Preeti burst into tears.

Preeti: “Won’t live in peace? Do you think I am at peace right now? It has been days since I slept in peace. Every day, every moment, all I do is wonder what made you accept such terrible charges. Day and night, I think about the possible reason again and again. Tell me the truth, Sahil, please. I beg of you!”

Tears welled up in Sahil’s eyes. Then, he gulped and nodded. Part of him had always wanted to share the awful secret with her. Moreover, the hidden truth behind the series of events in his past started to eat him up from within. So when the girl of his dreams stood in front of him today, he decided to pour his heart out to her.

Sahil: “Alright, Preeti! I will tell you everything today. I will tell you everything that I have hidden in a corner of my heart. But I have one condition. When you walk out of jail today, you have to wipe everything I tell you from your memory. You will never share it with anyone for the rest of your life. Do you agree?”

Preeti wiped her tears and nodded hastily without saying a word. Sahil heaved a deep sigh and began from the instant the goons killed Boney in front of his eyes.

Sahil: “Do you remember the night you saved me from those assailants?”

Preeti: “Yes, I do.”

Sahil: “Do you know the person who attacked both of us that night?”

Preeti shook her head.

Sahil: “Harak Singh!”

Preeti: “What? He was the one who attacked you that night? But everyone in court believed that he worked for you.”

Sahil: “Forget whatever happened in court. The court heard only what I wanted the court to hear, and delivered only what I wanted the court to deliver. Wipe from your memory whatever you saw and heard in court. Just remember the facts that I am going to reveal to you today.”

Preeti didn’t reply and continued looking at him curiously. She was eager to listen to his next words. After a pause, Sahil continued with his story.

Sahil: “I wanted to tell you about him the same night. But after you sustained a wound on your arm, you fell unconscious on the way back to the mansion. The events of that night had shaken me to the core. First, I lost my best friend Boney. Then, I discovered that Harak was the masked man who had killed him. Next, Mandana's betrayal before your arrival left me devastated. Finally, your injury blanked me out. I was going through so many horrible things all at once. Everything was happening so fast!"

Sahil sighed to regain his breath before continuing further.

Sahil: "Once I handed you over to Ma and Mandana's father, I looked around for Baba in the crowd. I thought it wise to speak to him first since Harak worked for him. Moreover, I did not want to create any sort of panic among the gathered people. Then, Bansi told me that Baba was at the chamber for an important meeting. As soon as a few men pulled you out of the vehicle, I drove to the chamber as fast as I could. I reached the chamber and parked my car. I entered the building and then…"

As promised, he revealed everything to her with utmost honesty and sincerity. He narrated all the events that had occurred until his conviction. Preeti's feet went numb when Sahil exposed Thakur's real identity to her. She shook her head. The news was like a bombshell. Her jaw dropped in disbelief as she fixed her gaze at him.

Preeti: "Baba? He is the one behind the Ratnagiri killings?"

Sahil sighed and nodded in disgust.

Sahil: "Yes! My so-called Baba! He is the one."

Along with Thakur's involvement, he described to her the roles of Tatya and all the others in the trade. He also explained his ploy to join hands with Thakur. He confessed to her that his ultimate motive had been to annihilate the empire. He told her how he had killed Tatya, Sikander, Rajvanshi, and all their men in the party hall. Then, he shared his long-kept secret. He revealed himself to be the one who passed all the information and evidence to Khan. A horrified Preeti held her head in her hands in anxiety.

Preeti: "Oh my God!"

With her heart beating fast, she gazed at him and asked him a heart-rending question in an agonized voice. She wanted to ease the heavy burden she had been carrying in her heart all these days.

Preeti: "Does this mean that my guess that you were never involved in the village killings was correct?"

Though the question had a straightforward answer, it caused a deep pang in Sahil's heart. All these days in jail, he had made up his mind to accept the lie to be the truth instead. He had accepted the charge whenever anyone asked him about it. But at that moment, he choked up as he was revealing the truth for the very first time. It was an intense and emotional moment. He found it hard to control his feelings. Without saying a word, he nodded.

Preeti: "Does this mean you took all the blame on your shoulders to punish Baba?"

Sahil clenched his jaw and started to weep in agony before nodding once more. Preeti crawled her hand through the prison bars and gripped Sahil's hands in empathy.

Preeti: "But why, Sahil? Wasn't there any other way to tackle this mess? Why did you kill Baba's men?"

Sahil looked at her with a straight face, and recalled Thakur's devilish face the night he found out his real identity.

Sahil: *"I...I...I will go and inform the police about this."*

Thakur: *"Go ahead! Any of my men will take the blame on his head, and I will continue to do what I'm doing. Everyone you see in this room would happily sacrifice his life for me."*

Sahil: *"I will tell everyone in Ratnagiri about your illegal activities."*

Thakur: *"Go try, my boy. And let me know if anyone believes you!"*

Sahil: *"What if Ma comes to know about you, Baba?"*

Thakur: *"I don't give a damn! Either she will die in shock or she will desert me forever. Whatever happens, I won't step back. If you still have a problem with this, you are free to abandon me as well, but I am not giving up this moneymaking venture."*

Sahil gulped and wiped his tears before replying to her.

Sahil: "I wish you had been there to witness his psychotic laugh, Preeti. I still remember his mad glee and tears of joy. He seemed to me like a crooked, devious, power-obsessed, fanatical psychopath that day. The despicable and obnoxious man I saw that night was not the one I had known all my life. The man standing in front of me was an incorrigible slimeball. He didn't give a hoot about Ma or the lives of any of the men who worked for him. He rejected every single plea of mine.

"But perhaps whatever he said that night was right. I did not have enough evidence to get any of them indicted. Besides, nobody would have believed my version of Thakur. The sly man has complete sway over the people of Ratnagiri. Though only a handful in number, the men involved in the murky trade were too powerful. Every one of them would have roamed scot-free before eventually getting back into the trade. Hence, I decided to destroy them all to bring an end to the ceaseless slaughtering in the village.

"But to accomplish my motive, I had to join hands and work with him. Though he and the others thought I was following the rules of the business, I was a decoy in his evil empire. I never condoned his actions. Finally, on the night of 12th February, I put my plan into action. In one go, I killed them all. It brought the curtain down on the otherwise never-ending and horrendous business."

Preeti remained silent as she heard every word he said with the utmost attention. She gulped and posed the next excruciating question to him.

Preeti: "But why this suicide, Sahil?"

Sahil sighed deeply.

Sahil: "Because I have sinned, Preeti, and it is too grave to be forgiven."

Preeti: "Sinned? And you?"

Sahil nodded with a miserable smile.

Sahil: "Yes. I committed a grave sin! Though I killed everyone involved, I spared the life of the mastermind. And the bastard is my mother's husband. Thakur was right when he said that she would die if she knew about him or if someone inflicts any harm on him. Every time I thought of putting my hands on his throat, Ma's traumatized face flashed before my eyes. My intent fluctuated between vengeance and forgiveness, and in the end, I pardoned his life for Ma. I didn't want to punish her for something she had no control over. I became selfish for her, Preeti."

As he said these words, he clenched his teeth in anger and slammed the bars with his hands. Tears of frustration trickled down his cheeks. The sight scared Preeti, and she gulped in panic. Sahil looked back at Preeti after he regained his composure.

Sahil: "But the night he mocked my suggestions and threats, he gave me a clue. He had rejected all my pleas with his savage reasons—things that would not have affected him. But he never mentioned one—my death! He did not care if I abandoned him, but he never said he could see me dead as he said about Ma. Hence, I decided to give him a taste of his own medicine. There was no other way, Preeti."

Preeti sighed desolately. But she was not done yet. She had a lot more questions, and she was desperate to know the answers.

Preeti: "If Tatya and the men working with Baba were involved in the trade, why did you prove them innocent in court?"

After he heard her question, he thought about a heart-wrenching moment in court. He recalled the instant when a desolate

Nitin had stood up and rebutted Batuk's claim. He could still hear his scream in his ears.

Nitin: *"NOOO! My father was a good man. My ahhh-ahhh-father was n-not a killer."*

Sahil: "Because of Nitin!"

Preeti: "Nitin?"

Sahil gulped and nodded with a miserable smile.

Sahil: "When I am gone, people might spit on my grave, but they will continue to love Thakur. The positive reputation he built over the years will remain intact. Though he may have turned into a fiend in his later years in the greed of money, he has done some commendable work for the people of Ratnagiri. But if the court had proven Tatya guilty, the cruel world wouldn't have been fair to Nitin. The child has his whole life ahead of him. I did not want the court to subject him to any kind of hate or disgust for something he was not responsible for. The same holds true for the kin of the other goons involved with Tatya. I wish that I could have done the same for the kin of Sikander, Rajvanshi, and their acquaintances. But unfortunately, it was not possible."

Preeti was quick to jump to her next question since they were running short of time.

Preeti: "How did you end up as the custodian of the school? Before Talwar revealed in the court, no one knew who the custodian was. Did Baba ever sign any such probate?"

Her question brought a smile to his face.

Sahil: "He did sign the probate. But he just doesn't know when he did it."

Bewildered, Preeti frowned at him.

Preeti: "I…umm…don't understand."

Sahil recounted his visit to Thakur the morning he had a migraine.

Sahil: *"Baba? Are you okay?"*

Thakur: *"Yeah, I am alright, just a little headache. My glasses fell off the table last night. Probably, my hand knocked them over accidentally while I was in my deep sleep. I tend to get a migraine if I don't wear them for long."*

Sahil: *"I need you to sign some payment checks that I would dispatch to the store in Khandala."*

Thakur: *"I….. umm…don't have my glasses on. How will I—"*

Sahil: *"It's just a matter of a couple of signatures."*

Thakur: *"All right. Hold my hand and place it where you need my autograph."*

Sahil chuckled as he recalled his actions that morning. Before asking Thakur for his signature, Sahil nicked the original probate from the safe vault in the study room. Thakur had always hung the key to the safe in the room itself, and it made it a lot easier for Sahil.

Then, he had crept into his bedroom while the old man was in deep sleep. He picked up Thakur's glasses from the table and dropped them deliberately. After the glasses broke, he sandwiched the revised probate between the two payment checks. Finally, on the pretext of getting the checks signed, he deceived Thakur and got his signatures on it. He knew that Thakur suffered from hyperopia and would not notice the hidden document. This amended and predated document named Sahil as the custodian of the school.

Things went exactly as he had anticipated. As soon as an ignorant Thakur signed it, Sahil became the undeclared custodian of the school for the past five years. Finally, at an appropriate time, he placed the revised probate back in the safe of the study. He knew that the police would seize it someday.

Preeti: "When did you click the photograph of the machinery in the school basement?"

Sahil: "I did that one evening when Tatya showed me the equipment installed in the creepy basement. I had hidden my camera in my trouser pocket, and I was waiting for the appropriate time to pull it out. Opportunity knocked on my door when Tatya sprinted back to his bike. He had forgotten his key in the ignition. I pulled out the camera at that moment and captured the visuals. I posted these pictures to Khan along with the picture of Rajvanshi and myself. One day before the party, I went to meet Rajvanshi in Pune. I asked one of his acquaintances to capture us in the same frame as a souvenir. That photograph was the last in the series of evidence I gathered."

Preeti: "And what about your picture with the body of that man…John?"

Sahil: "I stood with the corpse of John, the day Tatya throttled him. Then, I asked Tatya to click my picture with the dead body. Though I never sent that picture to Khan, I knew he would get ahold of it in the camera whenever he would raid the mansion."

Preeti: "Why did you send Baba out of Ratnagiri on the day of the party?"

Sahil: "I did not want him to be around when I killed everybody in the party. I did not want the police to point their needle of suspicion at him in any way."

Preeti: "You told me that you informed Khan about Tatya's plan to transport the dead bodies to Pune. Then why did you change the schedule of Tatya's travel? And the second time, you tipped off Khan but you did not tell Tatya about Khan's pursuit. Khan almost nabbed Tatya that night. What was the reason behind your contradictory behaviors on both occasions? If Khan had nabbed Tatya that night, his hands might have reached Baba as well."

Sahil remembered both instances. He recalled his first words to Khan as an anonymous caller to tip him off about Tatya's movement to Pune.

Sahil: *"Listen carefully, Khan. Tomorrow at 6 in the morning, a van with two dead bodies will make its way to the Ratnagiri checkpoint. Nab the van, and you'll get the man you are looking for."*

He then pondered and remembered his command to Tatya that night.

Sahil: *"Tatya! I want you to leave for Rajvanshi's place right now. Start moving!"*

Sahil further recalled the second incident that Preeti had mentioned, where he had tipped off Khan about the blue van heading for Pune.

Sahil: *"A blue van is heading for Pune. It should cross the checkpoint in about fifteen minutes. Get ahold of it. You will get everything you need to nail the bastards."*

With a chuckle, he recounted his little chat with Tatya after his narrow escape from Khan.

Tatya: *"Sahil…there's definitely a whistleblower. I had a near-death encounter with Khan on my way here."*

Sahil: *"I knew you would make it. That's why I assigned the task to you."*

Sahil looked at Preeti and gulped with a mild smile.

Sahil: "There is a famous saying—if the opportunity doesn't knock, build a door. From the day I pretended to work with Thakur and his men, I felt a lack of trust and confidence in their eyes for me. Even Thakur seemed apprehensive and had raised doubts over my suggestions at times. I still recall their irritated and frustrated deep sighs at me, whenever I listed any advice to the posse. I often found resistance from them on trivial subjects. The men, especially Tatya, found it hard to follow my commands because of my lack of experience in the field. Though they accepted me in the group since I was the Thakur's son, they often mocked and taunted me for my decisions.

"To accomplish my ulterior motive, I had to gain everyone's trust to then break it. Even though I had held them back from killing innocents, I knew this was temporary. They were desperate to resume the killings to feed their slumping trade. It was only a matter of time before the bubble of their constraint would have burst.

"But I finagled Tatya's trust the night I had asked him to change his schedule. After Tatya left early, he escaped the massive deployment of troops at the dawn of the next day. He soon comprehended that my advice saved his life. And after this, he started supporting me in my decisions. He was a prominent man who led Thakur's goons, and played a pivotal role in our alliance with Sikander. Once he came under my control, I enjoyed complete sway over all of Thakur's men, including Sikander. They considered all my suggestions much more seriously thereafter. And on one such suggestion of mine, they agreed to exercise restraint and refrain from killing innocents."

Sahil paused to take a breather.

Sahil: "But it was the second instance that proved to be the real turning point in the game. In one shot, Khan began to trust my words. And it was a must for me to win Khan's confidence.

"Khan is a wise, honest, and dedicated officer, Preeti. I did not want him to try his own innovative ways of cracking the case. Instead, I wanted him to approach things the way I wanted him to. And I agree that if Khan had nabbed Tatya that day, it would have all been over for me. All I could do was trust Tatya's abilities in dealing with such situations. Well-versed with the geography of the town, he knew all the detours in the case of any adverse events. That night, I sat in my room the whole time praying for Tatya's safety.

"Luckily, everything fell into place just as I wanted. What's more, the bloodcurdling incident shook Tatya and the others in the business. Scared for their lives, they became loyal to me like dogs to their master. The gamble that I had played finally paid off!"

Preeti fell silent as she tried to recover from the shock she was experiencing.

Preeti: "One part of the puzzle has been bothering me since I heard your story. Didn't you burn the evidence Baba asked you to? Then how did all those pictures and documents resurface in court?"

Sahil: "The answer lies in the question itself. Except for the original probate that declared Tatya as the custodian of the school, and Thakur's picture with Rajvanshi, I did not burn any other piece of evidence."

Sahil recalled the day he showed the packet he had snatched from Dhananjay to Thakur.

Thakur: *"What is this, Sahil?"*

Sahil: *"Our providence!"*

He recalled the shocked expression on Thakur's face when he saw his picture with Rajvanshi.

Thakur: *"Go… go and destroy everything you have with you."*

Sahil: *"Okay, Baba. I'll need a good quality matchbox."*

He continued narrating the incident to Preeti with a miserable smile.

Sahil: "Then, I returned to my room. Barring Thakur's photo and the original probate, I hid all the other pieces of evidence in my wardrobe. I slid the photograph and probate back into the envelope. Finally, I stepped out to the backyard and burned it. Do you recall the morning you asked me about the papers I set on fire? That answers your question."

Preeti frowned and looked at him in surprise. They locked eyes in a moment of silence, and she recollected her conversation with him.

Preeti: *"You behave so strangely these days. And what were you doing in the backyard last night? What did you burn? I saw you burning some piece of paper."*

Sahil: *"Preeti…there are things I wish I could share with you…things I wish I could explain, but…"*

Tears welled up when she recollected that moment. She choked back her tears and cleared her throat as she tried to control her emotions.

Preeti: "Mhmm…tell…tell me more about the day you visited Rajvanshi in Pune."

Sahil nodded and answered feebly.

Sahil: "I met him a day before I killed everyone at the party. Before I went to Pune, I visited the store manager in Khandala. I cleared my pending dues and collected the tools to disassemble the equipment in the basement. Then, I drove to Rajvanshi in Pune and invited him to the party. After I returned that night, I handed over all the tools to Tatya. Dog-tired after the long day, I made my way to Thakur's room. I still recall his words of concern."

Thakur: *"I am so glad you decided to remove the machinery from the basement. Good, timely decision! By the way, where were you? I haven't seen you since yesterday evening"*

Sahil smiled and looked into Preeti's eyes.

Sahil: "When Thakur had uttered those words, he was not aware that Tatya was busy disassembling the medical equipment that very moment. He had engaged all his men in removing the machinery from the basement of the school the same night on my command. He rang me up after I met you the next morning, on the day of the party. He confirmed that he had dispatched the equipment to Pune. It took a whole night for his men to dismantle the equipment."

Tatya: *"It's done, Sahil. We just finished the work and dispatched it. It was exhausting, and it took us the entire night."*

Sahil: *"Great! I hope no one noticed you guys."*

Tatya: *"Apart from a couple of two-wheelers that were passing by, I don't recall anyone else having noticed us. Moreover, our faces were covered."*

Sahil: *"Hmmm…Good! Today, I have received ten cartons of liquor for the party. Take them from me before you leave for the party. I'll reach a little late."*

Sahil fell silent after he narrated the entire sequence of events to Preeti. He gulped and finished the rest of the story.

Sahil: "Before the party, Tatya came to me in the mansion and took the liquor from me. The poor chap had no idea I had poisoned the liquor with cyanide. The death lord awaited them all. In the evening, Bansi and I drove to the chamber where he burned the copy of Thakur's picture with Rajvanshi. Then, we both made our way to the party hall."

Preeti was silent as she tried to absorb Sahil's words. Though things were pretty much crystal clear to her, one small doubt persisted in her mind.

Preeti: "In your first conversation with Khan, you swore upon your 'dead father.' What did you mean by that? Did you do it to make Khan believe that the informer was Dhananjay since Alok was dead at the time?"

Though Sahil had been calm all that while, Preeti's last question perturbed him. He recalled his conversation with Khan when he had tipped him off about Tatya's move for the first time.

Khan: *"You cheat! You gave me false information. Do you know that it is a crime to mislead the police?"*

Sahil: *"I swear on the soul of my dead father, Khan. One day, I will hand over the culprits to you."*

He looked up at her and replied to her question with a scowl.

Sahil: "That's just half the truth!"

Preeti: "What does that mean?"

Rage replaced the somber calm on his face. His scowl

deepened, and he replied to her in a stern voice.

Sahil: "My father died for me the day I heard his abominable cackle in the chamber. He died for me the night he puffed his chest out and challenged me."

He recalled Thakur's mirth and his vile words.

Thakur: *"My ambitions are too big, son. You can never defeat me. You simply can't!"*

With a trembling lower lip, he uttered his resolve.

Sahil: "My soul would be around when people would carry my dead body on a bier and would place in front of him. My soul won't rest in peace until I see him kneeling in the same stabbing pain that he had given to others over all these years. He will suffer the same trauma he has given to the families of his victims all these years. I will defeat him, Preeti. I certainly will!"

Preeti's voice quivered as she processed the horrible truth.

Preeti: "But this is insanity!"

Sahil gulped and spoke with a lump in his throat.

Sahil: "This might be madness, but there is a method to it. In fact, destiny wrote this as a script for me. There were too many events where I had no control over but they still pushed me into the situation. My chance encounter with Alok in his dying moments and an impudent lawyer of Batuk's caliber were some of them. Also, the recognition of the maroon balaclava by Khan and Tatya's escape from his hands helped me out.

"I had never even expected the seizure of the huge amount of cash and John's autopsy report from the party hall. Though small in nature, the events corroborated the facts and projected me as the kingpin of the trade. The appearance of Mandana and Dhananjay as witnesses in the second hearing left me baffled. Though I had anticipated that Dhananjay would testify against me, I never expected to see Mandana. Her testimony proved decisive in the trial. Destiny played an important role in bringing me to this point, Preeti."

Preeti: "Do you feel that whatever you did was justified?"

Sahil's eyes reflected the pang he felt, and he replied with a miserable smile.

Sahil: "Some days I feel that whatever I did was right. Other days I feel the exact opposite. Just let me die and meet my creator, Preeti. I will ask him the same thing, and I am sure he won't disappoint me."

Preeti broke down when she heard his woeful words.

Preeti: "And what about me? What about…us?"

Sahil fell silent and gazed at her. Then, feeling wretched, he replied to her in a trembling voice.

Sahil: "Forgive me in this birth, Preeti. I promise you that the next one will have something better in store for us."

A constable entered the room just then and interrupted their conversation. He reminded them that they had about two more minutes to spend with each other. They gazed at each other and exchanged pained looks as the constable walked out of the room. With profound emotions surging through them, Sahil bid a final goodbye to Preeti. There was one regret though. They both knew they loved one another, but the circumstances never allowed either of them to freely confess their love to each other. Their love remained undeclared. He slowly turned around to walk back to his cell. But before he could exit, Preeti wiped her tears and nervously called him out.

Preeti: "S-Sahil?"

Sahil stopped and turned around to face her again. Preeti stammered with a hint of embarrassment on her face.

Preeti: "I…I need to tell you something. Ma has f-f-fixed my marriage for next month. I don't know what to do…"

The news shattered him from within. He stood rooted to his spot as tears surged in his eyes. This was the most heartbreaking moment of his life. He knew that they could never be together. But his heart sank when he heard this confirmation of the fact from her mouth. He held back his tears and cleared his throat. His lower lip quivered as he tried his best to smile to cover up his melancholy. He replied to her once he swallowed his sob.

Sahil: "Mhmm…Mhmm…wonderful! Th-that is fantastic news! You idiot, you were busy listening to my crap all this time instead of telling me this great news? Congratulations, Preeti. Who is the lucky man?"

She shook her head ruefully before replying to him softly.

Preeti: "I…I don't know much about him. His name is A-Amit, and he works as a bank manager."

Sahil found it harder to control his emotions after hearing about the man. He replied with a heavy heart and a genuine smile.

Sahil: "I am glad I won't be around to witness it."

With these words, he turned around and stomped back to his cell. Preeti clenched the prison bars with her hands and lamented with her head lowered.

****

In a desolate state of mind, she knocked on the entrance door of the mansion. She had expected me to open the door, but the sight of Thakur standing at the doorstep shocked her. Her eyes widened in anger, and rage replaced the glum expression on her face. Tears of anger welled up in her eyes as she glared at him. Though she made a promise to Sahil that she won't talk with anyone about it, she failed to contain her emotions.

Preeti: "He bartered his life for yours, Baba!"

As soon as she uttered those words to him, tears dripped down her face when she blinked. Thakur's eyes widened in fear, and he gaped at her. She sighed and walked past a stunned Thakur, who watched her in despair.

Preeti opened the door of Sahil's room and sobbed as she looked around. With eyes brimming with tears, she walked close to Sahil's bed and caressed the mattress. The deafening silence in the room made her nostalgic. She recalled the mornings when she served tea to him in his room. They had sat together on that very bed once, and giggled for a long time. She could still hear his laughter in her memory.

She sobbed aloud. Then, she lay on the bed and put her arm around Sahil's pillow. With tears streaming down her cheeks, she fell asleep with bittersweet memories in her mind. To her, Sahil was still a man worth loving.

22. The Enlightenment

36 hours to the gallows – 7th April, 6:00 pm

A nervous Thakur sat in his room in despair. Perhaps he knew that Sahil's fate was inevitable. Deep in pessimistic thoughts, he picked up the receiver of his phone as soon as it rang. Hoping for some good news from any source, he answered the call anxiously.

Thakur: "Hello? Who is it?"

But he sighed in disappointment when he heard my voice at the other end.

I: "Thakur, can you come to the hospital as soon as possible? There's someone here who needs your help."

My unexpected and untimely request irked him.

Thakur: "Hospital? You know what I am going through and you want me to come to the hospital? I cannot come."

My next words sent shock waves through him.

I: "Sahil is in the hospital, Thakur. His condition is critical. You can save him, Thakur."

His feet went numb, and he stumbled out of his chair in a panic. His heart thudded in his chest while his eyes widened in fear.

Thakur: "S-S-Sahil? In the hospital? What are you saying Ban—?"

I gulped and disconnected the call being in a hurry. He ran out of his room and hired a rickshaw parked outside the mansion that brought him to the hospital. He sprinted to the emergency room and looked around in haste, hoping to catch a glimpse of either Sahil or me. Instead, he saw a doctor and nurse trying to stem excessive bleeding in a young man. They applied bandages to a wound he had sustained on his head.

Unperturbed by the bloody sight of the man, he continued to look around until he caught a glimpse of me. I was standing in one corner of the room with a glum expression, witnessing the pitiful state of the boy. Thakur ran to me and gripped me by my shoulders.

Thakur: "Bansi, w-where is Sahil? What happened to him? Is he alright?"

I looked at him with a grim expression and replied morosely.

I: "He is right beside you. Look around the ward, Thakur."

As soon as he heard my words, he turned around. Unable to find Sahil, he looked back at me and admonished me.

Thakur: "What rubbish? Is this a joke? Where is Sahil?"

But before he could reprimand me further, he found the answer to his question. He fell silent when he identified the injured young man. Named Sahil, the young boy was the only one in Ratnagiri to share his name with Thakur's son.

Thakur: "That's Sahil, isn't it? The grocer's son? What happened to him?"

I: "His bike overturned in a pile-up. I was on my way back to the mansion when I saw him lying on the road in a pool of blood. I brought him straight to the hospital. He needs a rare blood type, but the blood bank has run out of stock. I know you have a universal blood type. Would you like to help him?"

Thakur closed his eyes and heaved a sigh of relief once he realized that I spoke about a different Sahil. He wiped the sweat on his forehead and took a couple of deep breaths. Then, he glared at me and scoffed.

Thakur: "Why did you mislead me? Do you know what I went through the past half hour? Don't you know how tense I've been these days?"

But before I could explain, the doctor rushed to Thakur.

Doctor: "You have arrived in the nick of time, Thakur. He is in dire need of blood. Bansi told me your blood group is O-negative. That will serve our purpose."

Owing to his miserable state of mind, he was in no mood to agree to the request. But being a public figure, he felt pressurized into donating blood. Half-heartedly, he agreed to help the young man. The doctor injected the needle at one end of the intravenous line into the patient's arm. At the same time, the nurse injected the needle at the other end into Thakur's left arm. Once the blood transfusion began, the doctor asked the nurse to keep an eye on the patient and left. The nurse kept an eye on both of them, and after about ten minutes, she checked Sahil's pulse. Finding it stable, she finished some paperwork. Then, she left the ward after an assurance that she would return in about thirty minutes. With Thakur's permission, I made my way to a small eatery near the hospital. I had skipped my lunch that day since I had to carry the injured man to the hospital that afternoon.

Alone in the hall with the unconscious patient, Thakur glanced at the clock on the wall in front of him. It was exactly 6:50 pm. Deeply bored, he looked at the unconscious boy lying on the adjacent bed. He was a little frustrated, wanting time to pass as quickly as possible. He closed his eyes and soon drifted into a nap. He awoke from his slumber about ten minutes later. He could feel the sweat accumulated on his forehead; it was a hot evening. He wiped the sweat from his forehead, turned his face to the side, and glanced at Sahil again.

But as soon as he turned, a quiver of shock passed through him. Instead of the grocer's son, he hallucinated his son Sahil lying on the adjacent bed. Sahil was groaning in extreme pain, and blood oozed out of his mouth and nose. He wailed with his gaze locked at Thakur, and his lips trembled in agony. Thakur went numb when he witnessed Sahil in this abysmal state. With tears trickling down his cheeks, Sahil uttered some agonized words.

Sahil: *"Baba! Save me!"*

Thakur panicked when he heard Sahil's agonized words.

Thakur: "S-S-Sahil…how did you get here? It wasn't you a few minutes ago. W-w-what happened to you?"

But Sahil paid no heed to his father's words. He continued to repeat the same traumatized words in his dismal condition.

Sahil: *"Baba! Save me!"*

With a racing heart and shedding tears of pain, Thakur screamed again in a quivering voice.

Thakur: "Sahil…ahhh… D-d-don't worry, son. I won't let anything bad happen to you, as long as I am alive. I will save you."

But as soon as he uttered these words, shrill laughter resonated across the hall. It was coming from one corner of the hall. He frowned and looked around to see the man behind the loud laughter. And the sight of Harak Singh at the door with a bloody hole in his forehead stunned him. Thakur almost fell off the bed in shock. With unnerving glee on his blistered face, Harak Singh walked to Sahil and looked at Thakur with a smirk.

Harak: *"Heheheeee… I won't let you save him, Thakur… Heheee… I will own his soul… heheeheeee!"*

Droplets of sweat dripped down Thakur's face.

Thakur: "H-H-Harak?"

Harak began to dance and twirl as soon as he reached near Sahil's bed. With a psychotic smile on his face, he swirled his body in slow-paced dance movements. He began to croon a creepy song in a shrill voice that gave Thakur goosebumps.

Harak: *"Come on my dearrr…come on my friendddd… I am here to take youuu… to the new world that has no endddd… Come on, my dear… Come on my frienddddd!"*

With a deep sense of terror, Thakur gaped at Sahil. Sahil, too, locked eyes with Thakur and repeated his pleas.

Sahil: *"Baba! Save me!"*

Harak's spooky smile widened, and he extended his hand to Sahil. He continued to hum the same eerie song inviting Sahil to accompany him to the world of no return.

Harak: *"Come on my dearrrr… Come on my friendddd… I am here to take youuuu… to the new world that has no endddd… Come on, my dear… Come on my frienddddd!"*

Desperate to save his son's life, Thakur begged Harak.

Thakur: "N-n-no Harak. Leave him. He-he is innocent. T-take me if you want. I am the culprit. I am the one at fault. But please leave him!"

Harak fell silent. Suddenly, Alok appeared near Thakur's feet. With a scarred face and a slashed throat, he held a newspaper in his hand and looked straight into Thakur's eyes. Unlike Harak, Alok maintained a grave expression.

Alok: *"I was innocent too, wasn't I? All I wanted was some cash, Thakur. Why* *did you kill me?"*

Thakur looked at Alok with frightened eyes. But his horror crossed all bounds when he noticed Boney standing beside him. He was smiling, with a bouquet in his hands. His eye cavities did not contain eyeballs and looked like two small radiating black holes. Thakur recognized the bunch of flowers. The police had recovered the bouquet along with his belongings near the bus station. He had carried it for Sahil and Mandana's engagement.

Boney: *"And what did I do, Uncle? I was innocent too."*

Boney's question dismayed an already fretful Thakur. He gulped anxiously, as he had no words to reply to his son's best friend. But it was not over yet. Thakur gasped when he heard a kid's high-pitched voice coming from his other side. He went numb when he turned his face to the other side and saw Kaju standing next to his shoulder. With a teapot in his hand and blood streaming down his eyes, he looked possessed.

Kaju: *"Would you like to have some tea, sir? But, for what mistake of mine did your men kill me?"*

When Thakur failed to answer, Kaju's face turned livid. He pulled a paper cup out of his pocket and tilted the kettle to pour some tea into it. But Thakur jolted back in fear when he noticed blood, instead of tea, coming out of the pot's nozzle. Once the blood had filled the cup to the brim, it began to overflow and drip onto the floor. Some of the droplets rebounded off the floor and splashed onto Thakur's face. Thakur gasped in despair. He tried to wipe the blood off his face with his hand, and the act blotched his face. When he moved his hand away from his eyes, the sight of the numerous dead men standing around him terrified him. On his command, his men had killed them all over the years. Khatri and Murari were a few of the faces he recognized in the crowd. They all stood with their teeth bared at him.

Petrified by the visual before him, he looked back at Sahil. His heart skipped a beat when he saw the expression on Sahil's face. Unlike just a moment ago when he was whimpering, Sahil was staring at Thakur with a spooky smile on his face. Harak put a noose around Sahil's neck and held both of its ends. The psychotic smile on Sahil's face widened, and tears of agony flowed down his cheeks.

Sahil: *"You can't save me, Baba. My blood is on your hands. I have to go…"*

As soon as he spoke these tormented words, Harak's loud

laughter resonated all over the place. He tightened the noose around Sahil's neck. With his face and hands stained with blood, Thakur screamed in misery.

Thakur: "Noooooo… Leave him, Harak…Noooooo…please!"

But his tormented plea did not deter Harak, who continued to tighten the noose around Sahil's neck. Sahil's dry lips quivered in suffocation and he gasped loudly. Blood gushed from his nose, and his eyes began to bulge. With sweat covering his face, Thakur shuddered and clenched his teeth in agony. He screamed and broke down as he continued to beg Harak.

Thakur: "Noooooo… Leave him…leave him, please!"

He continued to shout until I grabbed him by the shoulder and shook him. I frowned and yelled at him.

I: "THAKUR! ARE YOU OKAY?"

He looked at me and gasped in terror. Then, he gripped my hand frantically, and began wailing dreadfully.

Thakur: "B-B-Bansi, h-help Sahil! He's going to kill my Sahil! Free Sahil from his clutches! Please, Bansi!"

I looked around in distress, as we were alone in the room.

I: "Who is going to k-kill Sahil? Did you have a nightmare, Thakur?"

My words jolted him out of his delusion. He fell silent and looked at me grimly. Then, he turned to his side and looked at the patient with frightened eyes. He sighed in relief when he saw the grocer's son lying on the bed instead. He gazed at his own reflection in the mirror fixed on the wall. A sense of calm washed over him when he saw his face without any blood smeared on it. He shut his eyes and exhaled in peace once he realized, everything he had seen happened in a dolorous dream.

Ten minutes later, the nurse returned to the hall and pulled the needle out of Thakur's arm. But as soon as she detached the apparatus from the patient's arm, she gasped.

Nurse: "Oh my God! He is sinking."

She checked Sahil's pulse and rushed outside to call the doctor. Sahil's condition deteriorated, and he started huffing loudly. Thakur got up from his bed and sprinted to the patient. And as soon as he reached his bed, he gulped in despair and cradled his head in his hands. Though the man only shared his name with Thakur's son, his pitiable condition ignited a twinge of pain in Thakur. He quailed at his struggle and uttered a few words of compassion.

Thakur: "Don't worry, son. You will be all right. Don't be afraid."

But Sahil's condition continued to worsen. Due to the extreme pain, he gripped Thakur's wrist with force. Amid erratic hiccups, he locked eyes with Thakur. His pleading eyes evoked a deep sense of sympathy in Thakur. Thakur sobbed and earnest tears streamed down his face. The behavior left me baffled since I knew that these tears were not feigned. He prayed for the young man to stabilize.

Thakur: "Don't go, please. Just hold on, son. Oh God, save him."

His words for the youngster came straight from his heart. He sniffled and looked at me angrily.

Thakur: "Why are you standing still? Go out, and call the doctor! The boy needs help! Go!"

Before I could step out to seek help, Sahil's grip on Thakur's wrist loosened. God had rejected all of Thakur's solemn prayers. The boy's eyes became still, and he let out a last, sudden gush of breath. He passed away!

Aghast at the boy's demise, Thakur began to sob. I still remember his grief-stricken and wailing remorseful words.

Thakur: "I COULDN'T SAVE HIM, BANSI... I COULDN'T... I WILL LOSE MY SON TOO.... WHAT SHOULD I DO, BANSI? WHAT SHOULD I DO? I AM SORRYYY.... AHHH.... I HURT SO MANY PEOPLE ... OH, LORD! PUNISH ME.... I AM THE SINNER, LORD... BUT, SPARE MY SON'S LIFE... SAHILLL... FORGIVE ME, MY SON, FORGIVE ME... AHHH...GODDD..."

Thakur's state baffled me. For the first time, I was seeing him in distress at the death of an unknown person. He looked nothing like the person who had earlier asked his goons to murder strangers to make some easy money. In an attempt to push him onto the right track, I had deliberately invited Thakur to the hospital. I had a feeling that the condition of the boy would have an impact on him. And his emotional distress confirmed my estimation. Aghast at Sahil's death, Thakur buried his face deep in my chest and sobbed in pain. I gulped and patted his shoulders to console him. It was a remarkable day, and Thakur had a change of heart. That was the day when the malevolent vermin residing somewhere in him died.

✳✳✳

32 hours to the gallows – 7th April 10 pm

There were no constables besides Khan in jail that night. They were all out as a security cover for a local politician who was on a visit to Ratnagiri. Preeti was waiting for Sahil in the visitor room. It was the last slot for a visitor in the day. Sahil entered the room and stood in front of Preeti on the other side of the bars. But when he looked at her, her avatar astonished him. Dressed in bridal attire, she had braided her hair and applied kohl to the contours of her eyes. With makeup on her face and bright red lipstick on her lips, she looked like a queen to him. Surprised by her makeover at that time of the night, Sahil looked at her from top to bottom.

Sahil: "Umm…something special today?"

Her coy smile widened as she nodded. And her next words shook Sahil to the core.

Preeti: "Sahil, I am getting married tonight!"

Stunned at the piece of news, he fell silent for a moment. He looked at her with a straight face. He wet his dry lips with his tongue, as the words sank his heart. Moreover, a brazen smile reflecting on her face left him flustered.

Sahil: "W-w-wedding? Wasn't it next month?"

Preeti shook her head with a teasing smile.

Preeti: "No, Sahil. It's tonight!"

Before he could comprehend her words, she pulled out a tiny metallic case and placed it on her palm. Then, she shoved her hand through the prison bars, and extended her palm with the case close to Sahil's face.

Preeti: "MARRY ME, SAHIL! RIGHT HERE, RIGHT NOW!"

Preeti's words left him thunderstruck. With a smile, she removed the lid of the case. Stunned, he looked down at the case on the palm of her hand. To his surprise, it was filled with vermillion. It was the scarlet powder a groom applied to the partition of his bride's hair in a nuptial ceremony. The sacred ritual would mark them as husband and wife.

Sahil frowned and gulped in shock.

Sahil: "What? What did you just say?"

Tears welled up in Preeti's eyes. With a tender smile on her quivering lips, she repeated her words.

Preeti: "You heard that right, Sahil. Marry me!"

Her plea infuriated Sahil.

Sahil: "Are you out of your freaking mind? You want to marry a man who will be dead in two days from now?"

Preeti nodded without saying a word. A disturbed Sahil turned his back to her despondently. He tried his best to control his emotions. Without looking back at her, he uttered his words in a quivering voice.

Sahil: "This is not a good time to play games, Preeti."

Preeti clenched the bars of the prison as she replied to him.

Preeti: "This is not a game, Sahil. I can't imagine living life without you. I beg you to agree to this one desire of mine. Don't deny me, please. It will give me some strength to pass through this aimless, long life of mine. Please don't refuse me, Sahil!"

After a brief pause, Sahil spoke with a lump in his throat.

Sahil: "You are thinking from your heart, Preeti. You need to use your brain instead."

Preeti: "When it comes to you, it is always my heart that speaks!"

Sahil punched the wall of the room with clenched fists.

Sahil: "No-no-no. I can't do it. I don't want to ruin your life."

Preeti: "Life? Do you think I have any left? Give me something to live by, after you are gone."

Sahil gulped and choked back his tears.

Sahil: "I am sorry, Preeti. I can't do this."

His refusal enraged Preeti. She stared at him austerely and made her resolve.

Preeti: "Alright, Sahil. If that is your decision, then listen to mine as well. When I step out of jail today, I won't go home. I will immerse my body into the holy waters of the Palanharini. I will consider myself fortunate to leave for the heavenly abode before you enter it."

With that vow, she turned around and walked toward the exit. Her words sent chills down his spine. He found a sense of deep commitment in her determined words. He loved her and did not want her to commit suicide on his account. He yelled in despair.

Sahil: "Preeti, stop!"

Preeti halted when she heard Sahil's agonized plea. She turned around and walked back to him. With a heavy heart, Sahil made one last attempt to convince her.

Sahil: "You have a wonderful life ahead of you, full of prospects and love!"

Preeti: "So did you!"

With these words, she placed the case of vermillion in front of him once again. Sahil looked at her with widened eyes. He gulped as he had run out of arguments. With a lump in his throat, he picked up a pinch of the vermillion with his thumb and forefinger. Tears sprung up in his eyes, and his lips quivered as he fixed his gaze at her. Then, after a pause, he applied the vermillion. Preeti shut her eyes as she felt Sahil's fingers running across her forehead. The Lord had answered and accepted all her prayers at that moment. It was an unforgettable moment.

Thin smiles crept onto their faces as Sahil wiped the tears dripping down her cheeks. They reached out through the prison bars and held hands. Lost in each other's eyes and with lips parched for each other, they yearned to kiss one another. Desperate to quench their thirst, they moved closer to each other.

But the double-layered bars turned out to be too much of a distance every time they tried to kiss each other. Every time they tried, their heads bumped against the bars and their lips remained apart by a whisker. After many failed attempts, they interlocked their fingers and wept in grief.

The scene aroused deep sympathy in Khan. He had stepped in to inform Preeti that her allotted time was up. But he halted when he saw everything that transpired between the couple. He had been a witness to the sacred moment when Sahil applied vermillion to Preeti's forehead. He found it hard to meddle the intense moment between the two made-for-each-other souls.

****

A rumbling sound echoed when Khan opened the rusted door of the dormitory in the front office. He looked around the dusty dorm before walking inside. But he was not alone. Sahil and Preeti had followed him to the dorm at his instruction. Khan cleared his throat and looked at Sahil grimly.

Khan: "Mhmm… It is half past 10, and my men will report back to me sharp at 2 in the morning. You both have about three hours to spend with each other. No one will barge in or disturb you two during this time."

With these words, he turned around and marched to the exit of the dorm. But before he could walk out, Sahil called out to him in an agonized voice.

Sahil: "Khan!"

Khan turned around and looked straight into Sahil's eyes. Though Sahil remained quiet, his silence said it all. He wanted to thank Khan for this favor. Khan was wise enough to understand the emotions running high within Sahil. It was an intensely emotional moment for him as well. He gulped and replied to him in a hoarse voice.

Khan: "Consider it…umm…a small wedding gift from me. I am sorry, my friend. I couldn't do much for you."

Khan sighed uneasily after he uttered these words and left for his desk in the front office. Sahil bolted the door of the room after Khan left, and looked back at Preeti. With a pinch of nervousness, he walked to her. They stood face-to-face, with their eyes locked on each other. Preeti was breathing heavily. Sahil cradled her face in his trembling hands. Then, he brought his lips close to hers. He wanted to capture her lower lip with his own, but before he could do this, she gasped and pulled back. She closed her eyes in excitement, and her breathing turned erratic. She could feel her heart pump loudly. Sahil chuckled at her state and held her hands. Then, with a naughty smile, he whispered in her ear.

Sahil: "I don't have time, Preeti!"

His words sank her beating heart. She looked up at him and her eyes widened with shock. Then, she grabbed his face and held his lower lip between her lips. Her bold action stimulated Sahil. He pushed his tongue into her mouth and touched her warm tongue with it. Preeti closed her eyes in immense pleasure and enjoyed every moment of the kiss. Breathless after sharing a passionate kiss, they slowly pulled apart. Preeti gradually opened her glittering eyes and eyed Sahil with a mild grin. There was a brief moment of silence between them. Finally, Sahil confessed his sincere love to her.

Sahil: "**I love you, Preeti!** I have never loved anyone as much as I've loved you. Thank you for being a part of my life!"

Preeti burst into tears as soon as she heard those words. She had been craving to hear him say those very words for the longest time. Though still in tears, she uttered the words that Sahil was desperate to hear too.

Preeti: "**I love you too, Sahil!** I've loved you since the day I realized what love is. I've loved you since the day I first held your hand as a child. I've loved you since we ran into the woods hand in hand. I've loved you all my life, and I will love you till eternity. Apart from being someone who loves you, I don't have any other identity."

Her words charmed Sahil. He moved his face close to hers, and their lips came together again. Lost in each other, they played with each other's tongues. Preeti's soft breasts pressed against Sahil's chest, and the feel of her hardened nipples turned him on. Feeling Sahil's hardened member against her bare midriff aroused Preeti as well. Sahil bent and put his arms around her waist. Then, he lifted her in his arms and carried her to the bed in the corner of the dorm. Sahil gently placed her on the bed. Lost in her eyes, he took off his shirt and flung it on the floor. Then, he nervously pulled off the long and wide drape covering her bridal dress. Preeti's breathing turned erratic, and she gave him an enticing look. Under a thin blouse, her breasts heaved up and down. Sahil was smitten by the view of her cleavage.

Meanwhile, seated at his desk, Khan cracked his knuckles in desperation. He had run from pillar to post all these days to save Sahil, but all his efforts had been in vain. As he sat lost in pessimistic thoughts, fortune smiled on him. His desk phone rang loudly, and his heartbeat sped up when he heard Ms. Usha at the other end.

Usha: "Hello, Khan."

Khan: "Hello, madam. I hope you'll give me some good news?"

Usha: "Oh, yes! I will for sure. Guess what? I got the orders from the court that puts a stay on Sahil's hanging. The court has accepted our plea for a retrial of Sahil's case. The judge will decide the date for the retrial in about a week. I received the document in the mail today evening. Sorry, I couldn't call you earlier. I was busy all day."

An ecstatic Khan jumped up from his seat as soon as he heard her words. He cackled and tears of joy welled up in his eyes.

Khan: "Really? HAHAHA… You've made my day, madam."

Usha: "I can understand your delight, Khan. Show it to the magistrate once he arrives at the jail to observe Sahil's hanging. He will defer the hanging. But…Ummm… there is a slight problem."

Her statement gave Khan heebie-jeebies. With a racing heart, he stammered anxiously.

Khan: "W-w-what happened, madam? Is everything okay?"

Usha: "I am flying out of the city early morning tomorrow since it is a long weekend. My office will remain closed for the next two days. Moreover, there is nobody around in the office to help me pass on the document to you."

Khan, too, was alone in the office as all his constables were on duty that night. He licked his lips and looked around in desperation.

Khan: "Madam, I can come to pick it up right now, if you don't mind. It shouldn't take me more than an hour to reach your office."

Miss Usha chuckled at Khan's request.

Usha: "Hahaha… As always, you will delay my plans to go home. I will be waiting for you in my office. Hurry up now."

As soon as he put down the receiver, he held his head in his hands in nervousness. It was too risky for him to leave for Ms. Usha's office with no one to keep an eye on the inmates. After struggling with the dilemma for a while, he decided to drive to Ms. Usha despite the absence of the other policemen. He needed to get a hold of that legal document that night. He decided to break the rules. He surrendered his duty to his inner conscience.

He got up from his desk and made his way to the dormitory. He wanted to share the wonderful piece of news with Sahil and Preeti as well. But as soon as he lifted his hand to knock, he stopped himself. He considered it too indecent to disturb the newlywed couple during their most intimate moments. He gulped and bolted the door of the dormitory from the outside. Hoping to get back within a couple of hours, he headed out to get his hands on the life-saving document for Sahil.

Behind the closed door of the dorm, Sahil lay on top of Preeti. His lips brushed against hers. Feeing Sahil's wet tongue on her neck, Preeti gasped and enjoyed the moment with closed eyes. They wrapped their arms around each other as they exchanged sweet, wet kisses. Preeti unbuttoned her bridal blouse and looked at him with a charming expression. She communicated her desire for love and lust through a blissful smile. Sahil licked his lips, and after a nervous pause, he pulled her top off. His heartbeat increased when he saw Preeti's breasts in a green bra. The thin fabric covered only the lower half of her otherwise naked breasts. He buried his face in her soft and juicy breasts, while she moaned and lightly bit into Sahil's shoulder.

Khan reached Ms. Usha's cabin within an hour. He went through every word on the stay order with the utmost attention. Ms. Usha was right. The document issued an order to defer Sahil's execution. A wide smile radiated on his face after he went through the document. He thanked her from the core of his heart. But Ms. Usha had a few words of caution as well.

Usha: "Pleasure's all mine, Khan. But there is something I need to tell you. In your excitement, you missed out on one small section of a clause."

She highlighted a small part of the text in the document and explained the details. Khan responded with a confident smile.

Khan: "Don't worry, Madam. Nothing of the sort will happen. I can vouch for it."

Ms. Usha nodded with a smile before shaking his hand.

Usha: "Good luck!"

He sprinted back to his car and started back for jail. The lucky break had energized him to the core. Feeling ecstatic, he began to croon an old folk song as he sped in the darkness of the night. The mild drizzle in the air and the freshness of the cool breeze took away all his stress. The fragrance of the wet soil invigorated him after a week of hopelessness and misery.

But his excitement ceased when the engine of his car smoked out, as he crossed a thicket in the dense woods. The vehicle came to a standstill with a loud grunting sound. He stepped out of the vehicle to seek help. But to add to his woes, he did not see anyone around; only the sounds of a few faint dog barks could be heard from a distance. He lifted the hood of the vehicle and tried to figure out the cause. But the glitch was too technical for a cop to fix. Annoyed, he sighed with frustration, and his mind went blank.

With clothes strewn all over the floor, Preeti lay and rested on top of Sahil. A thin quilt covered their nude bodies. Preeti kissed his cheeks, nose, and lips. Then, she slid down and gently bit his nipples. Aroused, he pivoted to get on top of her and returned the favor by planting a deep kiss on her forehead, eyes, nose, and lips. Then, he slithered down to reach her breasts. She closed her eyes and gasped, biting her own lower lip. She moaned and braced her thighs around his bare butt. And with their arms wrapped around each other, they made love. A blissful smile spread across her face, and tears of joy dripped down her cheeks as she gave her virginity to him.

✱✱

Standing in the middle of the forest, an impatient Khan stared at the mechanic busy fixing the jalopy. Earlier, Khan had got hold of a mobile mechanic who was passing by in the opposite direction. Once he spotted the stranded Khan, he stopped his vehicle and offered to help.

Khan: "How much more time will it take?"

The mechanic replied to him while tightening some screws.

Mechanic: "Almost done, sir. The carburetor had malfunctioned. I just finished replacing it. Your car should be fine now!"

His heart was beating fast. He glanced at his watch. The time was 1:53 am, and his men were due to report to him at 2:00 sharp. He still had more than half of the distance to cover.

After a couple of routine tests and a short test drive, the mechanic handed the vehicle back to him. He thanked the mechanic after paying him his due amount. Then, he got back into his car and raced back to jail without losing any time. He didn't want his men to encounter Sahil and Preeti together in his absence.

****

Sahil and Preeti lay beside each other, panting. Sahil caressed Preeti's long hair and ran his fingers through them. Preeti looked at him with a glum face and tear-filled eyes. She came out of the trance when Sahil whispered some words to her.

Sahil: "Take care of Ma. I know she still loves me a lot, even though she won't reveal it."

Tears welled up in livid Preeti's eyes, and she yelled in agony while looking at Sahil.

Preeti: "I will never forgive Baba!"

He stopped playing with her hair and cradled her face.

Sahil: "You don't need to hate a man who will soon go into a vegetative state. Instead, you should pity him for what he is going to lose! He is going to suffer something that no father ever wants to suffer in his lifetime."

Preeti broke down before uttering traumatized words.

Preeti: "D-don't go Sahil…or take me along with you… I-I…I can't live without you Sahil …Ahhh."

He embraced her and kissed her.

Sahil: "I will always be around you. I promise you, Preeti."

With these words, he removed the rosary around his neck and tied it around Preeti's neck. The priest's words were still fresh in his mind.

Priest: *"You can gift it to your bride if you want to."*

With quivering lips, she pressed her face against his arm and wailed. Sahil gulped and wiped her tears. They kissed and hugged each other in melancholy. It was time for the soul mates to separate, as the deadline approached. They both got dressed and walked to the door holding hands.

They unbolted the door and tried to push it open. But to their surprise, the door had been locked from the outside. The car skidded with a rumbling sound and halted on the gravel of the parking lot. Preeti wiped her tears as soon as she heard footsteps approaching. She didn't want to display her misery to Khan. They heard someone unbolt the door from the outside. But when the door opened, they both shuddered in fear at the sight of Aurangzeb standing in front of them.

Though the higher officials had set up an inquiry on him for

284

the charges of misappropriation of funds, they were unable to prove the charges. They had also failed to find a suitable replacement for Khan at the police station. They had no choice but to reinstate Aurangzeb. They needed Khan to take over things back in Ratnagiri police station as soon as possible. But before revoking his suspension, the officials instructed Aurangzeb to be a little softer in his approach to the inmates. They issued him an official warning letter too.

Aurangzeb had been asked to join on the 10th of April—a day after Sahil's execution. But he reached on the 7th itself. He considered Sahil to be the reason behind all the humiliation that he had suffered in the past few days. The evil man had a strong desire to witness Sahil's execution right before his eyes.

When he reached the jail, the absence of Khan and the other constables baffled him. He headed to the top-floored room allocated to Khan to have a word with him. But the heavy lock at its door surprised him. Finally, being tired, he thought of resting in the dormitory. But the presence of Preeti and Sahil in the dorm caught him by surprise. Besides the cleaning staff, no prisoners were allowed to enter the dormitory. Moreover, this wasn't a visiting time by any standards.

The wrinkles on his forehead deepened and he roared at Sahil.

Aurangzeb: "OYYEY! What are you doing here?"

His shriek terrified Preeti, and she clung to Sahil's arm. Sahil gulped in fear and braced his arm around her. He looked around desperately to catch sight of Khan. But to his disappointment, Khan was nowhere to be seen. He looked Aurangzeb in the eye and tried to explain things to the brute.

Sahil: "Umm… Kh-Kh-Khan he-he…"

But Aurangzeb paid no heed to Sahil's words. Instead, he was focused on Preeti's dazzling beauty. He did not take long to recognize her. She was a frequent visitor to the jail during his reign as the jailor. She always wanted to meet Sahil, but he always refused to meet her.

Though Preeti tightened her loose dress around herself, Aurangzeb couldn't stop peeking at her cleavage. Being a widower in his late forties, he was smitten by her dusky beauty. He concealed his lust with a fake smile.

Aurangzeb: "Ahhh… I get it. Khan let you spend some time together, isn't it?"

The couple exchanged puzzled looks in despair. It was hard for them to believe the unexpected kind words coming out of the devil's mouth. He cautioned them with concern in his voice.

Aurangzeb: "Listen, I think the girl should go back home and you should go back to your cell. If someone sees the two of you together, you guys might end up in some serious trouble. It will not only add to your woes but also create issues for Khan. He is not supposed to do what he did."

Sahil nodded without saying a word. Aurangzeb's words made sense. He gulped and gestured to Preeti to abide by Aurangzeb's advice. She wailed and embraced Sahil tightly. He kissed her forehead and separated himself from her with a gentle push. She sniveled and walked to the exit of the front office. She repeatedly looked back at him. He waved a forlorn goodbye to her with tears in his eyes. He found it hard to control his emotions. Finally, he turned around, wiped his tears, and headed back to his cell.

Preeti was about to exit when Aurangzeb's loud words fell on her ears.

Aurangzeb: "You forgot to enter your details in the visitor logbook."

She wiped her tears and turned around to face Aurangzeb.

Preeti: "I already did when I entered the building."

Aurangzeb: "I am sorry but you didn't."

Tired and stressed out, she was in no mood to argue with him. She could not recall if she had signed her entry. She returned to the counter and turned over to the last page of the logbook. But to her surprise, her entry had been logged and signed by her. And when she turned around to inform him of the same, she shivered in horror.

Aurangzeb was standing right behind her, at barely an arm's distance. He stood close enough, and she could smell the foul odor of his oily, dyed beard. With a vile glee, he chomped on a betel leaf, making a crunching sound. Sensing something terrible on the cards, she stammered in fear.

Preeti: "I-I-d-did sign it e-earlier."

Aurangzeb's wicked smile broadened.

Aurangzeb: "I know that."

His mysterious words terrified Preeti.

Preeti: "W-what do you mean?"

Aurangzeb: "You've fulfilled your lover's desire. And now, it is time for you to slake my thirst."

Outraged at his words, Preeti clenched her teeth and screamed at him in fury.

Preeti: "Shut up, you swine! Get away from me before I slap you."

But her warning did not deter him. He whipped off the leather belt around his waist and loosened his knickers. The very next moment, he gripped her hands and pulled her toward himself. Shocked at his impudent actions, Preeti screeched in despair.

Preeti: "Ahhh…Leave me, I say!"

Despite her attempts to free herself from his grasp, he tightened his grip on her bare midriff. Breathing heavily, he rolled his wet tongue over her neck. She tried to push him away in disgust. But he simply shut his eyes in pleasure and rubbed his nose against her cheeks.

Aurangzeb: "You smell wonderful, you pretty bitch!"

The abuse hurled at her was too offensive for her to bear. With a sudden jerk, she freed her hand and smacked his face. The sound of the whack resonated across the room. Her act infuriated Aurangzeb to the core. That too, coming that from a woman, who had always been meek creatures in his eyes, her slap insulted him deeply. He released her waist and frowned at her in fury. His lower lip quivered in rage. His glare petrified Preeti, who was unsure of his next move.

In a flash, he pulled down the top of her bridal dress violently. The vile move ripped her dress, exposing her upper body, which was now veiled only in her brassiere. She screamed and crossed her arms over her chest in a feeble attempt to cover her body. Aurangzeb jeered at her plight.

Without losing any time, Aurangzeb bent down and braced his arms around her thighs. Then, he lifted her in his arms and carried her to the couch at the corner of his cabin. A tormented Preeti wailed as she kicked in agony.

Preeti: "Please, leave me! Ahhh! For God's sake, leave me! Please!"

But her traumatized pleas did not melt the brute's heart. Moreover, his actions were fueled by his desire to take revenge on Sahil for getting him suspended. He shoved her onto the sofa and tried to force his hand up her skirt. Being the brave person she was, she continued to resist him with her full might. She did not let his rough hands slide past her knees. Next, he tried to pull off her brassiere. She scratched his face with her long nails and bit the back of his hand. This forced the crook to retract his hands for a moment. She cried out for help once again.

Preeti: "Sahil! Where are you, Sahil? Look at what he is doing to your Preeti! Sahil? Ahhh…ahhh…"

After he guffawed at her plight, he gripped her resisting hands and pinned them on either side of the sofa. This action rendered her completely helpless. Exhausted, she lost all strength in her fight against the strong man. With a victorious smile, Aurangzeb lunged at her. She closed her eyes in disgust and despair.

But before he could touch her, a strong hand smacked Aurangzeb's face. He fell off the couch and rolled onto the floor. Taken by surprise, he looked up at the assailant and caught sight of a furious Sahil baring his teeth. He stood between Aurangzeb and Preeti. She immediately got up from the couch and ran to her tattered dress strewn on the floor. She picked it up from the floor and draped it around herself. Then, she rushed toward Sahil and hugged him while breaking down.

Earlier, when Sahil had walked back to his cell, he noticed that the gate of the barrack was locked. He could see Ranga and Bheema in deep sleep on the floor of their cell. A lustful Aurangzeb had forgotten that the guards locked the barrack gates during the nighttime. Hence, Sahil returned to the front office for help in unlocking the door. But instead, the sight of Aurangzeb attempting to molest Preeti left him flabbergasted.

Preeti: "Sahil…this-this man tried to…"

But Sahil caressed her cheeks and nodded before she could narrate the horrific experience that she had suffered at Aurangzeb's hands.

Sahil: "You don't need to explain anything to me, Preeti. I can see what happened behind my back. And I promise, this man will pay the price for his evil deeds today."

Aurangzeb was back on his feet. Sahil's presence in the office stumped him. He frowned in anger and issued an austere warning to him.

Aurangzeb: "Go back to your cell before I gun you down."

But Sahil paid no heed to his command. Instead, he snarled at him.

Sahil: "I considered my job done when I brought down all the rogues at the party that night. But I was wrong, Aurangzeb. Until you, a filthy man, is alive, my task will remain unfinished. And today, I will mark it as done."

He marched toward Aurangzeb and punched him in the face. A thin stream of blood trickled from his cracked lip owing to the impact. Aurangzeb lunged at Sahil and shoved him to the corner of the room.

Preeti ran to the exit and climbed up the stairs to Khan's room on the top floor. But she gasped at the sight of a lock on the door and rushed back to the office.

Back in the office, no one seemed to be winning the battle. There were some moments when Sahil had an upper hand. At other times, the sturdy man seemed to be besting Sahil. But the scenario changed after Sahil got a hold of the belt that Aurangzeb had removed off his knickers. And that completely changed the course of the battle. Sahil put the belt around Aurangzeb's neck like a noose and pulled it taut. He clenched his teeth and tightened the loop around the brute's neck. Aurangzeb choked, and his eyes turned watery. He gasped for breath as he failed to free himself from Sahil's hold.

With her heart beating fast, Preeti rushed to Sahil and begged him to set the devil free. She did not want him to land in any further trouble. But her plea did not deter him. Aurangzeb flailed in agony as Sahil continued to suffocate the barbaric man. In his final moments, Aurangzeb's face turned red. His lips cracked, and his tongue hung out.

In a last-ditch panic effort, he got ahold of the emergency alarm on the table. With a trembling hand, he pressed the buzzer, and a loud siren sounded all over the place. The sound of the siren jolted every single prisoner out of his sleep. Bheema and Ranga exchanged bewildered looks. Moreover, the absence of Sahil in the barrack confused them. He hadn't returned since the time he went out of the cell to meet someone in the visitor room. A terrible fear crept into their hearts. They knew that something terrible had happened.

Khan was parking his car in the parking lot of the jail when he heard the siren. He jumped out of his car and rushed to the office. He knew that something dreadful had happened in his absence. Chills ran down his spine when he saw Sahil trying to throttle Aurangzeb. Without losing any time, he joined Preeti and tried to free Aurangzeb from Sahil's clutches. But it was too late. By the time they freed Aurangzeb from Sahil's hold, he had breathed his last. With eyes wide open, his lifeless body fell to the floor.

The moment left Khan devastated. As luck would have had it, the constables on duty that night to secure a politician, entered the front office at that very instant. Armed with guns, they marched inside and stood next to Khan when they heard the loud alarm.

Khan gulped in despair and stared at Sahil glumly. Tears flowed down Sahil's cheeks. He looked back at Khan with a miserable smile. Khan sighed and commanded his men in a dejected voice.

Khan: "Take charge of the body and take Sahil away to his cell. We will present his case in court tomorrow morning."

A group of constables gripped Sahil by his arms. And as they tried to tug him to his cell, Preeti began to wail and moved forward to embrace him. But Khan held her hand and stopped her forcefully, as he did not want to delay the proceedings. The killing of a cop was a matter of grave concern and scrutiny. Moreover, he had already given them enough time with each other. Preeti lamented and flinched in agony as she tried to free herself from Khan's firm hold. She screamed and pleaded in a tormented voice.

Preeti: "No, leave him, please! He did it to save me! Please leave him! Ahhh…ahhh…ahhh!"

The constables pulled Sahil forcefully to drag him back to his cell. But he resisted them all and stood his ground with a sad smile for one and only one reason. He knew that he would never see Preeti again. He knew that it was the last living moment they would share. He wanted to prolong the poignant moment between them as much as he could. He extended his hand toward her with a smile and tears streaking down his face. With one hand gripped by Khan, she lunged forward and grabbed Sahil's hand with her other hand. She sobbed as they looked into each other's eyes. It was time to part.

The constables yanked at Sahil once again, and his grip on her hand loosened. The constables' tug broke the clasp of their hands and separated them. Their fingers touched one another for one last time. Unable to control her emotions, she fell to her knees and lamented. Their eyes remained locked until the cops dragged him away from her sight.

A grieving Preeti knelt and wept. She touched the footprints he had left on the dusty floor as the policemen dragged him away. Then, she choked back her tears. With a sad smile and tears in her eyes, she caressed the marks with her cheeks. Then, she kissed the footprints to bid a final goodbye to the love of her life. She felt blessed to have had Sahil in her life.

Taking a cue from her tattered clothes, Khan reckoned what must have transpired in his absence. He took off his jacket and draped it around Preeti. Then, he gulped and patted her shoulder.

Khan: "Come on, sister. Let me drop you home."

His soothing words helped her regain some of her composure. She wiped her tears, and quietly followed Khan to his car. Soon, they headed back to the mansion.

****

Sunrise was around the corner. Seated in the front lawn, Vidya and Thakur waited tensely for Preeti's return from the jail. Though she had informed me before going to meet Sahil in jail, she did not whisper a word of it to anyone else in the mansion.

I had just served tea to Vidya and Thakur when the skidding sound of tires bewildered all three of us. Preeti's guise horrified us when she got down from the car. Khan remained behind the wheel on Preeti's request. She did not want him to recount all the events before us. He kept peeking at us through the window on the passenger's side.

Engulfed in deep sorrow, Preeti walked and stood before Vidya. She looked at her miserably and sobbed. She wanted to tell her everything that had happened between her and Sahil that night. But carried away by her deep emotions, she could not muster the courage to do so. Vidya frowned and looked at her from top to bottom. Though Preeti did not say a word, her appearance—Sahil's rosary around her neck and the vermillion on her forehead—revealed everything to her. Tears sprung up in Vidya's eyes as she gazed at Preeti. She walked to her and cradled her face in her hands. She wiped Preeti's tears and kissed her forehead with quivering lips. With her eyes locked at Preeti, she issued a command to me.

Vidya: "Bansi, I will be with my daughter-in-law. Send over two fresh cups of tea to my room."

With these words, the ladies walked into the mansion. Once Preeti was out of sight, Khan inserted the key in the ignition and turned on the engine. But before he could start, he caught a glimpse of the envelope in the cup holder of his car. The envelope contained the court order putting a hold on Sahil's hanging. He gulped in despair and picked up the envelope. As he pulled the paper out of the envelope, he recalled Ms. Usha's words.

Usha: *"Pleasure's all mine, Khan. But there is something I need to tell you. In your excitement, you missed out on one small section of a clause. As per this clause, Sahil should not commit any further felony until the result of the retrial is in our hands. If he does that, this legal document will become invalid. The stay on Sahil's hanging will be revoked, and the document will be deemed as null and void."*

Khan: *"Don't worry, Madam. Nothing of the sort will happen. I can vouch for it."*

He recalled the moment when Sahil throttled Aurangzeb, committing a grave felony. Following that moment, the legal document had turned into a mere scrap of paper with no value. He wept and rested his head on the steering wheel. He cursed himself for having left Sahil and Preeti all alone in jail the previous night. In sheer frustration, he clenched the document in his hand. Then, he ripped it into pieces and flung the shreds outside the window of his car. Finally, he looked ahead at the road and sped back to jail.

23. The Death Wish

11 hours to the gallows – 8th April 07:00 pm

Leaning against the backrest of his rocking chair, a crestfallen Thakur sat in his study. He looked up the doorway when he heard a knock on the door. He got up from his seat when Khan entered the room. Khan gulped in embarrassment, as he did not have good news to share with him.

Khan: "Hello, Thakur!"

A devastated Thakur remained silent. He licked his dry lips with his tongue, being in a terrible state of mind. After an uneasy pause, Khan explained the reason for his visit.

Khan: "Umm… Thakur… I came to…umm…inform you that the court has scheduled Sahil's hanging for tomorrow morning. As per the schedule, he will be hanged at sharp 6 in the morning. Since he registered himself as an organ donor, we will shift his body from the jail to the civil hospital first. After a couple of hours, an ambulance will bring the body to you. You don't need to go anywhere to claim his body. Do you have any questions?"

Thakur remained silent and continued staring at Khan with quivering lips. Tears streaked down his cheeks after he heard those dreadful words. With a heavy heart, Khan turned around and started walking to the exit. He wanted to give the old man some time alone. He knew that his excruciating words had shattered him from within. But before he could step out, Thakur cleared his throat and called out to him in a shivering voice.

Thakur: "Mhmm…Khan?"

Khan turned around and looked at Thakur. An anxious Thakur gulped and asked him a plaguing question.

Thakur: "You have been watching Sahil in jail all these days. Do you think he deserves what he will get tomorrow?"

His agonized query pushed Khan into deep thought. He pondered for a while before replying to him with a sigh.

Khan: "No, I don't. And I failed every time I tried to save him."

Thakur walked to Khan and held his hands. He had decided to reveal the undisclosed truth to him. With a lump in his throat, he confessed his crimes to Khan.

Thakur: "What if I tell you that he played a game to annihilate the empire I had set up over the years? What if I say that he surrendered himself on my behalf to punish his father? What if I say that it is me and not him who needs to be convicted for all those heinous crimes?"

Khan looked into Thakur's tormented eyes and smiled dejectedly.

Khan: "I can understand your pain, Thakur. But throwing lies around won't be of any help."

But Thakur was not ready to give up. He tightened his grip on Khan's wrist and continued to speak in a nervous but determined voice.

Thakur: "Trust me, Khan. It is not a lie! A few goons of mine killed all those innocents on my command. He never had any hand in it."

Thakur's words added to the puzzle Khan had failed to resolve till date. With a suspicious glance, Khan looked Thakur in the eye. Unable to believe his words, he asked for permission to leave.

Khan: "I…umm…need to leave."

Khan loosened Thakur's grasp on his hand and walked to the door with a glum face. But before he left, he halted his steps and turned around. Somehow, Thakur's words had caught his attention.

Khan: "Umm…do you have any evidence or any witness to corroborate your statement?"

Thakur's eyes glittered with hope. A rare smile flickered on his quivering lips.

Thakur: "Yes, I do! Do you remember the day I returned from Khandala, the morning after the catastrophic night? I was staying in the hotel *'Royal Exotica.'* That day, I had gone to a store in Khandala to pick up the tools that dismantled the equipment in the school. Just talk to the store manager, Khan. I spoke to him about the order that day."

Khan looked dejectedly at Thakur.

Khan: "Did you speak to anyone else in the store that day?"

Thakur shook his head in a jiffy.

Thakur: "No, I did not. But the manager would certainly confirm it."

Khan sighed and stole away his eyes from Thakur.

Khan: "We identified the store from the sticker on the tools we nabbed from Rajvanshi's haunt in Pune. We then went straight to the store, only to find that the store manager had died 10 days ago after suffering a massive heart attack. In the store's business register, the order was on Sahil's name. He was the one who picked up the tools. His signatures were on the check-out register."

Thakur gasped and tears streamed down his cheeks as soon as he heard Khan's words. He shook his head in despair.

Thakur: "Apart from that piece of information I don't have anything else to prove Sahil's innocence, Khan! He destroyed every little thing that could have proven him innocent or me guilty."

Khan remained silent for a brief moment.

Khan: "Thakur, I don't know what is true and what is false. I don't know whether to believe him or you. But you have time till 6 in the morning tomorrow. If you can give me some evidence that supports your statement by then, I can try to save him. Good day, Thakur."

With these words, he put on his uniform cap and rushed out of the mansion. Broken to the core, Thakur sat and gulped down some water. He didn't have any other proof. He sighed in despair and closed his eyes.

****

8 hours to the gallows – 8th April, 10:00 pm

Sunk in the gloom of the night, the forsaken mansion had an eerie look. Thakur restricted himself to the study to seek some solace. Vidya was all by herself in the mansion's temple worshipping Lord Krishna. An inconsolable Preeti had locked herself in Sahil's room. Though I rested on the cot in my dingy room, I was getting no sleep that night. I sighed in unease whenever I tried to imagine what the morning held for Sahil.

In the dull and moonless night, the scene was no different in jail. It seemed as though the moon too was in mourning, refusing to rise and light up the sky. The inmates refused to have dinner that night and the kitchen remain closed. They all flocked to the compound and hugged Sahil one by one. There wasn't a dry eye in the crowd of the gathered inmates. Ranga and Bheema, in particular, were inconsolable. Bheema thanked him for saving his daughter's life and embraced him. All his fellow inmates shook hands with him for one last time before walking back to their cells. The moment evoked deep nostalgia in him. He recalled his very last day of college when he had embraced all his friends one by one.

Unable to get any sleep as he lay on the floor of his cell, a

294

restless Sahil tossed and turned sides in anxiety. Being scared and nervous, he sat up and looked at the adjacent cell. He thought to speak to Ranga or Bheema to calm his nerves, but they had both slipped into a disturbed sleep by that time. He sighed and walked to the pot in the corner of his cell. After gulping down two glasses of water, he lay down on the floor again in the hope of getting some sleep. He yanked the blanket over him and drifted into an uneasy nap.

****

2 hours to the gallows – 9th April 04:00 am

A younger Thakur chuckled and walked to the window of a room in the mansion. He pulled apart the curtains to illuminate the room with sunshine. Then he made his way to the bed and removed the quilt draped over a child in deep slumber. A smile spread across Thakur's face as he looked at the innocent face of the snoring boy. He kissed the boy's cheeks before caressing his hair.

Thakur: "Sahil…wake up, son. It's morning. You are getting late for school."

The kid yawned and slowly opened his eyes. After a young Sahil caught sight of his father, he rubbed his eyes and embraced Thakur with a smile. His smile revealed a few missing milk teeth that had fallen only a few days ago. Thakur chuckled and put his arms around Sahil's back tenderly. Then, with another peck on his cheek, he lifted Sahil and carried him in his arms.

On one occasion, an impish Thakur pinched the young boy's butt mischievously while giving him a bath. Then, he chuckled and hugged Sahil as he faked a cry of pain.

One night, Sahil lay shivering in bed with a high fever. A distressed Thakur sat beside him the entire night and crooned lullabies to him. With a fretful look on his face, he applied cold-water bandages to his forehead from night till the crack of dawn. Being cranky and uncomfortable, Sahil wasn't getting any sleep. So, Thakur picked him up in his arms and rocked him to sleep gently.

On another occasion, seated on his father's shoulders, Sahil watched singing folk dancers in the village fête. A group of tribal men had gathered and played musical instruments to please the villagers. In their colorful long skirts, the tribal women moved in a circular formation and gyrated in sync. As the ladies danced, they placed brass pots on their heads and balanced them to perfection. With a wide smile on his face, a young Sahil had enjoyed every moment of the dance.

At times, an elated Thakur pumped his fist in the air in pride when the pellet fired from Sahil's pistol hit the bull's eye. Sahil loved the candy Thakur placed in his hand every time his shot hit the target. It was his initial greed for the sugar candy that drove him to master the art of shooting at a young age.

Moreover, as a child, Sahil cried every year when he had to leave for his maternal uncle's village during his vacation. Although he enjoyed his time there with Vidya, he hated leaving his father behind in Ratnagiri. Seated in the backseat of the car, he would lean out of his window with a sobbing face. He would then wave a forlorn goodbye to his father as soon as the car started to move. Then, he would weep in agony once the car accelerated and left the mansion. He would bawl at the diminishing sight of Thakur as the car moved ahead.

Sahil: *"Baba…Huuuu…Baba…Huuuu."*

Back in jail, Sahil sat up and shrieked in despair as the dream startled him.

Sahil: "BABAAAAAAAA…"

He felt the same pang inside him that he used to feel whenever he left Thakur alone in his summer vacations. The dream pushed him back to the sweet memories of his nostalgic past. Tiny beads of sweat covered his face and he looked rattled. His scream had awakened Ranga and Bheema as well. They jolted out of their sleep in panic and clutched the bars of their cell.

Bheema: "Is everything okay, Sahil?"

Ranga: "Did you have a nightmare?"

But before he could answer them, Khan unlocked the gate of the barrack and walked into Sahil's cell. An unsettled Sahil looked at him amid erratic breathing. Khan remained silent for a moment before he explained the purpose of his visit.

Khan: "Ummm…Sahil, two hours from now, you will be…hanged on the terrace. Is there any last wish of yours that you feel the authorities can help you with?"

Sahil remained silent, and tears welled up in his eyes. The words were enough to fluster even the most courageous man on the planet. He nodded and spoke once his breathing returned to normal.

Sahil: "Yes, I do have one."

****

1 hour to the gallows – 9th April, 05:00 am

Holding Thakur's hands, Khan entered the visitor room of the jail. In his death wish, Sahil had expressed his desire to meet Thakur, his Baba. The nostalgic dream rekindled Sahil's love for his father. It outweighed the anger and disgust he carried towards him for his heinous actions. In the remaining moments of his life, the malice he had for his father disappeared. He felt a sudden urge to meet his father, especially after their last meeting in jail.

Khan shut the room's door from the outside and left them alone. As Sahil had done last time, he stood with his back leaning against the prison bars yet again. He had his face turned to the other side and had his back turned towards his father. A nervous Thakur walked near Sahil with a thudding heart. His posture gave him a sense of déjà vu, reminding him of their previous meeting. Thakur gulped, as he expected the same rude behavior from Sahil again.

But then, something significant happened. Sahil turned around with profuse tears dribbling down his cheeks. Unlike last time, he looked at Thakur with a miserable smile. Then, in a shivering voice, Sahil addressed him with the word that Thakur did not hear from him in a long time.

Sahil: "BABA…"

Thakur broke down when he heard Sahil's voice. He had been craving to hear that four-lettered word from son's mouth all these days. He grabbed Sahil's hand through the prison bars and planted multiple kisses on the back of it. With a miserable smile on his face, Sahil fixed his tearful eyes on Thakur and repeated the word softly.

Sahil: "Baba…"

Heartbroken, Thakur began to wail. Unable to control his emotions, he glared at Sahil and clenched his teeth in anger.

Thakur: "YOU BETRAYED ME, SAHIL…YOU BETRAYED ME…. AHHHH… YOU WENT BEHIND MY BACK! SUCH TREACHERY! HOW DARE YOU? AHHH…AHHHH!"

Thakur's state petrified Sahil. Though he tried to console him, Thakur reprimanded him once again.

Sahil: "Baba… I—"

Thakur: "SHUT UP…DON'T INTERRUPT ME!"

Sahil abided by his father's command and fell silent. He wanted him to spit out all his frustration and anger. Thakur wailed and sniffed in an outburst.

Thakur: "WHO DO YOU THINK YOU ARE TO CURSE ME? SUCH A DOLOROUS CURSE! NO, BOY, NO! WHAT YOU'VE DONE ISN'T JUSTIFIED. I WILL NEVER FORGIVE YOU FOR YOUR TREACHERY. I WILL NEVER…"

But Thakur couldn't complete his words. He knelt on the floor. In remorse, he rested his face against the bars and spluttered amid hiccups. The heart-wrenching moment aroused deep sympathy in Sahil's heart for his father. He knelt as well. Then, he held Thakur's hand empathetically and locked eyes with him. The gesture calmed Thakur down a little. He wiped his tears and cleared his throat.

Thakur: "I can't live without you, Sahil. I can't! Take your curse back! Please, Sahil! I beg of you."

With a miserable smile, Sahil replied in a soft voice.

Sahil: "Who am I to free you from the curse, Baba? You wrote your destiny yourself."

Thakur: "Do you have any idea, without you, what my life would be like? It would be a lot worse than that of the living dead. Do you have any idea, Sahil?"

Sahil gulped and nodded before replying to him with a rueful smile.

Sahil: "Yes, Baba. I do."

Thakur gulped in panic and pleaded in a trembling voice.

Thakur: "Kh-Khan is a good man. L-L-Let's reveal the truth to him. I am sure he will help us. Let's tell him everything!"

But Sahil shook his head with a dejected smile.

Sahil: "It is too late, Baba. It's too late! Don't try to flog a dead horse."

Sahil's words pierced his heart. Thakur frowned and shut his eyes in remorse. His parched lips quivered.

Thakur: "Why didn't you kill me? It would have been a much easier death than the cruel life you have spared me for. Why didn't you seal my fate as you did for the others? Why didn't you kill me, Sahil?"

Sahil caressed the back of Thakur's hand in affection and smiled sadly after a sigh.

Sahil: "Do you really think I spared your life, Baba?"

Sahil's words were like a clout to his ear. Sahil was right! He hadn't spared him at all. He realized the irreparable loss he would bear after Sahil's demise. In fact, Sahil had subjected him to the worst fate a person could ever imagine for himself. Thakur gulped and gave him an abysmal look.

After brief eye contact with him, Sahil sighed and looked away. He stood up with a glum face, turned around, and paced a couple of steps. After a pause, he turned around and locked eyes with Thakur.

Sahil: "I sidetracked Preeti when she asked me the same question.

There exists an imperative and more essential reason that made me spare your life, Baba.”

His statement left Thakur shell-shocked. He gulped and his lips quivered when he realized that Preeti knew everything about him. Sahil’s words confirmed his suspicion. Her glare and admonishing words to him were still fresh in his mind.

Preeti: *“He bartered his life for yours, Baba!”*

He got back on his feet and looked down in shame. But he was not scared anymore. He was ready to expose himself to the whole world if it would save his son’s life. He remained silent, keen to hear Sahil’s reasoning.

Sahil: “Do you remember when I wished you a long life like Ashwathama’s?”

A wretched Thakur nodded with a lump in his throat.

Thakur: “Yes, I do. You wanted me to relive his curse.”

Sahil chuckled and shook his head.

Sahil: “That was not the only reason!”

Thakur frowned in confusion.

Thakur: “W-what are you trying to say, Sahil?”

Sahil: “After the Pandavas won the war, Arjuna visited Lord Krishna. A doubt had been bothering him since the day the battle had ended with their victory. He was keen to know the reason for the defeat of the Kauravas. That too, when the army of Kauravas had outnumbered that of the Pandavas by a ratio of eleven to seven at the start of the war. The Lord smiled before answering the Pandava. Do you know what he said to Arjuna?”

Unable to make head or tail of his words, Thakur shook his head with a straight face. Sahil smiled before he continued.

Sahil: “Krishna cited a tactical blunder committed by the Kauravas. As per him, the blunder led to their unexpected defeat. The Kauravas never appointed Ashwathama as the commander of their army in the early stages of the war.

“With a boon to lead an immortal life, Ashwathama was brave and one of the most intelligent men on the planet. As an intellectual, he had advised the Kauravas to refrain from the war. He had foreseen a certain defeat. He warned about the grief it would bring to everyone’s families. But none of the other warriors paid heed to his advice, and the war began against his wishes.

“When the battle started, he sensed a fast-approaching defeat with each passing day. Hence, in the middle of the war, he again advised the

Kauravas to call a truce with the Pandavas. But the Kauravas neglected his suggestion yet again.

"Having said that, he was a wicked warrior who got the job done by hook or by crook. Appointed as the commander on the last day of the war, he killed the progeny of Pandavas while they were in their sleep, all by himself. Though he later faced the wrath of Lord Krishna for his cowardly act, it hit the enemy where it hurt most. It dampened the pleasure of an otherwise resounding victory of the Pandavas."

As he recounted the enlightening words of Lord Krishna, Sahil sprinted back to Thakur. He held Thakur's hands in anxiety and continued in a divine voice.

Sahil: "The last time we met, I addressed you as Ashwathama for a reason. The world never witnessed the full potential of the mythological man we have always heard. History never gave him a chance! But I am giving you a second chance, Baba.

"Like him, your nuanced understanding of matters has no parallel. You have great insight into issues, and you have mastered the art of revolutionizing the lives of others. No one has a better ability to bring in innovations and reforms for the people of Ratnagiri. You are a born leader, and the masses bow to you. I know you can do wonders with your full potential.

"Think about your past, Baba! Recall the good things you did for Ratnagiri and its people before you succumbed to your greed for money and power. You were the first one to install greenhouse farming to help the farmers in the winters. You changed many lives when you brought biomass stoves to Ratnagiri. Your river-ice cooling systems have done wonders for the farming sector. Your multi-crop threshers eased the livelihoods of daily wage farmers. And Baba, I remember the school and roads you set up with the help of the local civic authorities. The state-of-the-art hospital has given respite to the residents in their hour of need. I can still recall your countless visits to the officials to clear the red tape getting in the way of its foundation. You were a pioneer, Baba. Then, something lured you away from the path of good."

Sahil's lower lip quivered as he spoke the next words in a powerful voice.

Sahil: "Oh old man, oh my Ashwathama, mend your ways! Re-channelize your energy! You have lived enough for yourself. Now, it is time for you to submit to the lives of others. The people of Ratnagiri consider you next to God and swear upon your name. Don't let them down. Live your life for them. Exceed the best you have given them so far. Get up, Baba! Awaken from the deep slumber you have been in all these years. It's time for you to burn like a lamp and guide others with the light. It is time for you to surrender yourself, Baba."

Thakur wailed in agony and cursed himself when he heard Sahil's heart-rending words.

Thakur: "I am sorry for everything I've done… Ahhh…I wish I could turn back this nightmarish time. I am facing the wrath of the almighty because of my malevolent and grave sins."

Sahil gulped in empathy. He knew that Thakur was a shattered man and his plight was not going to change any time soon.

Sahil: "You don't have the luxury to repent, Baba. Instead, atone for your mistakes in a way the gods in heaven admire your efforts. Be determined to do good deeds and take courage from every moment of suffering. Don't feel low if you ever remember the dark past. Don't let your guilt hinder your benevolence. A-a-and…do not stress yourself out! I am taking all the sins off your shoulders and carrying them with me to…ahhh…ahhh…"

Sahil couldn't complete his words as he broke down in tears of misery. After witnessing the dismal state of his beloved son, Thakur lost his composure and started to wail as well. But Sahil swallowed his misery and wiped his tears, as he did not want to prolong the poignant moment any further. He cleared his throat and pleaded to his father.

Sahil: "Start a new life! Be like a star guiding others. Promise me, Baba. You have to promise me!"

Sahil extended his palm through the bars and placed it in front of Thakur. He wanted him to keep his promise sincerely. Thakur gave him a sorrowful look. Then, he gasped and nodded before placing his trembling hand on Sahil's. He gulped and made his resolve in a quivering voice.

Thakur: "I promise you, Sahil. This life of mine doesn't belong to me henceforth. I devote it to the good of others from now on. The burden of my sins will always remain on my conscience. You will be my last living memory, and I will think of you till the day I die."

With that promise, they tried to embrace each other, but the bars kept them apart. Sahil smiled and held Thakur's hand in affection. Then, he knelt and started to weep as he touched Thakur's feet to mark his respect one final time. He broke down while struggling to speak, and uttered his next words in a raspy voice.

Sahil: "I seek your forgiveness if I ever hurt you or…if…I…belittled you…in-in any…anyway, Baba. I am…. s-so-sorry…"

Sahil found it hard to control his emotions any longer. Thakur, too, fell to his knees and cradled Sahil's face through the bars. He lamented before planting a kiss on his forehead. With tears trickling down his cheeks, Sahil smiled ruefully at his gesture. With his throat choked up, he held Thakur's hand and gave him a piercing message to pass on to Vidya.

Sahil: "Tell Ma I missed her in my last moments."

Before Thakur could have replied, Khan knocked on the door and entered. The sight of him terrified Thakur. His heartbeat escalated, and his eyes widened in fear. Khan walked to him and patted his shoulder with a somber expression. He sighed and said the words Thakur never wanted to hear.

Khan: "Time is up, Thakur. You need to leave. I'm sorry."

Thakur wailed at the thought of leaving the place. With a dreadful feeling, Khan held out his hand to support the shattered man. Then, he helped him get back on his feet. As Khan helped him walk to the exit, Thakur turned around and fixed his gaze at Sahil. Before leaving, he recited some poetic verses that Sahil recognized immediately. The verses were the ones that the crowd had sung during the funerals of Ratnagiri's past kings.

Thakur: *"O, righteous king!*
With everyone crooning your glory at will,
You will walk with your head held high like a hill.
The lives of your dear ones now dull and dry,
The void will make the world cry.
God will never bless any father ever again,
With a son like you, never to be born ever again!"

With a miserable smile on his lips, Sahil waved goodbye to his father. Thakur looked back at Sahil one last time before Khan ushered him out of the room. Sahil wiped his tears and made his way back to his cell. He was in complete peace now. His final wish had been fulfilled.

24. The Gallows

30 minutes to the gallows – 9th April, 05:30 am

I still remember the gloom in the early morning of that ill-fated day. With bated breath, I sat in the car and waited for Thakur to step out of the jail. As soon as I saw a lamenting Thakur, I jumped out of the car and ran to him. I put my arm around his shoulders to console him. He wailed and looked out of sorts when I helped him to get into the car. I started driving back to the mansion once we both settled on our seats. Though I wanted to console him, I remained silent. I couldn't gather the courage to speak any words of consolation to the wretched man.

It was still dark as our car neared the outskirts of Ratnagiri. As we sped ahead, a gloomy Thakur caught sight of the chamber of assemblies on the other side of the road. Though he had hatched vile plans in it all these years, a visit to the haunt always gave him immense peace. In a feeble voice, he asked me to pull over. He did not want to step into the mansion in his despicable state. Hence, to find some solace, he thought to spend some time alone in the chamber instead. And once he asked me to do so, I applied the brakes, and the car came to a halt with a rumbling sound. He got down of the car, and after a brief gaze at the deserted venue, he walked to its entrance. Seated on my seat, I frowned and inquired in a concerned voice.

I: "Thakur?"

He halted and replied in an austere voice without looking back at me.

Thakur: "I don't want anyone to disturb me, Bansi. Once I muster the courage to deal with this misfortune, I will walk home."

Located midway in between the jail and the mansion, the place was quite far from the mansion. I struggled to find words to converse with the mourning father.

I: "D-d-do you want me to pick you up later, any time after sunrise?"

Thakur: "The sun will never rise again for me. It has set forever."

With those words, he stepped inside the chamber and locked the door from the inside. I sighed and drove back to the mansion. And I regret that decision of mine till date.

The wooden floor creaked when Thakur stepped into the hall of the building. His eyes widened in despair as he looked around and walked into the hall of the chamber. After the fierce fight between Dara and Zola, the dilapidated place looked like a graveyard. The ruined furniture, tumbledown paintings, and broken statues added to the eerie look. I had already narrated to him the events that transpired between Dara, Sahil, and Zola on the day of the party.

The silence added to the spooky atmosphere of the abandoned building. The frightful place wasn't giving him positive vibes anymore.

To mollify his disturbed mind, he sat on a dusty chair to mourn the ill-fated moment. He closed his eyes and wept in melancholy. His heart pounded when he recalled Sahil's harsh words on his first visit to jail. In contrast, Sahil's affectionate behavior that morning shattered his heart. His lips trembled in agony, and tears streamed down his face. He gasped and looked around the place in despair. He recalled the night when Harak had killed Boney and Sahil had come to know his truth. He wept and cursed himself for rejecting his advice that night when he asked him to surrender to the police. Hounded by remorse, Thakur clenched his teeth and smacked his face three times in a row. He knew that he alone was to be blamed for the inevitable disaster.

Lost in his thoughts, he caught a glimpse of the safe vault in the corner of the hall. It reminded him of a critical piece of information that he had shared with Sahil on his fateful birthday. He had revealed to him the whereabouts of the picture of himself and Rajvanshi.

Thakur: *"The picture I snatched from Alok…I kept it in…umm…in the…s-safe vault of the chamber… at the mercy of the Death Lord."*

He stood up from his chair and walked to the unlocked door of the vault. As expected, he didn't find anything relevant. I had already told him that I burnt the envelope on Sahil's command. Dejected, he turned around to walk back to the chair. Suddenly, he stopped in his tracks. His eyes widened and his lower lip quivered as he made a disturbing discovery in an epiphany moment.

The night he killed Alok, a nervous Thakur made his way to the chamber. Though he had been orchestrating the killings for a long time, this was the first time he had killed someone with his own hands. He pulled out the picture from the envelope and glanced at it nervously. Being panicked, he had thought of destroying the picture at first. But then, he thought it wise to show the picture to Tatya first. He wanted Tatya to find out more details about the picture and details of Alok's trip to Pune in his pursuit.

Since Tatya was not in the village that night, he slid back the picture into the envelope and placed it inside the vault. But to his surprise, the locking mechanism of the safe did not work. Though he had correctly entered the secret combination 1,7,2,4,3,6,8 several times, the door refused to get locked. It was too risky to keep the picture in the unlocked safe. Moreover, he didn't consider it wise to carry the picture to the mansion. He didn't want any of his family members to accidentally catch a glimpse of the picture. Rajvanshi was a known criminal and everybody in Ratnagiri recognized him. A daily newspaper had published his pictures and his criminal details a lot of times. He didn't want Vidya or Preeti to suspect him if they ever manage to get a hold of the picture.

With that thought, he picked up the envelope from the vault and pulled out the photo from it. He then placed the empty envelope back in the unlocked vault and walked to a small table placed at the corner of the hall.

He slid out a trimmed drawer at the base of the table and placed the photo in it. The trimmed drawer was a safer place to hide the picture than the large unsecured safe vault. There was no other better place to hide the picture at that moment. He shut the drawer in, and sighed in relief before walking out of the chamber and driving back to the mansion. He had planned to destroy the picture after Tatya gets to see it once.

But since his dementia had been troubling him more and more by the day, he forgot about the drawer. As a result, he had asked Dara to secure the vault instead of the drawer. Though in reality, he never placed the picture in the vault as he had told Sahil in his drunken state. Instead, the picture remained secured inside the drawer, and the vault had always contained only an empty envelope. Hence, when I had set the envelope ablaze on Sahil's command, it didn't have any photo in it.

Stunned after he recollected the fact, Thakur glanced at the table with widened eyes. With his heart beating fast, he walked to the table and pulled out the slim drawer. And to his shock, the photograph was still in the drawer— it was the same one he had snatched from Alok, the night he killed him. He frowned in despair as he picked it up and brought it close to his eyes. Thakur fell to his knees and began to bawl. The picture had come as a blessing in disguise and could save his beloved son's life. Khan's words were still fresh in his mind.

Khan: *"You have time till 6 in the morning tomorrow. If you can give me some evidence that supports your statement by then, I can try to save him."*

After all his failed attempts to save Sahil, destiny had finally smiled upon him. But his celebration was short-lived. His eyes fell on the clock nailed on the wall. Chills ran down his spine—it was 05:44 am. Sahil's execution was due in fifteen minutes, and he had barely any time to make it to the jail. He panicked and ran to the telephone in the hall. He dialed Khan's office, but to his horror, no one picked up his call, as Khan was not at his desk. He groaned in fear and dialed the mansion's number. But once again, nobody picked up his call. Preeti had locked herself in Sahil's room, while Vidya had confined herself to the temple in the mansion. None of them heard the ring of the landline downstairs in the hall.

To make matters worse, he had no transport to get to the jail, as I had already left for the mansion on his command. The jail was at a distance of about a mile from the chamber. With no time on his hands, he rushed out of the building and started running towards the jail. With the picture in his hand, the old man sprinted as fast as he could. He was in a race against time. He had to beat the clock to save Sahil's life.

15 minutes to the gallows – 9th April, 05:45 am

Khan unlocked and opened the gate of Sahil's barrack. Seated on the floor of his cell, Sahil shook in fear when he heard the creaky sound of the gate. With erratic breathing, he clutched a book against his chest that he started to read a few days ago. He gasped and his eyes widened in fear as he looked at Khan with a straight face. Moreover, a magistrate entered in the cell as well, and stood abreast to Khan. In the adjacent cell, Ranga and Bheema gripped each other's hands in the glum moment.

Khan tried to cheer up Sahil with a sham smile.

Khan: "What are you reading, young man?"

Sahil gained control over his breathing and seemed composed by then.

Sahil: "Umm… I was reading this book called *The Curse to Ashwathama*. It's a well-written and interesting book. I have six more pages to skim through. May I?"

Bound by rules and regulations, Khan refused with a heavy heart.

Khan: "I…I wish I could have allowed it, but we are getting late. We need to move now. Sorry!"

Sahil looked up at Khan with a wistful smile. He gulped and nodded in melancholy.

Sahil: "I can understand, Khan. Let us go. I will probably read it on some other day."

With these heart-rending words, Sahil stood up and stepped out of his cell. Two constables held him by the arms and marched forward. Khan and the magistrate followed them. It was time for Sahil to walk to the terrace and face the gallows. As he started to move, he looked at Ranga and Bheema. They looked miserable and started to bawl inconsolably. With Khan's permission, Sahil moved close to them and shook hands with them to bid a final goodbye. Though in deep agony, Sahil tried his best to look cheerful.

Sahil: "Alright, friends! See you in some better place the next time."

Bheema and Ranga clung to his hands and ululated. Sahil gulped and uttered a few optimistic words to Bheema.

Sahil: "I hope your daughter gets a new life today. Break a leg, Bheema!"

In the heart-rending moment, Bheema sniveled, as he did not have any words in reply to his gratitude. With tears in his eyes, he planted a kiss at the back of Sahil's hand with the trembling lower lip. Sahil gulped and resumed his walk to the terrace after a sigh. He seemed calm and composed.

But as he walked past the other barracks toward the stairs, he witnessed something remarkable. Awake and standing in their respective cells, all inmates seemed to be in a pensive mood. With misty eyes, they held the prison bars with both their hands and had their glare fixed at Sahil. It was a moment of deep mourning for them as well. It was a peculiar view to witness in the early morning. Sahil looked at everyone and stepped onto the stairs.

But as he took his next steps, he experienced something even more stunning. He heard a sharp and shrilled clank. He frowned and halted his steps, as the jangle seemed familiar to his ears. He looked around and the view in front dazzled him.

With empty plates and mugs in their hands, the inmates clanged the utensils together. In nostalgia, he recalled the hunger strike when the inmates protested against Aurangzeb's atrocities in the same fashion.

There was a difference, however. Earlier, they clanged the utensils to mark their agitation. But this time, they did it as a tribute to Sahil. They shrieked in agony when Sahil started moving up the stairs. In misery, tears streamed down their faces. The hall buzzed with screams from all over the place. The tribute stunned Khan to the core. In his long career spanning decades, he had never witnessed such a frenzy. It was an extraordinary moment to witness.

Though Sahil tried to remain composed, he struggled to contain his emotions. His lips quivered in the intense moment. With a rueful grin on his face, he wiped his tears as he walked past the crescendo of the inmates. With every ring of the clanging metals, he recalled Thakur's words.

WHACK

O, righteous king!
WHACK
With everyone crooning your glory at will,
WHACK
You will walk with your head held high like a hill.
WHACK
The lives of your dear ones now dull and dry,
WHACK
The void will make the world cry.
WHACK
God will never bless any father ever again,
WHACK
With a son like you, never to be born ever again!

With trembling lips, he waved a forlorn goodbye to them all and climbed the stairs to the terrace.

****

Though Thakur had a powerful piece of evidence in his hand to save Sahil, he was running short of time. Soon, he lost his breath and halted his brisk run. He placed his hands on his waist and panted in loud snorts to calm down his erratic breathing. Stranded on a deserted road in the dark with sweat beading his face, he groaned in fear. The odds were heavily stacked against him. But then, his eyes glittered in hope.

With its headlights turned on, a speeding truck approached him with a vrooming sound. The view brought a grin on his fluttering lips. Amid heavy wheezing, he erratically waved his hand and gestured for help. But to his horror, the truck did not stop and sped past him. He huffed and shrieked as he ran behind the truck.

Thakur: "HEY… STOP … DO YOU HEAR ME? STOP!"

But the truck disappeared somewhere in the darkness. Thakur gasped and ceased chasing it when he ran out of breath. He gulped in despair and tiny droplets of sweat covered his face and forehead.

Bewildered, he screamed aloud amid tears, and looked around on the abandoned street. And probably, the luck smiled at him for one more time. A white sedan came near to him and slowed down. With a ray of hope, he clung to the window of the passenger seat and sprinted along with the moving car. A middle-aged lady sat on the wheel and drove the car with a frightened face. Thakur's insane behavior on an abandoned street terrified her. Running alongside the car, he wailed and begged her in a heart-rending appeal.

Thakur: "HELP ME, SISTER! PLEASE, HELP ME! JUST DROP ME TO THE JAIL. MY SON'S LIFE IS IN DANGER, SISTER! THOSE BARBARIC MEN WILL KILL MY SON! JUST DROP ME TO THE JAIL, SISTER! IT WON'T TAKE YOU LONG."

To Thakur's relief, the car slowed down and stopped near the curb. Thakur heaved a deep sigh of relief and walked to the car. A cheerful smile reflected on his face. But before he could reach her, the sedan accelerated and sped away. He gasped and ran behind the car in a panic. Thakur bawled and begged in a loud voice.

Thakur: "NO, PLEASE! DON'T LEAVE ME, SISTER! MY SON WILL DIE! HELP ME, PLEASE! AHHH!"

But all his efforts went in vain. The car disappeared in the dark, leaving behind a cloud of smoke and dust. Thakur was out of his breath. He stopped for a breather amid loud snuffles. Hoping against the hope, he looked around in panic and hollered for help.

Thakur: "IS ANYONE THERE? SOMEBODY HELP ME!"

But he didn't hear a sound besides the echo of his own voice. Dejected, he continued running towards the jail with faint hope.

Once Sahil reached the terrace, the constables released his arms, and Khan asked him to take a quick bath. A prisoner was required to take a bath before he faced the gallows. As instructed, Sahil walked to the open bathroom at the corner of the terrace. He took a mug out of a bucket filled with cold water and poured it over his head. With every mug of water he poured, he recited a few verses of the purification mantras. He had heard it quite a few times during the various funeral processions. With every chant, he prayed to God to free him of the sins he had committed.

Sahil: "*Om prann appann vyaann uddann smaanaa meee shudyantaam jyotiraham…*"

Meanwhile, Thakur groaned in despair while running as he still had a lot of distance to cover.

Sahil poured a second mug of water over his face as he continued chanting.

Sahil: "*Viraajaa-vipaapmaa-bhuyaa-sag-svaha…*"

With the picture in hand, Thakur shrieked as he ran.

Thakur: "I'M COMING, SAHIL! I'M COMING…"

Sahil poured a third mug of water over his bare chest.

Sahil: "*Vang mnaahaa shakshoo shrotra jigvaag graham reto budhiya kooti sankalapa mey shudhyantaam jyotiraham…*"

Running as fast as he could, Thakur clenched his teeth in frustration.

Thakur: "OH GOD, HELP ME! PLEASE!"

Sahil lifted the bucket and poured the remaining water over his shoulders as he finished his bath.

Sahil: "*Viraajaa vipaapmaa bhuyaa sag svaha…*"

Time to the gallows – 9th April 06:00 am

Dressed in a black shirt and black trousers, Sahil walked to the gallows in the twilight. The duskiness of the night glistened with light. With his heart racing, he glanced at the wooden structure before him, and the sight terrified him. The structure was about two meters wide and three meters high. Two giant upright parallel pillars marked the front boundary of the formation. And with a metal hook in its middle, a horizontal bar at the apex connected both the pillars. One end of a thick rope was tied around the hook, while its other end dangled midair. The dangling end held a noose that swayed in the strong breeze.

A bald and bare-chested hangman with an overgrown mustache stood beside the wooden arrangement. His hand was on the lever. He seemed restless and looked eager to push the lever and finish off the proceedings. The magistrate gestured to Sahil to walk to the floor of the gallows. Before stepping onto the ladder to reach the noose, he gave Khan a poignant look. Though Khan looked grim, Sahil smiled at him.

Thakur made his way to the bridge across River Palanharini. He was at a distance of about two hundred meters from the jail. Since it had rained cats and dogs the previous night, the areas around the river had flooded. The river was flowing above the marked danger levels. Amid the strong breeze and high tide, he could hear the rushing sound of the water. An agonized Thakur waved the picture in his hand. He roared with a trembling voice.

Thakur: "KHAN… LOOK WHAT I HAVE. WAIT … KHAN… WAIT FOR ME, KHAN…"

But he was still too far to be heard by anyone.

Sahil climbed up the ladder and walked to the noose. He gave the hangman a miserable look. The hangman reciprocated with an austere stare though. Then, the hangman walked to him and tied his hands together, and placed a black hood over his face. Finally, he helped Sahil walk to the two thin wooden planks loosely aligned with each other on the floor. The lever was responsible for controlling their position and keeping them aligned. If the executioner pushed the lever, the planks were designed to swing and rip apart. Following this, the body of the prisoner would drop. Held by the noose at the other end, the neck of the prisoner would snap instantly.

Thakur shouted at the top of his lungs as he reached the bridge. But nobody could hear him because of the loud sound of the flooding water.

Thakur: "HOLD ON, KHANNNN…I'M COMING, SAHIL… I'M COMING, SON…HOLD ON…."

The executioner tightened the noose around Sahil's neck and stepped back to the lever. With a stern expression, he looked at the magistrate and waited for his nod to press the lever. The magistrate raised his index finger. Sahil had only a few more seconds left in his tragic life. Thakur had almost crossed the bridge by now.

Just as he was about to cross the bridge, he suffered the final and the irreparable jolt. His foot tripped on a firmly rooted stone and he fell to the ground. He lost his grip on the picture, and the strong breeze snatched it up into the air. The photograph plunged into the flooded, cold waters of River Palanharini. Just then, the magistrate jerked his finger downward, and the hangman pushed the lever. The wooden planks on the floor gave way, and Sahil's body dropped. The birds resting in trees nearby flapped their wings in a frenzy and flew away. Lying on the ground, Thakur looked up at the jail. With his eyes widened in horror and fingers of empty hand spread out, he let out an agonized scream.

Thakur: "NOOOOOOOOOOOOOOO!"

****

Bansi gasped as he recounted the horrific moment to Rishi and Anu. He picked up a glass of water and gulped all in it. Rishi and Anu remained silent in melancholy and exchanged stunned glances. They understood that the old man who had grabbed the diamond ring from Bansi had been Thakur indeed. Bansi continued after he regained his breath.

Bansi: "Soon after Sahil's death, Khan retired voluntarily. He moved to his far-off village, and I never saw him ever again. A shattered Vidya turned into a recluse and confined herself to the temple of the mansion. She barely ever stepped out of it. Dhananjay, your father, sold all his assets and abandoned Ratnagiri. I never heard anything about him thereafter until you guys arrived here today."

Rishi pondered for a moment before placing his hand on Bansi's shoulder. With an embarrassed expression on his face, he asked for forgiveness.

Rishi: "I…I am sorry for my father's role in all this. I know he was wrong."

Bansi looked at him in deep misery when he heard his apologetic words.

Rishi: "But he didn't lead a peaceful life either. He lost all his money in gambling, but fortunately, the ring survived. His sister, Suhasini, whom he loved the most, died in a terrible car crash. And my mother died while giving birth to me. Even he didn't get an easy death. He was bedridden with paralysis for the last eight years of his life. Trust me, in his last days, he was remorseful for everything he did."

Bansi sighed and nodded empathetically after he heard the terrible piece of information. He spoke after a brief pause.

Bansi: "Sahil's tragic and untimely death brought about a miraculous reformation in Thakur. As promised to Sahil, he toiled day and night for the people of Ratnagiri to seek redemption for his sins. He led the life of an ascetic and worked relentlessly for everyone. Moreover, he initiated a slew of progressive measures. I'm sure you witnessed a few of them on your way to this place. The atrocity brought out the best in him. He was like a man reborn from the ashes. People responded quite well to him too. Time effaced people's memories of Sahil and his so-called sins. Out of sight, out of mind, I suppose."

But as soon as he uttered these words, his face turned grim.

Bansi: "But…"

Rishi: "But?"

Bansi gulped and looked up at Rishi despondently.

Bansi: "But as time went by, nature turned its wrath on Ratnagiri. With hardly any rains, the flora wilted and Palanharini dried up. Things turned murkier when Sahil's curse came true over time. Two years after Sahil's demise, Vidya passed away after a prolonged illness. She didn't forgive Sahil even in her last moments. He always remained a culprit and a sinner in her eyes. But I know that the real cause of her illness was the trauma of her separation from her son.

"Her death shattered Thakur completely. But destiny had worse in store for him. Soon, he developed incurable leprosy, and his dementia worsened over the years. Today, barring one or two people, he doesn't recognize anyone. He has lost his ability to speak and has confined

himself to a deserted corner of the backyard. He sits there for hours, lost in his thoughts. Though he doesn't remember much, he cries and howls at times. Perhaps the memories of Sahil have not been wiped from his mind. A few old friends often visit and pay their regards to him, but he never talks to any of them. I pray that the god of death visits him soon, and sets him free of all the suffering. It is hard for me to see him in this pitiful and pathetic condition. Fortunately, I won't have to endure it after about four months from now."
Rishi: "Why?"

Bansi smiled miserably before he answered.
Bansi: "Cancer is eating up my pancreas. I won't be around for long."
Rishi: "I…I'm sorry to hear that."

Bansi cleared his throat and nodded. After a momentary pause, he sighed and stood up from his chair.
Bansi: "Umm…never mind. Let me bring back your ring from Thakur. He must have gone to sleep by now. Thank you again for lending me that ring. Give me a couple of minutes; you'll have it back in your hands. You must be getting late. Wait for me, okay?"

But as he started to walk back to the mansion, Anu called out to him. Unable to control her urge to ask him something that had intrigued her the whole time, she spoke her first words to him.
Anu: "And…what about Preeti? What happened to her?"

He stopped in his tracks and looked at her in despair. Then after a brief pause, he gulped and replied to her with a sullen face.
Bansi: "Oh, didn't I tell you? She got married, poor girl."

With these words, he scurried back to the mansion. His terse reply confused Anu, as she had wanted a better answer.

And as they waited for him to bring back the ring to them, they heard a sweet female voice.
Female: "Would you like to have some tea and mango relish sandwiches?"

The words jolted the couple out of their thoughts, and they turned around instantly. They had heard the term "mango relish" quite a few times in the fascinating story. And the sight in the front left them stunned.

With most of her hair grey, a woman stood in front of them with a platter containing two cups of tea. Dressed in a simple white outfit, she appeared to be in her mid-fifties. She adjusted her glasses and gave them a humble smile. Though the couple had never met her before, they recognized her immediately. The rosary tied around her neck convinced them that the woman before them was none other than Preeti! Anu looked at her with widened eyes. Tears welled up in her eyes, and intense emotions surged within her.

Anu: "A-are…are you…"

The lady chuckled at Anu's incomplete query. Her reply confirmed Anu's guess. She was Preeti indeed.

Preeti: "Oh, sorry…Hahaha. I should have introduced myself first. I am Preeti Sahil Singh, the daughter-in-law of the house. I take care of things here since Baba, I mean my father-in-law, hasn't been keeping well these days. I got the news of some guests visiting the mansion, but some urgent work had held me up. I apologize for the delay. Can I help you with anything? Here, please have some sandwiches and some tea."

Before an elated Anu could reply, she caught sight of a young lady about her own age standing beside Preeti. She held a large plate with some stuffed sandwiches. Her appearance left the couple baffled. About twenty years younger, the young lady's features were a replica of Preeti's. And when Preeti introduced her, Anu could no longer hold back her tears.

Preeti: "She's my daughter, Sahiti. Sahiti Sahil Singh!"

Anu and Rishi looked at each other with mild grins and tears in their eyes. Sahiti greeted the couple and smiled before placing the platter on the table before them. Anu cradled her face in her hands and caressed her hair in affection.

Anu: "Sahiti means literature. May you enlighten the world with your knowledge and wisdom. God bless you!"

Following these words, Anu walked towards Preeti with tears streaming down her face. She held her hands in affection. The gesture perplexed Preeti, who gave Anu a puzzled look in return. Anu wiped her tears before speaking in a choked voice.

Anu: "I-I don't know how to tell you…how wonderful it feels to meet someone like you…"

Her conduct baffled the mother and daughter duo. Preeti frowned at her peculiar behavior.

Preeti: "May I ask who you are?"

With a wistful smile, an overwhelmed Anu replied to her after a pause.

Anu: "No one…in front of a sacrificial lady like you…"

****

Bansi hurried back to the backyard with the ring. But to his

314

surprise, he didn't see anyone in the backyard besides Sahiti and Preeti.

Bansi: "Preeti, where did the couple go?"

Preeti shrugged, looking equally surprised.

Preeti: "They left without saying much. They didn't eat any snacks either."

Bansi couldn't believe the couple had left without the ring.

Bansi: "They left? But why?"

Preeti: "I'm not sure. The lady was a bit strange though."

She recalled Anu's final words before the couple left.

Anu: *"No one…in front of a sacrificial lady like you! We need to leave now, Preeti. Once Bansi comes back, feel free to keep what he is carrying with him. Consider it a small memento from us. In reality, it's yours. We've had it all these years, but it never really belonged to us."*

Preeti: "Then they both left. What memento was the lady talking about? And who were they?"

Bansi sighed and replied with a miserable smile.

Bansi: "Someone atoning for the mistakes of a family member."

With these words, he extended his hand before Preeti. She gasped as soon as she caught sight of the ring on his palm. She recognized the ring immediately. Her eyes welled up with tears. In that nostalgic moment, she picked up the ring with a trembling hand. The memory of Sahil closing his one eye and peeking at her through the hoop of the same ring flashed before her eyes. She lost her balance and fell to her knees before bawling in agony. Bansi and Sahiti sat beside her and tried to console her.

****

Driving their way back home, Anu and Rishi sat with grim faces. They remained silent as the saga played in their minds. To dispel the moroseness surrounding them, they both looked at each other.

Anu: "I love you, Rishi."

Rishi replied with a smile.

Rishi: "I love you too, Anu."

Tears sprung up in Anu's eyes.

Anu: "Don't ever leave me."

A determined Rishi looked her in the eye.

Rishi: "I never will, I promise!"

Anu rested her head on Rishi's shoulder as their car sped back to their home.

****